FINDING MARIE

SUSAN PAGE DAVIS

HARVEST HOUSE PUBLISHERS

EUGENE, OREGON

Scripture quotations are taken from the HOLY BIBLE, NEW INTERNATIONAL VERSION®. NIV®. Copyright ©1973, 1978, 1984 by the International Bible Society. Used by permission of Zondervan. All rights reserved.

Published in association with the literary agent of Hartline Literary Agency, Pittsburgh, PA.

Cover by Left Coast Design, Portland, Oregon

Cover photos © Marili Forastieri / Digital Vision / Getty Images; George Glod / Super Stock

FINDING MARIE
Copyright © 2007 by Susan Page Davis
Published by Harvest House Publishers
Eugene, Oregon 97402
www.harvesthousepublishers.com

Library of Congress Cataloging-in-Publication Data
  Davis, Susan Page.
  Finding Marie / Susan Page Davis.
      p. cm.
  ISBN-13: 978-0-7369-2083-4 (pbk.)
  ISBN-10: 0-7369-2083-8
  1. Military spouses—Fiction. I. Title.
  PS3604.A976F56 2007
  813'.6—dc22

2007004336

Printed in the United States of America

07 08 09 10 11 12 13 14 15 / LB-NI / 10 9 8 7 6 5 4 3 2 1

To my cherished sister
Mim.

Next in age,
in childhood almost-twin and rival,
grown-up friend much loved,
you are a shining example to me and many others.

Acknowledgments

Several people helped me with many aspects of this book. Most of all, I want to thank my brother, Retired Coast Guard Warrant Officer Gilman C. Page, who taught me many things, like what to say when you're about to make an arrest on the high seas and where to get a cool catalog for marine stores. Gil, thanks for helping me work out the details and a super ending for this one!

Others who helped me with plot points, sailing, and Navy questions include my brother-in-law and awesome sailor Rondal A. Noyes Jr. and my friend and U.S. Navy Retired Machinist Mate Second Class Ken Lee.

Thanks also to my lovely and talented critiquers, who for this book included Lisa Harris, Lynette Sowell, Darlene Franklin, Vickie McDonough, and Candice Speare, all savvy authors.

ONE

Narita International Airport

Marie Belanger slid her arms around her husband's neck and looked up into his face. Pierre's brown eyes were troubled, and the dreamy expression she loved had fled.

"I'll miss you, *chérie*," he whispered.

"It's only three weeks." She smiled in an attempt to hide her own misgivings at traveling halfway around the world without him. They'd been married two and a half years, and his Navy obligations sometimes kept them apart for weeks, but it still felt strange. This time it was Marie's turn to leave.

"André will pick you up in Bangor tomorrow night."

"I know. Now, stop worrying. Your brother is very dependable." She stood on tiptoe and kissed him again, and he crushed her against him, stroking her hair.

A clipped feminine voice came over the loudspeaker, first in Japanese, then in English, and Marie reluctantly pulled away from Pierre.

"I need to get to my gate."

He nodded, his lips pressed together as he stared down at her. She knew she would have to make the move or he would hold her gaze all afternoon.

She stooped and grabbed the handle of her carry-on bag.

"At least you'll be with some people you know as far as San Francisco."

Marie glanced about the airport lobby. A dozen Navy wives, a few with children in tow, were heading for the escalators. Personnel whose rotations had ended would leave Japan to return to the United States. The dependents were booked on a commercial flight out of Narita. Most of the women's husbands would follow later on an aircraft carrier.

When the Belangers had first come to Japan, the tour had seemed interminable to Marie. But after some initial homesickness, she enjoyed the adventure and soaked up the experience. Suddenly it was done. Now she was eager to return to her sisters, her parents, her huge, crazy in-law family, and the green countryside of Maine. In just over a day she would be there. Much as she knew she would miss her husband, she felt the pull.

"Hey, Jenna Tarrington is going with you," Pierre said.

She straightened and followed his gaze. A flamboyant splash of red drew her eye. Of course. Jenna always made sure she'd be noticed.

Marie stood still. She couldn't hear their voices, but Jenna and her husband, who served in the same division with Pierre, seemed to be arguing. Jenna's face was set in a bitter scowl. Commander Tarrington stood with his profile to Marie. She could see that he was speaking rapidly, and his stiff posture and clenched hand told her that his parting words to Jenna were not sweet and loving.

"Wonder what her problem is today," Pierre said.

Marie swallowed hard. "Don't be so sure it's her problem."

"Right." He turned back to her, smiling. "Take care of yourself, *ma chérie*. I won't be there to look after you. When you get through customs in San Francisco, get right over to the domestic terminal and find your gate for Detroit."

"Oh, hush. I'm not a baby." She felt her face flush, remembering how she'd almost made them miss their connecting flight on the way out to Japan two years ago. "I'm a woman of the world now, and I can make a simple trip without a husband along to guide me."

He nodded, and his eyes went sober again. "I'll call you tomorrow night, at my folks' house."

"Terrific." The tears she'd determined not to shed sprang into her eyes, and she blinked. "Don't worry about me, baby. Pray all you want, but don't fret."

"Okay. Maybe those two need prayer as well." He looked toward the Tarringtons again. Jenna's lips contorted as she spat out her parting words. She wheeled away from her husband without touching him and pulled her black carry-on toward the escalator that led up to the international departure lobby and a heightened security area for passengers only. The strap of a leather laptop case hung from her shoulder. The commander stood rooted to the tiled floor, watching her and frowning, his eyes narrow slits.

As though feeling their gaze on him, Tarrington turned his head and focused on the Belangers. Pierre nodded and Marie attempted a smile, but colliding emotions hindered her.

She inhaled deeply and touched Pierre's sleeve. "I've got to go now."

"Are you sure you don't want me to go up with you?"

"No, you need to get back. You know they won't let you into the secure area, anyway."

He grimaced and slid his arm around her waist and walked with her toward the moving stairs. Ahead of her, Jenna Tarrington stepped off at the top and disappeared from view.

Marie turned her face up toward her husband one last time. Pierre kissed her gently and then stepped away.

"Au revoir," she whispered.

"À bientôt," he replied. "Soon."

He stood at the bottom of the escalator as she ascended, watching her, his dark eyebrows drawn together and his mouth set in mournful discontent. Marie faced downward so she could see him. Her handsome husband was usually more carefree, ready to laugh at the slightest excuse. Not today.

She wouldn't think about Pierre's duties for the next three weeks.

He hadn't confided his schedule to her, but it would no doubt involve one last official operation before he left the Orient. She would trust God to bring him safely home to her.

"Je t'aime," she whispered at the halfway point and blew him a kiss.

He nodded but did not smile.

Beyond him, she caught sight of Commander Tarrington, still standing where Jenna had left him, staring up at the level above her, his face set in displeasure. His eyes focused on something beyond her, and he raised his chin. Was it a reflex? An acknowledgment? A signal? The commander wheeled and strode for the exit.

Marie turned around as the escalator approached the upper floor. She stepped quickly off onto the solid surface, pulling her bag with her. She caught her balance and looked around, searching for the entrance to the secure area. A glance back told her she was now out of Pierre's line of sight, which was probably for the best. As long as he could see her, he would stay.

TWO

By the time Marie reached the security checkpoint, Jenna Tarrington had laid her bags on the conveyor belt and was removing her shoes. Several other passengers formed a line between them.

The queue crawled along beside the conveyor. Marie stooped and untied her running shoes. As she laid them on the moving belt, she looked ahead the length of the line and saw Jenna turn toward the gateway of the metal detector. Marie thought she'd seen the glint of tears in Jenna's eyes downstairs in the lobby, when she'd walked away from her husband. Funny, she wouldn't have described the commander's wife as a sensitive person. More brittle and angry. Jenna had always found something to complain about.

Marie felt inside all of her pockets to be sure she hadn't overlooked anything that should have gone into the basket on the conveyor belt. Her shoes and carry-on had already been engulfed by the ever-hungry scanner.

She gulped in air as she stepped into the metal detector. It shouldn't make her nervous, but it always did. It was the same unfounded feeling of guilt she'd had in elementary school when the principal entered the classroom. Even though she'd done nothing wrong, she felt he would focus on her and shame her.

The security officer nodded. She exhaled and slipped past him, fumbling for her sneakers and carry-on. Leaning against a wall, she pulled on her shoes and then walked to the seating near her departure gate. She sat down beside a blond woman holding a year-old baby.

The woman looked familiar, but Marie couldn't put a name to the decidedly Anglo-Saxon face.

"Hi. Are you Navy?"

"Yes. Linda Bailey."

"Marie Belanger." She settled her purse on her lap.

"Is your husband that doll of a lieutenant I saw downstairs?"

Marie couldn't help smiling. "Yeah."

"Lucky you. How long have you been here?"

"Two years."

"My guy's a third-class boatswain's mate. We've been here a year, but now he's been assigned to the *George H. W. Bush*, so I'm going home."

"Was the baby born here?" Marie smiled at the little boy and waggled her fingers before him. The baby rewarded her with a big grin. *Soon*, she thought. *A little boy with brown eyes and soft dark hair like his daddy's.*

"No, he was born in California, about a month before we came over."

Marie tucked her boarding pass into the front pocket of her carry-on. "Where are you headed?"

"San Diego. You?"

"Maine."

Linda's face went blank. "You mean..."

Marie smiled. "State of Maine. The Pine Tree State."

"Good grief! Could you get any farther away?"

"Not much. What's your baby's name?"

"Teddy."

"May I?" Marie held out her arms, and the baby came to her willingly.

"Is your husband staying here?" Linda asked with a smile.

"No, he'll be on the *Bush* too, but only as far as Pearl Harbor. Then he'll fly home. He's got thirty days' leave coming."

Linda shook her head with a chagrined smile. "Like I said: Lucky you. Danny will be on West Pac for six months."

Marie grimaced in sympathy while she hugged the warm, wiggly baby close. The long Western Pacific cruises were hard on families.

"No kids?" Linda asked.

"Not yet." Marie felt her cheeks flush. "After we get home. We thought we'd wait until we were in the States."

The chairs in the boarding area filled quickly. Teddy began to fuss, and Marie handed him back to his mother. Linda felt his diaper and stood up.

"Sorry. He needs a change. I'd better do it before we get on the plane." Teddy's whimpers became a wail, and Linda winced. "He knows something's going on, but he's not sure what, and he doesn't like it."

"I feel the same way," Marie said with a nervous chuckle. "See you later." She waved at the baby. He frowned at her and cried louder as Linda moved across the carpeted space. Marie inhaled, watching them and feeling more alone than before. Traveling with children must be difficult, but she would gladly accept the headaches if she had her own child to tend.

Someone plunked down in the seat Linda had vacated. Marie was startled that Jenna Tarrington had chosen that chair, but most of the other seats were taken.

"Hi," Marie said.

Jenna glanced at her and then back toward the open concourse, her eyes nearly shut.

Marie swallowed hard and told herself, *Don't take it personally.*

She wondered if Pierre had boarded the train heading back to the base. He'd managed to get the afternoon free so he could escort her, and she was thankful for that. Many of the women had come without their husbands. Then there was Jenna. Perhaps she'd have been happier if she'd come to the airport alone.

Jenna still watched the entrance to the boarding area. She rubbed the strap of her laptop case with her thumb as she stared from beneath her thick dark lashes.

Was she expecting her husband to follow her up here? He couldn't be flying out today. He was part of a unit that worked closely with Pierre's.

Marie followed Jenna's gaze but saw no sign of Commander Tarrington. Outside the boarding area, a Chinese man loitered. Perhaps he was flying on their plane but had not found a seat in the lounge. Marie looked around. Several Japanese families, a few unaccompanied women, and nearly a dozen men in suits were waiting with the flock of Navy dependents. A handful of other Americans and Europeans were also among the passengers.

The announcement for boarding came over the loudspeaker, and Marie stood up. Jenna seemed to notice her then. She wrinkled her face in a grimace of disgust as she picked up her bags.

"I hate flying."

Marie nodded. Was that supposed to explain her nervous detachment?

As Jenna gazed once more toward the concourse, her tense features showed something more. Fear, perhaps? Marie started to answer her comment, but the commander's wife grabbed the handle of her wheeled carry-on and rushed into the sloppy column forming before the door to the boarding tunnel.

Marie stared after her for a moment and then glanced back the other way. The Chinese man appeared to be deep in conversation with another man, and she noticed that both had briefcases and small suitcases. Neither of them looked Japanese. It was a subtle difference in the shape of their faces, but she had lived two years in this country and was starting to pick out the different ethnic groups. Chinese, she was certain, for the first man. His companion might be Korean.

The newly arrived man was wearing a cell phone headset. A dark line slashed his left cheek. From Marie's vantage point, it looked like a scar, or better yet, a healing wound. Sutures? She couldn't tell for sure at that distance. The two men ambled toward the check-in desk.

She picked up her purse and wheeled her carry-on over to the end of the line. As she reached the attendant at the door, she held out her boarding pass.

The immaculately groomed young woman took it, fed it into a machine, and handed Marie the stub.

"Thank you." Marie looked back. Linda Bailey slipped in at the end of the line, and Marie paused inside the boarding tunnel, letting other passengers go by her. Maybe she could take the diaper bag and help Linda get to her seat.

Linda showed her pass and advanced toward the doorway. She spotted Marie and grinned.

"Hey!"

"Let me help you."

As they shifted the quilted diaper bag between them, Marie glanced back toward the entry station. The two Chinese men hurried toward the back of the line. They eyed the boarding passengers with a clinical coldness that made Marie shiver. She turned away, not wanting to catch the attention of the scarred man with the headset, and shuffled with Linda and a few other stragglers down the tunnel that led to the plane.

THREE

1330 Friday, Tokyo

Pierre Belanger strode toward the stairway leading to the railroad station beneath Narita airport, determined not to look back. Marie was gone, or as good as. She'd told him not to linger until the plane was airborne, and she was right. He should get back to the base at Yokosuka and prepare for his last operation before boarding the *USS George H. W. Bush* for the States. One more run into China. He dreaded it, but it would be over in a couple of days, and then he could concentrate on home.

The afternoon was slipping away, and the train trip back would probably take at least an hour. The base had provided a shuttle bus for families with dependents leaving from the civilian airport today, but he knew the shuttle moved slower than the train, especially if traffic was heavy. With luck he'd get back in time to do a little more work tonight.

He passed a flower stall in the periphery of the train station and then a tea shop. He almost broke stride when he noticed Commander Tarrington sitting at a small table, talking earnestly with another man. Pierre looked away and kept walking. The commander had already acknowledged him inside the airport. Tarrington wasn't one to chitchat, and Pierre suspected he was no keener on interruptions, so he homed in on the platform he needed and put the two men behind him without making eye contact.

It did make him wonder, though. When he first arrived in the Orient, he wouldn't have noticed, but the nature of his duties required Pierre to be observant and discriminatory. The man speaking so earnestly to Tarrington had the facial structure he associated with Chinese heritage.

The platform was crowded with Japanese nationals and foreign travelers. Pierre found a pillar and leaned against it. The train must be due any minute, or there wouldn't be so many people waiting. He recognized an ensign from the *Bush* towering over the Asians and hailed him.

"Hey, Rocket!"

"Lieutenant." Ensign Laroquette grinned and eased through the crush toward Pierre. "Put the missus on the plane?"

"Yeah."

"Me too. Donna and the baby. Will wasn't happy this afternoon. I hope he doesn't scream all the way to Frisco."

The sleek train pulled up, and they let the civilian passengers board before stepping in. Pierre resigned himself to the long ride back to the base. He glanced out the window on the far side of the train, back toward the little tea shop where he'd seen Tarrington and the other man, but he couldn't spot them. He was used to setting up meetings for Tarrington and other officers and diplomats, and making sure they arrived safely at their appointments and got away afterward in one piece. But not here. Those secret meetings never took place inside Japan.

FOUR

Marie was surprised to discover that her assigned seat on the 747 was next to Jenna Tarrington, who had the window seat. They sat less than a third of the way back. Jenna glanced up from her in-flight magazine as Marie paused in the aisle but did not speak. Marie smiled mechanically as she wrestled with her carry-on.

Jenna turned back to the magazine, and Marie wondered if she did it to avoid conversation. She settled in and buckled the seat belt, and then she remembered the Asian men behind her in the terminal. An anxious glance down the aisle told her they hadn't boarded yet, unless they went into first class. Businessmen with expense accounts, maybe.

She sneaked a quick look at Jenna's reading material. She was studying the layout of the San Francisco airport. Calculating the time it would take to reach her next gate? Marie hoped customs wouldn't hold them up too long.

She wondered whether or not to attempt a conversation. During their time on the same military base in Japan, she had made a few overtures toward Jenna, but it was awkward with Pierre being lower ranked than Commander Tarrington. Most naval officers' wives behaved graciously and offered help to the younger women, but some seemed to assume their husbands' ranks and consider themselves above the rest. Jenna was cool and detached, and Marie had soon learned that she had earned a reputation among the other wives: snobbish and antisocial. Marie's private opinion differed. She believed Jenna was unhappy. Mrs. Tarrington declined most of the invitations for group adventures in the city. She appeared in public with her husband, but she also seemed tense and fidgety. And she rarely smiled.

Marie was sure the commander's high-stress job was partly responsible. She worried about Pierre herself when his unit went off on a classified operation. But she wondered if other reasons for marital tension simmered between the Tarringtons. Judging from things she'd heard Jenna say in the past, Marie was certain she was glad to leave Japan, yet Jenna's expression as she scrutinized the magazine was anything but cheerful.

Marie pulled her own copy of the magazine from the pocket on the back of the seat in front of her, and Jenna looked up.

"Nine hours," Marie said with a slight smile. "It'll be midnight here when we get to San Francisco, but it'll be seven a.m. there. I'll be exhausted."

"Yeah. Better try to sleep on the way."

"Say, can we use cell phones in here?" Marie looked around for a flight attendant, but the only one in sight was far down the aisle.

"If you're quick," Jenna said.

Marie punched the buttons for Pierre's cell, and he answered almost immediately.

"Hey, babe. Where are you?" Marie couldn't help but smile when she heard his voice. Jenna squeezed her lips together and went back to her magazine.

"On the train, just leaving the airport," Pierre said. "Any problems?"

"No, I just wanted to say *tu me manques.*"

"You miss me already?"

"You know I do."

"I miss you too." His voice took on the low rumble that sent anticipatory shivers through her. "Be careful, *chérie.*"

"I will."

Marie glanced up and saw a frowning flight attendant approaching.

"Gotta go."

"Call me later," he said.

"I will. Ta." She clicked off the phone and smiled up at the attendant. "I know." She slipped the phone into the pocket on the side of her purse and tucked the leather bag beneath the seat.

An hour into the flight, she felt some satisfaction. She'd succeeded in getting a little family information out of Jenna. Although Pierre was headed for home and an extended leave, it seemed the commander would stay in Japan for a few more months to wrap up his current assignment. Jenna was flying to Pittsburgh and would stay with her sister until the commander was transferred. In fact, she and Marie would be on the same flight again, from San Francisco to Detroit. The Tarringtons hoped for a new assignment in San Diego, but Jenna didn't want to move there until she knew for certain they'd be staying.

"I get so tired of this," she said.

"Moving around?" Marie asked.

"Yes, and having to do whatever the Navy tells Chris to do." Jenna shrugged. "I knew it would be like this, but I had no idea it would be like this. You know?"

Marie laughed. "Yeah, I guess. I was just so happy to be with Pierre at last, I didn't care where they sent us."

"Still feel that way?"

"Kind of." Marie felt a flush stain her cheeks. "I hate being separated from him again. Before we were married, he spent a year and a half away, and we didn't have much contact. That was really hard. I told him when he came home, 'I'll go to Antarctica with you if I have to. Just don't ever leave me alone again.'"

Jenna's delicate dark eyebrows drew together. "Well, he's high enough up now, and in such a specialized field, I doubt they'll send Belanger off on six-month cruises or anything like that again. He's too valuable for classified missions. I'm surprised they're letting him go before this one's wrapped up."

Marie swallowed and lowered her eyelashes. "I...don't know much about it. But he's been here two years. I don't think they can keep him longer, can they?"

Jenna shrugged.

"Maybe it's an ongoing thing that a new team will finish," Marie suggested.

Jenna leaned her seat back as far as it would go. "Who knows? You and I surely don't. I'm going to take a nap."

She closed her eyes, and Marie sat still for a moment, feeling dismissed. She wondered if Jenna knew more than she did about the classified work their husbands performed. She had certainly slammed the door on the topic. Marie knew only that Pierre worked in an office on the base, and every couple of months he and a few others took a trip that lasted from a few days to two weeks.

The first time he'd gone, she was so nervous she could barely eat or sleep until he returned. When he came home after five days of silence, she flung herself into his arms and burst into tears.

"What's wrong, *chérie?*"

"I was worried," she'd sobbed, amazed that he should think she'd be calm during his absence.

"But, baby, I'm home now."

She hiccuped and nodded, looking up at him and wiping her tears away with her sleeve. "I was afraid you were in danger. You know."

He shook his head in bewilderment.

"Combat," she whispered.

Pierre laughed. "My sweet Marie! If I were going into combat, would I have asked you to have my dress uniform cleaned before I went?"

She sniffed. "No. So...can you tell me now where you were?"

"No, but that doesn't mean I love you any less." He pulled her back into his arms, and she determined in that moment not to speculate, even when the dress blues stayed home and he traveled with only camos or civilian clothes. During his subsequent absences, she explored her new surroundings and signed up for a Japanese class. She discovered a small English-speaking church between the base and the business district, pastored by an American missionary and a Japanese seminary student. There she met Americans and Europeans in the country for both military and business reasons, and a few native Japanese families. At once her contacts and opportunities exploded.

After four months in Japan, Pierre had told her that the change in her astonished him. She no longer cried when he came home but greeted him with bubbly accounts of her adventures in his absence. He was jealous, he told her, and so on his days off she took him around Tokyo and Yokosuka to see the wonders she'd found, and on Sundays he attended the little church with her.

The memory brought to mind the New Testament Marie had tucked in her carry-on. She fished it out and opened to the book of Colossians, chapter 1. She and Pierre had agreed to read a chapter a day during their separation; the same chapter, so they could discuss it if they had a chance, and when they were reunited they would go on together.

"The faith and love that spring from the hope that is stored up for you in heaven," she whispered as she reread verse 5. She leaned back and smiled. Japan was a wonderful place. She was glad to be going home, but she would not forget the bustling streets, the courteous people who stared in delight when she greeted them in Japanese, the gracefully odd pagodas stuck between ugly contemporary buildings. And she would never forget that in Japan she and Pierre had found Christ under the missionary's teaching. That in itself was worth the time spent away from home and family, the homesickness, and early bouts of fear for her husband's safety. She would always love Japan.

She read on through the chapter. "That you may live a life worthy of the Lord…growing in the knowledge of God, being strengthened with all power…" She sighed and closed her eyes for a moment. *That's what I need, Lord. Strength. Knowledge.*

She looked at her seatmate. Jenna appeared to be sleeping. The cabin was quiet now, and Marie realized she hadn't heard a baby cry for quite some time. She decided to walk toward the back of the plane to find Linda and see how Teddy was doing.

When she returned half an hour later, Jenna sat with her laptop case open on the tray table before her.

"Hey." Marie smiled as she settled in her seat. "Did you sleep?"

"A little." Jenna closed the computer case and stowed it once more. "Was that a Bible you were reading before?"

Marie turned to scan her face. "Yeah."

"Do you...pray?"

"Yes."

Jenna's eyes narrowed. She looked away for a moment and inhaled sharply. Marie waited for her to speak.

"I'm a little nervous."

"About this trip?"

Jenna nodded. "If anything happens to me..."

Marie's pulse skipped. Jenna had admitted she hated air travel, but still, she didn't show signs of terror. No white knuckles and no digging her nails into the armrest, not even during takeoff.

"Would you like me to pray for you?" Marie could hardly believe Jenna's thoughts had turned in that direction, but as she spoke, Jenna's brow relaxed and she sighed.

"Couldn't hurt, right?"

"Absolutely."

"Thanks. I mean...well, Chris..." Jenna stopped and turned her face toward the window.

Marie touched the sleeve of her red silk blouse. "I'd be happy to pray for you, Jenna."

"Thanks." Jenna threw her an anxious half smile. "Not out loud or anything." She glanced around and gave a nervous chuckle. "I mean, I just thought..."

"Sure. God is always ready to hear our prayers, even if we don't speak them out loud."

"Right."

They sat in silence for a long moment, and Jenna continued to stare out the window at the swirling clouds.

Marie decided she was done talking. She settled back against the cushions and closed her eyes. *Lord, this is unexpected. I don't know what to pray. But You know what's on Jenna's heart. Please help her.*

FIVE

1600 Friday, Yokosuka

When Pierre left the train station near the main gate of the Yokosuka naval base, he was gratified to see a waiting Jeep, driven by an ensign assigned to his office. His official workday was nearly over, but he spent an hour finalizing arrangements for the unit's next trip into China. After sundown tomorrow, his small band of men would take three naval officers and two State Department lower level diplomats to Shanghai—Pierre's last such expedition, he hoped.

These undercover jaunts were usually uneventful, but they were never boring. His stomach churned from the minute they lifted off at Yokosuka to the moment they touched down again safely. His job, and that of the half dozen handpicked men he supervised, entailed making sure the officials engaged in negotiations with a vast network of Chinese subversives survived each session.

At six o'clock he pulled out his cell phone, stared at it, and sighed. She'd promised to call him later, but she wouldn't land in San Francisco for hours. He went home and ate supper, thinking all the time about Marie and how empty their apartment was without her.

At last he decided to forget about the huge amount of minutes the provider would subtract from his account and try to get through to his younger brother in Maine.

"Hey! Pierre! *Comment ça va?*"

"Bien!" Pierre grinned. André's voice came faint but enthusiastic as always over the airwaves.

"Marie get off okay?" André asked.

"Yeah, she's somewhere over the Pacific."

"Terrific. You do know it's five a.m. here, right?"

Pierre grimaced. "Sorry. I should have waited."

"Well, don't worry. I'll be there when Marie lands tonight. Just relax."

"I'll try."

"Portland, right?"

Pierre's stomach flipped, and he clenched the phone. "Bangor, you idiot! I told you! I e-mailed you her itinerary too." He stopped ranting long enough to hear André's laughter.

"I know," his brother chortled. "I couldn't resist. Now let me get a little more sleep, will ya?"

SIX

Marie breezed through customs in San Francisco smiling. Her trip was only half over, but she felt as though she were within the city limits of home.

She'd shipped most of the souvenirs she'd bought for her family and had little to show the agents. Just one item—a gift for her mother. An airline representative helped her check her two large bags again for the domestic flight. When the suitcases were safely on their way, Marie adjusted her purse strap, pulled up the handle of her rolling carry-on, and headed, yawning, into the bustling terminal. Uniformed agents of the Transportation Security Administration seemed to be everywhere, and she felt safe. Squinting to read the signs far ahead of her, she heard her name called.

"Marie! Wait a sec!"

She turned in surprise. Jenna scurried toward her, dragging her wheeled bag and struggling to keep her dangling laptop case under control.

"Where's the shuttle?" The strap threatened to slide off Jenna's shoulder, and she stopped to hoist it over her head, nestling the computer bag against her side.

"I think the stop is a ways down the concourse," Marie said. "We should have plenty of time."

"At least there's a flight out soon, and we don't have to sit in the airport all night."

"All day, you mean." Marie's body rebelled at the time change, and she longed to curl up in a comfortable bed and sleep.

Jenna fell into step with her, and they threaded their way through the crowd. Marie spotted a sign with the words "Shuttle Bus."

"This way."

Although Jenna kept pace, she swiveled her head frequently to look behind her.

Curious, Marie glanced back, past advertising kiosks and vendors' booths. An Asian man ten yards behind them turned quickly to examine the leather goods at a table to one side of the traffic flow.

Marie caught her breath. Wasn't that one of the men who had hurried to board the plane at the last minute at Narita? The one with the headset. She supposed it was possible, but then, it was also possible her mind was playing tricks on her. She'd seen him only for a minute in Japan, and now he'd turned his face away from her. She couldn't tell if he had a scar on his left cheek. An Asian man in a well-cut black suit, wearing a hands-free telephone headset. How common was that?

"Hey, do you know that man back there?"

"What man?" Jenna asked, swiveling to look.

Marie scanned the area where she'd seen him. "He's gone."

"Come on." Jenna quickened her pace, and Marie sped up to stay with her.

In moments they were outside and boarding a glass-sided van. Marie settled onto a bench, panting, with her purse on her lap and her carry-on nestled between her feet.

"When you want to move, you move." She threw Jenna a sheepish smile and leaned back as the shuttle made its way around the perimeter of the connected terminals. She wished she could reopen their brief conversation about God and prayer, but Jenna had slept or pretended to sleep for the remainder of their flight. Marie felt Jenna was embarrassed that she'd mentioned the topic and had raised the barrier between them again.

Ten minutes later they climbed down from the vehicle into already sweltering California air. Marie held the glass door for Jenna, and they hauled their bags into the domestic terminal.

"We made good time." Marie positioned her purse and prepared to drag her black carry-on down the open court toward their next gate.

"Hey, I'd like some coffee. How about you?" Jenna asked.

Marie stared at her.

Jenna shrugged. "It's like—what—almost one a.m. as far as my nervous system knows, right?"

Marie scanned the overhead signs proclaiming the gate numbers. "Okay. We're practically there, and we have time."

"Nearly an hour until we board." Jenna nodded ahead and to the left. "There's a gourmet coffee stall right over there."

"Why not?" Marie thought fleetingly of Pierre in Tokyo and hoped he was asleep. But the long flight had left her fatigued, and caffeine sounded good. Maybe it would raise her energy.

"Great." Jenna unzipped her purse. "Tell you what. I'll sit on this bench and watch the luggage, and you run for the coffee, okay? I'll take a caramel cappuccino. Get whatever you want. I'm paying."

Marie opened her mouth and then closed it. She parked her carry-on next to the bench, plucked the ten-dollar bill from Jenna's hand, and turned toward the coffee stand. Pierre had insisted she change her yen to American currency in Tokyo, but her cash was to last her until he arrived home or his bank account transfer came through. Since it was Jenna's idea, she would let Jenna pay.

Even though it was early morning in San Francisco, the airport was full of people. As Marie passed across the traffic stream in front of a newsstand, a constant flood of humanity parted around her. A graying man perusing a *Chicago Tribune* glanced at her over the top of the newspaper. Marie looked away from his penetrating gaze, feeling suddenly apprehensive.

What was it about traveling alone that put her on edge? She had to admit that knowing Jenna was waiting for her slightly calmed her nerves. She'd never done much of anything alone in her life, and the trip to Japan was her first long excursion. Her only venture outside New England before that had been a family trip by minivan to Quebec City. And she'd never lived alone. She was only nineteen when she married Pierre, and until that day she'd lived with her parents.

You're a big girl, Marie, she told herself. *A married woman and a world traveler. Relax. Enjoy this.*

Five minutes later she walked cautiously through the flow of pedestrians, back toward the bench where she had left Jenna, carrying two steaming cups and hoping her purse strap would not slip down her arm and slosh the hot liquid out through the slits in the plastic covers.

Her black wheeled carry-on, with a yellow chenille ponytail tie knotted around the handle, sat beside the bench. Jenna's, sporting a red-white-and-blue plastic luggage tag, was neatly positioned beside it. The near end of the bench was empty, and at the far end sat a woman in a burka, and beside her a young boy who stared at Marie with wide, black eyes.

Marie pulled in a deep breath and looked around as she approached, but Jenna was not in sight. She clenched the two cups in their cardboard holders and stifled the impulse to utter her frustration. Two teenagers, talking in low tones, edged toward the bags, and Marie quickly stepped forward and sat on the bench, placing the cups beside her and then drawing the two carry-ons close to her knees. The two young men nudged each other and moved on down the concourse.

Marie drew in a deep breath, picked up her chai tea, and sipped it through the cover. She scanned the crowd, sure she could spot Jenna's red blouse three gates away. The fumes of her slowly burning anger turned the tea bitter. How could Jenna do something like that—walk off and leave both their bags unattended? It was the first travel rule every novice learned, and the one the loudspeaker blared most often. Jenna was at least a decade older than Marie and far more experienced. It just didn't add up.

Marie sent up a quick prayer for calmness. Getting upset with

Jenna wouldn't help. She spied the sign for a restroom twenty yards away. That was probably it. Jenna thought she could make a quick trip in there and be back before Marie knew she was gone. But why on earth would she abandon the luggage? Couldn't she wait five minutes? Maybe she'd stayed put until she saw Marie heading back.

Her laptop. Jenna had carried a laptop. Did she take that along with her? Marie hoped so. If she hadn't, then it was gone.

"What a stupid thing to do!"

The woman in the burka turned her veiled face Marie's way, and the boy stared even more openly. Marie grimaced, realizing she'd spoken aloud. She glanced at her watch. They'd better get to the gate. But where was Jenna? Were the lines in the restroom that long?

After waiting five minutes, she considered towing her own bag and Jenna's to the gate and checking in. That would be better than waiting here and missing the flight. If Jenna didn't show up by the time she reached the check-in desk, Marie could leave the unwanted carry-on in care of the agent there. She stood, mentally slapping herself for agreeing to fetch coffee for Jenna. *You try to be nice...*

Far down the concourse, she noticed a flash of red. Marie set her half-empty cup on the bench beside Jenna's cappuccino and squinted toward the distant figure. Jenna was hurrying toward her with the laptop hugged against her side. But instead of making straight for the bench, she veered into the restroom.

Marie grasped the handle of one suitcase with each hand, trying to synthesize what she'd seen. Where had Jenna gone in the first place, if not the restroom? And why hadn't she come straight back? Marie looked at the coffee cups and made her decision. Pulling the bags, she struck off toward the ladies' room. No doubt Jenna would be upset that she'd left the drinks behind, but Marie's patience had evaporated. She would *not* miss that plane to Detroit.

Marie was still five yards from the doorless entrance when an Asian woman in a dark uniform ducked inside. On her back were large white letters: TSA. Marie followed, easing the two carry-ons behind her. Jenna's wobbled and tipped, and she paused to stand it up again. Moving on, she rounded a corner and gained the open area between rows of sinks. Her progress was blocked by the dark-haired security agent. The woman stood with her back to Marie, speaking sharply to the only other person visible in the room.

"You give it to me."

Marie stopped in the shadow of the entry, feeling that she was intruding. Over the security guard's shoulder, she could see Jenna clutching her laptop case.

"You give it now," the TSA agent said in slightly accented tones. She stepped toward Jenna.

"No," Jenna stepped back, her wide eyes on the other woman. "I called and told them I'm not ready to deal with you people. I'll make contact when I get to Detroit."

"Is too late."

"No. My husband—" Jenna gasped as the guard advanced toward her and seized the laptop case. "Stop! You can't do this. I'll scream and someone will hear me."

The security officer hesitated.

Marie's pulse hammered. *Lord, what's happening? Should I interfere?*

"Jenna? Are you okay?"

She took one step into the restroom, and the carry-on bags rattled over the tiled floor. The guard whirled toward her, and Jenna's eyes found Marie and locked on her face.

"Run!" Jenna cried.

Marie opened her mouth and then froze as the pistol in the officer's hand caught her attention. Her stomach plunged, and she felt suddenly weak.

"Call the police, not TSA!" Jenna's dark eyes held full-blown terror now.

Marie backed up, nearly tripping over the bags. The security agent seemed to hover for an instant, looking toward Marie with black eyes and then back toward Jenna, but the pistol stayed aimed at Jenna.

Two quick pops sounded, and Marie stared unbelieving as Jenna's eyes went blank and she crumpled to her knees, a darker red patch flowering on the front of her blouse.

Marie ran around the corner of the exit and crashed into a large, gray-haired woman.

"Don't go in there," Marie gasped. She squeezed past the woman and ran into the flowing crowd.

SEVEN

Marie hurried down the concourse, not seeing the people who dodged around her. She walked a long way before she looked back. She could barely see the sign for the restroom, and it hit her that she'd gone the wrong way, past the coffee stand and away from her next gate. She tried to think about what she should do, and at the same time tried not to think too deeply, but the image of what she had seen was permanently etched on her brain.

She reached with trembling hands for her cell phone. Whether he was asleep or not, she was calling Pierre. Her fingers sought the familiar rectangular case in the depths of her purse but came up empty.

Frantic, she dragged the bags aside and pulled out her wallet, her passport, lipstick, tissues, hairbrush, three pens, and a notepad. No phone. She checked her wallet, just to be sure, but her money and identification were intact. Helter-skelter, she loaded everything back into the purse. Maybe she'd stuck it in the carry-on. She checked each outside pocket methodically. On the plane in Tokyo, she had called Pierre. After that, she was certain she had returned her phone to her purse. Could one of the customs agents have pocketed it while checking her bags? Unthinkable with her standing right there, but she supposed it was possible. And why would they take a cell phone and not the three hundred dollars from her wallet? Her stomach felt queasy. She jammed her hand into the pocket of her slacks and inhaled only when she'd fingered the comforting lump of two hundred, folded up in a tight wad. She'd separated the cash into two stashes so that if part were stolen she wouldn't be destitute.

She stood for a moment, hunched over the suitcase. Her pulse throbbed in her temples. Jenna was dead, Marie was certain. Bile filled her throat, and she again thrust her hand into each outside compartment of her bag, hoping against despair that her fingers would find her phone. She was totally cut off from Pierre, and a woeful fear crept over her.

To be certain she'd checked everywhere, she opened the main compartment of her carry-on and rifled the contents. A small plastic case lay between her favorite jeans and her CD player. She grasped the case and held it up.

It was smaller than her phone, only about the size of a small pack of gum. Had a thief taken her cell phone and left this in her bag? She fiddled with it, and it slid open in two pieces. Marie stared at it. Something electronic, she decided. Pierre always laughed at her when she called on him to set the DVD player and fix her computer glitches. She was not a technology person. She liked to believe she was more artistic, thinking on the other side of the brain, whichever side that was.

Options flashed through her mind. She needed to check in very soon, but she couldn't get on the plane for Detroit with this... thing.

I need to turn this over to someone. She shivered, remembering the TSA uniform the woman in the restroom wore. How could she trust a security guard? They might be watching her right now! She looked around, but no one seemed to notice her, bending over her open suitcase. *Call the police,* Jenna had said. *Not TSA.* Somehow, TSA—or at least that one TSA agent—was involved in whatever it was that had gotten Jenna killed. Marie took three shaky breaths, exhaling slowly each time. Maybe that woman wasn't really a TSA officer. An imposter. But could she take a chance that the next one she encountered would be genuine?

She checked her watch and realized time was short. *I'll get to my gate and give them Jenna's bag and report that my phone was stolen.*

Two security officers hurried along in the direction she had come from, and Marie shrank against the wall. She pulled the zipper on the carry-on shut and watched them. They headed for the restroom entrance, where a knot of people had gathered. She heard one say, "We'll have to do crowd control until the police get here."

So far, her brain refused to form the word "murder." But as she watched the commotion down the concourse and saw hurrying people stop to stare at the officers taping off the doorway, she swallowed hard and faced it. Jenna was dead. She had witnessed a murder.

She looked down at the plastic gadget she clutched. *Call the police, not TSA.*

I would, she thought, *if I had my cell phone.* She had to call someone. There must be a bank of pay phones somewhere nearby. Calling Pierre would do no good in this moment, she realized. She could call 911, even though she had no coins. But there must be policemen already on duty in the airport. She needed to talk to one.

A man leaning against the wall across the way drew her eye, and Marie gasped as she focused on his craggy face. He stood on the edge of the crowd, perhaps ten yards from her, but she was sure of his identity. He was the man who'd stood by the newsstand earlier, and he was watching her.

Her heart seemed to stop, and then it lurched forward at a gallop. She exhaled slowly, fear overcoming the sick regret she'd felt when she thought of Jenna.

He turned and spoke to another man—an Asian man. The second man searched, searched, and then zeroed in on her. Marie wanted to hide, but it was too late. They had both seen her. The first man gestured to someone farther down the concourse and pulled out a cell phone. The Asian edged around the crowd in an arc that Marie feared was bringing him toward her position.

She shoved the tiny plastic case into one of the pockets of her purse and dashed back the way she had come, pulling her bag and

Jenna's behind her. As she passed the restroom area, she glanced across toward it. At least a dozen TSA officers were on the scene, but she didn't see the woman who had shot Jenna among them.

She shot a glance over her shoulder, but she couldn't spot the men who frightened her so with their cold, penetrating eyes. She was panting, and she slowed her steps as she threaded her way between herds of pedestrians with her awkward burden. She couldn't outrun those men. She needed to get out of the open central concourse. A gift shop featuring Southwestern art beckoned her, and she pulled the cumbersome bags inside and ducked behind a tall display of wooden carvings.

A wave of guilt hit her as she recalled her annoyance at Jenna's disappearance. She remembered her husband's cynical comment that morning at Narita. *Wonder what her problem is today.* What, indeed?

She tried to put together the pieces of her puzzle of fear. She'd seen Jenna eyeing an Asian man before they boarded the plane. Then two men, who might be totally unrelated to the restroom incident, had come through the security check at the last minute. After disembarking here in San Francisco, she'd thought she glimpsed one of the Tokyo men. Then she'd noticed a Caucasian man by the newsstand, and he seemed to be watching her. She'd followed Jenna to the restroom and seen her gunned down by an Asian woman wearing a security uniform. And then she saw the Caucasian man again, talking to…

"Jenna," she whispered. "What have you done?"

The man near the newsstand had seen her with Jenna. Was he stationed there to watch Jenna? He was connected to the Asian man. It seemed reasonable to assume they were also involved with the Asian woman who had shot Jenna.

Marie glanced behind her, scanning the gift shop with a shiver. *Dear Lord,* she prayed silently, *am I delusional, or have I fallen into a pool of evil?*

The act of praying calmed her, and she knew at once she should have used this weapon sooner. *Dear God, show me what to do! Make me wise.*

She forced herself to breathe slowly and peered from behind a coyote sculpture, surveying the entrance to the shop. No one stared back. Exhaling another wordless prayer, she made a decision.

Though her fear nearly paralyzed her, she had to elude the men. Every time she spotted one of them, she felt threatened and alarms clanged in her brain. But she couldn't wander around with Jenna's bag, hoping to find a policeman. She was close to the shuttle stop where they'd entered the terminal. Marie glanced at her watch. Only ten minutes to boarding time.

She hurried from the shop into the stream of travelers and wound her way back to the desk nearest the door where they'd arrived. A uniformed woman hovered over the computer behind the counter, with only one customer in line. Marie jumped into place. The young man in front of her had longish blond hair. She pegged him for a college student or a musician, or both. She flicked a look over her shoulder, saw no one suspicious lurking about, and pivoted forward again. *Don't show your face,* she told herself. The young man ahead of her turned away, and she was gratified to see that he was wearing a Pepperdine sweatshirt. College student for sure. She hadn't completely lost her reasoning ability.

"May I help you?"

The woman's generic smile lent a normalcy to the atmosphere. Marie slid Jenna's bag toward the counter.

"This belongs to the woman who sat next to me on a plane from Narita. Tokyo International, that is."

The agent nodded, her smile warping into a puzzled frown. "It belongs to someone else?"

"Yes. We got off the plane together and came over here from the other terminal, and then she…she left it with me, and she didn't come back. I need to get to my connecting flight, and I didn't want to just abandon it, but I couldn't wait any longer."

The woman reached for the phone, a carefully neutral expression on her face.

"Did you know this woman?"

"Slightly."

"Can you give me her name?"

Marie cleared her throat and looked toward the concourse once more.

"Uh, Jenna Tarrington. Her husband is serving with the Navy in Yokosuka." She supplied the flight and seat numbers, and then she seized the handle of her own bag and wheeled it around.

"Wait!" the woman cried.

"I'll miss my flight." Marie called over her shoulder as she hurried away without looking back. She was free! But she still felt guilty. She ought to do more, for Jenna's sake. Perhaps she could identify the shooter and help the police catch her. Yet she couldn't linger. That woman had not acted alone, and Marie felt that if she stayed here, the net of evil would close about her. Her pulse would not slow down, and she still felt the near nausea of fear as she left the desk. When someone came to pick up the bag, she needed to be far away. Best if she shed any association with Jenna as quickly as possible.

Walking rapidly toward her next gate, she kept an eye out for the mysterious men she'd seen before. She didn't see them, and breathing seemed easier, now that she no longer had Jenna's belongings.

Pushing her stride to just below a jog, she hurried as fast as she dared, warning oncoming people with her set expression that she wasn't prepared to stop or swerve. She tried to form another mental prayer, but breathing evenly and focusing on her destination took all her energy.

When they were dating, she and Pierre had talked about religion a few times. His faith was much stronger than hers, she was sure back then, during her naive high school days. She always thought she had plenty of time to figure out what religion meant to her, but from time to time she pondered it and felt sophisticated to be thinking about such weighty matters. She'd prayed for things she really wanted, even before she was certain God existed, but she had never felt a personal connection with God in those days.

Now she had a real, living faith. Thanks to the witness Pastor and Lori Lascomb had brought to the military personnel in Japan, she'd found Christ. Marie didn't have to shudder and hope everything would turn out well. Even in this horror tale she'd stumbled into, God was in control. She could know that no matter how this ended, she would be safe in God's hand.

Thank You, Lord!

That was settled, and the knowledge comforted her. As she approached her gate, she managed to string together another awkward prayer. Just for an instant she looked back, wondering if she had done the right thing. She remembered something her sister Lisa had told her once, when Marie was overwhelmed with planning the details of her wedding and her fiancé was thousands of miles away.

"Just make a choice, honey, and stick with it. Don't look back."

"But what if I choose the wrong thing?"

"Doesn't matter. Just go on from there. Ten years from now, no one's going to care if the flowers don't quite match and the cake is a little dry."

"Your gate has been changed," the man at the desk told her.

Marie gaped at him and then pulled in a sharp breath. "Okay. Where do I go?"

"Another wing of the terminal. Concourse C. It's quickest if you take the shuttle. The stop is back that way."

Marie's heart sank. He was pointing back toward where she had come from, and she recalled all too well the distant location of the shuttle stop, just beyond the desk where she had left Jenna's bag.

"But...isn't the plane boarding now?"

He nodded. "Yes, but we've posted a twenty-minute delay because there has been an accident over here. They're moving several departing flights to the other side of the terminal to ease the traffic flow. I'll call over there and tell them you're coming."

"Thank you!"

He already had his telephone to his ear.

Marie swiveled, flipping her carry-on around. She ran, making no pretense of courtesy this time, pushing between two men and dashing on without looking back when one snapped at her in a foreign language. Spanish, she thought. No, Italian. She ducked around a woman pushing a stroller.

Dear Lord, please don't let me miss my flight. Unless You want me to, of course. She clenched her teeth, yanking the bag around a post and slowing to avoid slamming into a plump man who waddled along with a large suitcase trailing behind him. What kind of crazy prayer was that, anyway? *Sorry, Lord. You understand what I mean, right?*

She didn't see any sinister men lurking, and she was thankful for that. So far she was coping, but if the severe man from the newsstand popped up, or one of the Asians from the Narita airport, she wasn't sure she could make a sane decision.

She realized she was even with the desk where she'd left Jenna's black bag. There was no line now, but the uniformed woman was still behind the counter, arranging a stack of pasteboard slips.

Should she stop?

No, of course not. That would be foolish.

But Marie's feet slowed. She stared at the low platform where she'd left Jenna's bag and wavered just an instant, inching into the shallows of the murky gray pool of horror again. This whole nightmare was far bigger than racing to catch a flight. Her feet slowed as two men in uniform cut across her path and approached the agent at the desk.

"Hi," said the taller one. "You called security about an unattended bag. We're here to collect it."

Marie whirled in confusion to hear what would happen next.

The woman stared at them. Her lips twitched. "You mean the Tarrington bag?"

"Yeah."

"I gave it to the FBI agent."

"What FBI agent?" the tall man asked.

"He was here a minute ago."

The second officer shook his head. "The FBI hasn't arrived yet."

Marie ducked her head. She plowed into the crowd. *Don't look back!* She zigged across to the door marked "Shuttle."

EIGHT

Marie veered to the right, slowing to a quick walk. The sinister Chinese man from Tokyo stood at ten o'clock, just ahead and to her left, talking to the graying Caucasian man from the newsstand. The reddish scar was plain on the Asian's cheek, leaving her no room for doubt.

She had to get beyond them to reach the shuttle stop. Falling into step with a hefty woman, she took a few steps forward and peeked around the bulk of her companion. A third man was joining them. Gleaming black hair, a dark suit. The other man from Narita?

Marie ducked behind two women buying souvenirs at a booth of silver jewelry and took a deep breath. Cautiously she leaned out and scouted the twenty yards of tile between her and her goal. The men appeared to be scanning the airport for someone and communicating with cell phones. They separated, walking slowly, searching.

Dear God, what do I do? They're looking for me. Make me invisible, Lord!

She knelt behind the edge of the booth's counter and unzipped her carry-on. Sunglasses. She clapped them on. Ah! Red Sox cap. Gathering her hair into a bunch at the nape of her neck, she shoved it under the cap and pulled the bill down firmly over her eyebrows. What else?

If only she could change out of her pink Mount Fuji T-shirt. That had to be attention getting. She slipped a plain blue blouse on over it. Maybe that would help make her less conspicuous.

Should I walk off and abandon my bag? She shot a furtive glance behind her. As she turned, she noted the jewelry booth's clerk staring at her. She yanked the zipper closed and dashed for the door leading to the shuttle bus stop, dragging the bag.

Several other people waited at the shuttle stop, and she careened to a halt on the tarmac just yards outside the terminal door. A middle-aged couple turned to eye her, and Marie attempted a smile.

"How long 'til the shuttle?"

"What terminal?" the man asked.

"C."

"It's coming now."

Marie edged away from the doorway and tried to blend in with the other travelers. A woman with two youngsters came out and stood behind her. Marie blew out a long breath. The shuttle pulled up. She scrambled aboard ahead of the family and plunked herself down on one of the hard, molded benches, keeping her carry-on between her feet.

The driver closed the door and pulled away, parallel to the terminal. Looking back, Marie saw an Asian man shove through the door onto the tarmac and run to the shuttle stop. She turned away from the window and ducked down in her seat.

Lord, help me! Should I get on that plane or not?

More than anything, she wanted to talk to Pierre. She wanted him—or someone else she could trust—to tell her what to do. But no human could do that right now. She'd have to rely on her own instincts and any guidance she felt from above.

She ran from the shuttle to her new gate, arriving just as the attendant reached to close the door to the boarding tunnel.

"Wait!" Marie gasped.

The woman looked up and checked her movement, taking Marie's boarding pass with a smile.

"You cut it close, but you made it."

"Thanks!" Marie gulped air as she pulled her bag along the passageway, over the bumps where the sections connected. She was beginning to hate the small, black suitcase. She could travel faster with only her purse. Still, without her stash of extra clothing, the men might have spotted her back there and...done what? She pushed the thought away as she entered the aircraft's cabin. The attendant in the doorway directed her down the aisle toward a seat midway along the body of the plane.

She tugged off her sunglasses and stuck them in her purse. Her legs trembled as she tottered along the narrow path between the seats wanting to stare at her feet and avoid eye contact. Instead she looked over her fellow passengers. None of the suspicious-looking men she'd outmaneuvered in the terminal could possibly be aboard, could they? She almost missed her row, she was searching so intently for a hostile face.

Her seat was next to an ample woman with glowing, dark caramel skin and abundant curly hair that spilled about her shoulders and framed her pleasant face.

The seat between them remained empty, and Marie was glad. She juggled her carry-on into the space beneath the seat ahead of hers and then glanced at the woman.

"Hello. I'm Caprice," the woman said, smiling, and Marie felt instantly more at ease.

"Marie." She extended her hand, and Caprice took it, looking her over with amusement.

"Had to rush, huh?"

"Yes. They changed my gate."

Caprice nodded. "I think everyone had to deal with that little surprise. But we're on our way now."

The seat belt lights pinged on overhead, and Marie struggled with her buckle. Her nerves still jangled, but she managed to fasten the belt with her trembling hands. She hoped Caprice couldn't tell how close to the edge she was. But perhaps she could put it down to almost missing the flight.

For a long minute she wondered if the plane was actually going to move. Had they folded back the boarding tunnel yet? They still sat motionless in the same spot beside the terminal.

Come on, move! We need to get out of here!

What if the men who were looking for her somehow convinced the airline authorities to hold the plane and let them search for her? She was sure they had lied to the woman in the terminal and told her they were with the FBI. Could they get away with that again? Would they come on board and force her to leave the plane?

A flight attendant came and stood in the aisle three rows ahead of her to demonstrate the oxygen masks and point out the emergency exits, while a recorded monologue of the instructions played. *I could use a little extra oxygen,* Marie thought, trying to steady her breathing.

The flight crew went to their seats, and the plane began to vibrate. Marie sighed in relief and looked past Caprice, out the window behind the wing, and saw that they were rolling away from the building.

She sank back against the seat cushions and closed her eyes.

Thank You, Lord!

The plane halted again, and her heart raced. Even now, would she be apprehended and hauled off the plane?

They began moving again, and the plane gained speed. Faster and faster, they rolled down the runway. Marie clenched her fists and gritted her teeth, praying. *Please, Lord, let us get airborne. Take me home safely, please!*

When the upward thrust and the pressure of their acceleration eased, she drew a deep breath and opened her eyes. Caprice was reading a fashion magazine, but she glanced over at Marie and smiled.

Marie pulled a catalog of overpriced merchandise from the seat pocket, opened it, and stared at a page of tiger eye accessories, not focusing, trying to keep her breathing smooth and even, and willing her hands to hold the paper steady.

Were those men really looking for her? Why?

Her mind went back to Narita, as she and Pierre had lingered, saying their reluctant goodbyes. She could see Jenna standing near her husband, her back rigid in the opulent red silk blouse, her face a mask of controlled anger.

Then Jenna's behavior as they waited within the boarding area. She'd been nervous, Marie thought, even though the commander was gone. She'd kept watching the entry to the boarding lounge. And when those two men had come in at the last minute, she'd fled into the crowd.

The more she thought about it, the more certain Marie was that the men from the Tokyo airport were now in San Francisco. Jenna had tried to elude them. Was that why she'd left the bags by the bench in the airport concourse? To try to throw them off her scent? Jenna wasn't nervous about flying. She was afraid of those men.

It was the only scenario that made sense to Marie, and she shuddered. Jenna's fear had transferred to her, and if her suspicions were right, she had good reason to be frightened.

Jenna was dead. And the people responsible for her death were now looking for Marie. Why? Because she'd had Jenna's suitcase for a few minutes? Chances were pretty good that her pursuers were now in possession of both Jenna's laptop and her carry-on. Why should they care about her? If Jenna had something they wanted, they had it now.

Of course, Jenna's checked baggage could be in the hold of the plane in which Marie now soared through the clouds. Would they follow Jenna's luggage to Detroit? Would someone claim it there? Hadn't Jenna said something to the woman with the gun about making contact in Detroit? And who was to say the sinister men hadn't planted one of their people on this plane to watch Marie, or that their cohorts wouldn't be waiting for her in Detroit?

She realized Caprice was watching her, and she offered a tiny smile, hoping to reassure her seatmate that she wasn't about to be sick or have a meltdown at thirty thousand feet.

"Excuse me for saying so, but you have fantastic skin," Caprice said.

Marie blinked and tried to process that, looking for a motive behind the words.

Caprice laughed. "Don't pay any attention to me. I own a cosmetics company, so I notice things like that."

Marie exhaled. "You started your own company?"

"Sure did. Six years ago, when I was twenty-two. We're grossing over two million a year now."

"I'm impressed." Marie shook her head, wondering what it would be like to head a successful business.

"What do you do?" Caprice asked.

Marie swallowed. What *did* she do? There was no answer that wouldn't sound puny next to Caprice's accomplishment.

"Well, my husband's in the Navy."

"Ah."

"We've been in Japan two years," Marie hastened on, hoping that would make her seem less unproductive. "But before that I..."

Caprice nodded, smiling in encouragement, her arched eyebrows telegraphing her eagerness to hear what Marie's feats had encompassed before she became a Navy wife.

"I used to waitress at my uncle's restaurant."

Caprice's smile broadened. "There you go. It helps to start at the entry level. Who knows? Someday your man's going to retire, and maybe the two of you will start your own nightclub or something. You just never know."

Marie leaned back, feeling more relaxed than she had since walking away from Pierre in Narita. She shut out all thoughts of tension and bloodshed. Girl talk she could handle.

It took only minimal encouragement to start Caprice on a monologue describing her line of makeup. Marie suppressed a yawn. She didn't want to offend the woman, but she was *so* tired.

"I'm just coming back from a big trade show in San Francisco." Caprice's eyes shone with enthusiasm. "They have it every year, and I go push my line to the buyers."

Marie straightened as a thought crossed her mind. "You don't have anything I could wear, do you?"

Caprice studied her for a moment. "I might. We started out with a line just for African-American women, but we're expanding to the general market." She reached down for a large tote bag and lifted it onto her lap. "That natural look suits you, but if you wanted to glam up a little with those big brown eyes, I think you'd look super in this new shade of eye shadow. It's amethyst with a copper sheen."

Marie frowned, trying to picture the shade, but Caprice was opening a small container of the product.

"Wait." Marie stared at the tote bag. "They let you bring a carry-on full of makeup?"

"Well, sure, just small samples. And most of what I've got here is in powdered form." Caprice settled back in her seat, studying Marie. "That's right. You just came over from Japan."

Marie nodded. "They let me have my lip gloss, but that was it. My other cosmetics are in my checked luggage."

Caprice shook her head in disgust. "Well, honey, pardon my saying it, but you've had a long night, haven't you?"

"I'll say. I don't even know what time zone we're in, and I'm exhausted." The stiffness in her spine seemed to have evaporated and left her lethargic. *If I wanted to get up and walk down the aisle, my legs wouldn't hold me.*

Caprice gave her a sage nod. "Well, just hold on and we'll get rid of those dark circles under your eyes. Take off that hat."

Hesitantly, Marie pulled off the Red Sox cap. Her hair cascaded down, and she shook her head gently, swirling it about her chin.

Caprice smiled. "Thick, healthy hair. Nice and shiny."

"Thank you." Marie felt very conspicuous as Caprice rummaged in her huge straw tote.

"Here it is. Look. My new foundation. It comes in liquid or a compact." She handed Marie a small plastic pot. "I'm not trying to sell you anything, okay? We'll just have some fun."

"Sure."

Caprice nodded. "That's a sample. It may be a shade darker than your skin, though. We're not trying to give you a tan. Let me see if I can go one lighter." She reached into the bag again.

"Thanks!" Marie unscrewed the cover of the container. Definitely darker than her usual foundation, but the eye shadow intrigued her. This was like trying on makeup with her sister Lisa or her best friend from high school, Alli. She smiled at Caprice. "Have you got any blush in there?"

NINE

0500 Saturday, Yokosuka

Pierre paced the living room of their tiny apartment. He couldn't sleep without Marie. He could fall asleep anywhere, anytime—on a helicopter, under a bush, or in a ditch—while on a mission with someone else on watch, but when he was home and she wasn't, sleep was as elusive as the agreement they were trying to get out of the Chinese.

In two hours he'd don his uniform again, even though it was Saturday, and he knew he needed to rest. Payback for calling André in the wee hours.

He picked up his phone and punched in Marie's number again, but the system took him immediately to her voice mail.

"Come on, babe! Please?" He figured she was in the air somewhere between California and Michigan, but he wished he knew for sure. If he could just hear her voice, then he could relax and go back to sleep.

He stared out the window. The street below ran past tall apartment buildings toward the main part of the base. He'd hoped she would call him when she landed in San Francisco, but her arrival time there was hours past. She'd probably figured it was too late in Japan, and she didn't want to rouse him. He snatched the printout of her itinerary off the floor and frowned at it, figuring the time difference. Another couple of hours, and she'd be on the ground in Detroit for a while. Maybe she'd turn her phone on then.

With a sigh he headed for the bathroom and prepared to get in the shower, leaving his phone balanced on the corner of a towel rack. They'd let the movers pack up and ship most of their household goods and given the rest away. He was left with a sleeping bag and a minimum of linens and dishes. The one remaining bath towel cushioned the phone. He'd turned the ringer up to maximum volume to be sure he'd hear it if it trilled while he was showering. Even so, he shut the water off after only a couple of minutes and checked the phone for messages before toweling dry, just to be certain she hadn't called.

Maybe he should call his parents and see if they'd heard from her. It was mid-afternoon in Maine. If André was at work at the busy post office, he wouldn't want to be bothered by his overprotective brother again. But his parents wouldn't mind. Or would a call from him just put them on edge, the way he was?

He yawned and stretched both arms out long, tightening and then relaxing his muscles. His fatigue was catching up with him. He had to be alert today and ready to leave tonight, if conditions were right.

Marie was probably fine. He had no reason to think otherwise. He decided to go over to the office at 0800 for a few hours, then come back and try to sleep through the afternoon. And sometime in the course of the day, he ought to be able to connect with Marie.

He wasn't exactly worried about her, but he knew he'd be thinking too much about her during his duties. He'd feel easier going into hostile territory if he heard her voice first and knew she was safe.

TEN

When the flight attendants came around offering complimentary beverages, Marie realized with a start that she and Caprice had talked nonstop for nearly half an hour. Many passengers had leaned their seats back and were dozing while she and Caprice chatted in muted tones. For a while Marie had almost forgotten her terrifying experience in San Francisco.

She ordered diet cola, Caprice took a bottled water, and they dove back into the conversation. Caprice drew item after item from her copious tote bag and smeared tiny dabs of different products on the back of Marie's hand.

"Now, you could wear this. It's good with light skin or dark. See the shimmer? That's really sexy eye shadow, girl."

Marie chuckled.

"Remember how you said before that this foundation would give me a tan?" She held up the sample Caprice had given her earlier.

"Sure."

"How different would it make me look? I mean, would it keep someone from recognizing me?"

Caprice turned her head slightly to one side and eyed her cautiously. "What do you mean? You trying to hide from someone?"

"Well, sort of." Marie gulped, wondering how much to divulge. "There's this guy…"

"Not your husband," Caprice guessed, "because, honey, you told me you're crazy about that guy, so it can't be him."

Marie winced. "You're right. There's someone else, and…well, I was thinking that when I get to Detroit, I wouldn't want him to see me. But if he found out when I was coming in and came to the airport…"

"Oh, yeah. Old boyfriend? No, don't tell me." Caprice's face went dreamy for a moment, and then she snapped her fingers. "Got it! In my other carry-on—it's up in the overhead bin—I have wigs."

"Wigs?"

"Yeah, they're great. The sisters love them because they can change instantly from an earthy, ethnic look to sleek and sophisticated. I only have three along that I used as models at the trade show, but I can show you. Hold on a sec."

Marie stood in the aisle while Caprice opened the compartment above them and took down a rectangular, rigid blue case. She sat down again and opened it on the seat between them.

The first wig was a short cap of downy black curls. Marie touched it gingerly.

"I don't know…" How much would it change her appearance?

"All right, something flashier." Caprice slid her hands beneath an elaborate creation of tiny, beaded braids and raised it so her seatmate could catch the full effect.

Marie caught her breath. The hairdo would snag attention, which was not what she wanted, and yet…

If they look at that, they won't look at my face.

"Take the case in the restroom and try it on," Caprice said softly. Her conspiratorial smile had a magic that made Marie believe anything was possible.

"You think?"

"I do. And here. Take this foundation. You don't want to go too dark, but a shade or two will make a big difference. And if you normally don't wear eye makeup, mascara and shadow would throw off someone looking for the girl next door, if he didn't look too close."

Marie put the samples Caprice handed her in her pocket and

carried the wig case down the aisle. One restroom was vacant, and she was glad no one waited in line.

In the small cubicle, she carefully took out the wig and settled it on her head. She wished Caprice had come with her to help her put it on right, but the two of them would never fit in this matchbox of a bathroom.

The startling transformation gave her hope. But the woman staring back at her was much too pale to carry off this decidedly ethnic hairstyle. Although she did not consider her skin to be light toned, she realized she needed a deeper tint to go with the glistening black tresses. She extracted the powdered foundation sample from her pocket. It took only a minute to smear the coffee-colored makeup over her cheeks, nose, and chin. She smoothed it up to her hairline, more and more satisfied with what she saw.

This can work! They'll never recognize me!

A tiny voice mocked her, asking who she was thinking of. *You've lost your mind, Marie! There's no one after you. The authorities are looking for a killer in the airport. Why would anyone be after you? You've gone paranoid.*

But the practical part of her brain told her she was not imagining things. She was a hunted woman, for reasons unknown to her but somehow connected to her brief association with Jenna Tarrington.

She applied the eye makeup and opened the door hesitantly. Two women and a man were waiting. They all stared as she pushed past them.

Marie forced a smile and pulled out what she imagined was a southern drawl. She'd never been to the South, but she and Lisa had practiced for weeks after seeing *Gone with the Wind*. "Sorry, y'all."

The nearest woman returned her smile. "No problem."

Marie tossed her head gently and felt the beads swing.

Were people staring? She walked down the aisle from the rear of the plane and forced herself not to look back. Probably no one noticed her. If anyone did, they would see a slim African-American girl in jeans and a blue blouse, with a mane of tiny braids.

She stopped at her row and lowered her eyelashes, unable to look Caprice straight in the face.

"Is this seat taken, sistuh?" she murmured.

Caprice burst out in a hoot of a laugh, but quickly stifled it as the man seated in front of them stirred and shot a scowl in their direction. Marie felt a blush flood her cheeks as she resumed her place.

"Here!" Caprice held out another sample. "You need to put it on your hands too."

Marie opened it and dabbed the foundation on the backs of her hands and wrists.

"What do you think? My...hair, I mean."

Caprice smiled. "You're a natural."

Marie licked her lips and took a deep breath.

"How much?"

"How much what?"

Marie glanced around at the passengers near them, but no one seemed to be paying attention.

"You know. How much does it cost? The wig."

Caprice smiled. "Well, if you was to order it new and custom tinted, seven hundred. But since that one's my model and I've been lugging it to shows and demonstrations for a couple of years, well...I'd let it go for three fifty."

Marie's spirit plummeted. That was a lot. But deep inside, she felt it was worth it. The wig could save her life. *How can I not afford it? If there's someone watching for me to get off the plane in Detroit...*

She made herself breathe slowly and consider that. Did she really believe someone was pursuing her? *Yes,* her quaking heart cried. *Assassins! That woman shot Jenna when she threatened to scream. I can't take the chance.*

"I'll take it."

Caprice's eyes opened wide, and then she grinned. "You sure?"

Marie clamped her lips together and nodded.

Caprice's eyes went dark and her lips thinned. "You're really scared of this jerk, aren't you?"

Marie looked down at her cappuccino-colored hands.

Caprice leaned toward her and lowered her voice. "Honey, if he's that mean, you ought to call the police."

"I…I'll think about it. But I'm pretty sure this disguise would fool him."

"Still…"

"If I see him, I'll consider what you said."

Caprice nodded. "Good. 'Cause if he'd go after you, he'd go after someone else. If he's not beatin' on you, he's likely beatin' on some other poor girl."

Marie hesitated. Was Caprice someone she could confide in? She seemed street smart. Maybe she could give some advice on how to handle this nightmare. On the other hand, Marie knew almost nothing about her. Could she really trust anyone right now?

She plunged her hand deep into her jeans pocket and brought out the small wad of bills. "Here's two hundred," she whispered. She unzipped her purse and rummaged in her wallet, then looked around before passing the rest of the money to her new friend. "Here you go. Another one fifty."

Caprice held the cash in her hand for a moment, looking deep into Marie's eyes. She unfolded the bills and smoothed them on her knee, down beneath the tray table, where the people across the aisle couldn't see. She covered a fifty-dollar bill with her palm and slid it, flat, across the seat between them.

"Here, honey. You might need this."

"But you said—"

Caprice closed off Marie's comment with a wave of her hand. "I reconsidered. It's getting shopworn. But it still looks plenty good on you."

ELEVEN

A half hour before they were due to land in Detroit, Caprice sent Marie back to the restroom to apply a few more touches. She'd given detailed instructions on applying more eye shadow and blush, eyeliner, and lipstick.

"If I didn't think it would attract too much attention, I'd do your face right here, but you can do it, girl." Caprice's confidence-inspiring smile burst out again. "Experiment. Just don't let that conservative Yankee blood show itself. Be a little daring. You don't care if folks look at you, right? Just make it so when they do, they'll think about the hot woman they're seeing, not that shy little gal from New England."

In the restroom, Marie doubtfully examined the products. Caprice's pep talk had buoyed her, but now she was out of sight and earshot of her mentor. Carefully she pulled the wand out of a tube of mascara.

When she returned to her seat, Caprice greeted her with a chuckle.

"That bad?" Marie asked.

Caprice shook her head. "Hold still." She reached over and smoothed the tender skin over Marie's right eye. "There. Just evening things out a little."

"The light is really horrid in those cubicles," Marie said.

Caprice sat back and squinted at her, nodding. "Do you speak Spanish?"

"No, but I speak French." A flood of high school memories deluged Marie. Her mother had insisted she take French in school so she could get in touch with her French-Canadian heritage. Marie had sulked. She wanted to learn German. But once she'd gotten into the first-year class, she had enjoyed it, more than she would admit to her mother. Besides, that was about the time Pierre Belanger started noticing her, and she'd learned that, with his grandparents living in their home, the Belangers always spoke French to each other. The first time he whispered *cherie* in her ear, she'd known she would study the language until she was fluent. She'd earned A's all four years.

"French?" Caprice raised her eyebrows in an alluring look. "Perfect! If anyone asks, you're from Haiti. And, by the way, you're gorgeous."

The seat belt sign went on, and the captain's voice came over the system. "We're about fifteen minutes from landing in Detroit. Please fasten your seat belts and return all tray tables to the upright position. Due to our late start in San Francisco, we'll be touching down about twenty-six minutes past our scheduled arrival. If you have questions about your connecting flights..."

Marie sank back into the cushioned seat and closed her eyes, pulling in a long, slow breath. She should still have plenty of time to get to her next plane. One more hop, and she'd be home. Pierre must be up and getting ready to report on the base. Was he wondering why she hadn't called him yet?

I'm sorry, mon chéri! Je le regrette. She wished her thoughts could wing across the continent and the vast ocean to his heart. Perhaps there would be time to call him from the airport in Detroit. But she couldn't call Japan from a pay phone. She frowned, wondering how to work that out. Maybe she could call her folks and instruct them to call Pierre and assure him she was safely on the way home. She looked at her watch. It must be about six o'clock in the morning in Yokosuka. She hoped Pierre had slept well. Now that he was up, he was probably waiting for her to call and worrying.

She sighed and looked past Caprice, out the window. The aircraft tilted and turned, and the earth was visible below them. What would happen when she left the comparative security of the plane? Maybe she could find a policeman in the airport and tell him her story, if there was no sign of the woman who killed Jenna or the men who had terrified her. She sent a swift prayer upward and shot off another heart message to her husband.

Je t'aime, Pierre!

TWELVE

"Take me with you tonight."

"Excuse me?" André Belanger frowned across the post office counter at Lisa Gillette.

"Mom said you're picking Marie up at the airport. I want to go with you."

André eyed the line of customers behind Lisa and glanced at his supervisor, Janet. She worked the other line, and patrons were four deep at each station. Janet flicked a disapproving look in return, and André faced Lisa again. Janet was death on employees chitchatting while customers waited.

"Uh, did you need any stamps or anything?" he asked.

"No, I just want to go with you. What time are you leaving?"

He cleared his throat, feeling the chill of Janet's frosty glare on his left cheek. "Um, I'll call you when I have my break, okay?"

Lisa scowled. "Okay, give me a book of stamps."

"First class?"

"Yeah, whatever." Lisa tossed her head.

"Do you want flags or birds or—"

"The top one. Now, can I go or not?"

"Cash or credit card?"

She sighed and tugged the flap of her brown suede purse open. "Here." She plopped a ten-dollar bill on the counter, and André began making change.

"I'll call you," he murmured as he handed it to her.

"Just tell me when you're leaving, for crying out loud!"

He glanced at Janet. Her attention focused on her postage scale, and her too-bushy eyebrows had almost morphed into one fuzzy hedgerow.

"Seven o'clock," he said quickly. "I'll pick you up."

Lisa grinned. "Well, thanks." She looked over at Janet, whose hazel eyes were now shooting invisible daggers at her. "I love this post office! Great service here!"

She whirled and edged past the six people now queued up behind her and shoved the glass door open. André kept his eyes straight ahead, avoiding the temptation to look into Janet's zip code again, and tried to smile at the next customer.

"Good morning. Set your package right up here, ma'am."

As he worked through the next hour, his mind took several detours in Lisa Gillette's direction, and he had to rein in his thoughts repeatedly. Lisa was Marie's big sister; his sister-in-law, sort of. A shirttail relative. André's older brother, Pierre, and Lisa's younger sister, Marie, had fallen in love while Marie was in high school and Pierre was at Annapolis. They were married a year and a half after Marie graduated.

André and Lisa had known each other all their lives. They careened through the Waterville public schools in the same class, some years in the same homeroom. It didn't seem right somehow for his big brother to have married Lisa's baby sister, but their passionate love was undeniable. Pierre had proposed when he was twenty-four and Marie was seventeen. They'd been married two and a half years now, and although they'd spent most of that time halfway around the world where their siblings couldn't observe the marriage firsthand, it seemed they were supremely happy.

Pierre was the oldest of the Belangers' eight active children. Marie, on the other hand, was the youngest of the three Gillette sisters. Stuck in the middle at age twenty-five were André and Lisa. Somehow, serious romance had eluded them both.

With relief, André saw the clock hands sweep toward his break time. He closed his station at the next lull in business.

"I'm going out back," he said to Janet.

She nodded, pulling a customer's receipt from her printer. As the patron went out the door, she called after André, "You'd better tell that girl to leave you alone during business hours."

He almost asked, "What girl?" But he knew. She was talking about Lisa.

"Is she stalking you or something?"

What a novel thought. Lisa, the plain-featured tomboy-turned-electrician, stalking him. André paused in the doorway.

"No, she's a relative. Sorry about that."

"Oh, she's one of the Gillette girls, isn't she?"

"Yeah. Marie is coming home tonight. We're picking her up in Bangor."

Another customer entered the lobby, and Janet turned back toward the desk.

André sighed and relaxed a hair. Janet could be a difficult supervisor, but she knew all about Pierre and Marie's grand romance and always wanted to see the postcards they sent from Japan. Maybe she wouldn't crab at him or make him shorten his break since she'd learned that Lisa the Pest was Marie's sister.

But he doubted she'd let up on him. Janet came from away—New Jersey, to be more precise—and she simply didn't understand the tentacles of large French families and how they slithered out to grab you and hold you close, even if you wanted to break loose. Young men like his eighteen-year-old brother Ricky fooled themselves into thinking they were getting away from the suffocation by going to Quebec all summer to work at a campground. But the sad truth was, the campground was owned by Maman's cousin Dennis.

And a woman like Lisa Gillette figured she had a right to bother you at work and make you include her in your plans just because you were almost related. But his older brother had entrusted him with this mission. Although he'd rather not share the long ride and wait for Marie with anyone, André couldn't think of a polite way to say no, and so he'd caved.

He sighed and got a bottle of root beer from the cooler. Any way he figured it, he'd spend at least an hour alone in his truck with Lisa tonight. Not that she was so horrible, but to his way of thinking she was a bit annoying. Her persistence, for instance. That might be admirable under other circumstances, but where was her sensitivity? She had none. A sensitive person would have seen how uncomfortable it made him when she accosted him under the nose of Janet, the postal dragon lady. And Lisa wasn't even pretty.

The thought surprised him, and he took a long pull of root beer, sending a spurt up through his nose. Slamming the bottle down on the tiny scrap of a table, he grabbed a paper towel and sponged his uniform shirt. Great. *This is Lisa's fault.*

He blew his nose and winced as his eyes watered from the pain in his sinuses. Okay, it wasn't directly her fault, and she wasn't ugly. But compared to her sisters…well, Lisa was just…Lisa. Guys never noticed her, except to complain about having a girl in their shop classes. André supposed she wasn't so bad as a person, but he had never gotten to know her as a person. In fact, he barely knew her. Sure, their families got together whenever Pierre and Marie were around—which wasn't often—but other than those occasional mandatory cross-family events, André's path rarely crossed Lisa's these days. In fact, he couldn't remember the last time he'd seen her in the post office. She probably never wrote letters.

He sat down with his soft drink in his hand and stared at the bottle. It was nearly empty. He'd shot a couple of ounces through his nasal cavities and guzzled the rest without thinking about it. Why did Lisa have to come around here today, anyway?

Only five minutes left before he had to go back to work. Maybe he could talk her out of going with him. He'd once gotten an A on a persuasive speech in English class.

The battered phone book lay on the table. Reluctantly he leafed through it, searching for the Gillettes. There was no listing for Lisa. Would L.E. Gillette be her? Or did she still live with her parents? He flipped to the back and scanned the yellow pages for electricians.

He recalled his mother saying that Lisa ran her own business now, after a few years of working under a master electrician.

Gillette Electric. How creative. He punched in the number, wondering if she had an office, or if it was a cell phone number and she just worked out of her truck, going from job to job.

"Hello, this is Lisa Gillette."

"Hey. It's me, André."

"Yeah? You said seven o'clock, right?"

"Well, yeah, I did, but…are you sure you want to go? Because you don't have to. Pierre asked me to pick Marie up and make sure she got home safe. She's staying with my folks, you know."

"I know. But I want to see her."

"You'll see her. But she'll be tired tonight, and…"

"What?" Lisa's petulant tone warned him not to push too hard. "You don't want me to go, is that it? Are you taking someone else?"

"What? No. You think I have a date for an airport run? That's stupid."

"No, you're stupid. I thought maybe your parents were going."

"Oh."

He swallowed hard. This wasn't going well, and the octopus feeling was choking him.

"André, she's my *sister*."

"Yeah. Well, listen, Lisa, I've got to get back to work, but I'll see you later."

"Sure. Hey, wait!"

"What?" he asked.

"Maybe we should go a little early and eat supper in Bangor. I mean, I'll be done here by five, and I can run home and change."

He pictured her with coveralls over the jeans and V-necked T-shirt she'd worn into the post office. Then he tried to picture her in a dress, but he could only conjure up the frilly rose-colored gowns she and Marie's friends had worn when they were bridesmaids.

"Well, I need to get out of my uniform too."

"So pick me up at 5:30."

"Uh…" Was he agreeing to dinner? Somehow it had zipped past him. "Well…uh…" Of course, she was right, they did have to eat. "Are you still at your parents' house?"

"Yeah."

The clock hands jumped a notch. "Okay, but quarter to six. I'll see you then."

He rushed back to his station behind the counter. Janet nodded at him and slapped her "THIS WINDOW CLOSED" sign onto the surface in front of her. He was glad she'd opted to take her break now. Maybe she wouldn't see the unnatural flush he felt suffusing his face, brought on no doubt by allowing himself to be set up by an ersatz relative.

"Good morning. May I help you?" he asked brightly as the customers shifted over to line up before his station. *Great. It's not morning; it's afternoon.* He felt his color deepening. Yup, this was Lisa's fault.

THIRTEEN

The crush of deplaning passengers separated Marie and Caprice as they edged toward the exit in Detroit. When Marie looked back, she could barely see Caprice's sleek, blue-black hair. She raised one hand and waved, and then she turned to scoot forward as the line progressed at a pitiful rate.

At last she reached the door and slipped into the long tunnel that extended to the side of the terminal. Once inside the building, Marie paused to gather her wits and adjust the strap of her purse. She was once more on firm ground. One more flight, and she would be home. André would be there to meet her at the airport, and he could tell her what to do. If he insisted, they would go to the Bangor police station before he drove her to the Belanger home in Waterville. That would be best, she decided. She'd already fled the scene in San Francisco. She might as well get safely to Maine and her loved ones before the questioning began.

She bent and wrapped her fingers around the handle of her carry-on and froze hunched over. Two men stood just beyond the gate exit, surveying all the disembarking passengers. She had no doubt this time. They were the same two Asian men from Narita and San Francisco.

She lowered her gaze and threw her shoulders back. If she looked confident, they wouldn't look twice at her in the disguise. But deep down, she knew they were looking for her, and it sent a chill to her heart. She prayed silently as she headed out into the concourse. As she passed them, she kept her eyes focused straight ahead.

A thought struck her: If they'd ridden on her plane, they might know about her wig. She hadn't seen them, but they could have stayed forward of where she and Caprice were seated, and she wouldn't have noticed them. It was a huge plane, and she hadn't walked forward during the flight. Or they could have taken seats in first class. If they knew she was on board, perhaps they'd decided to bide their time and confront her here, instead of on the plane. Making waves on an airplane was a sure way to draw unwanted attention. If they planned to confront her, they'd shown wisdom by waiting until they could carry out their plans in a less dangerous place.

Like an airport restroom. She shivered. What had she stumbled into?

People didn't seem to be staring, and Marie decided her disguise was a success. So far so good.

But I can't board the next plane wearing this wig and makeup, she told herself. She might have to show her identification, and if the airline agent couldn't recognize her as the person in the photo, the authorities would haul her aside and question her. They'd looked her over closely in San Francisco. Still, she'd had to go through customs there. In Detroit it would be different, she supposed. She would transfer from one domestic flight to another. Would she even have to show her ID, or was her boarding pass enough?

She arrived at her next gate after a short walk, but no airline personnel stood behind the desk. She checked the departure monitor overhead and saw that she had nearly an hour to wait. Better to remove the disguise now, in case she did need to show her identification. She could stay out of sight for a while and check in at the last minute. It was the best plan she could think of, and she moved on down the terminal.

When she passed a food vendor, tantalizing smells made her mouth water and her stomach growled. The airline's snacks were no substitute for the meals she had missed. The disguise gave her courage to stop and purchase a muffin and a bottle of juice. As she ate, she watched the foot traffic that passed the eating area. Five minutes later, she was on the move again, entering the nearest ladies' room cautiously.

She took a long time washing her hands, waiting for the others in the restroom to leave. Finally she decided it was just too busy a place and took an end stall, where she removed the wig and carefully tucked it into her carry-on. Then she used the rough, cheap toilet paper to scrape a layer of foundation off her cheeks. She removed the blue shirt and Mount Fuji T-shirt, choosing instead a chartreuse tank top, the last option in her small bag. She could pull the blue shirt or her sweater over it later if she needed warmth. When the room beyond her cubicle seemed quiet, she peeked out.

Only one woman stood at the sinks, and she turned to dry her hands. Marie went swiftly to the counter and washed her hands, scrubbing off the last of the tinted makeup. At least they had paper towels here, not just air dryers. The other woman barely glanced her way before she left the room, and for a minute and a half, Marie was alone.

She soaked a paper towel and carefully washed her face, and then she brushed out her straight, dark hair. Fumbling in her purse, she found a ponytail holder and pulled her hair back.

She stared at herself in the mirror. Her eyes were huge. She dampened another paper towel and used the folded edge to dab at her mascara and eye shadow. When she'd finished, her eyelids looked puffy, as though she'd been crying.

She heard someone pull the door open, and she spun around, remembering Jenna.

I'm crazy to stay in here alone! Lord, help me.

A young woman and a little girl came in together, and Marie exhaled and closed her eyes for a moment.

Thank You, she breathed. But she knew she had to leave the restroom. She was too vulnerable here, and the white tiled walls seemed closer than they had been.

The young mother smiled at Marie as she guided her little girl into a stall. Marie managed to return a grim smile and edged toward the exit door. A cluster of people passed by, and she stepped out, pulling her suitcase, and walked back to her departure area. Two uniformed agents were at the desk now, and a dozen passengers had formed a line. Marie took out her boarding pass and looked around. She couldn't see the Asian men who had frightened her when she left her last plane. She was grateful when a middle-aged couple came and stood behind her, partially screening her from view of anyone beyond the waiting area.

Immediately ahead of her was a young, blond woman who might be a teacher or a sales clerk. Marie's pulse slowed gradually, and she could breathe without gulping.

Ahead of the golden-haired woman, a passenger who had successfully checked in left the line, and a short man in a conservative business suit reached the desk. Marie pushed her carry-on forward six inches with her foot.

"I missed my original flight," the man told the agent. "Is there by any chance a seat available on the flight to Bangor, Maine?"

Marie froze. His clipped, precise English told her he was not a native speaker. Maybe she'd heard him wrong, but it sounded like a subtle Japanese accent as he inquired about a seat on her flight, like that of the assistant pastor at the church in Narita. She turned sideways, listening. Japanese or Chinese?

"The flight is fully booked," the agent told him, "but we can put you on a standby list. Sometimes we have no-shows, and there's a seat or two empty."

"Great," the man said.

Marie positioned herself behind the blond woman and stared after him as he went to the lounge area. Instead of claiming a seat, he stood to one side, looking slowly and methodically at the people around him. Even at a distance, across the lounge, she could see the scar on his left cheek.

She turned away before his gaze landed on her.

"Excuse me," she said to the couple behind her. Could they tell her heart was racing? A huge lump obstructed the airflow at the back of her throat. "I forgot something. You can go ahead of me."

While the couple moved their baggage up in line, Marie slouched lower and pulled her bag away on the far side of the line of waiting passengers. She made herself walk deliberately, without a hint of hurry. She emerged from the boarding area, back out into the concourse and walked away from the gate without looking back. She didn't allow herself to scan the area around her, though the temptation was painful. Instead, she focused on a snack shop a hundred feet away and made steadily for it.

Only when she had rounded the corner of the snack shop and could hide behind a juice cooler did she look back down the concourse. Halfway between her and the gate she had left, the graying man whom she'd seen at the newsstand in the San Francisco airport stood looking about and talking into a cell phone.

She turned away and strode quickly, putting as much floor space as she could between herself and the two men. Ahead was an escalator that led to baggage claim. She hopped onto the stairs and descended. Her head swam.

A crowd thronged around a carousel where baggage circled. The suitcases flopped down a ramp onto a conveyor belt and rode around, displaying matching leather pieces and battered canvas duffel bags. A group of college students stood chattering around a second carousel that had yet to present any luggage, and Marie eased to the fringe of their gathering.

I could pass for a college student. How hard would it be to blend in with this bunch? For a moment she wished she hadn't shed the wig and makeup.

She spotted a few chairs against the wall on the other side of the carousel and pulled her carry-on toward it. A girl sat down just before she reached the chairs and opened a laptop. Marie sat down and tried to breathe evenly. The girl glanced at her and smiled.

"Hi."

"Hi," Marie said.

"You're not with the Florida Tech group."

"No. I'm traveling alone."

The girl nodded, pressing buttons on her keyboard. "I'm Becka."

"Marie. Where are you headed?"

"We're going to Michigan Tech for a robotics competition."

"That's cool."

Becka reached into the pocket of her fleece jacket and took something out. Marie watched in fascination as she pulled the small, plastic case apart, stuck the larger piece into an opening on the side of the laptop, and resumed typing.

"Excuse me, what did you just do?"

Becka looked up at her, her green eyes wide. "Hmm?"

"You plugged something into your computer."

"Oh, yeah. That's my flash drive."

"Your…what does it do?"

Becka tossed back her flyaway auburn hair. "It gives you extra memory. You can store tons of documents on it and take it from one computer to another. I wrote my term paper on my desktop, but I saved it on the flash drive so I could bring it along on this trip and tweak it a little."

Marie's brain whirled. It made sense. Or did it? Of course that little thing she'd found in her suitcase was a computer accessory. She should have realized that at once. It gave the computer owner additional data storage. That part was logical. And the one she'd found must belong to Jenna. That would explain why the men who retrieved Jenna's suitcase under false pretenses were chasing Marie. The thing they really wanted wasn't in Jenna's bags. Marie's heart lurched and accelerated, making it hard to catch her breath.

Somehow the flash drive had mysteriously made its way into Marie's bag. It couldn't have been a mistake. No, Jenna knew what she was doing. She knew she was due for a confrontation, and she didn't want that tiny data storage unit on her when it happened.

The carousel started moving, and Becka closed her laptop with a snap. "There's my duffel." She smiled at Marie and stood up.

Marie watched her walk to the moving belt and pull her camouflage bag off. Other students grabbed their bags from the carousel. A fortyish woman reached for a tapestry suitcase, and a tall student wearing a college sweatshirt jumped to her side.

"Let me get that, Dr. Neverow."

Marie puffed out her cheeks and exhaled, thinking. The woman smiled and thanked the young man, and then she looked around at the people scrambling for luggage.

"Students, gather your bags and come this way," she called in a voice that could have been heard across a soccer field and two parking lots.

Becka hoisted her duffel bag, tucked her laptop under her arm, and strolled to the general vicinity of Dr. Neverow. Soon a dozen students milled around the professor.

Marie's legs felt rubbery as she stood and wheeled her carry-on toward them. She cast a glance toward the escalator that led back the way she had come. No skulking men from Tokyo. She stood on the edge of the cluster of students, avoiding looking at Becka.

The professor did a quick head count. "All right, Floridians. This way."

The group surged toward the nearest exit, and Marie fell in between two young men, not making eye contact with either of them. As they paused to take turns going through the revolving door, she made sure she wasn't in the last handful leaving the terminal, but as soon as they reached the sidewalk outside, she eased away toward a curbside check-in kiosk.

"Hustle, people!" Dr. Neverow called, and the students queued up to board a charter bus. Marie walked down the sidewalk a few more yards and spotted a cab parked by the curb. She hurried toward the taxi stand and leaned down to talk to the driver.

"Can you take me into town?"

"Sure. Climb in. You got luggage?"

"Just this." Marie opened the back door, swung her carry-on in, and then jumped inside.

"Where to?"

She swallowed hard. She'd never been to Detroit and knew nothing about the city.

"I need to find a hotel."

"Okay." The driver pulled away from the curb.

A rush of panic ambushed Marie. She was leaving the airport, and she was still a thousand miles from home. But she was too scared to go back to the terminal.

She looked out the back window. The last of the Florida Tech students were entering the bus when a man in a suit rushed out of the terminal and ran to where the professor watched the bus driver stow luggage in the compartment under the bus.

With a frightening kink in her stomach, Marie faced forward and whispered, "Dear God, I know what they want now. Should I just give it to them?"

That didn't seem right. If handing over the computer drive was the right thing to do, why had Jenna given her life to avoid that? And if she tried to enlist the help of a law enforcement officer, could she guarantee that the information would get into the right hands, or that she could safely turn it over before those men caught up with her? Seeking help at this point might only endanger other innocent people.

She huddled down in the seat and closed her eyes. "Lord, what am I going to do?"

FOURTEEN

0800 Saturday, Yokosuka

Pierre reached the building where he'd been assigned a cubicle and desk to use while on the base. He was about to open the door when it was opened from the inside, and Ensign James Laroquette hurtled through it.

"Hey, Rocket, what's your hurry?" Pierre asked as the ensign nearly collided with him and skidded to a stop just outside the door.

"Sorry, Lieutenant." He shifted a folder from one hand to the other and glanced back toward the building.

"Something wrong?" Rocket's hesitation and uncharacteristic frown told Pierre his guess was on target. "What are you doing over here, anyway?"

Rocket glanced down at the folder and then met Pierre's gaze with troubled blue eyes. "The chief sent me over here from the *Bush* with some paperwork for Commander Tarrington, but right when I got in there, a petty officer came in and told Tarrington the admiral wanted him in his office right away. I didn't know what to do, so I just stood there. At first Tarrington acted like the interruption was a big bother, but the petty officer said it was a sensitive matter, and he started looking kind of upset."

Pierre's inner radar began to ping. Emergency meetings and sensitive issues were bad news in his department.

"What's the paperwork you've got there?"

"It's the quartering assignments for your unit when we take you on the *Bush*."

Pierre held out his hand. "Why don't you just give it to me? I'll see that it gets to the right place."

Rocket's expression cleared. "Thank you, sir. That would make my life easier. I was going to just stick it on Commander Tarrington's desk, but he gave me a look and said, 'Dismissed, Ensign,' so I booked it."

Pierre took the folder with what he hoped was a reassuring smile. "Don't worry about it. Do I need to sign anything?"

"No, sir."

"Okay. I'll take care of it." He paused, his mind galloping away into places he didn't want to go. "Listen, Rocket…" He clapped a hand on the ensign's shoulder. Rocket was a good guy. Everyone liked him. He was also talkative. Pierre looked him in the eye and said softly, "Let's keep this under our hats, huh?"

Rocket's eyes widened, and then he nodded. "Sure, if you think…I mean, when I left, the commander looked all out of sorts, sir, but… well, yes, I sure will."

Pierre watched him walk away, hoping the man was as good as his word. All it took sometimes was a whisper of rumor to scuttle a covert operation. If something had gone bad with the China deal… He sighed. It was bad enough that when he'd reached his mother on the phone this morning, she'd told him they hadn't heard a word from Marie and assumed her journey was going as planned. Maybe he should call Marie's parents. Sometimes you just couldn't get a connection overseas. Marie would probably call the Gillettes first if she couldn't get through to him.

The door opened, and Tarrington came out with a petty officer Pierre recognized as the admiral's aide.

"Oh, Belanger, good," Tarrington said, landing a vague gaze on him. "Something's come up, and I need to get over to headquarters. Don't know what we're dealing with yet, but you'll keep a lid on things here, won't you?"

"Yes, sir."

Tarrington nodded and walked toward the waiting Jeep.

Pierre inhaled carefully. Rocket was right. Tarrington was worried.

FIFTEEN

In the relative privacy of the taxicab, Marie took the tiny flash drive from her purse and examined it. Even though she now knew its use, she still had no idea what it contained that had put her in such danger. And why did she have it now? Jenna must have slipped it into her carry-on while Marie was out of her seat on the plane. Perhaps she took the cell phone out of Marie's purse too.

I should have gone right to the security office when I got off that last plane. They would have done something to protect me. She grimaced in the twilight. *What will Pierre say? Probably that I've been very unadult.*

She'd only been in the cab five minutes, and already she regretted leaving the airport. A mature, logical person would have stayed put and sought official help. She'd run like a scared child, away from people who could protect her. Still, she couldn't help remembering the woman in the TSA uniform. She glanced at her watch. Her plane would be taking off right about…now.

Slumping back against the seat, she closed her eyes, fighting back the tears that prickled in her eyes.

Lord, please show me what to do, she prayed silently. She sat up and tried to focus on her surroundings.

"Excuse me."

"Yes?" The driver looked at her in the mirror. She tried to judge his trustworthiness, but it was impossible. His large dark eyes reminded her of her husband's, but his swarthy skin and bushy eyebrows were nothing like Pierre's, and he must weigh half again as much as the trim lieutenant did.

She cleared her throat. "Could you please take me to the nearest police station?"

His eyebrows drew together in a wrinkly frown. "Police station?"

"Yes."

"Well, I can, but it's a long ride.

"How far?"

"Well, I don't know. Let's see…"

Marie clutched her purse, which held her remaining two hundred dollars. Since she had run out on her prepaid flight, she'd have to somehow get all the way to Maine on that.

"Maybe twenty minutes, if traffic is good."

She exhaled with relief. "Okay." In silence she sat thinking about the situation. Yes, she should have sought assistance from the airport security personnel. They couldn't all be in on this conspiracy. Even if it caused a delay that made her miss her flight, it would have been safer than dashing off on her own. And the airline would probably have put her on a later flight if she'd gone right to them first. Now she had no chance of getting another plane out of Detroit without paying for it. She could use her credit card, though.

"Hey," the driver said, and Marie snapped to attention, peering at him in his mirror. "We're being followed."

SIXTEEN

0840 Saturday, Yokosuka

Pierre heard footsteps in the passageway. Several men, by the sound of things, but no voices. He leaned back so that he could see out of his cubicle, through the open door of the large workroom into the hallway. Commander Tarrington passed by with two men flanking him.

Pierre got up and followed them to Tarrington's office. While the other two men stood by, the commander opened a desk drawer and pulled out several file folders. He looked up when Pierre entered.

"Oh, Belanger." His eyes were vague and unfocused, and his face was ashen.

Pierre glanced toward the others and decided the escort was mandatory for Tarrington. His chest tightened. Something had happened, and it wasn't good, but he couldn't very well put a direct question to his superior.

"Is there anything I can do for you, sir?"

Tarrington frowned as he shuffled through a handful of papers. At last he looked up and met Pierre's gaze with haunted gray eyes. His jaw went slack for a moment, and then he inhaled, straightening his shoulders.

"Just carry on. Something's come up, and I may have to go Stateside." It seemed he would go on, but then he clamped his jaws together and closed the drawer. He picked up a stack of folders and loose papers, handed them to one of the petty officers accompanying him, and turned to Pierre again. "That's all, Lieutenant. If I have to go away, I expect you'll receive orders. Just…carry on."

Pierre followed the three men into the passageway and watched them walk to the door. He didn't like it one bit. He returned slowly to the workroom that housed his cubicle. Ensign Rodriguez, at the work station next to his, was just hanging up his telephone. He swiveled around in his chair and motioned to Pierre.

"What?" Pierre stepped next to Rodriguez's desk and instinctively kept his voice low.

"It's Commander Tarrington."

"What about him?"

Rodriguez gulped. "I'm not sure I should tell you this. I mean, it didn't come to me through official channels or anything."

"What?" Pierre snapped, and Rodriguez winced.

The ensign leaned forward and said softly, "I know it's unprofessional, but I think you should know."

Doucement, mon ami, Pierre counseled himself. Softly. He managed a tight smile. "So just tell me and don't worry. It stays between us."

"I've got a buddy over at headquarters. He says Tarrington's wife is dead."

Pierre stood very still. Jenna was on the plane with Marie. Was Marie all right? And did she know about Jenna?

"What happened to her?" His voice shook, and he took a deep breath.

Rodriguez shrugged. "I don't know. Hey, is Vinny going to get in trouble for telling me?"

"I won't say anything. Just… Did he tell you anything at all? I mean, the plane didn't…" Fear mushroomed in his throat, and Pierre swallowed hard. "The plane made it to San Francisco okay, didn't it?"

"I guess."

Pierre stroked his chin, fighting panic. "Listen, call your friend back. Ask him to tell you anything, anything at all. See if he can confirm that the plane made it."

Rodriguez nodded slowly. "I'm sorry, Lieutenant. I'm guessing Mrs. Tarrington was on the same flight as some other Navy dependents. Am I right?"

"At least twenty women and children connected to this base, including my wife."

"I'm sorry, sir. I'll see what I can do."

"All right, thanks. Be discreet, but if there's any trouble, I'll take the blame."

Pierre went back to his desk and sat down, elbows on the desktop, and sank his head in his hands.

"God, I don't know what to say," he whispered. "I don't feel as if I have a right to ask You for anything." He burrowed his fingers into his thick hair. Memories clogged his mind. Marie, dragging him to the bilingual church services that were so different from the church he'd grown up in. The dark guilt he'd felt when the truth of his own sinfulness struck him. And the joy, the liberating joy he'd found when he took the truth of the Scripture as his own and trusted in Christ. It was less than a year ago, and although he'd learned much in the services he and Marie had attended since then, he still felt spiritually ignorant. Would God let a new Christian, one who loved the Savior as much as Marie did, die?

He also remembered snatches of what Marie had told him about Jenna. She'd tried to befriend her, but Jenna was cool and turned down all her overtures. Marie had prayed for Jenna once, during their evening prayer and Bible reading time. It had stuck in his mind that she prayed for someone she didn't know well and didn't even particularly like. But she'd asked God to meet whatever hidden needs Jenna had and to show Himself to her. Pierre thought that was odd, but Marie had been to more church meetings than he had—he was away a lot on duty. And she also attended a weekly women's Bible study. Those women probably chatted up a storm. Anyway, he knew Marie had learned faster than he had. And she was maturing, right before his eyes. He had to believe her new faith had something to do with that.

I can't lose her now, he cried inwardly, the anguish tearing at his heart. *Lord, I love her so much! There's so many things we need to learn together. I'm begging You!*

"Sir?"

He looked up and straightened his shoulders. Rodriguez stood at the opening of his cubicle, making no attempt to cover his discomfort.

"What?"

"Vinny says he doesn't think it happened on the plane. Maybe she got in a car wreck or something, but it was definitely in San Francisco. The cops there contacted the Navy."

Pierre nodded, trying to breathe deeply. "Thanks. I appreciate it."

"No problem, sir."

Rodriguez disappeared.

"Merci," Pierre whispered. He took out his wallet and flipped to the picture of Marie that he carried everywhere. It was his favorite: Marie wearing one of his Annapolis T-shirts. Her eyes sparkled at him through the plastic film.

"Dear God, keep her safe."

SEVENTEEN

"Are you sure he's following us?" Marie looked out the back window. A dark sedan was tailing them, a few lengths back.

"I took a couple of turns I wouldn't normally take, and he's still back there."

"Can you lose him?"

"I can try."

They glided up to a traffic light, and the driver's shoulders tensed. He watched the oncoming stream of cars to his left, and when he saw an opportunity, he stepped on the gas and roared out into traffic, ignoring the red light.

Marie gulped for breath. "Awesome."

"If I get a ticket, lady, you're paying for it."

"Oh, no, they got out too! They're only a couple of cars back." She stared out the back window, keeping an eye on their pursuers.

"Hang on."

Approaching the next light, the cab driver veered into the break-down lane and skimmed past half a dozen waiting vehicles, and then he took a hard right and tore up the side street.

Marie watched behind them, her heart racing. Several vehicles moved through the intersection before she saw a dark car that might be their followers.

"Now, why was it you wanted me to take you to the police station?" the driver asked.

"I...I need some help."

"Lady, I don't want to get myself killed trying to outrun some gang."

"All right, all right." She held tight to the armrest as he careened around a corner into a different street and then overcorrected and straightened out. "Listen, if you can lose them long enough, you can just let me out someplace where they won't see me right away. I'll pay you extra, and you can be on your way."

He looked at her in the mirror, and their gaze locked for an instant.

"Are you sure?"

"Yes." Marie shivered.

"You should have a coat," he said. "Where'd you come from, Florida?"

"No." She almost said *Japan,* but decided the less the driver knew about her the better. She opened her carry-on and took out the sweater she had anticipated needing when she landed in Maine. In early May, the breath of spring could be downright chilly. She wondered if she would ever see her checked luggage again. She pulled the plain blue shirt and the sweater on over her tank. But the beaded, ethnic wig lay crushed in her carry-on.

"Hey, don't freak out, okay?" she said to the driver. "I'm going to change my hair."

As they whipped under a series of overpasses, she could tell he was watching her. She settled the wig on her head and tucked her own locks beneath it.

The driver said, "There's a mall not far from here. I'll drive around to the back, and if that car doesn't show, you hop out. I'll land you as close to an entrance as I can."

Marie nodded. It sounded as good as anything she could think of. "Thanks."

"So what kind of trouble are you in?"

She shook her head with a smile that strained her lips. "You don't want to know."

"Well, you look like a nice girl. If things were different, I'd ask you to have supper with me."

Her smile was genuine then. "Thanks. That's very flattering, but I'm married."

"Yeah?" He eyed her doubtfully in the mirror. "How come your husband's not here taking care of you?"

She pressed her lips together and stared out the back window. The twilight was deepening, and she couldn't be positive, but she thought they'd lost the dark sedan. She couldn't tell this man anything, not one tiny fact. Not that her husband was in the Navy or where she was going. How did she know she could trust him? And if those men caught up with him and questioned him, what would he tell them? Maybe she shouldn't follow his advice. He might lead her enemies to her.

"Listen, I appreciate your helping out," she said.

He nodded. "Well, when you get in there, find a pay phone and call the police. They'll probably come right to the mall and get you. Let them help you."

"I will. What's my tab going to be?" She unzipped her purse and took out her wallet.

"It's at twenty-two bucks right now. It'll probably be twenty-five or so when we get there."

She took out two twenty-dollar bills and held them over his shoulder. "Here. Keep the change."

"Thanks. It's not far now." He slowed for a turn.

"Can I walk from here?"

"You could. It's maybe half a mile."

"Then let me out. You keep going."

"You sure?"

"Yes. I don't want anyone to see you drive in there."

He pulled over to the curb, watching his mirrors. Marie watched, too, holding her breath.

"That's the mall up ahead. See the sign?"

"Yes."

"Okay, I guess you're on your own. And, lady?"

"What?"

"Be safe."

"I will."

EIGHTEEN

Lisa took her time to select the components of her salad. A bed of crisp lettuce, smothered in shredded carrots, thin-sliced cucumbers, grated cheese, chickpeas, pearl onions, and cross sections of mushrooms and pickled peppers, topped with French dressing and bacon bits.

André was back at the table long before she reluctantly left the salad bar. She eyed his plate with disdain. It held a large scoop of cottage cheese and a jumble of sliced peaches.

"That's what you call salad?"

He picked up his fork and stabbed some fruit. "I didn't call it salad. But the management does call the place where I got it a salad bar."

She smiled and spread her napkin in her lap. "You seem a little antsy tonight."

He glanced at his watch. "I just don't want to be late. I don't want Marie getting off the plane and finding nobody there to meet her."

"André." She paused until he quit chasing a slippery peach around his plate with his fork and looked at her. "We have an hour."

"But it will take them twenty minutes to cook the pizza, and—"

She shook her head vigorously. "We killed ten at the salad bar. It will be here in another ten. Give us twenty minutes to eat, five to pay, another ten to skip over to the airport, and *voilà!* We arrive with fifteen minutes to spare."

He put on a sugary smile and nodded. "Thank you, Teacher. I think I understand the story problem now."

She blinked in surprise at the slight hurt he had inflicted.

"What, are you saying I'm talking down to you?"

"Condescending, yes."

"Oh, so I'm the math teacher and you're the English teacher. Thanks for the vocabulary lesson."

He sighed and wiped his lips with his napkin. Lisa realized that his cottage cheese and fruit had disappeared, while she'd taken only three bites of her salad.

"Did you inhale that?"

He scowled at her. She ignored him and lifted a paper-thin slice of pepper, placing it delicately on her tongue and savoring its pungency.

André drummed his fingers on the table and looked around the restaurant.

Lisa swallowed the pepper and said quietly, "We will not be late."

He sighed. *"Je le regrette."*

She nodded. *"Ce n'est rien."* It's nothing. But it was something. He had apologized for his rather boorish behavior. Perhaps he was not so different from Pierre as she had thought. André had an innate courtesy, even though he was obviously on edge. Pierre would be much more gracious and would cover his impatience with more finesse. But still, André was making an effort.

He interested her, more than she ever would have admitted in high school or in those murky intermediate years since graduation, when she'd seen him only occasionally. Lately she'd thought how glad she would be when Marie and Pierre came home, and not just because she missed her sister. When the happy couple was in town, the Gillettes saw more of the Belangers. It was a fact of life. And she'd recently begun thinking it wouldn't be such a bad thing to see the Belangers more often.

She'd had to practically browbeat André into bringing her tonight. It wasn't the ideal way to convince a man to spend time with you, but it was a start.

He watched her mournfully, with the large, expressive brown eyes all the Belanger boys—men, that is—possessed.

"How is your brother Mathieu?" she asked between bites. Keep him talking and he wouldn't fret so about the time.

"He's all right. He's working down in Lewiston right now. The company keeps sending him to different places."

She nodded. "What happened with him and Michelle Murphy?"

"They broke up."

"I know, but what *happened?*"

"I don't know. They just…split up."

"Men!" She laid her fork on the edge of the plate.

"What do you mean, men?"

"Just that you guys never want to discuss anything personal."

"Depends on what it is," André replied. "Women want to know every little detail. But if it's something messy, or in this case, depressing for someone you care about, isn't it better to accept the reality and go on from there?"

"Oh, that's so noble."

His eyebrows drew down in a frown over those chocolate brown eyes that were now less dreamy and quite focused. "Women have to chew a thing all over before they swallow it."

Lisa laughed. "Maybe there's some truth to that. All right, we've established that Mathieu and Michelle are no longer an item, and they are getting on with their lives, so we will too."

"Wise choice. Thank you."

The waitress brought their pizza and refilled their drinks. André sat back as though relieved, both that the wait was over and the conversation was broken off. Perhaps he was more sensitive than she was giving him credit for. Unlike many of her friends, he hadn't seized the chance to badmouth the woman who had recently dumped his brother.

Lisa wondered why she'd never considered André worth pursuing before. Was it because he didn't seem to care what she thought of him? His even-tempered, unexciting personality had never snagged her notice. Sure, he had a job that paid well at the post office, but how ambitious was that? At least Pierre had demonstrated some initiative and leadership by joining the Navy and becoming an officer. He was still sweet and placid in nature, but he'd proved he had the most drive of all the Belanger brothers. And she'd heard about an incident where Pierre shot down a plane attacking his outpost on an island in the Pacific, saving the lives of his comrades. No wonder Marie idolized her husband.

"Eat," André said.

Lisa sniffed. "What's got you so wound up? You're not usually like this."

"I'm not?"

"Well…I don't know." She shrugged and reached for a piece of pizza.

"I'm doing this for Pierre. He doesn't ask much of me, but this time he wants me to do a job, and I intend to do it right."

"What's so hard about meeting someone at the airport? I'm mean, it's Bangor. It's not like you had to drive all the way to Boston and pick her up at Logan."

"I just want everything to go right for them."

Lisa chewed the meat-lover's pizza—not her choice—and considered that. She was trying to get past her childhood recollections of André and had fancied she saw some potential in him now. Was she wrong about that?

She swallowed and reached for her glass. "Well, I think it's sweet of you to try so hard, but it's nothing to stress over."

"Tell that to Pierre. He called me at five o'clock this morning to remind me to be up here on time."

"Well, I guess we'd better get over there, then, so you can tell your brother later that you did everything exactly right."

André just shook his head, as if she didn't understand at all.

"Hey, I want to get Marie home safely as much as you do," she said.

"*Vraiment?*"

She smiled. "Yes, it's the truth. I've missed her terribly." She studied his face as he finished his second slice of pizza. "I was always jealous of you in French class, you know."

He stared at her for a moment, and then he returned his attention to the food. "You did all right in French."

"Well, yes, but your family all speaks it so beautifully. I've already forgotten most of what I learned in high school."

"When your parents and grandparents force you to speak the language for the first ten or fifteen years of your life, you're not apt to forget it."

"What about now? Your grandparents died quite a while ago, right?"

"Well, Pépé died first, but we still had to speak French to Mémé—always. She passed on about ten years ago. After that, the English infiltrated pretty fast. Of course, we kids all learned it at school, but the younger ones, they speak English better than they do French. Annette and Eloise, for instance. They're struggling with their French classes now."

"Well, you boys always spoke it so well, you raised the bar for the entire class."

He smiled. "I could speak it only. I couldn't write it. That's because we never saw the French words or learned to read and write them until we had classes in high school. By then I found it a great nuisance to learn to spell all over again. And so I did badly my first year. I brought home a C minus and Maman hit the ceiling. No French boy should get C's in French class! And so she made me spend extra time studying, and I didn't get to play basketball that winter. I had to memorize verb endings."

Lisa nodded, smiling. "It was daunting at first, but now the way things are spelled in French kind of makes sense to me."

André shook his head. "It was confusing for me. See, I wasn't all that good at spelling in English, either. And I still can't spell, which is not so good in postal service."

She laughed. "Well, I may have pulled A's in French grammar, but if we drove over to Quebec tomorrow, I expect you would be the one to survive longest. I would be constantly asking people to speak slooooowly. You'd be jabbering away nine to the dozen."

He shrugged. "It is one of life's ironies, is it not?"

Before she could catch it, a giggle escaped Lisa's lips, and he stared at her. Something flashed across his features. His eyes widened momentarily, as though surprise had hit him, and then his lips twitched into a smile. His expression was open and warm, something she hadn't really expected. She'd felt him resist her earlier attempts at humor, but now, for a moment, he seemed receptive.

"What is so funny?" he asked.

"You. Your syntax is so European."

"Ah. Again, I have my *grand-mère* to thank. Precision, always, with her."

"I like it. I'm beginning to see why—" She stopped and pressed her lips together, ducked her head, and picked up the half piece of pizza she'd discarded.

"What?" His smile still peeked through, though he rested his chin on one fist in feigned seriousness.

"Nothing."

"I doubt it."

She felt her cheeks go crimson, and she avoided his gaze, taking a bite and chewing slowly, her eyes downcast.

That was brilliant. High school and technical college experience had taught her that the surest way to repel a man was to let him know you were attracted to him. She was on the edge of that precipice and had nearly blurted out that she was beginning to see why Marie had fallen so hard for his brother. But if she spoke her thoughts aloud, André would certainly make it clear that he didn't reciprocate. It was okay for his brother to marry her sister, but André had no interest in furthering the two families' alliance.

That was the way it always worked for Lisa. You find a guy who's interesting and decent, but as soon as you start thinking beyond casual acquaintance, he makes an excuse to exit.

Change the subject. That's the safest course.

"Do you still think in French?" she asked.

"Sometimes. Look, do you want any more of this?" He nudged the pizza box.

"No."

André crumpled his napkin, tossed it onto his plate, and stood. "I guess we can take it along, in case Marie is hungry."

"Good idea."

NINETEEN

Marie plodded along the sidewalk, pulling her wheeled suitcase. The beaded braids in the wig swung about her shoulders.

I should have ditched this bag! Dear Lord, give me some wisdom. Show me what to do now.

Ahead, in the dusk, she made out a covered pay phone against the wall of a brick building. Her heart raced, and she hurried toward it. She had no coins in her pocket except the few pennies she'd received in change when she bought breakfast. Why hadn't she purchased something else in the airport to get some quarters as change? She struggled through the recorded instructions to place a collect call to her parents' home in Maine. The unanswered ringing flooded her with dismay.

Mom, Dad, where are you? You should be home! She checked her watch. Her plane was due to land in Bangor in an hour. Pierre had asked his brother André to pick her up, and he'd probably left already. But her own family wouldn't be going to the airport, would they? They must have had plans for the evening.

She hung up the receiver and looked all around, staring into shadows and shrinking against the wall as an SUV passed.

I'm a target with this suitcase! The men from the airport might be the people in the dark car that had tailed her cab. And there were the usual urban predators. She would be easy prey out here in the open, alone.

She made another collect call, this time to the Belanger house, and again no one answered the prolonged ringing. Deciding to make one last try, Marie fished her tiny address book from her purse and held it close to her face. In the twilight she was barely able to read the number for Pierre's best friend, George Hudson. It seemed crazy to call George, when he lived in Hawaii. But George was Mr. Efficient. He would be able to get a message through to Pierre.

A familiar voice accepted the charges and greeted her through a humming connection.

"Rachel! It's Marie."

She had only met Rachel Hudson once, on the way to Japan. Pierre had managed an overnight stop in Hawaii so that he could see his best friend. George and Rachel were newly married then and had just left Frasier Island, where they'd battled together against terrible odds and come away with nothing but their love for each other and their faith in God. Pierre and George were closer than brothers, and Marie and Rachel had bonded immediately.

"Hi, Marie. Where are you?"

"Detroit. Or near Detroit. I'm not really sure exactly where. But I need help."

"Honey, what's wrong?"

Rachel's warm, sympathetic voice was enough to send tears gushing through Marie's ducts painfully fast.

"Someone's following me. On the plane from Japan, I sat beside the wife of one of Pierre's supervisors. We got off in San Francisco, and—"

A car approached slowly.

"Rachel, I'm scared. Jenna went into the airport restroom, and a woman went in there and shot her. I saw it. And now some men are chasing me. I made the plane to Detroit, but then I panicked and took a cab."

"Marie, slow down."

"I can't. They'll kill me!"

"What—"

"I think I have something they want, and they killed Jenna for it."

"Can you just dump it somewhere?"

"No. They wouldn't know. They'd think I still had it, and besides, it may be critical that it not get into the wrong hands."

"You mean, it's some kind of classified material?"

"I don't know, but it seems like it. Or maybe she was smuggling, but—" The car passed and rolled on down the block. Marie watched as it turned at the next corner. "Rachel, I'm at a pay phone on the street. I can't stay here. My cell phone was stolen. Can you and George call Pierre and tell him where I am? He's probably going nuts right about now."

"Of course, but Marie, you've got to get help! Go to the police!"

Marie gulped and turned her back to the street as another car approached. She stood between the driver and her suitcase, hoping to shield it from his view.

"That's my plan. I'm near a mall, and I think I can get help there. But I need to move now."

She jammed the receiver onto its base and grasped the handle of her suitcase. Far down the street, she could see the lighted sign of the mall entrance. She threw back her shoulders and walked toward it.

TWENTY

1030 Saturday, Yokosuka

Pierre paused outside Captain Wheeler's office, turned his cell phone off, and handed it to the ensign on duty outside. As much as he wanted to receive Marie's call, he knew better than to take electronics into a high-security meeting.

He was a bit surprised that no other personnel were in the room with him and Wheeler. He closed the door behind him and took the chair opposite Wheeler's desk.

The captain looked up from his keyboard and swiveled to face him.

"Belanger. Good. Listen, we've had a change of plans on tonight's run."

"Sir?" The run into China was planned down to the second. But covert operations were scrubbed close to execution if something came up that caused the commanding officer to believe the men involved would be in excessive danger or that the project was at risk of discovery by their adversaries. Pierre couldn't help wondering what had brought on this change of tactics in Operation Lion Gate, but he usually didn't get the full details in such cases. If he was lucky, he'd have a general understanding of what had alarmed Wheeler, but just enough so he could help make informed decisions as they configured plans for a new foray.

Wheeler nodded, inhaling and focusing on a point beyond Pierre's left shoulder. "I'm afraid so. We still need to meet with Yuan as soon as possible, but we have to change the location."

"The alternate we discussed earlier?" Pierre strove to keep his features relaxed and neutral.

"Negative." Wheeler opened a file folder on the desktop. "That was my first inclination, but today's events preclude that. We've chosen a new location. It's one that you suggested a month ago, but we'd ruled it out because of the difficulty of access." He shoved a sheet of paper across the desk, and Pierre glanced at it.

"I remember. You felt it was risky, and I agreed, though it would be ideal if it weren't so far inland."

"Right. You and I discussed it. No one else."

Wheeler's eyes measured him as he spoke, and Pierre involuntarily sat a little straighter.

"We'll make it work, sir. You can count on me and my men."

"We'll have to push the timetable back forty-eight hours, while our contact makes sure that location is secure."

"Yes, sir." Forty-eight hours. Would this delay his departure for the U.S. and his leave? Poor Marie, always waiting for him. At least she didn't know the fixes he and his men got into on their secret assignments.

Wheeler leaned back in his chair, allowing his stiff shoulders to slump just a bit. That and his lowered eyebrows tipped Pierre off to the depth of the captain's worry.

"This project…"

"Yes, sir?"

"We've had a security breach. You need to know, Belanger. We're taking steps to close it, but we need to be extra careful now."

"But the operation is still a go?"

"Yes." Wheeler steepled his fingers, and a philosophical air enveloped him. "Amazing what we go through, hoping to leave the world a little better than we found it. Not perfect, just a little better." He met Pierre's gaze and smiled. "I gave our contact two new passwords. He should be in touch with you tonight, and again six hours before liftoff. Belanger, if this falls apart now, after all the work we've put into it…"

Pierre watched him carefully. The captain's fatigued voice and drooping posture sent a wave of anxiety over him. Wheeler was always upbeat about this project. He saw the potential of fomenting unrest in China to the point of collapsing the current government, provided a faction with democratic leanings was ready to step in and stabilize things. It would take an enormous surge of energy from the contingent that craved relief from the yoke of communism. The leaders would have to exert all their charisma and confidence as they called upon the masses for a cohesive push toward a new order.

And the United States would stand by and watch, without giving overt support to the insurgents until it was certain how the chips would fall. And then…yes, then. The president would announce his support of the new government, with certain reservations, and promote the birth of a new—and huge—democracy.

Free elections in China? It was unthinkable. Yet there were men in the State Department who thought it was possible and who whispered to the undercover negotiators that it could be done in less than two years. American involvement would be minimal but crucial. And the reality of the aid being promised to the Chinese insurgents must be invisible. It would never be confirmed, never acknowledged, until and unless a new Chinese government took hold and maintained its power through the inevitable mess that followed a coup.

"Well, sir," Pierre said cautiously, "when I am sure we have a safe meeting place, should I report to you?"

Wheeler shot him a keen glance before picking up the sheet of paper and returning it to its folder. "Yes. You'll brief me and Commander Reginald."

"Yes, sir." A strained silence hung between them.

"It's probably in your best interest to know," Wheeler said at last, "that Commander Tarrington has had a personal emergency. He needs to go back to the States immediately."

Pierre hesitated. He didn't want to cause any trouble, but he wanted information. He had always liked Wheeler. The captain was fair and considerate of his men, and he wanted to see the Chinese people freed from the oppressive government that enslaved them. Pierre cleared his throat, and Wheeler's inquiring blue eyes focused on him, open and nonjudgmental.

"Sir, I heard a rumor. It may be just that, or it may be the truth. My wife left here yesterday afternoon from Narita. I put her on the same plane Mrs. Tarrington boarded. If there's anything you know that might have a bearing on my wife's safety…"

Wheeler clamped his lips in a straight, harsh line and swiveled his chair back and forth, just a little. After a moment he stopped the motion and looked Pierre in the eye.

"Belanger, I know you'll honor my word when I tell you this is classified. Mrs. Tarrington is dead, but so far as I can tell, it has nothing to do with your wife or any of the other dependents who left here yesterday. And I pray it has nothing to do with this operation."

Pierre gulped for air and nodded. "Thank you, sir. That's a comfort. I mean, the part about my wife not being caught up in it."

"Well, keep it to yourself. Mrs. Tarrington's death will become public knowledge. In fact, it's probably already being broadcast in California. But the circumstances of her death… If you hear rumors, tell me what you hear but don't pass them on."

"Aye, aye, sir."

Wheeler smiled. "I don't need to tell you that. But I wouldn't have thought I needed to tell anyone in my chain of command."

Was he hinting that someone within the small cadre involved in the China op had leaked top secret information? Tarrington? What about the six men who served directly under Pierre to ensure the safety of the covert diplomats as they with the Chinese insurgent leaders?

"Sir, with your permission, I'll call my unit in immediately and brief them on the change of plans. Not the new location, but just to tell them things are on hold and we're not moving tonight. I'd like to meet face-to-face with all of them."

Wheeler nodded. "Good. And, Belanger, I haven't forgotten you're due for leave. If we can untangle things over the next day or two, you should ship out on schedule."

"Yes, sir." Pierre tried not to let anything show on his face—not the wave of homesickness that engulfed him; not the uneasiness Wheeler's briefing had brought on; certainly not the anxiety for Marie that would not lie down and keep silent as he left the building, but continually screamed through his brain.

TWENTY-ONE

Lisa and André didn't talk much on the short ride to Bangor International Airport. Her silence met with André's approval.

So she wasn't a perpetual chatterbox, the way his sisters sometimes appeared to be. It gave him time to mull over the topics they had touched on and the transformation in his feelings about Lisa. Maybe she wasn't so bad after all. At first she'd seemed a little bossy. Assertive to the point of annoying. Now he wasn't sure. Maybe that was a cover for insecurity. And single women had to be somewhat assertive, didn't they? They had to take care of themselves. Did Lisa believe she'd be alone for the rest of her life?

He glanced over at her as he put the car window down for the parking lot ticket. She was biting her upper lip and craning her neck as she looked toward the terminal.

She looked his way as though sensing his attention and gave him a smile. "Now you've got me worrying. You do think Marie's okay, don't you?"

"Sure. She's fine. It's just that Pierre and I were really close, and now we've been separated most of the time for the past ten years or so. I don't know. I suppose I want to keep that bond we used to have. This is the only thing he's asked me to do for him, and..." André shook his head, grabbed the ticket, and then eased into the short-term parking lot.

Lisa said softly, "I guess that's sort of why I wanted to come. Marie and I used to share a room at home. I miss her so much. And now we have a chance to have her all to ourselves for a few weeks, until Pierre gets home." She flexed her shoulders in a tiny shrug. "I admit I was disappointed when she told us she'd be staying with your family, not ours."

"Well, I'm sure she'll spend as much time with you as she can. She'll love being with you again. I guess she just figured it would be simpler to stay with us and not have to move her things when Pierre gets here."

"Yeah, probably."

He parked his pickup exactly in the center of the parking space and put the transmission into park. Before Lisa could unbuckle her seat belt, he was out and circling the vehicle. But she opened her door before he could get to it and swung her legs out—long, slender legs clad in soft, faded jeans—and looked up at him with a surprised smile.

"Hey…thanks."

She stood on the pavement and slung her suede purse over her shoulder. André reached past her uncertainly and grasped the edge of the door. Her face looked a bit pinkish. Did she feel as awkward as he did? How long had it been since he'd opened a car door for a woman? Of course, the "rules" were no longer rules, just options. Lisa was an independent woman. Maybe she would take his attempt at courtesy as an insult.

Yet she wasn't scowling at him. Her expression was guarded but almost sweet. A half smile. In that moment she was decidedly pretty. Not beautiful, but pleasant to look at. He was glad for the first time that she had come with him. All sorts of thoughts zinged through André's mind, but he reminded himself of his mission and flipped the lock button before swinging the door to.

"Twenty-five minutes 'til she lands," Lisa murmured.

"Good. Let's go in and check the monitor."

Inside the small airport they stood beneath one of the arrival screens mounted near the two baggage carousels in the downstairs lobby.

"Looks like they're on time," André said. "Coming in upstairs."

Lisa nodded. "You want to go right up?"

She looked up at him inquiringly, which was a mild surprise. He would have expected her to lead the way.

"Sure." He walked beside her to the base of the escalator and stood back for her to hop on first. He mounted two steps below, and after a moment's hesitation, stepped up so that he was directly behind her. She turned and faced him, and they were nearly at eye level.

"Maybe when Pierre gets back, we can do something with him and Marie," she said.

He liked the idea. A year ago, he would have backpedaled and found an excuse to decline, but now the prospect appealed to him.

"Yeah. Maybe we can do some waterskiing while they're home."

Lisa shivered. "I don't know if his leave is long enough for that. I never swim before Memorial Day."

He laughed, and they both stepped off the escalator. Lisa staggered, and by the time she caught herself André was clutching her wrist.

"You okay?"

"Yeah. Sorry."

He nodded, looking down into her eyes. They were lighter than Marie's, almost golden. He took her hand in his without allowing himself to analyze the move and drew her away from the escalator.

"Where do you want to sit?" He didn't look at her, knowing he would blush if he did and fearful that her eyes would register shock and perhaps disapproval.

"Over there near the security gate? Then we'll see her as soon as she clears."

"Great." He walked toward the row of empty seats she'd indicated, noting two things. Lisa did not pull away from him, and her hand was deliciously warm.

They sat down facing the glass wall of the gate area. She wasn't hard to talk to at all. They ran through a slew of high school tales, and he found himself laughing a lot. Why had he dreaded this? She was funny and smart. And her eyes had that swirled caramel color.

"Hey, that's her flight." Lisa swiveled her head toward the gate, alert and expectant.

André cocked his head and listened to the announcer's high-pitched voice. It was Marie's plane, all right. He glanced at his watch. Two minutes early. No sense standing up yet. It would take them a while to enter the terminal.

Fifteen minutes later, he and Lisa stood together near the security barrier. Dozens of incoming passengers had swept past them and into the arms of their loved ones. The flow had slowed to a trickle, and now it appeared to have ended.

Lisa looked up at him, her face pale. "Where is she?"

André started to respond, but he noticed the flight crew coming through the gate. He bounded forward.

"Excuse me. My sister-in-law was supposed to be on this plane, but she hasn't come out yet."

The flight officer eyed him warily. "All passengers have de-planed."

"But…" He turned and looked at Lisa, and he knew from her bewildered expression that he couldn't accept that answer.

"Go to the airline desk downstairs and inquire," one of the flight attendants told him. "They should be able to tell you whether the person you're looking for was on the plane."

André stepped back and let them pass. Lisa's hand clutched his, and he tried to pull out a reassuring smile for her.

"Let's go down."

She nodded, and they went down the escalator, silent this time.

In the lobby André located the desk of Marie's airline and stepped up with a show of confidence he did not feel.

"Excuse me, I'm here to meet a passenger from the flight that just landed. She's my sister-in-law, Marie Belanger. She was supposed to arrive from Detroit, but she didn't come into the terminal. The crew said to ask you about it."

The uniformed woman huddled over her computer. "What was the name again?"

A few moments later she looked up at André and Lisa.

"I'm sorry. That passenger did not get on the plane in Detroit. I have no more information."

TWENTY-TWO

The parking lot lights dazzled Marie, and she approached the side entrance of the mall with hesitation. This was bigger than anything she'd encountered in Maine. Her legs dragged as she crossed acres of pavement filled with cars. Big American cars. SUVs, pickups, and minivans. Even a Humvee.

A group of young people sauntered, laughing, toward the entrance. Marie followed them inside and along the open foyer area to a directory sign. The array of businesses overwhelmed her. It reminded her of a huge shopping center she'd been to outside Tokyo, except the individual stores were larger here, and all the signs were in English. Hundreds of people roamed the central atrium. She couldn't remember ever seeing so many tall blond people. She hovered between a miniature pagoda where ear piercing was the specialty and a kiosk offering custom T-shirts. The food court must not be far away. The smell of pizza dominated those of onion rings and coffee. Over it all the steady beat of rock music thrummed.

She found an empty bench with its back to a fountain and sat down. Her fingers had molded around the handle of her small, black suitcase, and when she let go of it, they ached and refused to straighten. Her stomach clenched as the food smells did their work.

It's not safe here. Too open.

She stood, grabbed the bag, and walked swiftly to the nearest shop. Country decor, handwoven baskets, and soothing music nearly

covered the distant rock beat. It was a good choice for her to gain
her bearings and make sure she wasn't followed. The clerks wouldn't
think it odd if she lingered.

Of course, she hadn't renewed her makeup job. In this light, her
ethnic wig might seem oddly mismatched with her complexion.
Furtively, she studied the other patrons. Spotting a sixtyish woman
with blue-and-purple hair convinced her that her own hairstyle would
not give her away. But the suitcase would draw attention.

In twenty minutes she had three offers of assistance. She'd better
buy something. They probably suspected she'd come to fill her bag
with their merchandise.

A display of specialty chocolates caught her eye. They were pricey,
but they would serve two purposes—legitimizing her presence and
taking the edge off her growing hunger. She snatched up one of the
smallest packages and went to the counter.

Emerging into the mall again, Marie was ready to call the police
and ask them to come pick her up. She ambled toward the food court,
unable to resist the penetrating odors of food any longer.

As she approached the open area between the food vendors, the
volume of the music increased. She turned and came abruptly into a
large courtyard filled with tables and chairs. To one side, a platform
had been erected from plywood on wooden pallets, and a four-man
band stood on it with their instruments, singing and playing. If
their earnest expressions were any indication, this performance was
critical. Marie read a large placard posted next to the drum set on the
platform: Music for Monkey Bars. Concerts May 12–15 to benefit
Smith Street Playground. Donations welcome.

On the far side of the courtyard, past the tables in the center of
the restaurant booths, was a bank of pay phones, and beyond them
a short hallway led to a side entrance.

Marie made her legs move slowly, nonchalantly. She was not
afraid. She was not desperate. Not on the outside, anyway.

She walked between the tables, not making eye contact with any
of the patrons, and reached the line of phones. Relief swept over

her as she lifted the receiver of the nearest one. *Punch in 911*, she thought. *Three digits, and I'm safe.*

She let go of the suitcase. As she raised her hand to punch the 9 button, she glanced behind her. Nothing unusual snared her attention. The musicians still sang, and people still bought chow mein and hot dogs. She turned her back to the tables and punched in the number.

The ring sounded twice.

"What is your emergency?"

Marie drew in a breath. "I need—"

A hand closed about her wrist, and the air rushed out of her lungs. Adrenaline shot through her veins. She pivoted and stared into the black eyes of a Chinese man a few years older than her. A prominent red scar reached across his cheekbone from just below his left eye to his earlobe.

"Hang up." His fingers dug into her wrist as he bent it. "Do it now."

TWENTY-THREE

1115 Saturday, Yokosuka

With great effort Pierre pulled his thoughts away from his wife and back to his duties. He'd made short work of the quartering assignments on the *Bush* by delivering Rocket's folder to Captain Wheeler's aide. Tarrington wasn't the only one who could keep things rolling.

After retrieving his cell phone from the ensign on duty at the door, Pierre headed toward his own building. As he walked, he turned the phone on and checked the screen. One missed call. Marie! Who else?

But the message was from one of the men in his office, telling him that new equipment he'd requested had arrived.

Back at his desk, he unlocked the drawer that held the details on transportation for the impending China trip. He glanced at his watch. Was it still morning? It felt like years since he'd left the apartment. Marie should be on the ground in Maine now, maybe even back at his parents' house. André had better have been there on time to help her get her luggage and drive her down to Waterville. He should have told André to ask her if she'd had supper. She'd be hungry if all they gave her on the plane was pretzels and diet soda.

Why hadn't she called him? He couldn't wait to be sure she'd made it safely, and he pressed the buttons on his cell phone, praying for a good connection.

Immediately, he was kicked to Marie's voice mail. She must have turned the phone off. He groaned silently while her message played, a quick, bright greeting in English and French. The beep sounded, and he tried to put all anxiety out of his voice.

"Hey, *chérie*. Where are you? Give me a ring and let me know you're home."

He pressed the disconnect button. Almost at once, the phone rang. He grinned as he pushed the talk button.

"Allo."

"Pierre?"

He was mildly disappointed to hear his brother's voice, not Marie's.

"Oui, c'est moi. Comment ça va?"

"Not so good."

The knot in Pierre's throat resurrected and nearly choked him. "What's wrong? Where's Marie?"

"I don't know," André said. "Lisa and I are at the airport, and she didn't get off the plane."

Pierre swallowed, processing that. "Lisa who? Marie's Lisa?"

"Yeah, her sister. She's with me. Marie didn't show up. She wasn't on the plane from Detroit."

"Are you sure?"

"Yeah, we asked the airline agent. She says Marie never got on the flight."

The air Pierre inhaled tasted thin. He needed more oxygen, fast.

"What about San Francisco?"

"What about it?" André sounded confused and slightly stupid, but that was nothing new. He'd always given an impression of being mentally slower than he really was.

"Did she get on the plane at SFO?"

"I...don't know."

"Find out. Find out, man! It's important."

"We're trying, but it's evening here and they're shorthanded." Now André sounded hurt.

"Tell them this is critical." Pierre jumped up from his chair and sent it flying backward to bump the file cabinet behind him. "You don't understand. I need to know if she made the flight from San Francisco to Detroit. André, something's wrong, and I can't tell you any more than that, but I need to know what's happened. Trace her back. Can you do that?"

"I'll try. A troop plane just landed from Ireland, and they're bringing two hundred Marines into the terminal. They've been in Iraq for who knows how long, and this is their first stop on American soil. It's chaos here."

"Right." Pierre was well aware of the pride the city of Bangor took in being the port of entry for overseas troops. A group of "troop greeters" met every military plane that landed, and they distributed phone cards, stuffed animals, and hugs to the returning soldiers. It was great. Anytime but now.

Pierre paced the three steps across his cubicle and back. "Oh, God."

After a second's silence, André said, "Hey, bro, you don't swear."

"I'm not swearing. I'm praying. Look, I'll put someone on it at this end, but you try, do you hear me? Make that agent call someone higher up in the airline. Be obnoxious. Insist that they tell you where she left them."

A new voice came over the airwaves.

"Pierre, this is Lisa. I'm here with André, and he's letting me listen. You sound really worried. Is there something you're not telling us?"

Pierre sank into his battered chair. "Yes. Please, do what you can."

"I've had assertiveness training. If anyone can force them to tell us something, it's me."

"Good. Thanks, Lisa."

The connection went dead, and he sat for only a moment, winging off a more complete prayer for wisdom and results. Then he rose and entered the large workroom.

"Rodriguez, Miller, Corson! Whatever you're doing, put it aside. I need you."

TWENTY-FOUR

Lisa stood beside André, watching the officers herd the Marines back through the security gate. A hush fell over the waiting room as it emptied. On impulse, she stepped over near the movable barrier that formed the path boarding passengers followed. Two women with graying hair had planted themselves outside the barrier, close to where it met the glass wall of the restricted area. Probably members of the local VFW auxiliary, Lisa surmised.

"Goodbye," the ladies called to the soldiers as the line inched past them. "Thank you so much for serving. We're glad you had a safe trip home."

A girl in a camouflage uniform moved through the line between two men who towered over her. She met Lisa's gaze with an uncertain glance. Lisa smiled and held out her hand.

"Thank you. I'm glad you're heading home."

The girl smiled, and her dark eyes lit up for a moment. The satisfaction there overshadowed the lines of fatigue that creased her skin and the purple shadows beneath her eyes. "Thanks. This is great, y'all being here."

As the last of the Marines passed through the gate, Lisa realized André was at her elbow. She looked up at him. He tensed his facial muscles and shook his head slightly.

"Makes me want to enlist."

"I know what you mean." She turned away with a sigh. "What now? It's still half an hour until the next plane from Detroit lands."

"Let's check back with the airline. You never know." He led her downstairs again. Lisa was sure the airline agent was tired of dealing with them after the blistering tirade she'd delivered half an hour ago, but she followed André over to the desk.

"Oh, hey!" The woman looked up with a tentative smile. "We haven't located your sister yet, but her bags were on the earlier plane."

"Really?" Lisa hadn't considered the possibility that Marie's luggage had come through without her. "Where are they?"

"We've set them aside in the back."

"Can we have them?"

"You'll have to show some ID."

Lisa fumbled with her purse and hauled out her wallet to show her driver's license.

"Okay, you're Lisa Gillette. Now, how do I know you're related to Ms. Belanger? Any proof that she's your sister?"

Lisa gulped. "Well, I didn't exactly come here expecting to have to prove that sort of thing. But I have a picture of me and Marie together."

"And she's married to my brother," André said, producing his wallet. "I can give you my ID too."

The agent frowned. "Well, it would be best if Mr. or Mrs. Belanger claimed the bags in person."

"Pierre is in Japan," Lisa said quickly. "And obviously Marie would claim them if she were here."

"I don't..."

"You could call our parents," André suggested. "Our families are both in the Waterville area."

The woman's eyebrows lowered as she tapped a few keystrokes on her computer. "We've got a passport photo of Marie Belanger." She held the photo Lisa had supplied up next to her monitor and smiled. "Anyone who takes a passport picture that good has got to be beautiful in real life."

"She's gorgeous," Lisa agreed. But that wouldn't help establish their relationship. Marie had the glistening dark hair, the deep brown eyes, the perfect olive complexion. Lisa had the mousy brown hair, butternut-almost-hazel eyes, and indifferent skin. Sisters? Strangers were amazed when they learned of the bond.

"Hey, listen." The agent leaned toward Lisa in confidential closeness. "The suitcases have tags with an address on them. Can you tell me what it says?"

André stooped to enter the huddle. "It's probably my folks' address. She's going to stay there." He rattled off the address of the forty-acre farm on the outskirts of Waterville.

"Yeah, that's it. Can you tell me anything that's inside the bags?"

"If I know Marie, lots of shoes and cosmetics," Lisa said. "She's been away two years, and I have no idea what clothes she would bring along."

"Any gifts or souvenirs she mentioned?"

"Hmm...my mother's birthday's next week." Lisa felt a pang of hope. "Marie told me she was going to try to get her a traditional silk kimono, but I'm not sure if she managed it. We got a few things she shipped in the mail last week, but that wasn't among them."

The agent still wavered.

"Look, you *know* she's my sister." Lisa leaned closer and stared, forcing the woman to hold her gaze. "What can I tell you that will convince you it's okay to give me that luggage?"

"It's just that I could get in trouble, you know?"

"Happens to me all the time," said André. "I work at the post office, and we're not allowed to give mail to anyone whose name isn't on the list for a particular mailbox."

Lisa scowled at him, a you're-not-helping scowl.

"Hey, my uncle is the postmaster in Newport," the woman said, flashing him a smile. "You don't know him, do you?"

André's brow furrowed. "Newport, Newport. Let's see, I did a substitute run up there for a week last summer. Let me think. Brown?"

The woman's featured lit in confirmation.

"Harry Brown," André said. "No, wait. Not Harry. Henry. Gray hair, glasses. He told me a funny story about how he was restoring a '57 Chevy."

The woman laughed. "That's good enough for me. Oh, by the way…" She glanced at Lisa. "There's a package marked 'Mom' inside one suitcase, and a ton of makeup. Also a picture of a naval officer with a smile to die for."

André nodded. "My brother."

"You got a photo?"

"No, afraid not. Not on me."

She shrugged. "I'm satisfied, and I need to get ready for the next flight. You'll have to sign for them, though. Give your complete address, phone number, cell, e-mail—any way to reach you." She handed Lisa a clipboard and disappeared through a doorway behind the counter.

Lisa pulled the pen from a holder on the clipboard and scowled at André. "My photo of me and my sister isn't good enough, but you know about her Uncle Harry's car, and suddenly you're golden."

"Henry."

"Oh, right." Lisa scrawled something resembling her name across the bottom of the release form.

The agent returned with two bulging black suitcases and hoisted them onto the scale between the counters. "Here you go, and I hope your sister's on this next plane."

TWENTY-FIVE

1200 Saturday, Yokosuka

Pierre returned to the apartment on his lunch break. He doubted Marie would leave a message on the landline phone, but it was possible. He scowled as he unlocked the door. He was supposed to have the phone disconnected before he left. Marie had left him a list of chores to perform before he headed home on the *Bush*. What had he done with it?

The message indicator was blinking, and he jabbed the button.

"Pierre, *mon copain*, this is George. Rachel took a call from Marie a few minutes ago, and she gave us a message for you. She's in Detroit, and she's okay, but there's more to it. Give me a call and we'll talk this thing over. *Au revoir!*"

Pierre grabbed the phone and dialed the international code. When he heard his friend's placid greeting, his words gushed out.

"George, *c'est moi*. What is going on with Marie? My brother told me she didn't get off the plane in Maine."

"Rachel told me Marie sounded a bit frantic when she called here a couple of hours ago."

"Frantic? What does that mean?" Pierre tore open the drapes and stared down at the parking lot.

"Her cell phone was stolen, and she couldn't get through to you. She said someone was following her."

Pierre froze, his breath sucked away. He clenched his fingers around a clump of drapery fabric and forced himself to pull air into his aching lungs. *"Qu'est-ce que c'est?* She is in danger?"

"Easy, now." George's maddeningly calm voice only sent Pierre's adrenaline surging. That was the voice George had used when the three of them—George, Pierre, and Rachel—had been targeted on Frasier Island by an international cartel of enemy forces. Back then, it meant *Stay calm but be ready to fight for your life.* Pierre read the same message now in that deadly even voice.

"Who could be after her? And why didn't she get on her plane?"

"She told Rachel she'd witnessed a shooting, and someone is following her. Maybe the shooter. Rachel advised her to go straight to the Detroit police."

"A shooting? But she's okay?"

"Yes, but she's scared. So scared she apparently didn't want to stick around the San Francisco airport. She took her flight to Detroit, but left the airport there."

Pierre inhaled slowly. "All right. So, what now? We just wait until she checks in again?"

George hesitated, which was not like George. "We could call the Detroit PD and see if they've heard from her."

"I don't like it. I mean, if this is connected to Jenna Tarrington somehow—"

"Whoa! Rachel said Marie mentioned the name Jenna. She said this Jenna was shot in the airport. The wife of someone you know?"

"Yeah. Her husband's a commander I work under."

"Okay, that's progress. Rachel tried hard to remember everything Marie said, and she wrote it down for me."

Pierre stared down at the cars and Jeeps wending through the parking lot. "Tell me."

"She said she's near Detroit. Someone's chasing her, and she's afraid they will kill her. She has something they want."

Pierre inhaled sharply. "What on earth?"

"I don't know. Just that she has this—whatever—contraband or something—and she can't dump it."

"And it's connected somehow to Jenna Tarrington."

"That's a leap, but from what little we know, it seems possible."

"Yeah, well, my CO told me an hour ago that Jenna Tarrington is dead. So far, the word is that her husband is going stateside because of that, but I'm positive he's going under escort."

"What are his duties?"

"He's deep in a clandestine operation that my unit provides secure transportation for."

George was silent for a moment, and then he sighed. "You're coming home soon?"

"If they don't send me back to…the place I go to now and then."

"The place that's in the color of my wife's eyes?"

Pierre couldn't help smiling. He vividly recalled the leap of joy he'd felt the first time he talked to his friend after George and Rachel's miraculous escape from Frasier Island. "We just got married, *mon ami*, and I thought you'd want to know," George had said, his exultation charging over the airwaves.

China blue.

That was the way he'd described Rachel's eyes, and Pierre knew that George was hopelessly, irrevocably in love. After months of keeping them from throttling each other, it had been a moment of triumph for Pierre. And now George was using the color of Rachel's eyes as a code.

"Three points for you, my old friend," he whispered.

"Thought so."

"It's supposed to be a secret. If you know, the world probably knows."

"The world doesn't have the intuition I have."

Pierre laughed. "So, tell me. What do we do to help Marie?"

"I could go to Detroit."

"I couldn't ask you to do that."

"Hey, you know me. I have so much leave stacked up, I'll never use it all. Rachel's been hounding me to take some time off."

"With her."

"Well, sure, but she only gets so much. The Marine Mammal Center keeps her busy. But I could easily take a couple of weeks and fly over there."

"This...death. It happened in San Francisco."

"I could go there first. It would mean arranging a flight from Honolulu to San Francisco and talking to the police there, that's all."

"The brass will put an NCIS team on it."

"Probably."

"For sure. They're probably already on it." Pierre turned away from the window and paced the room. "Maybe FBI too. And if it is really connected to Commander Tarrington's assignment, the CIA may be mixed up in it."

"I'll get clearance."

"Just like that?"

He could almost see the gleam in George's eyes. "You doubt me, *mon ami?* I already have high-level access, and my CO will listen when I tell him bringing Marie home safely is critical. You know I have connections in high places."

Pierre nodded. "Yeah. All the way to heaven. But we need more information. Will you pray with me? I'm all on edge over this."

TWENTY-SIX

Marie writhed as the man twisted her wrist.

"Hang up the phone."

She barely heard him over the pounding beat of the music.

With her free hand, she reached the receiver toward the wall-mounted phone box but missed. It clunked against the base and fell, dangling by the metal cord.

"Let me go!"

The music stopped suddenly.

"Calm down or you'll get hurt, Marie," he whispered.

She froze at the sound of her name on his lips.

"That's better. Now, come on. There's an exit right over there." He jerked his head to his right, and Marie glanced toward it and then back beyond him. The crowd in the food court gave a smattering of applause for the band, but most people were too busy eating. At a nearby table sat two men in leather jackets, with motorcycle helmets resting on an empty chair between them. They dove into their pizza, paying no attention to Marie.

The Chinese man pulled her wrist. "I said move." He poked her in the side, and she wondered if he had a gun in his pocket. A vivid image crossed her mind. Jenna falling to the white tiled floor, dark blood seeping through the front of her red blouse.

Marie whirled and wrenched her wrist, kicking at the same time.

The man yelped and released his hold on her arm. He leaped back, whipping a pistol from this jacket pocket.

Marie stood staring at him for an instant. The food court had gone deathly still.

"Gun!" a woman screamed.

A shuffling and scrambling erupted behind Marie, a baby wailed, and people shouted. "Run!" "Get under the table!" "Call security!"

In a flash one of the bikers stood and flung a metal chair at Marie's attacker. The Chinese man's pistol flew from his hand and skittered across the floor.

Her pursuer grasped his empty gun hand and stared at Marie, his mouth gaping, and then he faced the biker. The leather-jacketed man and his partner came around the table toward them.

The Chinese man leaped at Marie and seized her arm. His other hand grasped her head. A sudden rush of cool air told her the wig was off.

"Leave the lady alone," said the chair-throwing biker. His buddy towered over the smaller-framed Asian.

In her peripheral vision, Marie saw the band members leave their makeshift stage. She expected them to fade away from the action, but instead all four boys strode toward her. They formed a circle with the two bikers around the Chinese man. They appeared to be teenagers, but each of the musicians held a blade in his hand.

"Get out of here, sister," said one of the band members and the Asian released her.

The lead guitarist nodded. "We've got this jerk. Eldon, go make someone call that security dude. You know, the big guy."

She opened her mouth to say thanks, thought better of it, and turned to look for her things. The wig lay in a humble heap on the floor. Her small suitcase still sat by the phone with the hanging receiver, a dozen feet away. Beside it on the floor rested the Chinese man's pistol. She gulped and clutched the strap of her purse. Somehow she'd managed to keep hold of it. She looked toward the main part of the mall. In the distance, she saw a uniformed officer approaching. But coming faster, from the opposite direction, were the craggy-faced man and the second Chinese who had pursued her at the airport.

She ran for the side exit.

TWENTY-SEVEN

"What now?" Lisa asked. "More coffee?"

André sighed and leaned against a pillar in the airport lounge. "There's not much point in us waiting here any longer. That was the last plane due from Detroit tonight."

"There's one from Philly at twelve twenty-five."

"She didn't go to Philly. She went to Detroit."

"So far as we know."

André closed his eyes for a minute. He was too tired to think straight, and he had to work in the morning. "If she comes in tonight from some other city, she'll call."

"Yeah."

They stood for another moment without speaking. André looked down the bleak corridor of the future. What would he tell Pierre? *I'm sorry, big brother, but the love of your life has vanished.*

The airline desk was closed, and they walked silently past it toward the exit, each pulling one of Marie's suitcases. The chilly air slapped them, and André wished he had a jacket. Lisa buttoned her sweater as she walked. When they reached the truck, he unlocked her door and opened it for her.

She climbed in without comment, and he shut the door, lifted the luggage into the back, and then went around to the other side.

After he stopped at the booth and handed the attendant his parking ticket and six dollars, Lisa stirred.

"This rots."

"Yeah." He pulled out into sparse traffic and headed for the interstate.

She said nothing for several minutes as he maneuvered onto I-95. Her silence confirmed André's knowledge that he had failed.

"Pierre and Marie don't deserve this," he said.

"I'll say. I hope she's all right."

"Yeah."

Lisa looked over at him, her eyes catching the glint of headlights in the distant northbound lane.

"Hey, did Pierre ever say anything to you about church and the Bible?"

"No."

"Really? Because lately Marie has been bugging me to read the Bible and go to church. Every time she wrote home, she'd tell us about this strange church they'd been going to in Japan."

"Strange how?"

"It meets for services in a school, with all the grown-ups and kids together. They have an American preacher and a Japanese preacher. And the American military personnel and the Japanese locals worship together."

"What's weird about that?"

"Maybe not weird, but unusual, I guess. And they study the Bible all the time."

"You mean, at church?"

"Well, yeah, but Marie was going to some other group that met every week in a Japanese lady's house to read the Bible together. She talked about it a lot." Lisa frowned and shook her head slightly. "Do you ever read the Bible?"

"No."

"Me either. I don't even have one, do you?"

"Yeah, somewhere. Mémé gave it to me a long time ago."

"But you never actually read it."

He shrugged and swerved around a dead skunk on the pavement.

"Oh, Mathieu and I used to look up the Sodom and Gomorrah story once in a while. We liked that. And David and Bathsheba."

Lisa grimaced. "Boys. I assume you've grown up since then."

"One can hope." He drove on, trying to ignore the skunk odor and thinking over what she had said about Marie's new religious fervor. "You know, Pierre did say something to me today. He said he was praying."

"I suppose anyone would pray in his situation." She watched him, her eyes sober, as though trying to glean every nuance from his expression. "Was he in the habit of praying before they left for Japan? Because I figured your family was pretty conservative. I mean, you believe in God, don't you?"

"Sure. And we used to go to church. When I was a kid we went a lot. I don't go so much now."

Lisa stared forward through the windshield. "We didn't, not much. Once in a while. On Easter and Christmas for sure, but the rest of the time, it was kind of hit or miss."

"We had to. Mémé wouldn't let my father hear the end of it if we kids weren't all lined up in the pew on Sunday."

She turned toward him, her eyes wide, and he felt that she had dropped the mask of Lisa Gillette, self-sufficient business owner. Instead, she looked young and vulnerable, the way she had the first day of ninth grade. That was the last time he ever saw Lisa looking scared. Somehow she'd brought her fears under control, or at least the outward manifestation of her fears, and managed to look purposeful and confident.

But now she had that dazed look, like the timid girl facing the first day of ninth grade alone. He wondered how many people had seen her in the transparent mode.

"You okay?"

"Yeah." She licked her lips. "I just thought it was really strange that Marie jumped into this church thing over there. I mean, she never did here. All she cared about was boys and fashion and music. And then Pierre and fashion and music."

André chuckled and nodded, watching the taillights ahead. "Sounds just like my sisters."

"A couple of months ago she wrote to me about a church here."

"Really?"

"Uh-huh. Apparently their pastor over there contacted someone here to find a church for her and Pierre to go to when they come home. What he calls a 'good' church. Wouldn't you think all churches were good?"

"Well…"

"I mean, any church is better than no church, right?"

"My mémé wouldn't have said so. She would have had a fit if any of us kids had tried to switch churches."

"Grandmothers are like that." Lisa's lips pursed and her eyebrows drew together as she stared out into the darkness. "For some reason, Marie thinks this church their pastor in Japan heard about is special, and she wanted me to find it for her and…and even go to a Sunday service. Kind of check it out and tell her and Pierre about it, you know?"

"Pierre never said anything to me about it."

The miles slipped away beneath the wheels of the pickup. André sneaked an occasional glance at Lisa, but she seemed absorbed in her thoughts. After a long time, he asked, "So did you find it?"

"What?"

"That church."

"Not yet. It seemed too…"

She is scared, he thought. *She doesn't want to walk into a strange building full of people she doesn't know, and who maybe don't think the way she does. That would be too much like high school all over again.*

"What should we do when we get home?" he asked.

She ran her hand up and down the shoulder strap of her seat belt. "I guess I'll wake up my folks and tell them."

"Maybe you should let them sleep and tell them in the morning."

Lisa shook her head. "No, they'd want to know. I mean, what if we found out later that…something had happened to Marie, and I didn't tell them tonight that she's missing?"

"I guess you're right. But they might know already. My mother might have phoned them after I called her." He cringed just remembering his mother's high-pitched demand that he stay at the airport until Marie arrived, or at least until every plane from Detroit had landed. He was sure Maman would be waiting up to receive Marie. He ought to have called her again and told her he was returning empty handed, but he didn't think he wanted to hear her outrage and fear while he was driving.

Lisa leaned back against the headrest and closed her eyes. As they left the interstate at the Waterville-Winslow exit, the streetlights illuminated her face. He didn't think she was sleeping. Probably thinking about Marie. Her features were so poignant, he would have guessed she was praying for her sister. Except, Lisa had implied that she rarely thought about God. Still, in a crisis people often found faith.

He hoped their two families had no reason to run desperately to God.

TWENTY-EIGHT

1900 Friday, Pearl Harbor

"Admirals don't impress me, but apparently they do my boss. He says you've got clearance and you should be in the loop, and that's the only reason I'm talking to you, Lieutenant Commander Hudson." FBI special agent David McCutcheon's impatience and disapproval survived the tenuous phone connection between California and Pearl Harbor.

George suppressed his own irritation. He didn't like working with civilians who disdained the military. Then again, he didn't like working closely with anyone. He was a loner and worked best when he was in charge, but he managed to charm the surly and placate the irate when necessary. Right now this arrogant agent McCutcheon was in charge, and George knew he'd have to step warily if he wanted any information from him.

"I'm sure we can work together. The Navy has confirmed reports that the wife of one of our officers was killed in the San Francisco airport terminal."

"Are you with NCIS?" McCutcheon asked.

"No. I'm working on another matter. Another Navy dependent is missing, a woman who was on the same plane with Jenna Tarrington from Tokyo, and I'm trying to establish whether there's a connection between these two incidents."

McCutcheon said nothing for a long moment, and George waited, tapping a soundless tattoo on his desktop and looking out the window of the tiny apartment he and Rachel were allotted in Pearl Harbor. One thing he knew how to do was wait. He was an expert at sitting, alert and silent, anticipating the action that would come.

"Well, Hudson, I'm told an NCIS team is on the way. I expect them any time. I'll be working with them on this Tarrington thing. We don't have the autopsy report yet. Right now we're interviewing airport staff and looking for women who entered the restroom around the time Ms. Tarrington went in there, and also for the woman who was her seatmate on the plane she arrived on."

"Her seatmate?" George sat up straighter.

"Yes, we'd like to talk to her and see if there was any interaction between them on the plane, and if she knows anything about what happened to Ms. Tarrington in the airport. But apparently she took a connecting flight to Detroit, and we haven't made contact yet."

"Well, sir, I may be able to help you there. I believe the woman I'm looking for was Jenna Tarrington's seatmate."

"You don't say."

"Marie Belanger."

After a moment of silence, during which George thought he heard paper rustling, McCutcheon said, "Yes. What can you tell me about her?"

"She's young and naive. Her husband's a lieutenant serving at the naval base in Yokosuka. Apparently she was slightly acquainted with Mrs. Tarrington, and their husbands' duties sometimes intersected."

"Okay. That's interesting. We have a passport photo, and we've had police officers showing it to the witnesses. No one has placed her in the restroom yet, but that doesn't mean she wasn't there." He paused. "Looks like we've got one airline agent who says she spoke to this Marie Belanger after the shooting was reported. But that's not for the media until I say it's for the media."

"I understand. Just so we're clear, sir, I don't intend to do any press conferences."

"Okay, what else can you tell me about Ms. Belanger?"

"She made telephone contact with a friend a few hours ago. She said she was in Detroit, and she was frightened. The friend advised her to go to the police there."

"Good. We'll contact them and see if she's come in."

"Yes, sir, but I'll tell you now, I've already talked to the police chief and their detective sergeant, and at that time they'd heard nothing from her."

"That's not good."

"No, it's not."

"You think Ms. Belanger's mixed up in this, though?"

"No, not directly, but I think she may have stumbled into something that's over her head."

"I have to consider her a suspect."

"Well, I believe she's in danger. She may know something. It's possible she witnessed the shooting, but she's not a killer."

"You know her personally?"

"Not well, but her husband and I are as tight as they come. He's trustworthy for certain."

"I don't trust anyone, Commander. Not in this business."

George inhaled while willing his blood pressure to stop skyrocketing.

McCutcheon asked, "Do you think this shooting has to do with military operations? The husbands' assignments, maybe?"

George gritted his teeth, not liking where the FBI agent was going. He put a light tone in his voice. "Do you?"

"To be frank, sir, I have no idea what the motive in this case could be, but I'm looking for one."

George sat back and consciously relaxed his back and shoulder muscles. "Look, I'm only interested in Jenna Tarrington's death because of her proximity to Marie Belanger. If I find Mrs. Belanger alive and well, I'll be out of your hair."

"All right, Hudson, we'll get onto the Detroit angle. If Ms. Belanger saw something, we need her testimony. But we're still processing what we've got here in San Francisco. I doubt very much your buddy's wife brought a gun in on the plane."

"Absolutely not."

"If you hear any more on her whereabouts, you keep me informed."

"I'll do that."

George hung up and stared at the notepad where he'd scribbled a dozen names and phone numbers during the evening. With great reluctance, he made one more call, to the ensign who was his right hand in the office.

As he hung up, his wife came into the room carrying a steaming mug.

"Coffee, babe?" Rachel asked.

"Yeah, thanks."

"It's decaf." She placed the mug in his hands and ruffled his hair.

"You shouldn't have told me."

Her smile did more to perk him up than the first sip of coffee did.

"Learn anything new?"

"A little. I've got confirmation that Jenna Tarrington was shot in the airport restroom. She was dead when they found her. The FBI is also looking for Marie as a witness."

"They don't think she did it?" Rachel's blue eyes flared, and her mouth quirked, sending a flash of protectiveness through George. If Rachel were the one who was missing…

"Well, the bird who's on it for the FBI is keeping an open mind."

"In other words, she's on their wanted list."

"Mmm, sort of. I didn't tell him Marie said she'd witnessed the shooting." George pulled her toward him, and she stooped to kiss him.

"Are you going to keep at this all night?" Her husky tone could be mistaken for nothing other than an invitation, and he ran his fingers through her gleaming chestnut hair.

"No, I'm done. I just talked to Ensign Fuller and told him to put the office staff on notice. I'm going to have to use up some of that accumulated leave they keep reminding me of."

"For Marie?"

"Yeah. For Pierre and Marie. He's going nuts."

"He can't afford to do that."

George nodded and took another sip of coffee. "He has people who depend on his being clearheaded. I asked Fuller to set up transportation for me."

"You're leaving first thing in the morning?"

He winced as he looked up into her eyes. "Afraid so, sweetheart."

She nodded. "I figured. I started packing for you."

He raised his mug again. "The earlier I get there the better. I told Fuller to get me a seat on the first plane out of here for San Francisco. You sure this is decaf?"

"Affirmative." He took a sip, and she removed the cup from his hand, set it on the desk, and then wriggled onto his lap. "Let it rest until morning."

"What, the coffee?"

"No, Marie."

He wrapped his arms around her. "I wish I knew she was safe tonight."

"I know. But if she tried to call again, we'd know it. That's what call-waiting is for."

"You're right." He rubbed his eyelids. "God knows where she is."

"Yes, He does. Let's pray for her."

TWENTY-NINE

Marie awoke befuddled. A motor thrummed, and her resting place vibrated. She rolled over and slammed against a wall. Cigarette smoke. Slanting waves of light interrupted the darkness.

The truck.

In a flash she recalled fleeing the mall through a side door and sprinting across the parking lot toward a highway. As she'd panted up the incline beside an on-ramp, a trailer truck had rolled to a stop beside her, the brakes whooshing out air.

From high above her a woman's voice had called, "Where you heading, honey?"

"Uh…Maine."

"Main Street?"

"No, Waterville, Maine."

After a pause, the door opened and a pudgy woman twice her age climbed down to stand beside her.

"I'll give you a boost. No backpack or anything?"

"No. Just my purse."

Before she'd quite fathomed her new circumstances, Marie was climbing into the cab of the truck between Harold and Trixie. She sat shivering and trying not to think about the men who had come to her aid in the mall. She only knew that she didn't want to be there when the other two adversaries clashed with her rescuers. She doubted one security guard would have much influence on the sinister trio that had followed her. How had they found her? Marie welcomed the distraction of her new companions.

Harold, it seemed, was trying to quit smoking after twenty years' practice. He chewed a large wad of bubble gum, which restricted his speech somewhat. Trixie declared several times that she was proud of him for quitting, but she continued to chain smoke as they drove. Marie fought nausea, wondering if Harold really believed he was doing himself any good by quitting when his seatmate was smoking for him.

After several attempts at pleasant conversation to which Marie responded vaguely between yawns, Trixie shooed her into the sleeping area at the back of the cab. The last things Marie remembered were a musty pillow and country music.

She rolled over, wondering how long she had slept. Her head ached.

A crackly voice that had to be a scanner reached her, but the words were indecipherable.

"'Bout time for some breakfast," she heard Trixie say, and Harold grunted a reply.

Before long, the truck slowed and shifted as they left the highway. Marie sat up, reaching for her purse. The little plastic case that had caused her so much trouble was still there, with her wallet and hairbrush. She assessed her disheveled state. The wig was gone, but that didn't matter. Somehow her enemies had learned of her disguise and followed her to the mall. But she would miss her carry-on bag. No change of clothes. At least she had her sweater on over her tank top and blue shirt. She groped for her sneakers in the darkness.

She poked her head out into the cab and wrinkled her nose at the smoke and sweat.

"Where are we?"

"Oh, look, hon, she's awake!" Trixie grinned at her, her plump face only inches from Marie's.

Marie tried to keep from reacting outwardly to the blast of Trixie's smoky morning breath.

Harold cranked his head around and ogled her.

"Hey, there, sweet pea! We're just coming up on Battle Creek."

Marie frowned, trying to visualize a map.

"That's in Michigan, right?"

"Sure is." Harold sounded almost jovial, in spite of his bubble gum.

"How long did I sleep?" Marie asked, stretching.

"Only four or five hours. There, Harold. There's Bernie's." Trixie turned and smiled sheepishly. "We hit bad traffic back near Ann Arbor. It was one lane for a while because of construction, but at night it hadn't ought to be so slow."

"Well, there was that wreck," Harold reminded her, flipping on his turn signal. "You sure you want to eat now? It's awful early for breakfast."

"I'm starved. But you're right about that accident. We sat in that snarl for pretty near an hour." Trixie rummaged in a pile of belongings at her feet. "Hey, where'd I put that coupon book, hon? Bernie's had that special."

Marie's brain was beginning to function, and she didn't like the conclusion she was drawing.

"Isn't Detroit on the east side of Michigan?"

"That's right." Harold eased the big rig up to a stop sign. "We're about halfway across the state now. If traffic's not bad, we'll have you in Watervliet in an hour or so. That's after we eat breakfast, of course."

"Where?"

"Watervliet. You know. The place where you're going. It's right on the way to Chicago." Trixie smiled at her with such eagerness that Marie hated to burst her balloon of expectation.

"I…" She gulped in air and said carefully and distinctly, "I'm going to Water*ville*, Maine."

Trixie's jaw dropped.

"Maine?" Harold bellowed. His mouth opened so wide, Marie was afraid his gum would plop out onto his shirt, which strained over his protruding belly. "You mean, the state of Maine? Lobsters and all that?"

"Yes."

The muscles in Trixie's cheeks began to twitch as she stared.

Oh, no. She's going to cry.

"I'm sorry. I thought…"

Trixie sniffed. "I thought you said you was going to Main Street in Watervliet. That's what I told Harold."

Marie felt lightheaded. If she didn't get some fresh air soon, she might collapse back onto Harold and Trixie's bunk and sleep through their two a.m. breakfast. At least they were stopping. The brakes sighed heavily as Harold brought the huge rig to a stop in the parking lot of an all-night restaurant. The street lights and neon sign cast shadows that made the couple look old and tired.

Harold switched off the engine and turned with a shrug.

"Oh, well. Nothing we can do about it now. You got a nap, and we got to meet someone from a place we've never been."

"I've been to Maine." Trixie lifted her chin a good two inches, as though daring Harold to contradict her.

"When?"

"Back when I was flying from Boston to Montreal, and some idiot said he had a bomb in his briefcase. They made us land at a little hick town, name of Banger."

"Bangor," Marie said gently. "Bang-gore."

"Huh. Anyhow, that airport was so small, there wasn't nothing open at night. Not even the newsstand. Nothing to eat. Well, there was a vending machine, but they only had three kinds of candy bars."

Harold shook his head and made a sympathetic clucking sound. "I recollect you told me about that."

Trixie gave a vigorous nod, setting her short, graying curls bouncing. "Yup. It was a couple of years before I met you. The worst thing was, they called it an international airport."

Marie opened her mouth to explain about the uniqueness of Bangor International Airport but thought better of it.

"Well, come on," Harold said. "We might as well go in and get some pancakes. You can drive afterward, Trix. I'll get some shut-eye, if Marie here is done snoozing." He opened the driver's door, and a blast of cool air wafted through the cab.

Marie inhaled deeply. "I think I'd better try to find a ride going east."

"Aw!" Trixie frowned, and her eyes took on a sadness that seemed genuine. "I was hoping we could talk. I spend twenty-four hours a day with this chump, and I don't get to talk to girls very often. Why don't you just stay with us to Chicago? You can find a ride east from there easy, at the truck terminal."

"Ah, that's nutty," Harold said. "She doesn't want to go that far west. Who do you think she is, Wrong Way Corrigan?"

Trixie glared at him. "All I want to do is chitchat for a little while."

"You gals can talk over breakfast. She wants to get home, and we've took her a hundred miles or more out of her way, even with the construction and the wreck."

Trixie brightened. "I'll pay for your breakfast, Marie. Do you like pancakes? They have the best strawberry pancakes here. We stop at Bernie's every time we come through Battle Creek and have breakfast, no matter what time it is."

Marie struggled with a sudden urge to giggle. "That's kind of you. Now that I think about it, I'm hungry too."

"Too bad we have to make up the time we lost." Trixie shook her head. "We're not far from the Kellogg's factory. They give tours, you know."

"Not anymore," Harold said. "It's that Cereal City thing now. It's for kids."

Marie smiled, amazed that he hadn't categorized her as a "kid." "I really need to get going, anyway."

He nodded and held the door to the building open for her and Trixie. "Maybe we'll see someone we know heading east."

"Sure!" Trixie was all smiles again. "We can help you find a ride. Just don't get into a cab with Jud Vanderhof."

"Jud…" Marie followed Trixie to a booth at the side of the restaurant. She was surprised that half the tables were filled at this hour.

"She's right," Harold said, squeezing in on the other side. His belly creased around the edge of the table. "Jud's a bad'un. Preys on kids that hitchhike."

Marie nodded. "Got it."

A man wearing a stained, grayish apron plodded toward them. "You need a menu?"

Trixie shook her head. "Strawberry pancakes all around. Right, Marie?"

Marie nodded. "Thanks."

"And coffee," said Harold.

"Um…do you have any hot chocolate?" Marie looked up into the waiter's weary face.

Trixie chortled. "She's just a baby, hon. Hasn't graduated to coffee yet. Bring her some cocoa."

"I'll see if we got any." The man shook his head and turned back toward the counter.

Marie sank down on the booth bench, tempted to rest her head on her hands, but she knew that if she did, she'd be asleep in seconds. She tried to count the hours since she'd had a real meal, but between her fatigue and the time changes, she lost track. The waiter passed them, carrying a huge platter of eggs, fried potatoes, and bacon to another table. A sharp twinge squeezed Marie's stomach. In her mind, she formed a plea. *Lord, help me to stay awake long enough for those pancakes.*

THIRTY

1700 Saturday, Yokosuka

"I can do this, Captain." Pierre met his commanding officer's cool gaze. "Really. I've planned everything, and I know we can complete the operation tomorrow night."

Wheeler shook his head. "It's too risky. For one thing, I'm not sure you're fit to go into hostile territory without knowing the status of your wife."

Pierre inhaled sharply and looked away.

"You still haven't heard from her?" Wheeler's voice dropped into an almost fatherly tone.

"No, sir."

"I'm sorry."

"She called my friend's wife this morning, but she hasn't called me or anyone in my family or hers since. I've been trying all day not to think it, but something's got to be wrong." He gripped the visor of his hat with both hands to keep from fidgeting. *God, keep her safe,* he prayed silently.

"You're certain she hasn't contacted anyone else in the States?"

"My brother's called several times. She never made it home, sir." Pierre raked a hand through his hair. "I just don't know what to do."

Captain Wheeler nodded. "I've been relying on you since we lost Commander Tarrington from this project."

"I know, and I'm sorry. I've tried to give it my full attention, but…" Pierre shook his head. "Look, I'll be there for the men who are taking this jaunt. I have to be."

"No. I'm more convinced than ever that you shouldn't go."

"But, sir—"

"We've had too many setbacks this time. It's just too iffy. I'm going to scrub this op."

"But they're so close to reaching an agreement with the chieftains in the southern provinces. We can—"

Wheeler held up one hand, and Pierre stopped talking.

"I've made my decision, Belanger. It's too risky right now. I'm not just talking about your mental state. We don't know how much of our data has been compromised."

Pierre noted the troubled look in Wheeler's eyes. "Yes, sir."

The captain sighed and tipped his chair back. "The FBI is investigating the murder of Jenna Tarrington, and our NCIS team is working with them."

"It was definitely murder, then?"

"Afraid so. She was shot in the San Francisco airport. How anyone got a gun into the secure area, I don't know." Wheeler eyed him cautiously and set his chair down solidly on the floor. "Your friend, Lieutenant Commander Hudson…"

"Yes, sir?"

"I received word from the admiral that Hudson is cleared to look into this matter on your behalf."

Pierre's spirits rose. "He'll help investigate Mrs. Tarrington's death?"

"No. Hudson's not qualified for that, but he'll have access to the NCIS team's data and have liberty to search for your wife if need be. We were hoping you'd have heard from her by now. But the way things are, I think you might be more effective stateside than here."

"Sir?" Pierre could hardly believe what he was hearing. "You think…I should go look for Marie myself?"

"It would be unofficial. You could meet up with Hudson. I can get you stateside immediately, Belanger. You can start your thirty days of leave now."

Pierre tried to breathe evenly, but it was difficult. The captain was sending him home. That meant the brass in Yokosuka were worried about Marie. They didn't want her to meet Jenna's fate. But did they also think Marie was embroiled in the same trouble Jenna had been part of?

"Is NCIS looking for Marie now?" He watched Wheeler's face. If the captain couldn't look him in the eye, it might mean they considered Marie a suspect in some crime. But if they thought Marie had something to do with Jenna's death or something else—smuggling, say, or espionage—would they let him go look for her? Maybe, Pierre decided. If they thought he would lead them to her.

Wheeler shuffled the papers on his desk. "They're working with the FBI on Mrs. Tarrington's murder, and they've put out bulletins saying they'd like to speak to the woman who sat beside her on the flight from Tokyo to San Francisco. I believe that's all they've done so far to look for your wife." He looked up and gave Pierre a bleak smile. "I'm hoping Lieutenant Commander Hudson can do more for you. I'd like to see that part of this case resolved quickly, as I'm sure you would."

"Yes, sir."

The captain gazed into his eyes, easing Pierre's anxiety. "I've got my aide looking into possible transport for you, either civilian or Navy. I suggest you go home and rest this evening. Pack your seabag. I'll call you as soon as I know your schedule. If we can't get you out of here tonight, just relax. And if you hear anything from your wife, let me know. If Hudson, the FBI, and NCIS can't locate her right away, we'll send you over there. And if the press gets hold of it, you might need to make a statement about your wife's disappearance."

Pierre flinched. It was official—his wife was a missing person, not just a delayed traveler. He nodded, hating the classification.

Wheeler opened a file and squinted at the document inside. "The FBI is in charge of the case, but if a whiff of Operation Lion Gate leaks out, the CIA will probably take over. The admiral is preparing a statement for you, in case you need it. You mustn't say anything you're not authorized to say. And keep quiet about your duties here in Yokosuka."

"Of course."

"It would be best not to admit that your wife knew Mrs. Tarrington, or that you worked with her husband. Let's keep that connection low profile. If this turns into an espionage scandal, you want to be as far from it as possible. The two women were Navy dependents flying home on the same plane. That's all."

"You said Marie sat beside Mrs. Tarrington on the plane. George Hudson mentioned that possibility to me the last time I spoke to him. Is that definite?"

"The airline is sure Mrs. Belanger was Mrs. Tarrington's seatmate. But then your wife flew to Detroit and somehow left the Detroit terminal without connecting for her flight to Maine. We don't know if she knew Mrs. Tarrington was dead when she boarded the plane for Detroit."

Pierre nodded. "That's more than I knew. All I have to go on is that one phone call she made from somewhere near Detroit. I keep thinking I'll hear from Marie or the Detroit police, saying she's safe. But so far...nothing."

The captain's mouth squeezed into a grimace. "It's a tough situation. Do you pray, Belanger?"

"Yes, sir."

"Good."

Pierre was satisfied that the captain was being as frank and open with him as he could under the circumstances. "Sir, do you think this business is enough to compromise the entire China project?"

Wheeler clenched his teeth and shook his head slightly. "I hope not. But we need to find out who killed Jenna Tarrington and why. If we learn that her husband was somehow involved, it could mean the whole operation's been betrayed."

Pierre wondered if he should voice their unspoken thoughts. At last he said, "It sounds as though you think Commander Tarrington has gone rogue. That he's maybe turned classified information over to the Red Chinese."

Wheeler sighed and tipped the chair back again, leaning against the wall. "I don't know anything, Belanger. It's all speculation until we either find your wife or…"

"Or what, sir?"

"Or Tarrington starts talking."

Pierre called George as soon as he was outside the building that housed the captain's office.

"I can't believe they're letting me come work with you, George. We can conduct our own investigation."

"Whoa, *mon ami*. We'll have to work with the official investigators on this. It's the only way. We'll lose our authorization otherwise, and that wouldn't help Marie. I'm flying out of here as early as I can in the morning. Are you coming through Pearl Harbor?"

"I don't know yet."

"Hmm." George cleared his throat. "Well, I guess we'd better just plan to meet up in San Francisco tomorrow. If you're delayed, at least I can touch base with the FBI and the NCIS there. You can meet me as soon as you're able."

"All right." Pierre walked quickly toward the apartment building. "I'm going to start packing. And I've got to make a few phone calls before I leave. Marie will be mad if I don't get the list of chores she left me checked off." It struck him suddenly how stupid that sounded, considering that her life was in danger. "I mean… Oh, man, I'm so confused."

"It's all right. I understand."

"Does Rachel? Is she okay with you doing this?"

"Hold on a second."

Pierre climbed the stairs to the second-floor apartment. As he pulled out his key ring, Rachel's voice came over the airwaves.

"Pierre, this will turn out all right. You and George will find her. And I'll stay here in Hawaii and pray until you call and tell me Marie is safe."

"Thanks. That means a lot to me."

"You know how much we love you," Rachel said. "God loves you even more. Keep trusting Him."

"I will. Thanks. And Rachel, you said Marie told you a woman shot Jenna."

"That's right. She said Jenna went into a restroom, and another woman went in and shot her."

"And Marie was there."

"She said she saw it."

"Anything else?"

"Not that I can think of. Except that she seems to have contraband the killers want."

"George told me." He scratched his chin. "I guess there's nothing more we can do until we get stateside. *Au revoir, mon amie.*"

Pierre let himself into the apartment. He always parked his keys on the nightstand overnight, but now the nightstand was gone, and he checked his movement toward the empty spot beside the bed. He stooped and placed them carefully on the floor.

The bed. Did the new tenants want it? He decided to stop fretting about it and just leave what was left of the furnishings. Only Marie mattered now.

He opened the closet and pulled out his bag. As he stuffed his clothing into it, he began to pray silently. Marie and the China project. That was enough to occupy his prayers all night long.

Was the China mission really behind Jenna's murder and Marie's disappearance? He'd worried about the safety of the men involved, but not about their families. Had the communist Chinese learned of the plan to help subversive groups splinter the People's Republic? If so, they would stop at nothing to counter the coup.

The United States government had covertly planned for years to launch a movement undermining the central government of the huge communist nation. In the two years he'd been involved, Pierre had learned the basics of the plan, though he wasn't directly active in the negotiations and strategizing. The undercover agents and Chinese contacts would encourage the rural people to rise up against the communists. So far the plan looked promising. Merchants in the cities backed it, as they craved economic freedom. Peasants approved of the plan that would allow them to own their own land and enjoy the liberty their grandparents knew.

The American government had taken its time, making sure the subversives would succeed before committing to help them. Commander Tarrington coordinated the liaison team that dealt with the rebel Chinese contingent. He was one of a handful of men who had access to the specific plans promoting the downfall of the People's Republic of China.

And now his wife had been murdered. Pierre could read between the lines. Navy authorities suspected Tarrington was using Jenna to pass critical information about the plot to communist contacts in the United States. If the details fell into the communists' hands, the subversives would be crushed and an international incident could follow. Especially if the Chinese Communist Party had evidence the U.S. was backing the subversives.

Pierre inhaled carefully as he packed his dress uniform. He didn't want to think about the possibilities, but they darted into his mind, anyway. Nuclear war. Sending in ground troops would be ridiculous against China's billions.

He sat on the edge of the bed and took out his wallet. Marie had shipped all their photo albums home weeks ago, and all he had was the one picture.

"Oh, *chérie!* Where are you?"

He stared at her sweet, lovely face.

"Lord, You've got to help us. Please keep her safe. Help me and

George to find her. No, Lord. Belay that. Please, make it so we don't have to look for her. Let me hear from her soon."

He took out his cell phone and checked it to make sure it was on.

THIRTY-ONE

When Harold and Trixie left the truck stop at three thirty a.m., Marie hovered in the booth, nursing a nearly cold cup of cocoa. Trixie had assured her that any of the eastbound truckers with room in their cabs would be happy to accommodate her, but Marie lingered, uneasy in her new role.

Hitchhiking was taboo in her family. Her mother had made it clear that her three daughters must never consider such a rash act. Only runaways and serial killers stood by the highway with thumb extended.

Of course, this was a little different. She sat in the booth and studied each of the early morning patrons. Men. All men. Apparently the gender gap was still huge in the trucking industry. She wondered how long she could sit here waiting for a female driver to come in. She'd probably have to buy something else, at the very least.

After mentally rejecting a dozen or more potential chauffeurs, she slipped into the ladies' room, or gals' room, as the sign indicated, opposite the door for guys. The lights were dim, and the quiet swept over her. If no women came to the restaurant during the night, no one would enter this room. She chose the corner stall and locked the door. She peeled off her sweater, removed the long-sleeved blue shirt, and put the sweater back on. She spread her blue shirt on the floor and sat on it, refusing to think about germs and bugs. Wedging her purse into the corner between the walls and the toilet, she drew up her legs.

She rested her head on her knees and she wondered if she could sleep this way. Her stomach was full, and her body screamed for rest. Exhaustion claimed her, but not before she noted with satisfaction that, thanks to Trixie and Harold, she seemed to have eluded her pursuers.

A sharp rapping jerked Marie from sleep. The dream in which she'd snuggled toasty and safe against Pierre's back shattered.

"Excuse me. Honey, are you okay?"

Marie blinked and stretched her cramped arms. She'd apparently fallen asleep and let her right foot extend beneath the stall door while she was in oblivion. That would be enough to scare any woman entering a restroom.

"Uh, yeah." She scrambled to her knees and pushed herself upward.

"Okay," the nasal voice replied. "Just checking."

Another stall door clicked, and she took stock. A glance at her watch told her it was five thirty a.m. She'd slept at least an hour, maybe two, but she still felt sluggish. Her arm tingled where she'd leaned on it too long, and her head ached.

She picked up her purse and shirt and then opened the door. As she walked over to the double sink, the image in the mirror almost sent her back to her hideout. Huge brown eyes stared at her. Beneath them were dark smudges that could be mistaken for bruises. Her hair was flattened from the time it was crammed beneath the wig, and her complexion had a wan, unhealthy cast.

She found her brush and vigorously attacked her hair. If only she could get a shower. After debating whether or not to put the shirt on again, she folded it up as small as she could and was pleased to find she could cram it into her purse and still close the bag.

Behind her, the door of the occupied stall swung open. A blond woman wearing a short-skirted uniform approached the other sink, glancing over at Marie.

"Did you sleep in here?"

Marie winced. "Sorry about that. I need to catch a ride, but I was really tired, and none of the customers seemed like the right person to approach."

The woman nodded and turned on the faucet. "I'm Cathy. I work here for the breakfast shift, which is getting into full swing."

"Do you get any women drivers in here?"

"A few. Just take a booth and keep a cup of coffee in front of you."

"It's so hard..." Marie looked directly at Cathy, trying to size her up, but concluded that she didn't have the instincts to know whom she could trust. "It's hard to tell if somebody's decent, you know?"

Cathy grabbed a paper towel and wiped her hands. "I hear you. Maybe I can point out someone to you. Just don't sit at the counter or near the windows. Those spots are popular, and if Bernie thinks you're hanging around too long, he'll peg you for a hooker and toss you out."

Marie's throat went dry. She stared at herself in the mirror. Did she look like...one of those? She didn't think so. Her wedding and engagement rings screamed otherwise. Her jeans and sweater missed the provocative mark by a wide margin. But from what Cathy said, Bernie wasn't very discerning. She swallowed hard and reached for her purse.

"Thanks."

Cathy served Marie her breakfast in the dining room and filled an ironstone cup with coffee.

"You don't have to drink it. Just pick it up once in a while and sip."

Marie reached beyond her fatigue and smiled. "Got it."

She ate the scrambled eggs and hashbrowns slowly, though her stomach rumbled for her to fill it. Surprised that she could be ravenous again just a few hours after the pancake platter, she made herself pause between bites. Cathy and another woman worked the room, carrying steaming plates to the eager drivers and swinging coffeepots about as though they were permanent appendages.

Half an hour later, Cathy stopped by her table and dribbled a bit more coffee into Marie's mug, though it was still three-quarters full.

"I haven't found the right ride for you yet, but be patient."

"Thanks. I appreciate it."

Cathy picked up her empty plate. "Did you get enough to eat?"

"Plenty, thanks. If I pay now, can you bring me some quarters? I really need to call someone."

"Yeah, sure." Cathy pulled out her sales pad and flipped through it until she located Marie's bill and tore it off.

Marie unzipped her purse and extracted a twenty-dollar bill. She thought about using her credit card but rejected the idea. She'd save that resource until she needed something large. Like a bus ticket, maybe. When she got to Toledo, she'd see what bus fares were to Maine. That would be better than hitchhiking more than a thousand miles.

As soon as Cathy brought her change, she counted out a generous tip in spite of her instinct to hoard her cash. The pay phone mounted on the wall between the restroom doors at the back of the eating area drew her.

She hesitated only a moment. She wouldn't try to call Japan. It would cost a fortune, and she couldn't call collect. She punched in her parents' number, suddenly desperate to hear her mother's voice.

It rang three times, and her stomach knotted. Would she miss them again? Where were they? Dad would be at work, but surely her mother would be at home.

"Hello?"

"Mom!" Marie's legs went wobbly. She closed her eyes and leaned against the wall.

"Marie! Honey, where are you? Are you okay?"

"Yes, yes, I'm fine. I'm just...sort of stuck in Michigan."

"Michigan? Still? We heard you were there last night. Pierre called and said you'd talked to a friend of his."

"Yes. Listen, Mom, I'm trying to get—"

Someone tapped Marie's arm, and she swung around.

"I've found the perfect ride for you," Cathy whispered, her eyes widening with her smile. "But you have to hurry. He's paying his check now."

"Thanks." Marie's mother rambled on, and Marie turned her attention back to the phone conversation.

"What happened? Why did you miss your plane? Nobody tells me anything. Did somebody try to hurt you?"

Marie's heart wrenched. "No, I'm okay. Really."

"Can you just stay where you are, and Daddy will drive out and get you?"

"No, Mom, it's too far." She winced, trying to hold back prickly tears. Wouldn't it be wonderful to just stay here and wait for her father to walk through the door of Bernie's? But she couldn't do that. It would take her father a day or two to get here. And besides, if the men chasing her had escaped and were still trying to track her down, they would probably realize she'd hitched a ride. Truck stops would be the first places they'd look.

"Can you take the next plane home?"

"Mom, listen. Call Pierre and tell him I'm all right and I'm heading home. Please?"

"Well, sure, but—"

"I've got to go. Don't worry about me, okay?"

"Of course I'll worry about you."

Marie glanced toward the checkout. Cathy was slowly counting change into the hand of a gray-haired man with large, dark-rimmed glasses. When Marie caught her eye, Cathy wiggled her eyebrows and nodded toward the paying customer.

"Goodbye, Mom. I need to leave. I love you."

Before her mother could protest further, she hung up and scurried toward the cash register.

THIRY-TWO

The post office closed at noon on Saturdays. Janet didn't work weekends, which made André's shift much more peaceful. He and the other clerk, Nancy, served the customers who came in. Traffic was always light in the post office on Saturdays.

André watched the clock hands inch toward quitting time. He used every spare second to tidy his workspace and take care of his end-of-shift duties. Nancy agreed to lock up. When noon came, he was ready to walk out the door.

Leaning against his green pickup in the back parking lot was Lisa Gillette, clad in jeans, a black turtleneck, and a green fleece pullover. André checked his step, expecting a surge of annoyance. Instead, his pulse accelerated slightly, and he felt something he couldn't name, but it wasn't bad. She smiled, and he realized that he no longer associated annoyance with Lisa. What he felt was anticipation.

He strode toward her, determined not to stress over this revelation. He would worry about it later and try to pinpoint the moment he started liking her. All morning he'd fretted about Marie and racked his brain for ways to trace her, but when he saw Lisa waiting for him, he actually felt upbeat.

"Hey." Her smile twitched with apology. "I didn't want to bother you at work again, but there's news. Sort of."

"You heard something this morning?"

"Yes. Marie called my mother about eight o'clock, but she didn't say much. Dad was at the store, and I had left early for a job up in Pittsfield."

"Well, what did Marie say? Where is she?"

"Still in Michigan."

"That's a relief. Sort of." Lisa's expression was anything but carefree. The corners of her mouth crinkled, and her eyes were narrow, not the wide, hopeful orbs she'd shown him last night. "Are they putting her on a plane today?"

"We don't know. All she said was that she was all right, to call Pierre and tell him, and that she was heading home. My mother's a basket case."

"Well, maybe we should call the airline. They might be able to tell us if she's booked another ticket."

Lisa's grim expression moderated just a little. "I tried that. If she did, it's not on the airline she was with originally."

"Okay. What now? Call other airlines that fly through Detroit?"

She bit her upper lip. "I don't know. Mom said Marie was in a big hurry and had to run. Maybe her plane was boarding. But why didn't she give us a flight number? André, I'm scared."

"Hey, come on. She's probably fine. I'll bet she left the airport to get a room for the night after she missed her flight."

"Hotel rooms have phones. She would have called us or Pierre last night and explained if she could have."

André tried to keep his expression from betraying his own fear. Lisa was right. If nothing was wrong, Marie would be home safe. She would at least have let them know she'd found refuge. This had to be more than a missed flight.

Lisa reached toward him, her hand hovering in the air. "We've got to do something."

He nodded. "I was thinking of going to the airport again. It probably won't do any good, but…"

"Let's. If she caught a plane this morning, she could be sitting in Bangor right now." The furrow between Lisa's eyebrows smoothed out. André was glad he'd made the suggestion, if only because it eased Lisa's anxiety a little. Action always helped in stressful times. Driving the hour to Bangor again might not do anything for Marie, but it would make Lisa feel better. Himself too, for that matter. They would know they had tried.

As he unlocked the truck, he noticed her fire engine red pickup parked beyond his. GILLETTE ELECTRIC. The letters were a foot high and ran the length of the truck's body. Lisa's phone number was beneath the words.

"Do you mind taking my truck?" he asked.

"Not if you don't." She pulled a cell phone from her jacket pocket and checked the screen. "I keep it on all the time. She knows my number."

He opened the door and looked down into her toffee-colored eyes. Something in their depths—a bleak desperation bolstered by her pleading gaze—stayed his movement.

Gently he brushed a lock of hair back from her cheek and tucked it behind her ear. She took a quick breath, and her eyes never left his. He let his fingertips glide across her warm, smooth cheek to her chin.

"We'll find her."

She nodded, still staring up at him. As he watched, liquid pooled in her eyes, swirling about the toffee irises, and she pressed her lips together.

"Aw, Lisa, don't cry on me!" He pulled her into his arms, and they stood in the parking lot, holding each other close. He stroked the soft contours of her pullover, across her shoulders and down her back. She clung to him but didn't sob. Her warmth transferred through the sweater, and only then did he realize how chilly the air was on this cloudy day. Snuggling against her and resting his chin on her hair felt right, and he hoped she thought so too.

They didn't speak, but André didn't feel a need to fill the silence. After a little time she stirred.

"Thanks." Her voice was hoarse, and she pushed away from him a bit, batting at a stray tear with her sleeve.

"You okay?"

She didn't quite meet his gaze. "Yeah."

"Marie's a smart girl. She'll come out of this okay." He wanted to say more, to promise her things he couldn't guarantee. He wanted to ease her burden of fear and worry and fill her heart with joy. But he couldn't.

Lisa edged toward the open truck door.

"Let's go."

THIRTY-THREE

Marie hated to leave the grandfatherly driver who had adopted her at Bernie's truck stop. Buzz had driven her back along Interstate 94, all the way to Ann Arbor, chatting as they rode about his kids and their kids and how much he missed his late wife, Emma. Marie liked him. He reminded her a little of Grandpa LaChance.

But now Buzz had pulled over for fuel and lunch, and she knew she'd have to leave him.

"Too bad." He shook his shaggy white head mournfully and took a huge bite of his BLT.

Marie ate the sandwich he'd insisted on buying her.

"Of course, if you wanted to go back to Detroit, you could keep riding with me. But you said you want to go east, so that would probably just hold you up. You need to get a ride south, down Route 75 toward Toledo. From there you shouldn't have any trouble finding somebody going east."

Marie nodded and swallowed the bite she'd been chewing. "Thanks. I'll do that."

He sighed. "I hate to see you go. It's a rough world out there, you know."

She smiled at that. If he only knew. But she simply said, "Yes, it is."

Five minutes later, both had finished eating. "You want pie?"

"No, thanks. I'm full. But you go ahead."

"No. The doc says I sit too much and I need to quit packing away the sweets."

She gave him a sympathetic nod. She would miss him.

"Well, missy…" He polished off his coffee and stood up. "You take care now, you hear?"

"I sure will."

He walked out of the café, and Marie pulled in a shaky breath, watching through the smudgy window as he headed for his rig without looking back. He fired up the engine and pulled out onto the highway again.

She crumpled her paper napkin and looked around at the others in the room. The only women were a waitress and a girl who looked like a teenager. The girl's face was coated with foundation and blush, and when she finished eating she reapplied a shocking red lipstick. Then she hung on the arm of the man who occupied the stool beside hers and giggled. He looked a couple of decades older than her, but it was hard to tell since the girl's age was questionable. Under all that eyeliner and shadow, she might be thirty-five, but Marie doubted it. That girl needed a lesson from Caprice on how to apply makeup correctly.

A man stopped at Marie's table, and she glanced up in surprise.

"Hey. Anyone sitting there?" He nodded at the bench on the opposite side of the booth.

"Uh…no."

As he sat down, she reached for her purse. He seemed friendly, but he also seemed inordinately interested in her.

"Where you going, babe?" he asked with a crooked smile.

"I…um…" She looked down at her leather purse. He was good-looking in a rough way. He needed his hair trimmed, and a day's stubble darkened his chin, but his handsome face and lean figure would draw attention no matter where he went. The fact that his biceps bulged under the thin knit shirt made her feel even less at ease. Unlike Buzz, this man must work out between runs with his rig. Marie had a feeling he liked distracting the women he met.

"I'm just traveling." She slid to the edge of her bench.

"By yourself?"

She ignored his question and stood.

"Do you need a ride?" he called after her.

Marie headed for the door, certain that every eye in the café watched her. She felt a blush diffusing over her cheeks. How could she approach anyone and ask for a ride? She'd heard that most truckers would help hitchhikers without harming them, but she found it impossible to trust them. How could she be sure?

That fellow looked nice enough. In fact, he looked so good she was embarrassed that she'd noticed. And he'd tried to hit on her. She wasn't used to that. Pierre had been her watchdog since high school. Even when he was overseas with the Navy, the young men in her neighborhood had known better than to try to make time with her. Pierre's class ring, hanging from a gold chain around her neck, and his protective brothers had kept the guys away.

And now here she was, on her own, frightened, tired, and in dire need of a bath, and a handsome, muscular man had tried to flirt with her.

She inhaled the cool air deeply and scouted the rows of trailer trucks in the parking lot. If only she could find a married couple driving together. Or two women. Cathy, the waitress who had been kind to her that morning at Bernie's, had told her she knew a pair of middle-aged women who drove a rig together.

That's what I need, not some—

"Excuse me, miss."

She turned around. A large, sandy-haired man was walking toward her from the door of the café.

"Can I help you?" She tried to put a cool authority into her voice.

He stopped and looked down at the ground, fidgeting and avoiding her direct gaze.

"I just couldn't help notice…well, that fella, Max, he's a bad 'un."

"Oh?"

"Yup. You don't want to ride with him none."

She nodded. "Thanks. I won't."

"Well, if you need a ride…"

She bit her upper lip and looked him over. He gave an impression of excruciating shyness.

"Are you driving?" she asked.

"Uh-huh."

"Where are you headed?"

"Where you going?"

"I asked you first."

He grimaced. "Sorry. I'm going to Ohio."

"South."

"Yes, ma'am."

"I'd like to get down to Toledo and catch a ride east on Route 80."

He nodded, frowning as though puzzling it out. "Sure. You can do that."

"Are you heading that way?"

"Uh-huh." He jerked his head toward the row of tractor trailers. "That's my rig yonder, the third one."

She studied it. The trailer was hitched to a tractor that wasn't as new and shiny as some. Marie didn't know anything about trucks, but the brown cab looked a bit frumpy and out of date.

"Would you take me?"

The man's face lit up. "Sure would. I've got to pay for my meal, but if you want to wait out here, I'll be right along."

She waited, feeling the sun warm her shoulders. At last the clouds had moved out, and the afternoon sparkled, bright and promising. The terror of the past thirty-six hours was behind her. She was heading home.

The man hurried from the café, and he smiled when he saw her standing beside his tractor. He unlocked the door, and then he put his hand on her elbow to boost her up into the cab.

When he'd clambered in on his side, he switched on the engine and nodded to the dashboard. "Like music?"

"Oh, you've got a CD player."

"Uh-huh. I like just about any kind of music. I've got jazz, country western, and classical, plus a little light rock. No rap, though. I hate rap."

She chuckled. "Whatever you want is fine."

He shot her a glance and then focused on the road as he eased the big truck out onto the highway. "What's your name?"

"Marie."

"Pleased to have you along, Marie."

"Thank you." She sat back, almost able to forget that a few hours ago she'd witnessed a murder, and then been held at gunpoint by a man she was pretty sure intended to kill her. "What's yours?"

He smiled slightly and put on his turn signal to pass a slow-moving van.

"Some folks call me Jud."

THIRTY-FOUR

1200 Saturday, San Francisco

George Hudson strode into the conference room allotted to the FBI team at the San Francisco International Airport. Three men and a woman sifted through photographs and documents scattered on a table. A man in a charcoal gray suit and geometric-patterned green tie advanced to meet him. His bland features were enhanced by a full brown mustache.

"Agent McCutcheon?" George asked.

"Yes. Special Agent Heinz?"

George suppressed a smile. "No. I'm Lieutenant Commander Hudson. We spoke last night."

"Oh. You're the one from Pearl Harbor." McCutcheon eyed his uniform insignia and shrugged. "You made good time."

"I take it I beat the NCIS team?"

McCutcheon winced. "They've had some mechanical problems and had to change planes. Should be here anytime, though." He turned to the others and called, "Agent Calloway, would you please get Lieutenant Commander Hudson some coffee? He just flew in from Hawaii, and I'm sure he'd appreciate some caffeine."

The female FBI agent raised her chin and looked around at them. She was pretty in spite of her severely masculine outfit. Early thirties, George judged, single and not happy about it. From the glint in her eyes, he anticipated a tart comeback for McCutcheon—something along the line of women not being domestic slaves any longer. But when her gaze lit on George, she checked and lowered her lashes, and a becoming flush colored her cheeks.

"Certainly. Cream and sugar, Lieutenant?"

George couldn't help smiling then. Civilians always had trouble getting a handle on his rank. "No, just black."

"You might as well see the photos of the crime scene," McCutcheon said, leading him to the table. "Mrs. Tarrington was shot twice in the chest. We assume the shooter used a silencer since no one reported hearing gunshots."

"Technically, that's not true, sir," one of the other men said.

McCutcheon waved his objection aside. "When the word was out, a few people said they thought they'd heard popping noises in the vicinity of the restroom. But I expected that. The power of suggestion."

George examined the stark photographs and felt a little queasy. He'd seen casualties before, but not many female gunshot victims. It brought back memories. *Rachel hefting a rocket launcher on Frasier Island.* He was glad he'd never made Jenna Tarrington's acquaintance.

"Here you go, Lieutenant." The female agent had returned with a Styrofoam cup of black coffee. George thought she'd renewed her lipstick.

He laid down the folder of photographs and reached for the cup, giving her a smile that he hoped was friendly but not provocative. "Thank you, Agent Calloway. It's lieutenant commander. You can say Commander Hudson or...well, why don't you just call me Hudson?" He'd almost said *Call me George* but decided that might be construed as being a come-on, and he had no desire to have to explain his happily married status.

She nodded, her lips slightly pursed and her speculative gaze darting to his hands and back to his face. *Checking out my wedding ring?*

"Is a lieutenant commander higher than a captain?"

He laughed. "No, but sometimes I wish it were."

McCutcheon laid out the evidence he had accumulated. George scanned the printouts of witness statements given by airport security personnel and travelers.

"Of course, the person I'd really like to talk to is the husband." McCutcheon frowned and rested his chin on his fist. "Commander Christopher Tarrington. I'd give my eyeteeth to know if he's mixed up in this."

"You haven't interviewed him yet?" George asked.

"No. They said they're bringing him in from Tokyo, but they won't tell me if he's here yet, or where they're holding him."

Agent Calloway said, "I understood the NCIS team was going to question him first."

"That makes sense." George shrugged at McCutcheon's unhappy expression. "They need to determine whether his testimony will compromise any classified data. If not, I'm sure they'll let you talk to him."

"I still don't like it. And what about the other husband?"

George arched his eyebrows.

"Belanger," said the FBI agent. "The one whose wife is missing."

"What about him?"

"You're here on his behalf."

"Yes. He's eager to cooperate with the investigation."

"When was the last time he had contact with his wife?"

"She called him on her cell phone after she was on the plane at Narita. He expected her to call again after she got to San Francisco, but he did not hear from her."

"I'm not surprised."

"You're not?"

McCutcheon shook his head. "The cell phone registered to Mrs. Belanger was found on Jenna Tarrington's body."

"Well, what do you know."

"Maybe Mrs. Tarrington borrowed it." McCutcheon's eyebrows shot up as he awaited George's response.

"Or lifted it from Marie's purse."

McCutcheon grunted. "The last call on it was made between the time they went through customs and the time the body was discovered."

"To whom?"

"Now, that's very interesting." George waited, and after a moment McCutcheon sat back and smiled. "Whoever used the phone placed a call to the office of Chen Trading."

"Chen Trading?"

"It's an import business owned by a second-generation Chinese immigrant."

"I don't believe Marie Belanger made that call. If they're in on whatever deal Mrs. Tarrington was trying to cut, she may very well have lifted Marie's cell phone as a way to contact them from the airport, hoping it couldn't be traced back to her."

"And told them what?"

"Assuming you're right that her husband was using her to pass classified material, maybe she told them that the deal was off. But she wasn't counting on their people following her into the airport."

McCutcheon shrugged. "We don't know, do we? But however it happened, I'd like to talk to either of the Belangers."

George cleared his throat. "As a matter of fact, Lieutenant Belanger phoned me late last night. He's due for leave, anyway. His commanding officer approved transportation for him on a commercial flight out of Tokyo."

"So what time will he be here?" McCutcheon scowled at his watch.

"Not until morning. They're refueling in Honolulu. I'll meet him when his plane lands here at the international terminal."

McCutcheon sighed. "In that case, why don't you get something to eat, Hudson? Did you have lunch?"

"No, I didn't. My stomach doesn't know what time it is. I think it wants breakfast."

Agent Calloway laughed. "I can get some bagels or breakfast sandwiches."

"That suits me fine." George took out his wallet and handed her a twenty-dollar bill. "Thank you. I'd just as soon stick with you people and observe, if you don't mind."

McCutcheon shrugged. "Fine. I'm heading over to Terminal C soon. I talked to the agent who checked Marie Belanger onto her Detroit plane yesterday, but I want to speak to her again. And we've located the woman Mrs. Belanger sat next to on that flight. She's quite a character. Says she just met Marie Belanger yesterday and talked to her for three or four hours, and she swears up and down that the woman you're looking for is innocent."

George smiled. "Marie has that effect on people. You can't know her and not trust her. If you meet her, you'll see what I mean."

McCutcheon's lips compressed in a firm line. "Like I told you, Hudson, I don't trust anyone."

One of the younger FBI agents entered the room and said to McCutcheon, "Hey, boss, we may have something. A TSA agent reported a stolen uniform."

"When?"

"She reported it this morning, but she hadn't worked for two days. Her locker was broken into."

McCutcheon frowned. "She?"

"Yeah." Agent Packard consulted his notebook. "Marcella Reed."

George cleared his throat. "Best check into that right away."

"You know something?"

"Nothing definite." McCutcheon glared at him, and George shrugged. "When Marie Belanger made her phone call from Detroit, she said something that led her friend to believe she'd seen the shooting. I told you that was a possibility."

"Did she say it was done by a TSA agent?"

"No, but it would be the perfect disguise. No one would think twice about a woman in a security uniform entering the ladies' room."

McCutcheon stroked his mustache. "We'd already figured it might be a woman. No one has reported seeing a man go in there."

"You have videotapes," George said.

"Not inside the restroom, but there's one a few yards from the door."

"Check them for a uniformed guard."

McCutcheon nodded. "You bet. Good job, Packard."

THIRTY-FIVE

Marie couldn't relax. Every time she tried, her leg muscles tensed as though ready to leap from the truck cab. She sat forward, trying not to look over at the driver every few seconds. Jud maintained his humble, almost nervous manner. Could he possibly be the man Harold and Trixie had warned her about?

He didn't talk much after Marie had chosen a jazz CD. Once he caught her looking at him and flashed her a sweet smile and then turned back toward the road ahead. He seemed awed by her presence. If the dark warning weren't tumbling in her mind, Marie would have thought he had an innocent crush on her.

"Too bad you don't have a backpack," he said. "Most people take one when they go hitching."

"Oh, I…" She let the sentence go. Should she tell him she'd lost her luggage? Not likely. That would make her more vulnerable. And she wasn't going to lie to explain away her situation. So she kept quiet.

She stared out the side window at the rolling farmland.

I haven't lost much, she told herself. *A few clothes, some makeup. My Bible.*

Her Bible.

She missed it. Had Pierre read the chapter they'd agreed on this morning? Other than her phone, she most regretted losing her Bible.

That realization led her thoughts to the spiritual aspects of her trouble. She hadn't prayed about finding rides today. This morning at

Bernie's, she'd been relieved to let Cathy arrange things for her. And Cathy had done a good job, introducing her to Buzz. But now…

Lord, if this is really the man Trixie told me about, I need Your help! I'm sorry I didn't ask for it earlier. Please show me how to get out of this situation and away from him.

Silently she repeated a verse she had learned for her ladies' Bible class in Yokosuka. *Never will I leave you; never will I forsake you.* She breathed her thanks.

After riding in silence for more than an hour, she cleared her throat.

"Mr.…. Jud, were you planning to stop soon?"

He glanced at her, his eyebrows drawing together in a frown. "I don't like to stop too often. Have to keep my schedule, you know?"

"Oh. Sure."

"Do you need to stop?"

Marie felt her cheeks flush. "Not really. I mean, sometime, but not yet."

He nodded.

They rode without speaking for another ten minutes.

"So…what's your last name?" she asked.

"Folks just call me Jud."

"But you must have a last name on your driver's license."

He chuckled. "Smith."

"Smith?" She almost laughed. It wasn't him! Then a sober thought froze her. He was teasing her in a sinister way. He wouldn't tell her his real name because he didn't want her to be able to report him.

She wondered if he had a cell phone. If he did, he wouldn't let her use it, though. And if she asked, he'd know she had no means of communicating with anyone outside the truck.

The citizens band radio crackled, and other drivers chattered back and forth about the traffic and road conditions. She wondered if she could figure out how to use the CB. Maybe if Jud got out of the truck, she could put out a quick call for assistance. Or if he stopped at another truck stop, she could run inside and get help. But he'd filled up at the stop where he picked her up near Ann Arbor. He probably wouldn't need fuel again for hours. A weigh station? Buzz had stopped for one that morning, and she'd seen a police car parked near the scales. Maybe they would come to another one soon.

More trees edged the highway now. The afternoon was waning, and Marie shivered. She'd thought they were traveling through a well-populated area, but this highway seemed to bypass most of the towns. They appeared to be heading into a stretch of woods. Was this the type of place where Jud Vanderhof liked to take advantage of his helpless riders?

He'd have to get off the highway to try anything. Did he have a place in mind? A rest stop, maybe. Or would he leave the road at an exit where he was familiar with the rural area? Traffic was light. She sent up another prayer for safety and wisdom.

A loud pop startled her, and Jud clenched the steering wheel as the truck swayed. Marie grabbed the armrest with one hand and braced against the dashboard with the other. The rig hurtled sideways and then jerked to career around as Jud struggled to straighten it.

"Hang on!"

He gritted his teeth and manhandled the wheel, judiciously applying the brakes. Marie's pulse stampeded. Her chest hurt. She whipped against the door, held in place only by her seat belt. At last the huge tractor and trailer straightened. Jud slowed and eased it to the side of the road.

Marie took a deep breath. "Flat tire?"

He grunted. "Happens now and then. I've got a spare and tools in back. Stay put. It's on my side, so I had to pull way over." He opened his door and climbed out of the cab.

Marie swallowed hard and waited a few seconds before opening the compartment where she'd seen Jud stow his log book. She flipped the cover of the notebook up and leaned down to read the name inside. Thomas Vanderhof.

She sat up and closed the compartment so quickly that the lid slapped shut, and she caught her breath, half expecting Jud to open the door and scream at her. When nothing happened, she eyed the radio transmitter. Why hadn't she forced herself to learn more about technology? Her sister Lisa could probably operate this thing like a pro. On impulse, she opened the glove compartment. Maybe she'd find a cell phone. She fumbled through odds and ends, her breathing shallow and rapid. She tried to stay alert to any sound of Jud's return, but there was no phone.

Instead, she found a small coil of clothesline, a roll of duct tape, and a large, ugly knife.

THIRTY-SIX

André sat with Lisa on the porch swing at the Belanger family's farmhouse.

"Thanks for inviting me for supper," Lisa said. "I should go help your mom."

"Nah, she told me to treat you like company."

"What does that mean?"

"Well, you're sort of family, and you're sort of not." He smiled at her. "If she gets to know you a little better, she'll have you tossing salad and setting the table next time you come."

Lisa nodded, but her sober expression told him she wasn't in a teasing mood. "Do you think we should have gone to Portland?"

"No. They said on the phone they'd check to see if Marie was scheduled on any plane landing there instead of Bangor and get back to us."

"But will they really try hard to find Marie? They might get busy with other things and just let it go. But if we went down there to…"

"To nag them?"

Her lips twitched. "I was thinking *to keep them focused.*"

"Ah. Well, I don't think driving all the way down there and back would do anything but burn six or seven gallons of gas."

She sighed and leaned back, closing her eyes.

André pushed gently with his feet and set the swing gliding back and forth. Lisa lifted her feet slightly. Without opening her eyes, she turned her head toward him.

"This is nice."

André slid his arm around her shoulders, and she didn't object.

"You must have loved living out here," she murmured.

"It was a great place to grow up."

The swing swayed forward and backward.

"Why'd you leave home?" she asked, her eyes still shut.

"Well…" He was about to say, *I grew up*, but she might take that as an insult. They were the same age, and she still lived with her parents. "I guess because my folks had enough kids to deal with. I'm sure when we older ones left they were happy to have a little more space and fewer mouths to feed."

"Is that all?"

"No." There was the independence thing. And he'd grown tired of squabbling with his younger brother, Ricky, who'd shared his room for years. But those weren't things he wanted to talk about with Lisa. He contracted his arm a little, easing her closer, and she allowed it, settling her cheek against his shoulder.

"Do you ever think of moving out?" he asked.

"Sometimes. But Mom and Dad seem to like having me there. Especially Mom. With Marie and Claudia gone, the house seems kind of empty. If I left, she'd probably get lonely."

"Oh, I don't know." André smiled. "My dad's always saying what good times he and my mom will have when all the kids are grown and gone. Mom can have a sewing room, and they'll turn Annette's bedroom into a family room."

"With no family left?"

"I think he wants a big screen TV, but they have no place to put one. No money, either, with Lucia in college."

The front door opened, and Lisa sat up quickly, putting a couple of inches between them and smoothing her hair. His mother came out onto the porch holding a cordless phone.

"André, there's a man asking for you. That friend of Pierre's. You know. Hudson."

André took the phone. "Thanks, Mom." He held it to his ear. "Hello? This is André Belanger."

"Hey, André. George Hudson here."

"Hello, George. Pierre's told me a lot about you. Is there any news?"

"Your brother's en route from Japan to San Francisco. That's where I am now, and Pierre will join me this evening. We spoke just before he took off from Tokyo, and he asked me to clue you and the rest of the family in on what's going on. I've been working with the FBI agents investigating this case."

"The FBI is looking for Marie?"

"Well...there's more to it than that."

"We figured there was a lot we don't know. Is Marie all right?"

"So far as I know. I believe her mother heard from her this morning?"

"Yeah. That was the last we heard."

"Pierre and I don't have anything fresher than that as to Marie's whereabouts. But the fact that she called her family is a good sign."

"She said she was headed home."

"Yes. Pierre told me he hoped that meant she had a ride of some sort. A different flight or perhaps a bus ticket."

"She hasn't called. We've contacted the airport in Portland and hounded the one at Bangor. But if she were coming in on public transportation, she'd let us know, don't you think?"

"Mmm. Maybe she's riding in a private car."

"With who? This doesn't make sense."

"That's why Pierre and I are going to try to trace Marie's steps."

André realized that Lisa and his mother were both watching him with the same hungry expression. He sat forward and looked away, so their anxious eyes wouldn't distract him.

"You say the FBI is involved?"

"Yes. A crime took place in the San Francisco airport shortly after Marie's plane landed here yesterday morning."

André jolted straight in his seat. "I think I heard about that on the radio. A woman was killed in the airport."

"That's right."

"But…" Horrible things rushed through André's mind. "It wasn't Marie. My mother spoke with her after that. Please tell me Marie has nothing to do with that murder."

"I don't think she's directly connected to it. However, it's possible she witnessed the crime, or in some other way crossed paths with the killer. I didn't want to be the one to break this to your family, André, but Pierre felt you should know. Marie isn't just lost or stuck in an airport. She believes she's in danger, and…we think she's right."

"I don't understand."

André's mother came over and laid her hand on his shoulder. He glanced up at her.

"What?" she whispered.

He stood and walked to the porch steps, his back to her and Lisa.

George Hudson's calm voice went on. "An NCIS team arrived here this afternoon."

"Naval Criminal Investigative Service?"

"You're good."

"No, I just like crime shows."

Hudson chuckled. "Well, NCIS is a real organization, and they're investigating the murder at the airport here, along with the FBI."

"Why is the Navy involved?"

"Because the woman who was killed was the wife of a naval officer. The husband happens to be stationed at Yokosuka with Pierre, and they've worked together."

André leaned against the pillar at the side of the steps. "I still don't see how Marie fits into all this."

"We hope she doesn't. Pierre hasn't been able to speak to her in person. He only has bits and pieces we've put together from the two phone calls Marie managed to make after her phone was stolen. But we believe that whoever killed the other woman is after Marie now. Pierre is landing here in a few hours, and we plan to fly out together as soon as we can. We're going to follow Marie to Detroit. If she calls home again, we need you to get a location from her and tell her we'll come and get her, wherever she is. Then you contact us and tell us where to find her."

André nodded. "Sure."

"Good. Can you write down my phone number? After Pierre lands, I assume you'll be able to call him on his cell phone too. I'm arranging to have a new sim card ready for his phone so he can use it once it gets to the States. But take my number just to be sure you can reach one of us."

André turned around. "Mom, get me a pen and some paper. Quick."

"Here." Lisa rummaged in her handbag and came up with a pen and a small notebook.

André scribbled down the number George gave him.

"I still don't understand what these people want with Marie."

"Neither do we, but NCIS is going to interview the dead woman's husband and see what they can learn. I expect Pierre will call your parents as soon as he can."

After he'd disconnected, André turned slowly. His mother and Lisa stood side by side, waiting.

"You said someone wants Marie. Someone's after her?" his mother asked.

"Yes. No. I don't know. Look…" André winced and pulled in a breath, choosing his words. "Mom, they don't know any more than we do about where she is. But Pierre and George Hudson are flying to Detroit. If Marie calls here, we need to tell them where to go and pick her up."

His mother clasped her hands together. "Oh, I'm so glad!"

"Pierre's coming home?" Lisa asked.

"He's supposed to land in San Francisco soon. Then he and George are flying east together."

"I'd better make some pies."

André smiled. His mother always made Pierre's favorite—apple and peach pies—when she expected him home.

"They won't get here tonight, Mom."

"Well, I'll start after supper. I feel like baking." She headed for the door, but turned and looked at him and Lisa. "Oh, we'll be ready to eat in fifteen minutes."

"Can't I help you, Mrs. Belanger?" Lisa asked.

"No, no, you just keep André company. I've got Annette in there helping me."

She went inside, and Lisa sat down again on the swing. André joined her and reached for her hand.

"It's going to be okay," he said.

A tear spilled over Lisa's eyelid and trickled down her cheek. "What did he say to you? Marie's in danger, isn't she?"

André chewed his bottom lip. How much should he tell her? "She could be. They don't know."

"What was that business about someone being killed?"

He inhaled slowly. "Another Navy officer's wife was shot." He wrapped his arms around her, and Lisa slid in against his chest, slipping her hand up around his neck. "It's going to turn out all right," he whispered.

"You don't know that."

"A lot of good people are looking for her. They've got the FBI and NCIS looking for the murderer, and Pierre and his friend are going to Detroit tonight."

They sat in silence for a long minute, and André gently moved the swing back and forth.

"Did I tell you my mother called Claudia?" Lisa asked.

"No."

"She's trying to get a flight home tomorrow." Her voice cracked. "It's like...like Marie died or something."

"That's not going to happen." André squeezed her. He wasn't surprised that the Gillette clan was closing ranks, though. The oldest daughter coming home did give the situation an undeniably grave slant. Claudia was taking time off from the fancy magazine she worked for so that she could be with her parents and Lisa when the word came—that Marie was safe or that she was not. They would rejoice or grieve together.

Lisa collapsed in his arms as though the starch had gone out of her. "I found that church."

"The one Marie asked you to find?"

"Yeah. I drove past it this morning."

He stroked her hair. "Do you want to go there tomorrow?"

"I'd like to. I think Marie would be happy if she knew."

"All right. We'll go."

Lisa sighed. "Maybe we can say a prayer for her."

He held her close until his thirteen-year-old sister Annette came to the door and called, "Hey, lovebirds! Supper is ready."

THIRTY-SEVEN

A metallic clank reached Marie's ears, and the truck shifted ever so slightly.

Now or never, she thought. *Lord, help me to be smart and fast!*

She pulled up on the latch and paused, holding the door nearly closed and listening. She heard metal on metal, and the truck shivered.

With her purse tucked against her side, she swung the door open, careful not to let it swing free and make a noise. She lowered herself cautiously onto the running board and held on to the handle on the side of the seat as she eased out of the cab and down onto the grass. The truck was off the edge of the road in the breakdown lane, and the verge slanted downward, away from the highway. She stumbled and caught herself, and then she looked back.

Beneath the truck she could see Jud's legs as he knelt beside one of the wheels. She wished she had shut the door, but now she stood far below it, and closing it would be awkward. She couldn't risk him hearing her or seeing her feet beneath the trailer body.

She hauled in a deep breath and ran across the grassy buffer zone between the highway and a clump of woods.

When she reached the trees, she ducked within their welcoming shelter and looked back. The truck still pointed south on the edge of the road. A few cars whizzed past. She plunged into the chilly shade. For ten minutes she ran, expecting every second to hear a shout behind her or the tramp of heavy boots.

At last she stopped, gasping for breath. How far could she be from a house or another road? She'd half expected to burst through the edge of the forest onto a farmer's field, but so far she couldn't see any break in the trees ahead.

Mosquitoes buzzed around her, and she swatted at one that landed on her cheek. Where was the sun? They'd been driving south; she knew that. She wanted to head west, away from the highway. Toward the sun.

The trees all but obliterated her view, but she guessed at the direction that seemed to hold the source of light. The shadows deepened, and she knew dusk would come soon.

She trudged over the uneven ground until she was exhausted. Beneath a big pine she pulled up and squinted at her watch. Six fifteen. Could she have been in the woods more than an hour? She slumped down onto orange pine needles. The tree trunk oozed pitch, and she lay on the ground, careful not to touch the sticky bole.

Lord, please get me out of this mess! I know You know where I am, but honestly, I didn't know there was this much woods in Ohio. If I'm in Ohio. Maybe I'm still in Michigan. Lord, where are all the people?

A faint, humming whir grabbed her attention. She opened her eyes and sat up. It had to be a car. Did she hear the wheels crunch gravel, or did she imagine it? She scrambled from under the low pine branches and stood listening. The sound was fading, but she thought she'd pinpointed the direction. She set out with new determination.

Ten minutes later she tripped over a tree root and sprawled down a shallow embankment. She lay panting for half a minute and then raised her head. A dozen feet away was a dirt road. Overjoyed, she heaved herself to her feet and climbed to the level surface. Which way?

Off in the distance to her right, she could see pink clouds. To the left was twilight and more woods. That must be east. Back toward the highway—but also toward home.

Thank You, Lord. This is great. But if it's not too much to ask…I need a place to sleep tonight. If You want me out here in the woods, I guess that's okay. I won't freeze. But I figure You brought me to this road for a reason. Now I'm going to walk east. Is that what I should do?

She waited, uncertain. How did one really know what was best in a situation like this? In the Bible study a few weeks ago, they'd read about how God had told Hezekiah He would give him a sign. Would God give her a sign for something as simple as which way to walk?

Raising her eyes to the darkening sky, she said aloud, "Okay, Lord, I'm going. If You don't want me to go this way, put a skunk or something in my way, all right? I'm too tired to think up something better, but if there's anything disagreeable or scary down here, I'll turn around." She paused and swallowed hard. "And please take care of Pierre. Tell him I'm safe, so he won't worry too much. Thank You. Amen."

She lowered her chin and focused on the bend in the road a hundred yards ahead and began to walk. Tiny black flies and mosquitoes swirled around her in a dark cloud. She shook her head, whipping at them with her hair. Despite her eagerness, each step was harder than the last, and by the time she reached the bend, her feet dragged.

Behind her, a distant motor thrummed, and a streak of light from a vehicle's headlamps washed over her.

Not Jud, Lord!

Too late to scramble down into the ditch and hide. She held her breath, knowing she would jump down the bank and run into the woods again if she recognized his tractor trailer.

But the oncoming vehicle materialized into something smaller. An SUV, she discovered, as it pulled to a stop beside her.

A man rolled down the window and looked out at her. Marie could see another person beyond him, in the passenger seat.

"Need a ride?" the man asked.

"No. Thanks. I'm fine." Marie stepped back a little, but found herself teetering on the edge of the deep ditch.

"Going to the campground?" the driver asked.

"Uh…yeah."

"Hop in. We're heading back there."

"I'm just…hiking," Marie said.

"Okay. Suit yourself."

He drove on, and she watched the red taillights shrink in the gloom. It was probably all right. She should have accepted the ride. Maybe she could have found a place to sleep at the campground, even though she didn't have a tent or a camper.

The SUV's brake lights came on just a little farther down the road, and the vehicle turned to the right.

Marie swallowed hard. Was she this close? By the time she reached the side road, her lungs burned and her side ached. She bent over beside the sign, clutching her side. Belle Glade Campground.

Twenty paces into the road, she sat down on a rock to catch her breath. A pickup truck rolled past her, leaving the campground. She got up and walked with confidence. *Lord, You've brought me this far. And no skunks. I take that as a sign. You've got a place for me here.*

She reached a small cabin with signs reading "Office" and "Pay here." No one seemed to be about. Beside the door hung a poster headed "Campground rules," and Marie scanned it. No sleeping in cars. She guessed that meant they would turn away a pedestrian without a vehicle or a tent. Still, they must get backpackers. Of course, as Jud had pointed out, she had no backpack.

The road divided into three branches, and she picked one at random. Almost at once she was wandering amid campsites. Nearly every one had a trailer or tent set up, and campfires burned invitingly at several. Two teenaged girls passed her, carrying buckets. They barely glanced at Marie. She walked on, observing each campsite with anticipation.

Which one, Lord?

She rounded a curve in the roadway. Off to the left, nestled in the trees, was a large campsite tucked away by itself. Two dome tents huddled at the back of the clearing. Closer to the road, a minivan sat in the drive, and in the middle a fragrant wood fire blazed in the requisite stone fire ring. A woman bent over the fire, supervising a boy feeding sticks in under the grate. Three more children scurried about the campsite, chasing each other with whoops and laughter. A second woman unpacked provisions from a cooler on the picnic table.

"Hey, kids, settle down," the woman by the fire called.

"Yeah," said the other woman. "It's almost suppertime. Get your hot dog sticks ready."

Marie hovered for a minute, watching the scene. No men appeared while the women doled out hot dogs, buns, and small bags of potato chips to the children.

A car pulling a travel trailer came slowly down the road, and Marie stepped into the campsite's driveway. When the car had passed, she turned to look at the campers again. One of the women had noticed her.

"Hi," she called, waving with a speared hot dog.

"Hello." Marie walked toward her, and the woman advanced a couple of steps, meeting her between the van and the picnic table.

"Are you camping here?" the woman asked. Her expectant expression and pleasant, rounded face gave Marie hope.

"Well…I'd like to." Marie hesitated. *Here goes, Lord. Let's see what You can do.* She cleared her throat and glanced around at the children, who were squabbling over the plastic condiment bottles. The second woman was moderating the tussle but kept glancing toward Marie and her friend. "This may sound strange, but I need a place to sleep tonight."

The woman who had greeted her arched her eyebrows. "Are all the campsites taken?"

"No, but…I don't have a tent. Or anything. Just…" Marie held out her hands, palms up. "Just what you see."

The woman stared at her for a moment. Her facial muscles went soft and her mouth drooped. She turned toward her friend and called, "Hey, Rita."

The second woman set the ketchup bottle on the table and joined them. Her long, dark hair hung in a braid over her shoulder.

"What's up?"

"This gal needs a safe place tonight."

Rita looked her over. "Are you okay?"

Marie nodded. "Yes. Thanks. I just…I had to leave the situation I was in fast, and I don't have any luggage. I thought I'd look for a hotel, but I was way out in the boonies, and…well, I wound up here."

Rita nodded. "That's rough." She and the first woman looked at each other.

"Why not?" her friend asked.

"Right." Rita extended her hand. "I'm Rita, and this is Jill."

Marie smiled and clasped each hand eagerly. "Marie. Thank you. Thank you so much."

"My tent's a little bigger than Rita's." Jill turned to her friend. "Can we come up with an extra blanket or two for Marie?"

"I've got an old wool blanket I was going to put under Maddie and Rory, but it's warm tonight."

"Good. I've got a throw in the van."

Marie nodded. "I'm very grateful. Is there anything I can do to help you get ready for the night?"

"I think we're all set," Rita said.

A boy of about eight came and tugged at Jill's sleeve. "Mom, can we have the marshmallows now?"

Jill laughed. "Time for s'mores. Say, Marie, I think we've got a few hot dogs left. You want one?"

"That'd be great. Thanks."

She stepped forward and claimed one of the toasting sticks from the picnic table.

While Jill dispensed marshmallows to the children, Rita rifled the cooler.

"Well, what do you know? Three hot dogs. They left us one apiece."

Marie took hers with a smile and skewered it.

Rita lowered her voice. "Do you need some help? I mean, officially?"

Marie froze. "What do you mean?"

"I don't want to pry, but you said you had to get out of a sticky situation in a hurry. If your boyfriend is hitting you or—"

"No. No, it's not like that." Marie clamped her lips tight. Now what? Did she need to explain? And if she did, what would happen?

"Actually, I'm married," she whispered. "But my husband's away."

Rita frowned.

"He's coming home soon, though. Things should be okay once he's home."

"Is someone bothering you while he's gone?"

Marie shivered. Would telling her story bring Jud or Jenna's killers down on her? Worse yet, would it endanger these kindhearted women and their children?

Rita rushed on, "Because we've been there. Both of us. In fact, Jill just got her divorce papers in the mail yesterday, and we brought the kids up here for the weekend to distract them. That and to keep her ex from knowing where they are. He keeps calling her at all hours and demanding that she let him take them. It's been pretty rough for her."

A great sadness welled up in Marie's heart. She wasn't sure if it was for Jill or the children or herself.

"I'm really sorry."

"Yeah, well, it happens. She doesn't dare let the kids visit their father unsupervised."

"Has he hurt the children in the past?"

"She doesn't think so, but he's abusive in other ways, you know? What you might call verbal or mental abuse. Jill's making an appeal to the court. They think the guy's a saint. She really needs to get a different judge. The hearing's at the end of the month."

"That's really tough." Marie glanced toward Jill. "She seems to be holding it together for the kids."

"Yeah. She's doing her best to protect them. The trouble is, most people won't listen when she tells them all the things Jerry's done to her."

"Why not?"

Rita grimaced. "Because for years she kept quiet. She loved the guy, so she hid the evidence. Bruises, cuts, a broken wrist. Everyone thinks he's a great guy because she let them think so. Her ex is a well respected, highly decorated state trooper."

THIRTY-EIGHT

1530 Saturday/Sunday, International Date Line

"We are now crossing the international date line. Welcome to Saturday...again."

At the pilot's words, Pierre scowled at his watch. *Great. I get to live one of the worst days of my life over again.* No sense setting his watch to local time until he landed in California. He leaned back in his seat and shut his eyes. Despite the few hours of sleep he'd had last night, he knew he wouldn't nap on the plane. But he hoped playing possum would keep the large motherly lady next to him from trying to chat. He'd already seen photos of her eight grandchildren and two great-grandchildren and heard all about her gallbladder surgery.

What would George do in this situation? During the eighteen months he'd served under George Hudson, Pierre had formed the habit of asking that question before he took action. While George sometimes looked on the dark side of circumstances, Pierre doubted his friend would be pessimistic now. Regaining half a day by traveling east would give him a chance to find Marie earlier. He puzzled over the paradox of real time. Where was Marie now?

It was Sunday noon, Tokyo time. But in the eastern United States time zone, it was ten p.m. Saturday. The refueling stop in Honolulu would hold him up a couple of hours. He ought to be stepping off the plane in San Francisco in another fourteen hours. He'd missed church, no matter what time zone he reckoned it in. He hoped Marie was safe and had a chance to worship, wherever she was.

He pulled out his cell phone, looked at it, and shoved it back in his pocket. No way he could get an update from George or anyone else until they hit the tarmac in Honolulu.

God, You've brought me this far. I never expected Captain Wheeler to get me a flight out so fast. Please keep Marie safe. Let us find her soon!

THIRTY-NINE

Marie lay awake in the tent, listening to the staggered breathing of Jill and her two children. The magnitude of what she'd been through almost crushed her. Terrifying images raced through her mind. Jenna's anguished cry of "Run!"; the hard-eyed Asian woman who held the pistol; the Chinese man who grabbed her at the mall; and the grim boys from the rock band, encircling her and her attacker with their knives drawn.

She wondered if those boys had been arrested for carrying illegal weapons, and if the security guards had taken the Chinese man into custody. Or had his friends somehow helped him elude capture? Had she fled the mall before the outbreak of a bloody battle?

The thought that she might have caused harm to innocent people—the band, the bikers, the food court patrons, the security officers—made her stomach roil. Or maybe it was putting a charred hot dog and a dozen blackened marshmallows into an empty belly.

She rolled over and stared at the tent door. Jill had zipped the screen door but left the canvas flaps up. Marie could still see a faint glow around the fire pit, an aura that reminded her of happy times with her own family.

She heard a car drive slowly along the gravel road. Her heartbeat quickened at the thought that somehow the evil men had traced her here. But the vehicle rolled on without stopping, and she drew a deep breath.

Please, Lord, let me sleep while I have the chance. And tomorrow, let me get home.

She awoke to sunlight through the blue tent fabric and the sound of four-year-old Maddie's whines. "Mommy, I have to go. Mommy!"

Jill groaned. "Okay, okay. Hush, now. Don't wake up Rory and Miss Marie. Just let me find my sneakers. Put your shoes on."

Maddie wailed.

"Quiet!"

"I have to go bad."

Marie sat up.

Jill showed her teeth in a grimace. "Sorry."

"It's okay." Marie shuffled the blankets and located her own shoes. "I'll go up to the latrine with you, if you don't mind."

They left Rory sleeping in the tent, snoring softly, and walked along a wooded path toward the restrooms.

"Hurry, Mommy!" Maddie danced ahead of them.

"Shh. People are sleeping. Walk like an Indian."

At once, Maddie began lifting her feet high in exaggerated tiptoes.

Marie chuckled. "I don't suppose you have a cell phone."

"Rita does, but I don't think the service here is very good. She tried to call her mom after we got here yesterday, but she couldn't get a connection."

Marie nodded. "It's okay."

She busied herself about camp when they returned, helping prepare breakfast and going with Rita to buy a bundle of firewood at the office afterward.

"Mom, can we go swimming?" Rita's son, Caden, asked.

"Are you nuts? That water is freezing."

"Oh, please?" six-year-old Stacie chimed in.

Jill turned with the frying pan in her hands to catch Rita's gaze. "Maybe they could wade?"

Rita inhaled deeply, clearly wavering. "All right, but let's get this camp shipshape first. Who wants to get water?"

"I'll do it." Marie hurried to get the plastic bucket they used for water.

"So, Marie, do you want to stay with us tonight?" Rita asked. "We'll be here one more night and break camp tomorrow morning."

Marie pondered her options. She needed to get home, or at least to get to a place where she could contact Pierre or her parents. "I should probably get moving today."

"Please stay," Stacie teased, bouncing up and down as her mother tried to run a brush though her dark hair.

"I'll think about it while I get the water," Marie promised with a smile.

"Let me go with you!" Stacie pulled away from Rita and scurried toward Marie.

"Hey!" Rita cried. "I'm not done yet."

"I'll take the brush with me." Stacie ran back and snatched it from her mother's hand.

Rita looked questioningly at Marie.

"I don't mind." Marie chuckled and reached out to smooth the rambunctious little girl's hair. "We'll only be a few minutes."

Stacie insisted on keeping one hand on the pail's handle as they walked down the path together. She chattered incessantly. At last they reached the water spigot at a fork in the trail, and Marie filled the bucket.

"Ooh, it's heavy!" Stacie said, grimacing as she tugged at the handle.

Marie knew it would be easier if she carried the load alone, but she kept the pail low between them and hobbled along at an awkward pace that allowed Stacie to keep her hold. Halfway back to the campsite, they set it down for a minute to rest.

"You okay?" Marie panted.

"Yup. Are you?" Stacie stared up at her with huge, brown eyes.

"I'm fine. But maybe we should go a little slower so that we're not huffing and puffing when we get there, or everyone will think we're wimps."

Stacie giggled. "We're not wimps!"

Marie smiled. The little girl was beginning to carve a niche in her heart, and the two women had been kind to her beyond her expectations. Why not stay with them one more night? Perhaps she could walk up to the office and see if it would be possible for her to call her family. Or maybe Jill would drive her to the nearest pay phone.

When they at last reached the campsite, the two boys were gathering twigs for future kindling, and Maddie sat at the picnic table eating a banana. Jill and Rita stood close together near the van, talking in low tones and examining a sheet of paper. Marie and Stacie carried the bucket of water to its spot beside the cooler.

"Look, Stacie. There's a chipmunk!" Marie pointed to a rock where the quick little animal had paused to peer at them.

Stacie caught her breath. "Oh! Oh!"

"Shh," Marie warned her. "Be quiet, now. You'll scare him."

"Can I feed him?"

Marie glanced toward Jill and Rita. They threw worried looks in her direction but did not approach her. Marie felt a prickle of uneasiness. She opened the cooler and pulled out a bread wrapper.

"Here, take a chunk off the bread heel. There you go."

Maddie climbed down from the bench and reached for a piece of bread too, and Marie watched the two little girls tiptoe toward their quarry. The chipmunk sat motionless until they were within a yard and then scampered away to a fallen log a few feet beyond.

Marie turned and walked to the two mothers.

"Hi. What's up?"

Jill eyed her cautiously and bit her lower lip. Marie's chest tightened. She looked at Rita, who hesitated and then said, "The campground manager brought this around. He said a state trooper brought a stack of them for him to hand out."

Jill blinked hard and crunched her face as though determined not to cry. "When he said a state trooper was here, I thought it was Jerry, looking for me and the kids. But it wasn't that at all."

FINDING MARIE   193

Marie's mouth was dry, and her knees began to shake. "What was it?" Her voice croaked.

Rita's eyes hardened. "The police are looking for a woman who may be involved in a murder at the San Francisco airport. Travelers are supposed to beware and contact the authorities if they see her."

She offered the paper she was holding, and Marie stared down at the flier. For an enlarged photocopy of her passport picture, it wasn't bad.

FORTY

0700 Sunday, San Francisco

Pierre's spirits brightened when he spotted George waiting for him in the boarding lounge.

"*Georges, mon copain! Comment ça va?*"

His old friend drew him into a quick bear hug, swinging his soft briefcase over Pierre's shoulder.

"Look at you! You haven't changed a bit except for your rank. Pretty snazzy." George nodded toward the concourse. "I checked on where to pick up your luggage. Come on. We'll get your phone switched over too." As they walked, he quickly filled Pierre in on what he had learned the previous day from the FBI agents, Navy investigators, and airport security personnel.

"Just between you and me," George said, leaning close to Pierre's ear as they stood near the baggage carousel, "NCIS is pretty sure Jenna was carrying information on the matter we mentioned."

Pierre nodded. "I was afraid of that. Just before I left, Captain Wheeler briefed me. He said we had to be prepared for this because things were not looking good for the commander."

George nodded and glanced about before he spoke again. "They've got him here, over at the San Francisco PD."

"Really?" Pierre didn't like thinking Tarrington had betrayed the project. The solidarity and comradeship he'd felt with his Navy associates seemed false, and their patriotism tainted. If the China plot failed, it would be worse than wasting two years of concentrated effort. The story would be used as propaganda to paint the Americans with the hue of power mongering.

"They're keeping him in tight custody. Afraid he'll run."

Pierre inhaled slowly and stared at the belt on the carousel as it began to move. "Let me get my bag. Is there someplace secure where we can talk?"

"Sure. But let's have breakfast first."

"Okay. You can catch me up on things in Pearl. How's Rachel doing?"

"Fine. She sent you something. And get this: Norton's retiring."

"You don't say. That will change things for you."

George nodded. "I'll take over the five units he supervises."

"So where's my present?"

George unzipped a pocket on his briefcase and pulled out a manila envelope. Pierre opened it and drew out the sheet of heavy paper inside. He smiled as he studied the detailed pencil sketch of a slim woman standing on a pool deck, tossing a fish out to a huge sea lion that breached the water.

"Self-portrait?"

"Yeah. She loves training the sea lions. They do amazing work, training them to do deep water recovery."

"That's great."

"It saves our divers a lot of headaches when the sea lions take a line down and hitch it to whatever we want to pull up."

Pierre grinned. "We could have used one of these fellows on Frasier." He glanced toward the carousel. "There's my gear. Can you carry this for me?" He handed the envelope back to George and reached for his seabag.

After an hour of intense questioning with McCutcheon and his investigators, Pierre itched to move on. He and George had learned all they could in San Francisco, and they were wasting precious time. They needed to get to Detroit, the last place they knew Marie was alive and well.

"Relax, buddy," George counseled as they left the conference room together. "In another hour, we'll mosey over to the boarding gate and check in. We can't move any faster than the airlines do."

Pierre nodded. He'd called his parents and learned nothing, except for the family's anguish. He'd tried André's cell phone and connected to voice mail.

George stopped at a newsstand. "I want to get a local newspaper and see what the media's putting out about all this."

Pierre's phone rang, and he flipped it open as George stepped up to the counter.

André. Well, it was better than nothing.

"Hey, brother," he said.

"Hi! I just got your message. You're in San Francisco?"

"Yeah. Where you been?"

"Lisa and I went to church."

"What say?"

"Church. You know. Choir, sermon, preacher."

"Oh, yeah?"

"Yeah. Lisa found the church Marie told her about, and we decided to go to the service there this morning."

"Marie told her about it?"

"Yeah, supposedly your minister in Japan recommended it."

"Sure, I know about that. I just didn't realize Marie had told Lisa."

"She did. We went."

Pierre chuckled, suddenly less downhearted. "That's great. How was it?"

"Interesting. Different from what I remember about church, but we can talk about that later. Have you and George found out any more about Marie?"

"Not really. But we're heading for Detroit. Our plane leaves here in a hour, and we'll land at six o'clock your time."

"Good."

George walked over to join Pierre, browsing the front page of the newspaper he'd bought.

"Keep your phone on," Pierre said to André. "I'll call you the last thing before we go airborne. And if you hear anything—*anything*—you call me."

"Right."

Pierre closed his phone and slid it into his pocket. "My brother," he said to George.

George nodded. "The *San Francisco Chronicle* is making hay with this story."

Pierre looked over his shoulder. "But they don't mention Marie, right?"

"Not by name." George winced. "They do say the police and FBI are looking for a woman who sat beside Jenna on the incoming flight. They want her for questioning."

"They make it sound like Marie's a suspect in the murder."

George looked at him. In his gray eyes, Pierre saw an empathy and regret that he didn't like. George grasped his arm and pulled him to a niche where they could sit on a vacant bench with nothing at their backs but the wall.

"What?" Pierre asked him.

"Brace yourself. The media runs with stories like this. Right now there may be TV news anchors broadcasting Marie's name and description all over the country."

"You're joking."

"No. The FBI has distributed her photo to police here and in Michigan. It's only a matter of time before they set up a hotline and Marie's picture is broadcast on TV."

"A manhunt? For my wife?" Pierre's stomach lurched.

George started to speak, but then he looked away. "I hate to say this, but it could come to that. McCutcheon wasn't exactly forthcoming with you, but I've been shadowing him for almost a day, and I can tell you this: The NCIS and the FBI are being cordial on the surface, but the FBI will do just about anything to solve the murder and claim credit. The NCIS won't allow them access to any classified data. That means they're not letting McCutcheon interview Commander Tarrington. The Navy will try to keep his involvement in the subversion plan quiet. We don't want that to leak out, no matter what."

Pierre stared at him. "You think the Pentagon would sacrifice Marie to protect the China op?"

George's mouth twisted into a grimace as he shrugged. "I'm saying they might let the spotlight fall on her to keep it off the reason Jenna was killed. If the FBI can be sidetracked for even a couple of days with looking for Marie and figuring out her connection to Jenna, that will give the brass time to hide whatever they want hidden and get Tarrington out of range of local cops and the FBI."

Pierre put one hand to his forehead and shoved his hair back. "But Marie… It's bad enough that Jenna's killers are after her. I know these people, George. They'll be ruthless."

"I'm aware of that."

"If she finds out the police think she's a murderess…"

"She's done a good job of keeping her head down for forty-eight hours."

Pierre leaned back and took a deep breath. "Do you think that's why she hasn't checked in? She's afraid of the cops too?"

"I don't know. And I'll never lie to you. Every shred of information I learn about Marie, I'll share with you. That doesn't mean the investigators will, though. You're too close to this, and it's too personal. I'm not sure they're telling me everything, either, because they know I'm tight with you."

"That means a lot."

"Do you know what it was that Jenna was carrying? Don't give me specifics. I'm just asking if you have an idea of what she might have had on her that would get her killed."

"Yeah, I have ideas. If someone got hold of a list of all our China contacts, that would be worth a lot to the communists. It would tell them who all the leaders of their enemies are, who's organizing the rebel factions. A lot of heads could roll if they get that information, George."

His friend held up one hand. "Don't tell me any more. I figured it was something like that."

Pierre closed his eyes. "I just don't know what I'll do if anything happens to Marie."

"You'll get through it. God will hold you up."

Pierre looked over at him. "How did you handle it when Pam died?"

George folded the newspaper and tucked it under his arm. "Not very well, I'm afraid. I wasn't relying on God then. But we're going to find Marie."

"Assassins are chasing her. She's an amateur, and she's all alone."

"Don't think that way. God can do anything. Trust Him to do this."

Pierre nodded. "It's hard. How can she be safe and not let us know?"

"God knows, and He can take care of her."

"I hate to even ask Him to do anything for me." Pierre shook his head at the memory of his own callousness, not so long ago. "I used to think that if I said a few prayers now and then, lit a few candles, and kept my nose clean, I'd be okay with God, you know? But now it's different. That church we went to in Japan… Well, I'm glad Marie found it and we found Jesus Christ. It's made a huge difference in our lives."

George smiled. "I'm glad too. If I'd been at that point a few years ago, things would have gone better for me, I'm sure, and I wouldn't have made a lot of other people's lives miserable."

"Yeah." Pierre chuckled. "You did have your obnoxious moments. Hey, let's pray about this together. I mean, if it's okay with you."

"Definitely okay."

They bowed their heads and offered brief prayers for guidance and for Marie's safety as the airport crowd swirled around them. When Pierre opened his eyes, George was smiling.

"We'll find her."

Pierre stood up. "I'm not sure I believe that just because you said it, but I do believe God is in control."

At the boarding gate, they found seats among the waiting passengers. Ten minutes later, the airline agent positioned herself behind the desk and began to check in the first-class passengers.

"Hey." George nudged Pierre, and he looked up.

Hurrying into the boarding area were David McCutcheon and another man. George and Pierre stood as McCutcheon spotted them and strode across the lounge.

"Agent McCutcheon," George said easily.

"Hudson. Looks like Special Agent Heinz and I will be on the same flight as you and Belanger."

George turned to Pierre. "I don't think you met Special Agent Heinz of the NCIS."

The man was not uniformed, and Pierre assumed he was a civilian investigator for the Naval Criminal Investigative Service. He extended his hand.

"Pleased to meet you."

"You're both going to Detroit?" George asked.

"Yes," McCutcheon said. "We've decided that finding Mrs. Belanger and hearing her testimony is crucial to the case."

"Any word on the stolen TSA uniform?"

"Not yet. We've got a possible on one of the videotapes, but no ID yet. My team will carry on here with what evidence we've got, and the NCIS team will do whatever they're doing." McCutcheon scowled, and Pierre wondered what had passed between him and Heinz, where it came to the custody of Christopher Tarrington.

"We've done some advance work by phone," Heinz said. "The local authorities are on it, trying to find where Mrs. Belanger went from the Detroit Metro Airport."

"We know she'd already left the airport when she spoke to her mother yesterday," George said.

Heinz nodded. "Yes, and a CIA team will meet us there."

"CIA?" George asked.

"I'm afraid so."

McCutcheon's mustache twitched. "Apparently the Navy thinks we need them."

Heinz's smile was almost apologetic. "Well, the international aspects of the case look suspicious. You understand."

George and Pierre both nodded, and Pierre wondered how much the NCIS team had revealed to McCutcheon and his people about Tarrington's classified operation. And why was the CIA going to Michigan, where Marie was, instead of to San Francisco, where Tarrington was in custody?

"I assure you, Lieutenant," Heinz said to Pierre, "we will do everything in our power to help you locate your wife and bring her in safely."

Pierre flicked a glance at George. As usual, the lieutenant commander's gray eyes were noncommittal, but Pierre could read him. George wasn't buying it, either.

FORTY-ONE

"I had nothing to do with that murder." Tears filled Marie's eyes as she stared at Jill and Rita. She blinked hard, but one escaped anyway, spilling down her cheek. "Really. I'd never hurt anyone."

"Then why is your picture making the rounds?" Rita demanded.

Marie's lips trembled beyond her control, and it was difficult to fill her lungs with air.

"I was there in San Francisco. I went into the restroom and…and a woman was killed in there. But I had nothing to do with it."

Stacie and Maddie careened across the campsite and screeched to a stop beside their mothers.

"Are we going wading?" Stacie asked.

"In a minute," Rita replied. "Go straighten up the tent first."

Maddie's cheeks and mouth formed the ultimate pout. Marie would have laughed if she hadn't been so distressed.

"Come on, Maddie." Stacie took the little girl's hand and led her toward the dome tents.

"So how come they're looking for you?" Jill asked. Her blue eyes held Marie's gaze with unrelenting mistrust.

Rita touched her friend's arm. "Take it easy, hon." She turned to face Marie. "You knew Jill's ex was a state trooper. I told you last night."

"Yes."

"When the manager came here and told us a trooper had been to see him, Jill was scared stiff. What if Jerry had come around the campground himself with these fliers? He would have seen us, and then he would have started harassing Jill again."

"I'm sorry."

Rita exhaled sharply and shook her head. "I don't care what you've done. You're not going to put Jill and her kids in danger."

Marie nodded, not quite able to meet Rita's eyes. "You're right. Forgive me. I'll leave." She walked toward the larger tent to pick up her purse.

"Hold on," Jill called.

Marie pivoted and waited for her to speak.

"Look, we'll take you to the nearest town. You can get a motel or a ride, or at least phone someone who can help you."

A painful lump formed in Marie's throat. "I wouldn't want to put you out. You two were really nice to me. I don't deserve…"

Jill shook her head. "I don't think you're a killer, but if you are…well, we want to get you away from our kids in that case, don't we?"

Rita started to speak but refrained.

"Right," Jill said. "Rita, you keep the kids here, and I'll drive Marie into town."

Rita pulled out her car keys. "No, you should stay out of sight. I'll take her. Just don't let Caden swim until I get back."

Marie moistened her lips, unable to express the anguish in her heart.

"Come on," Rita said, walking toward the van.

Marie glanced at Jill. "Thank you. And I'm truly sorry."

They rode together in silence for twenty minutes. At last they reached the outskirts of a town.

"Where do you want me to leave you?" Rita asked. "A restaurant? A pay phone?"

Ahead Marie could see the tall sign for a motel.

"There."

"Meadow Inn?"

"Yeah." All of the things she wanted to explain ran through Marie's mind as Rita pulled in and stopped the car before the motel's office.

"Listen, I didn't do anything wrong, and I want you and Jill to know that. I saw someone get killed, and I got scared and ran. Probably I should have stuck around and talked to the police."

"Why didn't you?"

Rita's unyielding gaze was more than Marie could bear. She reached for her purse. "I can't tell you, but I promise I'm not a criminal. And I sincerely hope that I haven't brought trouble down on you and Jill. Thanks for everything you did for me."

Rita held the stare a few more seconds, and then she looked ahead, inhaling and thumping her hands on the steering wheel. "Sure. I hope everything turns out okay for you too."

Marie hesitated. "I'd like to be able to contact you later and explain some things."

"No. I think we'll just leave it right here. Good luck, Marie."

Marie nodded. Her heart was like a stone. She opened the door and left the car without looking back.

The sun beat down on her shoulders as she walked to the office door. In the motel's dim office, a fan pushed the warm air about the small room.

"Help you?"

An olive-skinned girl about her age jumped up from a chair behind the desk.

"I'd like a room."

"Okay." The young woman glanced up at the clock. "Check-in is noon, but it's only fifteen minutes early, so you can get in now."

Marie nodded, cutting through the thick Hispanic accent for the sense of her words. "Thank you." She read the name tag on the girl's glittery black-and-gold top: Angela.

The clerk pushed her long, black bangs aside and tapped a few keys on a computer screen. "Your name?"

Marie hesitated. If she used her real name, would the men from Tokyo find her? She was low on cash. If she did use her own name, she could also use her credit card and save her currency for meals and other needs.

"How much for one night?"

"Seventy-nine dollars."

"Here's my credit card. My name is on it."

It was a split-second decision. Depleting her cash might be more dangerous than giving out her name. Once she was in the room, she could call someone. And she could get a shower. *Oh, glory! Thank You, dear Father in heaven!*

"And what is your car license number?"

Marie's voice shook. "I…don't have one. Someone drove me here."

Five minutes later Angela handed her the key and pointed her toward her unit. "Checkout is ten thirty a.m."

"Thanks."

Marie strode quickly to the door of her room and inserted the key card. When she closed the door, she exhaled and sent up a prayer of thanksgiving. Security, if only for a short time. Privacy. Hot water. And a phone.

She tossed her purse on the bed and picked up the telephone, skimming the printed instructions that lay on the nightstand. Eagerly she punched in the access code and Pierre's cell phone number. A recorded message told her the call was being forwarded to a new number.

"Hello?" Pierre's voice said a moment later.

"Baby, it's me!"

"Chérie!" Pierre sounded breathless.

"Oui, c'est moi."

"Grace à Dieu! Où es tu?"

She let her tears flow unheeded and flopped back on the poofy pillow with a sob.

"Where am I? I don't know."

"How is that possible?"

She sighed. "I'm in a motel."

"Good. Are you alone?"

"Yes."

"Better. Now, where is this motel?"

"It's in a little town called Cafford, but I don't know if it's in Michigan or Ohio. It could be near the border. I was on Highway 75, going south out of Michigan, but I left it on the west side of the road."

"*Bien!* Can you wait there for us?"

"I...guess so."

"Good. I will have the FBI man look it up on his laptop computer."

"FBI man? Where are you, Pierre?"

"I'm in the San Francisco airport, where you landed Friday morning, but George and I are about to get on a plane for Detroit. That is where you went, yes?"

"Yes, but...you and George Hudson?"

"*Oui, ma chérie.* We are coming to get you. Just stay where you are."

"All right."

"What is the name of the hotel?"

"The Meadow Inn, room 16. When will you be here?"

"Well, it depends on how far it is from Detroit. We'll look it up and let you know. We land in Detroit at..." there was a pause and a shuffling of paper, "a little after six o'clock, and we'll have to get a rental car. Can you stay at the hotel until we arrive?"

"Yes. I'll try to get some sleep."

"Good. Just make sure your door is locked and the safety chain is on."

Fear surged through her, overpowering the joy the sound of his voice brought. "Pierre, what's going on? Why are the police hunting for me? I'm scared."

"Oh, my sweet one. Settle down and rest. All will be well."

"But...Jenna Tarrington..."

"She is dead, my love."

"Did they catch the woman who did it?"

"Not yet. But the FBI and the NCIS are working on it. Tell me—you saw the shooting?"

"Yes."

"Describe the killer for me, quickly."

"She was an Asian TSA agent. Chinese, I think. About five-two."

"Wearing a uniform?"

"Yes."

"Hold on." She heard another voice speaking to her husband but didn't catch the words.

"Marie, *ma chérie,* I have to get on the plane. They will make me shut off the phone. But you've given us a lot of help. The officers will pass that information on to their men. I wish I could talk to you until we get there."

She sniffed. "I wish you could too."

"You swear you're all right?"

"Yes. Now I am. Just hurry!"

She hadn't meant to cry, but tears streamed down her face as she said a quick goodbye. The last thing her husband said to her was, "We'll be there soon, *mon amour. Je t'aime.*"

FORTY-TWO

Marie jolted awake and sat upright on the bed. Her heart hammered. It took a second to remember where she was…the motel…the delectable hot shower…sinking into the soft, fresh bed.

The phone was ringing. She lunged for it and fell back on the pillow, holding the receiver to her ear.

"Hello?"

"*Chérie!* We are in the airport in Detroit. Good news. George thinks we can be where you are in a couple of hours. He's renting a car now."

A surge of warmth flooded her. "Honey, I'm so glad."

Pierre chuckled. "Me too. I've missed you so much! Did you rest?"

"Yes. I was sleeping when you called."

"Well, go back to sleep if you want to. We'll be there soon."

"I love you."

Reluctantly she hung up the phone and nestled down under the cozy covers once more. This horrific dream was almost over. She would be in Pierre's arms soon. *Thank You, Lord!*

I ought to get up and dress, she thought. But the comfortable bed and the proximity of sleep were too tempting.

Someone pounded on the door. She jackknifed into a sitting position and glanced at the illuminated clock. Half an hour had passed since Pierre's call. Could they be here already?

"*Señora!*" a raspy feminine voice called. "*Señora,* open!"

Marie jumped out of bed and stumbled to the door. She squinted and peered through the peephole. Angela, the Latina girl from the office, stood outside. The streetlights in the parking lot sent glints off her black hair. She looked over her shoulder and then called out again.

"*Señora,* open *por favor!*"

Marie threw on her jeans and tank top, and then she fumbled with the safety chain and flung the door open.

"What is it?"

"Please!" Angela pushed her back into the room and followed her inside, shutting the door behind her. "*Señora,* tell me quick, are you legal?"

Marie blinked and rubbed her forehead, trying to make sense of that. "I'm sorry. I don't…"

"Two men came into the office just now. They are asking about you."

Marie came wide awake and stared at her. "They asked for me by name?"

"Yes. Marie Belanger." She mangled the last name, but Marie ignored that, reaching to grasp her wrist.

"My husband and his friend are coming to get me. These two men—is one of them tall and dark haired? Brown eyes. And the other is only a little shorter. He's about forty. Light brown hair and gray eyes. Both very handsome men?"

Angela shook her head, distress distorting her pretty features. "One is Asian and the other is white, but he is not handsome. He's older, and he has an ugly face."

Marie's throat tightened, and she gasped for a breath.

"My father is stalling them," Angela said. "I thought at first they were policemen, but they didn't show badges. So then I am thinking, *Immigration!* They asked to see the register. I told them they would have to talk to my father, and I got him to come to the desk, then I ran over here. *Señora,* if you're not legal, you need to run!"

Marie swallowed hard and then dashed to the bedside and jammed her feet into her sneakers. Angela's description left her no doubt.

"My brother and his family were deported last February." Angela's voice trembled. "We don't want to see that happen to anyone else. You go, and we will keep them away as long as we can, but you must be quick!"

Already Marie had her sweater on. She grabbed her watch and purse from the nightstand.

"Thank you!"

She squeezed Angela's arm and slipped out the door.

Raindrops pelted her as she ran along the length of the building and around the corner into darkness. She stopped, panting, and edged her face to the corner and looked back. Angela had left room 16 and was walking toward the office. Light spilled out of the office doorway as three men exited. One was a small, hunched man who might be Angela's father. It didn't take Marie a second glance to recognize the other two, even in the uneven lighting of the motel parking lot. Somehow her pursuers had found her again. She turned and ran around to the back of the motel, dodging a dumpster.

FORTY-THREE

Marie dashed into the recessed back doorway of a school building and tried to ignore the drumming rain. Splashing droplets reached her and began to soak through her jeans. She pressed tighter against the locked door and hid her face in her arms.

Lord, You've got to help me! How on earth could they know where I was?

She went over every move she'd made that day. Had she somehow spilled her location to the enemy when she spoke to Pierre on the phone? Or did they trace her through the use of the credit card? If only she'd had time to call Pierre again before fleeing the room. She had run only a block or so from the motel before sheltering in the school doorway. She didn't want to go too far from the Meadow Inn. Pierre and George would come there soon, and she didn't want to miss them.

There was a lull in the rain. She stepped cautiously out of her refuge. Silently, she flitted along the backs of buildings, from the shadow of a bush to a tool shed and back toward the motel.

At last she was once more behind the Meadow Inn. She sneaked to the spot from which she'd observed the men and gingerly peeked around the corner.

She ducked back. Several men were talking outside the door of the room she'd occupied, and she'd seen the glint of light on a gun barrel. She heard loud knocking and then a shout, "Open up!"

Against her better judgment, she snatched another peek. The largest man drew back and kicked the door viciously. It flew open, and he stumbled forward into her abandoned room.

Marie turned and ran.

FORTY-FOUR

Lisa had trouble sitting still and talking to the Gillettes' company. The stress of Marie's disappearance kept her fidgeting and springing up to fetch things that didn't need to be fetched. Her mother had insisted they call the Belangers on Sunday evening and invite them to come over and share the family's misery.

Claudia was home. Lisa's parents had picked up their older daughter themselves in Portland that afternoon. The two families crowded into the living room and dining room of the Gillettes' two-story Victorian house.

Lisa felt the tiniest bit awkward. Both sets of parents, while consoling each other and issuing reassurances that Marie would soon be found, seemed to avidly watch her and André. The fledgling romance was a diversion, she supposed, and the hawks were lined up, waiting for it to move. She was sure she and André provided their mothers with plenty of fodder for chitchat when they were out of earshot.

Claudia found it amusing. When their mother had first hinted that Lisa was interested in one of the Belanger boys, she'd laughed. "Really? Which one? Mathieu, I suppose." Mathieu was in Claudia's class.

"No, not Mathieu," the girls' mother said.

"Well, who's next in line? André?"

"He's the one."

"Not as smart as Pierre, but he's just as cute," was Claudia's verdict.

Lisa had found an excuse to dive into the dim, old-fashioned pantry and rifle the shelves.

"What are you hiding in there for, Lisa?" Claudia called, with a knowing lilt to her voice.

"I'm not hiding. I'm looking for the cheese grater."

"It's right here on the sideboard, where you left it."

Now they were all here—Mr. and Mrs. Belanger, André, Lucia, Eloise, and Annette. Three of the boys were away, of course—Pierre on his quest to find Marie, Mathieu presumably at his job in Lewiston, and Ricky at his summer job in Quebec. Giselle was away at school in Indiana, working on a master's degree, and Lisa wished she could have made it; Giselle was only a couple of years her junior, and they got along well. Lucia, the next younger Belanger sister, had come home from the University of Maine for the weekend.

The suffocating feeling increased in Lisa's chest. The four parents sat around the dining table, drinking coffee and talking. The younger Belangers lounged in the living room, oddly quiet, accepting the snacks Lisa and Claudia offered with murmured thanks.

Lisa longed to sit down on the sofa beside André, but she felt as though that was exactly what everyone was waiting for, so she didn't. Instead, she perched on the arm of Claudia's recliner.

"Anyone want to play a game?" Claudia asked.

Annette perked up a little, but Eloise shrugged and looked away, as though embarrassed that Marie's sister had suggested a frivolous pastime while Marie's life might be in danger. Eating pie was bad enough.

The telephone rang in the kitchen, and Lisa jumped up.

"I'll get it, Mom."

She lifted the receiver in the middle of the third ring.

"Hello?"

"*Allo*. Lisa?"

"Yes."

"It's Pierre. *Comment ça va?*"

She laughed with relief. "Much better, since you've called. What's the word on Marie?"

"George and I are on our way to pick her up. We expect to have her with us in about half an hour."

"Fantastic." Lisa leaned against the wall, suddenly wobbly. "Where is she, anyway?"

"A little town in northern Ohio. We'll be there soon. Can you tell my folks? I called their house, but no one answered."

She chuckled. "That's because they're here. I'll tell them."

"*Bien!*"

"Pierre, call and let us know when you've got her, will you?"

"I will. Talk to you soon."

She walked into the dining room, unable to hold in a grin. "That was Pierre."

Everyone exclaimed, and the younger generation moved in from the living room to hear every word.

"He and his friend George are almost at the spot where they're supposed to pick Marie up. He said they'll have her soon."

"Wonderful!" Her father looked expectantly toward her mother. "Is there any more of that apple pie?"

"Lisa, get your father more pie," her mother said. "Michael, would you like more?"

Mr. Belanger shook his head. "No, thanks. But maybe a drop more coffee."

Claudia headed for the kitchen. "I'll get it."

Lisa followed her sister and was through the kitchen door before she realized André was shadowing her.

She made a face at him. "What are you after? More pie?"

"No, the waitress serving it."

"Claudia, did you hear that? André wants to flirt with you."

Claudia laughed. "Come now, little sister, you were never this dense when we were kids." She put the dessert plate with their father's pie on it in Lisa's hands. "Go give this to Dad. I'll get the coffeepot.

And then I think you and André should go out for a walk. Work off some tension."

"Who's tense?" André asked.

"Oh, did I say that?" Claudia shrugged. "I meant to say calories. Work off some calories while I start a game with your little sibs."

Claudia breezed into the dining room.

"I like her," André said.

Lisa studied his face, at once insecure and proud. He was here to be near her, after all—in fact, he had spent the entire day with her. And yet… Did he like confident Claudia more than he liked her? Claudia was prettier. And she had a nice job in Atlanta. She had great legs and creamy skin, like Marie.

"You want me to take that?" André asked, reaching for the pie plate.

"No, thanks. I'll just give it to my dad."

He nodded. "Okay. Then do you want to follow Claudia's advice?"

"Do you?"

"I think that would be great."

"We might miss it when they call and tell us they've found Marie."

André tilted his head to one side. "We don't have to go far. We just haven't had a chance to talk about this morning. The church service and all."

"Okay." *It's me he likes.*

He held her gaze for a moment before she looked away and headed for the next room. Her father smiled and reached for the pie but never stopped talking to Michael Belanger. Lisa caught André's eye and nodded toward the door. They'd almost made it outside—André was holding the front door open for her, when her mother called, "Put your jacket on, Lisa Josephine! It's chilly."

She sighed and turned back to snag her velour jacket from the coat closet. André held it for her and then opened the door. The cool evening air and quiet of the nighttime street were a relief.

"So," he said, reaching for her hand. "Josephine, eh?"

"Guilty."

"It's not a bad name. Lisa Josephine Gillette."

Belanger, she added mentally and then flushed in the darkness. It was way too soon to be thinking that way.

"Do you think Claudia's pretty?" she asked and then wished she hadn't.

He raised his shoulders and eyed her cautiously. "I suppose. Kind of. Do you?"

"Sure. Oh, not beautiful. Marie's the beautiful one. But..."

"What?"

"Nothing."

They walked on in silence to the end of the block and paused beneath the streetlight.

"Do you want to go back?" he asked. "I know you don't want to miss that call."

She looked up at him. "Well, I did want a chance to ask what you thought of the service."

He focused on something in the distance and nodded. "It was different. Powerful."

"Yes. Compelling, almost."

Their gazes locked.

"I felt small," she whispered. "Like God is much bigger than I ever knew."

"Yes. And more awful and glorious and majestic."

His words suited her own nebulous impressions. "It made me want to study the Bible."

"Me too." They began to walk back toward her house.

"I guess tomorrow after work that I'll go to the bookstore and get one," Lisa said.

"You'll have something to discuss with Marie."

She smiled at that. "It's hard to believe they're actually going to bring her home. Do you truly believe everything will turn out all right?"

"We could pray. That minister said God is right there. I mean, right here. With us."

She inhaled the moist, chilly air. "That's what Immanuel means. God with us. I like that."

"Yeah." He tucked her hand into the crook of his arm, covering it with his warm palm. "I don't think I ever thought of God as a person before. Just an idea."

"Well, there's Jesus."

"Yes." He strolled on with her, his face thoughtful. "I just didn't get it."

"But you do now?"

"Not completely, but today was a start, I think."

"You want to go back to that church?" She was almost afraid to ask, but an eager hope had kindled in her heart.

"I do. Do you?"

She pressed her lips together and raised her eyes to meet his. "I decided when we left the church today that I would whether you wanted to or not. I think Marie is right, and it's important. I want to quit missing out on something that critical."

He stopped and drew her into his arms. Lisa looked up into his dark eyes that reflected a speck of light from the nearest house's porch lamp. He bent toward her.

The realization shocked her. André Belanger was going to kiss her. She'd only been kissed once, by Sid Wyman, an introverted boy from her shop class. She'd worked up the nerve to ask him to the prom seven years ago to avoid the humiliation of having no date, as usual. By then all the cute boys were committed, and of course none of them had asked her. She couldn't remember who André took that night. While he was fairly popular, he wasn't on the A list of hot boys. And when Sid Wyman took her home, he'd kissed her on the front porch. It was awful, like kissing an uncooked fish stick. She'd told herself then that kissing wasn't all it was cracked up to be, and she didn't care if no one ever kissed her again. She'd believed that lie all of a week.

She inhaled suddenly, just before André's lips met hers, and he froze. His eyebrows rose, and he drew back a little.

"Should I apologize?" he asked.

Lisa gulped. "For what? You didn't do anything."

He opened his mouth and then closed it. He stood poised, his arms halfway around her, frowning.

"What?" she asked.

"I'm trying to decide what's the best course of action right now. It seems to me that what you said is kind of like that sign on the picket fence in front of the historical society. You know?"

"Uh-uh."

"It says, *Stop before hitting the fence.* Every time I see it, I wonder how many drivers have stopped their cars and then floored the gas pedal and hit the fence."

She stared up at him, wanting to laugh but afraid he wasn't amused. "And?"

"And I think I was about to hit the fence. Should I back up or…?"

Lisa thought she would explode if he didn't stop talking. She didn't mean to let it, but her pent-up tension escaped with her breath in a tiny sob.

He blinked. "I'm sorry. I didn't mean to—"

"Hit the fence, André."

"Huh?"

"Hit the fence."

"Oh."

He kissed her then, eradicating all associations in her mind between fish sticks and kisses. In fact, if the dowagers of the historical society had been present, Lisa figured they would have been outraged at the blatant demolition of their pristine picket fence.

When he at last released her, she refused to let go of him but embraced him fiercely, burrowing her face into his denim jacket just below his collarbone. He held her for a long time, until someone came out of the house across the street and started a car engine.

"I guess we'd better get back." He lifted his chin and looked around. "Are we almost to your house?"

She straightened and ran a hand through her hair, wondering how much he had disarranged it with his ardent caresses. "We passed it two blocks back."

FORTY-FIVE

Marie plodded on, her head down against the gentle rain.

Could be worse. It could be pouring rain and lightning.

She'd run away from the lights and cars, afraid to be seen. A side street had taken her to a less traveled road leading out of town. She clung to her soggy leather bag. It would probably be ruined. She just hoped her passport and the other things inside weren't getting wet. She stuffed it under her arm and trudged on beside the pavement.

This is stupid. I should go back.

But she couldn't make herself turn around.

Pierre might be there now, the logical side of her brain said.

I could get us both killed, the other retorted. She kept walking.

Her shadow sprang long before her, and she knew a car was approaching behind her. She scurried off the roadway and behind a tree, hoping the headlights had not silhouetted her clearly.

This was too much like when she'd fled Jud Vanderhof.

I won't think about that!

Her head ached, and the memory of Jud sent a shiver down her spine. Or maybe it was the chill of her wet clothes and the shock of seeing the men she'd thought she'd eluded. She dashed away a tear and sobbed out a laugh. Why bother to wipe away her tears? It was easier to ignore them and let them mingle with the rain.

The car had passed. She stepped out onto the verge of the highway once more. As she walked, she deliberately turned her thoughts away from the men who kicked in the motel room door and were most likely cohorts of the woman who killed Jenna. Instead, she thought of home and her parents. Lisa would be with them. What were they doing tonight? Watching TV together? Eating popcorn?

They're probably sitting around fretting over me!

And with good reason. She had a multicultural mob chasing her. The Chinese men and the Caucasian who had stalked her since San Francisco intruded once more on the mental images cycling through her brain. They must have something to do with Jenna's time in Japan, Marie decided. Which might very well mean there was a connection between Jenna's murder and Commander Tarrington's military duties. Which meant the secret missions Pierre went off on might also be linked to this whole mess. He'd never told her where they went on those trips, but she'd always suspected China or North Korea. Which meant...

Again she harnessed her uncooperative thoughts. There was nothing she could do about whatever international intrigue Jenna and her husband had gotten into. But what did it all mean to her and Pierre?

Pierre. She would think about him. She imagined his handsome face and the sweet, contented expression he wore when they were at home together in their little apartment in Yokosuka.

Dear God, please help me. Let him find me soon! Keep me safe. I don't want to die, Lord. Show me how to get away from the men who are chasing me. I don't feel smart enough to outwit anyone! Even if I weren't so tired and my head didn't hurt, I'm not a genius. I'm just an ordinary person. Help me!

Of course, God knew that already. It came to her that the Creator knew exactly what she was made of. He had put her together Himself.

Thank You, she prayed. *Give me courage...and wisdom. Make me invisible when they come near. I know You can do that. And please, please help Pierre to find me.*

In the distance the glare from a streetlight shimmered on the wet pavement. As she approached it, she made out a road sign. She realized she must be close to a highway, maybe the one she'd left when she ran from Jud.

I should hitch a ride.

Again the memory of Jud chilled her more than the clammy night air. But there were also people like Buzz, and even Trixie and Harold.

I'm going to head east, Lord. Show me what to do.

FORTY-SIX

2100 Sunday, Cafford, Ohio

"I don't know this person." The young woman behind the hotel desk threw her chin up and stared defiantly at Pierre.

"I think you do."

"I have never seen her before in my life."

"She's my wife. She phoned me and told me she'd checked in here. Room 16." Pierre leaned on the counter and stared back. "She was waiting for me to come get her, but the door to the room she rented is all smashed in. Now tell me what happened to her!"

"No! I don't know her."

Pierre felt George's strong hand come down on his shoulder, and he straightened. His own technique wasn't doing any good. Better let George try. He stepped away and shoved his hands into his pockets, staring at the rack of tourist brochures on the wall.

George spoke gently, and Pierre knew without looking that he was smiling at the clerk.

"Look, Angela, we don't want to cause you any more trouble. I get the feeling you've had enough of that tonight."

The clerk was silent, and Pierre shot her a glance. She was eyeing George with frightened brown eyes.

George went on, "Mrs. Belanger is very dear to her husband, and they are good friends of mine. We only want to help Mrs. Belanger and take her to safety."

Angela's upper lip quivered. "Please, *señor.* Do not ask me."

"Why not?"

She blinked at tears filling her eyes. Pierre almost stepped forward. He was eager to press her for the information he was certain she had. But George's relaxed, easy manner was eroding her terror. He waited.

"My father…" Pierre could barely hear her whisper, but George picked up on it immediately.

"Your father? What about him? Angela, is your father angry?"

She shook her head. "No, no. He is… They hurt him."

Pierre's stomach clenched. It was all he could do to keep quiet and let George continue his "good cop" routine.

"Who hurt him?"

"Some men. They came here and they hurt him. How do I know you aren't like them?"

George kept his voice low and fluid. "Angela, we won't hurt anyone. I'm speaking the truth. We're here to help Marie Belanger. Is there anything we can do for you and your father?"

"No, nothing."

"Did you call the police?"

She shook her head.

"Why not?"

"I was afraid."

"Some men came here and intimidated you and hurt your father, and you were too scared to call the authorities?" There was no recrimination in George's tone, only sympathy.

Angela nodded. "I thought…I think…they are authorities."

George cocked his head to one side. "It was policemen who came here?"

She shrugged. "I don't think police. Immigration, maybe. There was a Japanese man with a scar on his face—"

"Japanese?" Pierre couldn't keep out of it then. "What happened to my wife? Tell me now!"

Angela gasped and backed up a step.

"How do I know you are really her husband? She told me two men are coming, and both…" She paused and looked them over carefully, first Pierre and then George. She nodded. "I guess you are them, but I'm so afraid. I don't want to do anything more that will harm her."

Pierre took out his wallet and opened it to the photo of Marie. He held it out, and Angela glanced at it, and then she reached out, drawing it closer.

"What did they do to Marie?" George asked softly.

Angela's eyes flared. "Nothing. She got away. I told her the men from immigration were here, and she ran. I thought she mustn't have a green card, and that is why they were after her."

Pierre's pulse hammered as he returned his wallet to his pocket. "Where did she go? We have to find her."

Angela spread her hands in helpless defeat. "Away. That is all I know. They broke the door on number 16, and when they saw she was not there, they hit my father. And then they left."

Pierre put both hands to his throbbing head. "We need to find her, George."

"I know, buddy."

"What do you suggest?"

George winced and wagged his head sideways. "She knows we were on the way here. If she hid from those men, chances are she'll come back here and wait for us, once she knows the coast is clear."

"Maybe we should walk around the neighborhood and look for her. She was on foot, right?" Pierre whirled to stare at Angela again, and she cringed.

"Yes. On foot. I'm sorry I could not help her more. I did all I could."

George leaned on the counter again, lacing his fingers together. "Is your father going to be all right? Does he need to see a doctor?"

Her lips twitched, and she swallowed hard. "He is resting. He won't go to the doctor. It is too expensive."

George said nothing for a moment, and then he looked at Pierre.

"I think we should take a room. We have no idea what direction to start looking in, so we might as well stay here and get some rest. If Marie comes back, we'll be here. If she calls you from a new location, we'll head out and pick her up."

Pierre nodded. He didn't like the plan. It was too stagnant, too uncertain. But he couldn't think of a better one.

"Do you have a room we could rent?" George took out his wallet. "Preferably near the one Mrs. Belanger had."

Angela eyed him cautiously. "Number 18 is vacant. But we cannot afford more damage."

"Will your insurance pay for what those men did?"

"I don't know."

He nodded. "Well, I promise you, Lieutenant Belanger and I are law-abiding people, and we won't be doing any damage to your property. Here's my credit card. And if Mrs. Belanger contacts you, tell her that her husband is in room 18. Let her call us on the phone and speak to him so that she knows it's really us."

Angela nodded slowly. "*Sí.* I will do it."

In the spartan but clean room Pierre tossed his duffel bag on one of the beds and headed for the shower. The rigors of the trip were catching up with him, and the warm water lulled him. He knew he would sleep, even though Marie's life was at stake. It seemed disloyal. He ought to be too wound up to sleep. But he'd seen men sleep standing up, leaning against the gunwale of a boat, when exhaustion overcame them. It wouldn't help Marie to allow himself to reach that point. George was right about that. Better to rest while they waited and hoard their strength for the future. The moment would come. He had to go on believing it would. Marie would contact them again, and she would need them.

When he came out into the chamber again, drying his hair with a towel, George was sitting on the second bed, talking on the phone.

"All right, sweetheart. We'll keep you posted." George hung up and turned to look at Pierre.

"How's Rachel?" Pierre asked.

"Good. She's at the Marine Mammal Center, but I caught her on a break. She's doing some training with the sea lions today. And speaking of family, you probably ought to call yours."

Pierre nodded. "I hate to. Did you let McCutcheon know?"

"Yeah. He and Heinz located the mall Marie went to Friday night on the southern edge of Detroit. They got quite a story from the security guards. Apparently Marie was attacked right there in the food court. She was trying to use a pay phone, and a man pulled a gun on her."

Pierre dropped his towel and reached for his pants.

"What are you doing?" George asked.

"I can't stay here. She's running for her life, George."

"Sit. That was forty-eight hours ago, and we know she was here today. There's nothing we can do right now. We need to stay where she can find us."

Pierre hesitated and realized George was right. He dropped his slacks back on the luggage rack with a sigh and sat down on the bed.

"All right, what happened? How did she get away from the mall and come here?"

George shook his head, frowning. "McCutcheon says an Asian man grabbed Marie and waved a gun at her. Several civilians came to her defense. They detained the man who attacked her and knocked the gun out of his hand. But before the guards could get there, two more men with weapons came on the scene. Marie ran out the side exit, and the civilians blocked the men from following her. By then several guards arrived, and all the pursuers vamoosed. One of them managed to snag Marie's suitcase."

"Must have been her black carry-on." Pierre tried to make sense of that.

"The police have several witnesses who say Marie ran outside into the parking lot, but they couldn't trace her from there. They have some poor quality security tapes that may help them identify the men who attacked her, but they have no idea what happened to

Marie between the time she left the mall and the time she showed up here."

"But when the FBI talked to them, they already knew she was here in Cafford. I told McCutcheon and Heinz at the airport, right after Marie called me."

"Right. But they were hoping to get a line on those men. Who are they? Why are they chasing her? McCutcheon said maybe they just wanted the suitcase, and they've got what they want now. But I told him how they followed Marie here, so that kills his theory about the suitcase." George leaned back on his pillows. "Seems the mall was a dead end."

"Not quite. We know at least one of them is Asian."

"Yeah, and Angela, the desk clerk here, said one of the men who came and asked for Marie was Japanese."

"Japanese, Chinese. She probably doesn't know the difference." Pierre gritted his teeth. "This isn't good, George."

"I know."

"We ought to be able to do something."

"We can't. Not yet."

Pierre sighed and stretched out on his bed. "Anything else?"

"Yes. They found a wig on the floor, and one witness said Marie was wearing it, but she dropped it when the gunman grabbed her."

"A wig?" Pierre sat up again. "Marie doesn't own a wig."

George shrugged. "Can't help it. That's what McCutcheon told me. It was a black wig with beads on it."

"Did you say beads?"

"Uh-huh. An ethnic wig, he said. Lot of little braids."

Pierre scowled at him. "That's crazy. Marie wouldn't wear something like that. Blonde, maybe."

"Marie as a blonde?" George's eyebrows drew down in concentration. "Nope. Can't picture it."

Pierre lifted his shoulders. George's calmness frustrated him. He'd always been this way. Cool as a Maine sea breeze when the pressure was on.

"Could be it belonged to someone else," George conceded. His eyelids drooped. "Things got wild when the guns came out. Maybe a woman in the eating area lost it when she tried to scramble under a table or something."

"So when will McCutcheon and Heinz get here?"

"Probably another couple hours. I told McCutcheon I'd hold a room for them. The CIA hasn't arrived yet. Heinz wants to bring in a couple more of his own team members too. If they need more space, they can take care of it. But I'd better go over to the office and tell Angela they need at least one room so she doesn't panic when they show up." George sat up and yawned.

"You could call."

"I think Angela will take the news better if I deliver it in person, with a smile."

Pierre nodded. "Okay. I'll call my folks." He looked at his cell phone, just to be sure it was on and no new messages had come in while he was in the shower. "You know, George, this really rots."

George paused with his hand on the doorknob and looked back at him. "It's going to get better, buddy. We're closer. A lot closer. Something will break soon."

"I hope you're right."

"If you're still awake when I come back, we'll pray about it."

Pierre nodded and scrolled through the phone numbers programmed into his cell phone. George left the room, and all was still as he pushed the button for André's number.

"Hello?"

"Hey, bro." Pierre took a deep breath.

"Hey! Have you got Marie?" André asked.

"No, not yet. We had a setback."

"What kind of setback?"

Pierre stared at the badly framed landscape print on the opposite wall and inhaled carefully, thinking. "Are you with the folks?"

"No. Lisa and I went for a walk, and we're just getting back to her house."

"Well, listen, this is kind of difficult to tell you. I hate to do it, but you've got to tell her folks too. We lost her again."

"What are you saying?" André's stark voice told Pierre that his brother felt his own despair.

"Someone got here before us, to the location where we were supposed to meet her."

"What? They kidnapped her?"

"No, I don't think so. The hotel clerk says Marie got away. But we don't know where she is. George thinks we should just wait here, in case she comes back or calls my cell phone. I suppose he's right, since we have no idea which way she headed, and we both need sleep."

It sounded sterile; uncaring. This was Marie he was talking about so coldly. He knew the task of analyzing every clue meant shelving his emotions for now, but his own helplessness slapped him like a wave of cold seawater. She was out there in the rain, alone, running, hiding.

"We were so close."

He realized he'd spoken aloud when André replied.

"I'm sorry."

He heard Lisa then, her voice tight and urgent, saying, "What? Tell me, André! What happened?"

Pierre pulled in a breath, past the painful mass of fear in his chest. "Look, don't tell her folks about the people chasing her."

"I have to, Pierre. I mean, what else can I say? You went to where she told you to go and she'd disappeared? They'll want to know why."

Pierre exhaled and stared down at his bare toes. *This is too hard, Lord,* he pleaded silently, and at once felt that he wasn't alone.

"Look, George and I are praying. Just tell everyone we're doing all we can, and we're ready to go to her as soon as we hear from her again. We have to trust God to keep her safe, and if anyone feels like praying along with us..."

"Lisa and I said a prayer for her when we went to church," André said.

Pierre found it impossible to speak. His sinuses filled and tears burned his eyes. It had been a long time since he'd cried, but he recognized the onset. "That's...that's great. Thanks. And tell the folks...I don't know. Just tell them I'm doing everything I can, and I believe God will work this out."

There was a moment's silence, and he heard Lisa's voice, low and soft, but he couldn't understand her words. Then his brother's voice came, gentle over the miles. "I'll tell them."

The door to the motel room opened and George came in, peeling off his dripping jacket.

"Hey, I'll call you if we hear anything," Pierre promised his brother, and closed the connection. He looked up at George and raised his eyebrows in question.

"Angela's holding a double room for them. I paid for it in advance. And she let me see her father."

"Is he okay?"

George frowned and sat down to remove his boots. "Hard to say. I get the feeling he wasn't in the best of health to begin with. They roughed him up pretty badly, though. I offered to drive him to the nearest hospital, but he refused."

Pierre shook his head and considered the events that had led them here. He focused on the blank television screen. "How did they get onto her before us? How did they find her again?"

George leaned back on his pillow, raising himself on one elbow so he could look over at Pierre. "Marie used her credit card when she paid for her room. Angela just told me."

Pierre swiveled to look at his friend. "You think they found her tonight because of that?"

"Maybe."

"But they'd have to have some kind of connection with the bank...or a law enforcement agency that could check on it."

George sighed and lay down. "There's something in what you just said. I'm not sure what. Let me sleep on it."

"She's out there on the street, George."

"I know."

Pierre imagined the woman he loved more than life slinking through back alleys in the rain, shivering and crying. *No, Marie isn't crying now. She's strong. God, protect her. Don't let her cry. Tell her I'm here, waiting for her.*

He looked over at George. "If she goes to another hotel and uses the credit card again, they'll find her again."

"Yes."

"What can we do?"

"Nothing."

"George, I'm going nuts."

"I know."

"Can we pray now?"

"Yeah."

"Hold on." Pierre reached for his pants once more.

"What now?" George asked.

"If she calls while we're praying, I want to be dressed and ready to go."

"I thought you agreed to try to sleep for a while."

"I can sleep in my clothes."

Pierre stood and pulled the slacks up around his waist and fastened his belt. "If the FBI or the local police come around here and show one of those fliers with Marie's face on it, Angela will freak. She'll think Marie is a murderer."

"Then we'll just have to tell her that it's not true. The police are looking for her, but not as a suspect."

"Are you sure?" Pierre caught his gaze and held it. "Maybe in San Francisco they do think Marie killed Jenna. And how do we know the FBI and NCIS don't think that?"

"Come on, buddy. Let's not get paranoid. They're helping us. And there's the stolen TSA uniform, don't forget. It corroborates what Marie told Rachel."

Pierre said slowly, "And Jenna took Marie's cell phone, probably while they were on the plane."

"Right. She called Chen Trading in San Francisco, and the FBI is digging into that company right now. They think someone in Chen Trading is a contact for the Red Chinese government. We need to work with any agency that will help us find Marie."

"But she's in danger. What happened here proves it. George, it's got to be thugs sent by the Chinese communist contingent chasing her."

George looked away and drew in a breath. "You're convinced."

"Aren't you? Look at the facts. Chris Tarrington had access to the complete blueprint for the coup they were planning. Lists of names. Leaders in all the rural districts. The plan for coordinating the uprising. Things were supposed to move forward this summer. I'm not talking theories here, George. It's been in the works for years, and it's going to happen."

George was silent for a moment, his mouth folded in a tight line. "Tell me you didn't have access to the same data."

"I didn't. I knew about it, but I couldn't get at it in a million years. I don't have that kind of clearance. But if Tarrington put that data in a portable form and gave it to Jenna..." Pierre walked to the window and slid his fingers between two slats on the blind so he could look out on the parking lot. Everything was quiet.

"I don't like to think that's what we're dealing with here," George said. "Espionage. Treason."

"It has to be." Pierre tried to come at it from another angle in his mind and couldn't. "I'm telling you, Tarrington struck a deal with them, and Jenna was the courier. They want the data she was supposed to give them. But for some reason, Jenna didn't hand it over like she was supposed to. I'm guessing her husband put her up to carrying it, but she didn't want to be part of it. So she refused to give it to them. They killed her, and now they think Marie has the data."

George eyed him carefully. "What do you think? Has Marie got it?"

Pierre stared into his friend's gray eyes. A sick feeling clutched at his stomach. "I think we have to find her before the communists do."

FORTY-SEVEN

Marie had no idea where her meandering had taken her. She had left her pursuers behind. That was all that mattered. Out of sheer necessity she had overcome her terror and hitchhiked several short rides, and she staggered into a service station while her current driver gassed up his car. Five a.m. The smell of gourmet coffee lured her to the front of the little store, and she chose a large thermal cup. Vanilla bean. Her stomach growled as she watched the dark liquid swirl into the container, and she knew she needed some solid food too.

She approached the counter with her coffee, a bag of potato chips, and a packaged cinnamon bun.

"Where are we?" she asked as the man behind the counter rang up her purchases.

"We are just outside of Akron, Ohio," he replied, holding out her change.

Marie held her palm up, and he let the coins trickle into her hand.

"Is there an airport there?" she asked. "I mean a commercial airport."

"Akron-Canton. It's about an hour from here. You'd need to go down Route 77."

"Thanks. Oh, and is there a pay phone here?"

"Outside, around to the right."

She gathered her things and went out. The rain had stopped just before sunrise, and everything smelled a little dank, with a petroleum overtone.

She found the wall-mounted telephone and set her coffee on the ledge beneath the phone box, holding her purse and bag of snacks under one arm while she dialed Pierre's number.

The relay kicked immediately to his voice mail. She stamped her foot. How could he not have his phone on? Maybe he was talking to someone else. She left a quick message and hung up. Her driver was coming out of the store.

"Hey! You coming with me?"

She hesitated. The man she'd been riding with would keep going east. Maybe she should stay with him. She didn't like him much, but as long as he behaved himself that didn't matter. She sent up a quick prayer and shook her head.

"Thanks, but I'm heading…a different way."

He waved and headed for his car without another word.

Marie considered her options and dialed zero, then her sister's phone number.

FORTY-EIGHT

0515 Monday, Cafford, Ohio

George awoke to the soft but insistent ringing of his cell phone. He rolled over and groped for it in the magenta light of the digital clock.

"Hudson."

"Commander! I'm sorry to call you this early, but I had to. This is André Belanger."

George sat bolt upright and swung his legs over the edge of the bed.

"You've got something?"

In the other bed, Pierre snorted and rolled over.

"Marie called her sister," André said. "I guess she tried Pierre's phone and couldn't get him."

"And?"

"She told Lisa to call you if she couldn't get Pierre, but Lisa—oh, that doesn't matter. What matters is, Marie is heading for Akron, Ohio."

"Akron," George said. "Wait, let me write this down."

He snapped on the lamp, and Pierre sat up and blinked at him.

"Go ahead, André. How is she traveling?"

"I'm not sure, but she says she's going to the airport there, and she'll fly home if she can."

George barely made sense of his words as Pierre scrambled across his bed, tossing the coverlet and sheet aside.

"That's André? What happened?"

George slashed the air with one hand to quiet him. "Akron. Good. We can deal with this."

"You sure?" André asked.

"Yeah, we'll hit the road now. We've got an NCIS agent here, and an FBI man. They're bringing in more people. Maybe they can contact the airlines and see if she's booked a ticket. But if she calls again, tell her to stay there, and we'll pick her up."

"I'll do that, sir."

George hung up and looked at Pierre, who loomed over him.

"Why didn't she call me?" Pierre rubbed his stubbly chin.

"Your brother said she tried."

Pierre dashed around the beds and grabbed his cell phone from the other nightstand. He groaned.

"I shut it off when I went to charge it. How could I do that?"

George stood and reached for his shirt and pants. "Check your messages. She probably left one."

Pierre punched the keys, glaring at the phone. George tugged on his clothes as Pierre listened with arched eyebrows. He moaned. "*Chérie!* No, no, don't do that."

"What?"

"She's going to hitch a ride to an airport and try to fly home."

"Right. Tell me exactly what she said."

"Here." Pierre pushed a button on the phone and handed it to George. He put it to his ear and immediately heard Marie's youthful voice, low and urgent.

"*Mon chéri,* I'm sorry. I couldn't stay there. Those men came and broke the door down. It was the same men who followed me from San Francisco. I had to move fast, so I hitched another ride. Honey, if you get this, don't worry. I'm way over near Akron now. I'm going to try to get to the Akron-Canton airport and buy a ticket to Maine, okay? I guess I'll try to call home, but if you don't hear from me again soon, just assume I'm trying to fly home from Akron. I love you."

George saved the message and hit the "off" button. "I wish I had a laptop." He opened his duffel bag and pulled out the road atlas he'd bought when they rented the car in Detroit. "Akron...Canton..."

"She's going to use her credit card again," Pierre said. "They'll get to her before we can get there."

George frowned, tracing a line on the map with his finger. "She must be going down 77. She said she's near Akron, but the airport is between there and Canton. She's probably hitching with truckers. Maybe we could put out a bulletin via CB radio."

"No!"

"Why not?"

"Don't forget those killers are out there. They might have a CB."

George let go of the idea with reluctance. "I suppose you're right. Let's ask McCutcheon what he thinks."

"Look," Pierre said, "Marie didn't have a ride when she left that message. She said she'd try to get one. I'm afraid if we try to locate her through the trucking network, we'll waste a lot of time and put her and whoever she rides with in danger."

"Well, you're right about one thing: The men stalking Marie have access to a lot of information. Whether they found her here through tracing the credit card or the phone call or some other means, I don't know. But they beat us to her."

"Exactly." Pierre reached for his boots. "We've got to be careful, George."

"Well, we have to tell McCutcheon and Heinz we're leaving. We can't just take off at five a.m. and not tell them."

"You want to wake them up? Fine. You call their room." Pierre stomped his foot into the boot and tied it. "McCutcheon will probably want to hold another press conference and tell the world once again that they're looking for my wife in connection with a murder."

"It's not that bad, Pierre."

"Yes, it is! People think Marie is an assassin. She doesn't dare ask anyone for help. But don't you let him and Heinz mess with truck-speak or credit card companies. I don't want to give our adversaries

any more help. Me, I'm grabbing my stuff and heading for Akron."
He threw his razor into his duffel bag. "You coming?"

"Hold on, *mon ami*. I have the car keys."

Pierre scowled at him, and George laughed, tossing him the key
ring. "Here. You drive. Just give me a sec to call McCutcheon. He's
not going to like being awakened after four hours of sleep."

"So let him snooze. We can call him when we've got Marie."

"No, we promised we'd tell them the minute we heard anything.
I'll meet you in the car."

Pierre pocketed his cell phone and went out, slamming the
door.

FORTY-NINE

0700 Monday, Ohio

George clicked "off" on his cell phone for the fifth time in half an hour and sighed. "I never use all my minutes, but this month I might come close."

"Use mine," Pierre offered, keeping one hand on the steering wheel as he fished in his shirt pocket for his phone.

"It's okay. I may be done for now. Heinz put one of his NCIS people on talking to all the airlines that fly out of Akron-Canton, and no one will confirm that Marie bought a ticket. And no one seems to fly directly from Akron to Maine."

"But they checked on connecting flights to Portland and Bangor?"

"Yes, but they don't think she's booked yet. She might not even be at the airport. It's only been two hours since she left the message on your phone."

"I suppose it could be taking longer than she thought to get there."

"I advised them to ask about tickets to Manchester, New Hampshire, like you said. So far, nothing."

George studied his friend's profile. The stress was beginning to show. Pierre's youthful face was creased with fine lines between his brows and at the corners of his eyes. The beard stubble gave him a wild, volatile air. Usually Pierre looked on the bright side of events, but not now. George hadn't seen that hollow look in Pierre's eyes since their bleakest days on Frasier Island.

"Maybe I should ask my brother to go to Bangor in case she shows up there."

"How far a drive is that for him?"

"An hour." Pierre reached up and adjusted the sun visor. "He probably has to work today, though."

"We don't want to send him up there and find out she's flying into Portland, anyway. That's the other direction, right?"

"Right. But my folks would probably go. Dad could have someone cover for him, and Maman would go at the drop of a hat. I'll bet Lisa could go too. I think her schedule is flexible, and she'd do anything for Marie. They're close."

"But until Marie books a flight, we don't know which way to jump."

"Maybe that's good," Pierre said. "If we have no idea where she is, neither will they."

George said nothing. He knew who "they" were. He wondered if Marie was deliberately not contacting them to avoid leading her enemies to her. They drove for several minutes in silence. He turned over in his mind all the information he'd gathered over the last four days. Marie…Jenna Tarrington…the men who had beaten the motel owner…the sketchy outline Pierre had given him about the operation he'd worked on. China. The thought of the giant nation fragmenting scared the daylights out of George. It could mean chaos in Eastern Asia for years. Political and financial anarchy. A crumbling infrastructure. Possibly a global war, if support of the movement was traced back to America.

He wondered exactly what part the United States would play in the upheaval. Bankrolling it, perhaps? Supplying weapons? Intelligence? What if the plan backfired, and the Chinese people suffered more than they gained? And would America be able to let the people rule themselves if they broke free from the bonds of communism? *Lord, I know You're in control of this, and every aspect of the operation*

is in Your hands, from the highest official to the poorest peasant. Give us
wisdom. I'll trust You to work this out the way You want it to go.

He focused on the highway signs they whipped past. "What do
you say we stop for breakfast?"

"Nah, we've got to find her before something else happens." Pierre
glanced over at George. "Unless you're starving."

"I'm a little hungry, but I can wait. You're right. If we push on
through to the airport, we can grab something there."

Pierre puffed out his cheeks and blew his breath out, staring
down the highway.

"She'll call us again," George said.

"I hope so."

George sensed the young lieutenant was near snapping.

"Hey, chin up. She called Lisa just a couple of hours ago, and she
was healthy and confident."

"Thank you, *mon ami*. I'll keep remembering that."

"And if it will make you feel better, I'll call your brother and ask
him if someone from the family can cover the Bangor airport."

"Let's pray again." Pierre glanced over at him. "I mean, you pray.
Would you? I'll keep driving."

"Sure. But, you know, you can pray while you drive. Just keep
your eyes open."

Pierre cracked a smile at that.

FIFTY

Marie's feet dragged as she walked along the sidewalk. Her last ride had let her out at a highway exit marked "Airport," and she'd headed out full of hope. It couldn't be far now, but her fatigue held her back. She needed rest and a meal.

Ahead she spotted a service station and approached it slowly. She was so weary, she told herself she didn't care what happened now. But as she studied the sign—Randall's Auto Body, Specialty Foreign Cars—she knew she did care. More than anything she wanted to be with Pierre.

There were no gas pumps, and disappointment brought tears to her eyes. Likely they didn't have a pay phone. One of the big garage doors was open, and a metallic clanking noise emanated from inside the building.

She walked to the open bay and peered in. A small green car was perched on ramps a foot off the floor. As her eyes adjusted, Marie realized that beneath it a man stood in a pit in the floor, working on the underside of the car.

"Excuse me."

He looked toward her, and then he shaded his eyes and looked again.

"Help you?"

She stooped down so he could see her better. "Do you have a pay phone?"

"Nope."

"Thanks."

She couldn't keep her shoulders from drooping as she turned toward the street.

"You can use the phone in the office," he called.

Marie pivoted toward him. "Are you sure?"

"It's an unlimited calling plan. Help yourself." He flipped his wrench toward a door inside the building.

She smiled at him and stepped inside, out of the sun. She could see his gray-speckled hair and callused hands plainly now. His coveralls were stained, and a smudge of grease darkened his cheek.

"Thank you."

He nodded. "I'm all alone today, or I'd come show you. I usually have an apprentice mechanic helping me, but he had to be in court this morning. It's right in there on the desk. Make yourself at home."

"That's great of you. Oh, what street are we on? I'm going to have someone come pick me up."

He told her, and she went into the tiny office. The grease-smeared telephone peeked out from beneath a muddle of papers. She sat gingerly in his ragged swivel chair and placed the call.

It rang four times before she heard Pierre's voice, cautious but hopeful.

"Allo."

"Pierre."

"Ma chérie!" His exuberance revived her, and she straightened.

"I'm almost to the airport. It took a while to get rides after I called Lisa, but now I'm nearly there."

"Hold on. I've got to pull over. I can't do this and drive."

A moment later a soothing, deep voice said, "Marie, it's George. I'm just holding the phone while Pierre stops the car. We're going to switch drivers."

"George, tell me what to do. I'm exhausted and I'm scared."

"I'm so sorry. Are you at the airport now?"

"No, not yet. I'm close, though. Someone told me it's about half a mile. I'm on foot."

"We're on the way. Keep praying, and I'm sure we'll be with you soon. Here's Pierre. Just tell him how we can find you."

A few seconds later, Pierre came on again.

"Baby, don't take the plane."

"What?"

"My love, we're close to you. We left the minute André called."

"André? I called Lisa."

"Those two are as thick as Mémé's beef stew now."

She chuckled. "Lisa and André? How did that happen? I didn't think either of them knew the other existed."

"Oh, they knew. They just didn't care until you disappeared. Right now they're playing Poirot and Hastings, trying to help us bring you in safe. We'll see if the attraction lasts when I take you home and things settle down."

"That's sweet. I'm glad you told me."

"Something good came out of all this, I guess. Marie, I miss you so much. Remember what we talked about that last night we were together?"

She felt the blood rush to her cheeks. *"Oui. Je me souviens."* Of course she remembered. She would never forget. They'd whispered late into the night about their future family. Pierre had insisted they wait until he was transferred back to the States before they started a family, but the longing for a child never completely left Marie's consciousness.

"Well, that time is coming soon," he assured her. "I'm officially transferred. Captain Wheeler is fixing it. I'm done in Yokosuka, *chérie.* When we pick you up, we head home, and I don't have to leave for a month."

She couldn't say anything, but she brushed at the tear running down her cheek and smeared it.

"We'll be there soon," he said, and she wanted to believe it.

"I…" She looked over her shoulder, into the mechanic's shop. For the past two minutes she'd forgotten how close she'd come to death, and that danger still followed wherever she went. *"Mon chéri,*

I'm afraid to sit still for long. They always find me. And I used my credit card at the motel—"

"Don't use it again."

"I'm sorry. That was a mistake, wasn't it? I hope Angela and her father are all right."

Pierre said nothing for a moment.

"There are okay, aren't they?" she asked.

"Yeah, they'll be fine. Now, just sit down and wait for us."

"But every time I do that, those men find me."

"You think they know where you are now?"

"I don't know."

"Tell me where you are."

"At a mechanic shop." She gave him the address. "Are you and George on 77 South?"

"Not yet. We're on Route 80."

"Well, take 77. Exit 113. It's not far once you get off. It's Randall's Auto Body Shop. On the left."

"*Bien.* You sit tight, *chérie.* You hear me?"

"Yes. Can I get something to eat?"

Pierre chuckled. "Sounds like you're as hungry as George. Find something close by, but be careful and stay near the body shop. We'll be there in ninety minutes, tops."

"But what if—"

"No, *chérie.* No what-ifs. We'll be there."

"But the men. What if they come here?"

There was a dreadful pause. She hoped he would tell her that her pursuers had been caught and could not chase her anymore. But he didn't. She heard voices murmuring and supposed George was giving his opinion.

"George says to set a rendezvous point," Pierre said.

"Besides here, you mean?"

"Yes, an emergency plan. Whatever happens, don't go to the airport. They'll expect you to go there."

"Where, then?"

"Hold on. I'm looking at the map."

She waited, watching the street through a dirty window.

"All right," Pierre said. "There's a street off of the one you're on, back almost to the highway. It goes east to a little town called Greenwood. If those people come to the repair shop and you feel threatened, you go there."

"Greenwood?"

"Yes. It's not very big, and it's near a state park. If you think they're on to you, go to the post office in Greenwood. We'll find you there. You got it?"

"Yes."

"Good," he said. "Watch for our car. It's a red Toyota Corolla. But try not to show yourself too much. The FBI agent is holding another press conference this morning. Your face is all over the TV news, *chérie*."

"I'm scared."

"It'll be okay. We've got the FBI and the NCIS. They're helping us, although right now they're a ways behind us. We told the NCIS team to go straight to the airport, so they'll be in the area very soon if we need backup. I expect we'll see you shortly, right where you are now."

"Je t'aime," Marie whispered and hung up. She tried not to let the what-ifs creep into her mind. She went out of the office. The man had left the pit and was working at a bench at the back of the garage.

"Did you get through?" he asked.

"Yes, thank you. My husband is picking me up here in an hour or so, if you don't mind."

"Fine by me."

She went outside and stood in the paved area in front of the building, surveying the block. Not far down the street, on the other side, a tall sign for a strip mall rose above the sidewalk. She hurried toward it. At a convenience store, she bought a bottle of apple juice and a packet of protein bars.

Outside again, she unwrapped a bar and wolfed it, alternating bites with swallows of juice. She opened another bar and ate it more slowly, savoring its sweetness. A few steps away was a trash can, and she ambled toward it as she ate and read the signs of the other shops.

It was still early, and most of them were closed, but a woman approached one of the small businesses and unlocked its door. Marie looked up at the sign and smiled. Wendy's Closet—Gently Used Apparel.

The owner was friendly and talkative. She pointed out the new hosiery and lingerie she sold, along with the used clothing on consignment. Marie threw away her inhibitions and went for an entire new outfit. White pants, a plaid blouse, underwear, a floppy sun hat, and a tote bag to carry her soiled clothing in. She almost picked up an adorable pair of natural leather sandals, but decided she'd better not. Though she didn't want to think so, she might have to hike again, and her sneakers would serve her better. The proprietor let her pay for her choices and then change in the fitting room.

Marie studied herself in the mirror. It wasn't her usual style—a little housewifeish, but that was probably good. If her adversaries showed up, they wouldn't be looking for this image. She might regret the white pants. If only she could bathe! *Ah, well, you can't have everything. Thank You, Lord, for what I'm getting.*

She walked out into the sun and headed back toward Randall's with a spring in her step. Pierre was on his way! She strode down the sidewalk on the side where the strip mall was situated. The thrift shop owner hadn't charged a lot for her clothing, but her cash was getting low. But Pierre was coming. She wouldn't have to worry about that anymore.

When she was nearly even with the auto body shop, she paused. A belated warning flashed across her consciousness. It would be another half hour at least before George and Pierre arrived. Better look things over before she plunked herself down on the curb by Randall's. Now that she thought about it, this wasn't a very good meeting place. Too conspicuous.

She glanced back toward the strip mall. She could go back and hang out there a little while longer. Maybe one of the other shops would open. Or she could walk around the block. That might be best. She strolled on and turned at the next corner.

A new anxiety began to nibble at her serenity. She wanted to call Pierre again and see how close they were now. Maybe she could stay on the line with him until they arrived. The mechanic was friendly and generous. He would probably let her do that.

She turned and walked back toward Randall's. Opposite the building, she waited on the sidewalk for a break in traffic. Just as she was about to step into the street, a dark red sedan drove into the body shop's parking lot. Marie's pulse quickened. But it was too early. She hesitated, one foot on the sidewalk, the other down on the street.

A man got out of the passenger seat and walked toward the repair shop, looking around as he went. Marie gasped and turned away. It was the middle-aged Caucasian man with the homely face. He'd changed his clothes and now wore a blue polo shirt and tan slacks, but she'd know him anywhere.

She tried not to run. Her knees wanted to buckle, but she kept going. In her imagination, his gaze settled on her as she walked away. She didn't look to find out if he really saw her. She took the corner where she'd turned earlier, walking swiftly. Along the sidewalk, into the shade of another building. It must obscure her from his view now.

She ran.

At each cross street, she looked left and right. If the street led toward a built up area, she turned the opposite way. After ten minutes, she panted as she hitched along. Her side ached. This was wrong. She was supposed to follow the main street back toward the highway and go east. She tried to locate the mid-morning sun, but couldn't.

Houses loomed on either side of her. She was out of the business district. She cut across a small park and again chose the way that led toward the least populated vista. There were no sidewalks now. On one side of the road a brick wall stretched for a hundred yards. A private school or an opulent estate? She hurried on, through a wooded area to a road that could have been in Maine, except it was better maintained than New England country roads. Far ahead she saw a boy on a bicycle coming toward her.

Her heart pounded, and her head ached. She stopped and put both hands to her temples.

Should I hide, even from this boy? Please, dear God, give me a clear mind. I don't know what to do!

The boy's blond hair ruffled in the breeze as he pedaled. He couldn't be older then ten, and as he came closer, she studied his freckled face and knew she had nothing to fear from him.

"Hey," she called when he was only a few yards away. "That's a neat bike."

He slowed down and eyed her as he rolled nearer. Marie stepped aside so he wouldn't think she was forcing him to stop or swerve into the road.

"I don't suppose you'd sell it?" she asked as he passed her.

He braked and looked back at her over his shoulder.

FIFTY-ONE

0930 Monday, Akron, Ohio

"There! Randall's Auto Body." Pierre pointed, and George pulled in. One garage bay door was up, but Pierre couldn't see anyone working. He looked around the small parking area and up and down the street. No Marie. Just traffic and commercial buildings and fumes.

"Come on." He climbed out and made for the building. He was almost to the open door when a young man burst from it and stopped short, panting. Pierre stood his ground.

"Help me!" The kid's breath came rapidly.

Pierre's pulse picked up. "What's up?"

"Mr. Randall's hurt. It's bad."

"And who are you?"

"Ron Spelling. I work here part time."

George came up beside them. "Where is your boss?"

"In the pit."

They followed Ron into the garage and past a little green Fiat sitting on ramps. A droplight gleamed in a mechanic's pit under it. Pierre squinted down into the dim recess. He made out the body of a man in dirty coveralls sprawled facedown at the bottom.

"Here." The kid took them to the far end, where concrete steps led downward.

"I have some first aid training," George told Ron.

Pierre stood back and let him go down. Ron followed. George stooped and touched the prone man's shoulder. He moaned. Pierre descended two steps, but there wasn't really room for him at the bottom. George turned the injured man over. The lower part of his coveralls was stained dark.

"Sir, where are you hurt?"

"My leg. I think I've been shot."

George looked up at the young man. "Call an ambulance."

As the kid pushed past him, Pierre looked to George. "What do we do?"

George frowned. "He's bleeding a lot. Get me something to use for a pressure bandage."

Pierre went to the workbench at the back of the shop and looked around. Nothing clean here that would do. He spotted an open door to a small restroom and found a roll of paper towels above the sink. He grabbed the whole roll and went back to the edge of the pit and tossed it to George.

"Best I could do. Maybe the kid can find something better."

George tore off several sheets and wadded it into a ball. He pressed it against Randall's thigh, and the man gasped.

Pierre squatted at the top of the steps, his mind racing.

"George, if we're here when the cops arrive, they won't let us go for hours."

"I know. But if we walk out of here now, this man could bleed to death."

"Is he conscious?"

"In and out. He's lost a lot of blood."

"Ask him about Marie."

George hesitated, and then he leaned close to the man's face.

"Sir? Mr. Randall? Sir, can you tell me who did this?"

The man moaned again. Pierre couldn't stay still. He got up and went to the office door. Suppose the kid did it? He might have a gun. Pierre wished he had his service pistol, but he couldn't carry it on the plane. He'd left it in Japan to be shipped with his other gear.

Ron Spelling held a telephone receiver and twisted the cord around one hand. "Yes, okay. We're staying with him. I don't know what happened. I think he said someone shot him. But I had an appointment this morning, so I came in to work late. When I got here, he was just lying there bleeding."

Pierre stepped outside, listening for a siren.

"Pierre, *viens!*"

He rushed back inside and peered down at George.

"Mr. Randall talked to Marie," George said.

Pierre edged to the back of the pit and went down the steps. He looked up warily at the Fiat and squeezed in next to George.

"Here. Put pressure on the wound." George took Pierre's hand and placed it where his had been, on a saturated wad of towels. Then he ripped another section from the roll, folded it, and inserted it between Pierre's hand and the bloody mass. "See if he can tell you anything. I'll go topside and call McCutcheon. Maybe he can get his FBI team in here before the locals show." George slid past him and up the steps.

Pierre looked down at Randall. The man stared up at him.

"You spoke to my wife?" Pierre asked, bending down.

"Cute girl?" Randall gasped.

"The cutest."

"Dark hair? Big eyes? Plaid blouse?"

"That's her. I don't know about the blouse."

Randall panted. His eyes roved over the undercarriage of the Fiat, and then he focused again on Pierre's face. "She asked me...what the name of the street was."

"Yeah."

"Used the phone."

Pierre nodded. "She called me. Then what happened?"

"She left. But she said..." He moaned, lying back on the cold concrete.

Pierre waited, feeling guilty. A man in this condition shouldn't be bothered, but it might be his only chance to find out what Randall knew.

"Mr. Randall, when she called me, I told her to stay here until I came to pick her up."

He shrugged, and his face contorted in pain. "She went out. A while later, a man came in."

"How much later?"

Randall closed his eyes. His breathing was shallow, and Pierre wondered if he'd lost consciousness. "Half an hour, maybe. Big guy. Ugly as sin."

"Is he the one who shot you?"

"Yeah." He started to say something else, but winced and raised one arm, clenching his fist. Pierre pushed on the towels, wishing he could do more. Randall swore. "I'm gonna die, aren't I?"

"I don't know." Pierre swallowed hard. "I don't think so." The blood that soaked Randall's clothing and pooled on the concrete seemed excessive for a flesh wound. "You said you've been lying here a while. If the bullet hit your femoral artery, I don't think you would have made it this long."

Randall inhaled, squirming to shift his position, and then he lay still. "I thought no one would come, and I'd just bleed to death here by myself. Then Ronnie came in…" His voice grew faint. Pierre thought he heard a siren in the distance.

"Hold on, sir. Medical help is coming. They'll get you to a hospital."

Randall's eyelids quivered, and his lashes flicked upward. "She told me…you were coming to get her."

Pierre nodded. "That's right."

"I didn't know she was in trouble. That other guy…he was mean. I could see that. Asked if she was here."

"What did you tell him?"

"That I hadn't seen her."

"At all?"

"Yeah. Then he pulled a gun. I thought…"

The annoying siren grew louder and then stopped. George's voice came from above them. "EMTs are here, buddy. Just keep the pressure on until they get to you."

"Take it easy, Mr. Randall," Pierre said. "Help is coming."

"Thanks," the mechanic gasped. "I thought at first he was her husband. But if he was…" He closed his eyes and took several shallow breaths. "I didn't want him to find her."

"You did the right thing, sir. I don't know how to thank you. But I promise you, we'll find the man who did this to you."

"He told me…if I didn't give her up, he'd kill me."

"I'm sorry."

"Your friend…" Again he closed his eyes.

"Stay with me, Mr. Randall."

"He said…FBI…coming."

"That's right."

"Are you guys legit?"

"Yes."

A uniformed man came down the concrete steps carrying a case.

"You holding a pressure bandage?"

"Yes, sir," Pierre said. "Paper towels is all."

"Good. Just let my partner get down here and we'll relieve you."

A few minutes later, Pierre and George washed the blood from their hands in the restroom. When they emerged, the EMTs were lifting Randall out of the pit onto a stretcher. Ron Spelling stood by, wild-eyed.

"Is he going to be okay? I don't understand. Who would do this?"

"Take it easy, son," one of the EMTs said. "We'll get him to the hospital, and they'll take care of him."

Spelling's voice rose. "I shoulda been here!" He turned to George. "Oh, man, there's so much blood."

"The police and the FBI will be here soon."

"FBI?" Spelling's pupils grew large. "What for? I don't get it."

George drew him toward the office doorway. "Just stick around and tell them how it was when you found him. They'll want to know which hospital the EMTs are taking Mr. Randall to. Do you know how to contact his family?"

"Sure. His home number's inside."

"He's married?"

"Yeah."

"Give the number to the police so they can call Mrs. Randall."

"Who are you? Did you come to get your car fixed?"

"No. I'm Lieutenant Commander George Hudson. I've already called the FBI. Agent David McCutcheon will be here soon. He's investigating a case that involves a suspect in another shooting."

"I can't believe he was shot. I thought at first something fell on him."

"Well, the FBI's case may be connected to this incident. So you stick around and tell Agent McCutcheon everything you know."

"I will." Spelling's blue eyes jumped back and forth as he stared first at George and then at Pierre. "Mr. Randall will be okay, though, right?"

"I don't know," George said. "If he makes it, remember that you helped save his life."

"I didn't do anything." Spelling ran a hand through his unruly hair.

"You got us to help control the bleeding, and you called 911. That's good stuff."

The kid nodded, still staring. Pierre wondered how long it had been since he'd blinked.

"My partner and I need to leave now," George told him. "We're trying to catch up with the thugs who did this to your boss."

"Okay. But...why did they do it?"

George gritted his teeth. "I can't give you any more information about the case, Ron. We need to get going. Another person's life may depend on us catching up with the shooter soon."

Pierre took the cue and hurried to the rental car and started the engine. When George piled in, he turned the red Toyota around in the parking lot and drove past the ambulance, into the street. "Is it kosher for us to leave before the cops get here?"

"I'm sure it's not, but as you mentioned earlier, expedience sometimes overrides protocol."

"Greenwood?" Pierre asked.

"You got it. Quickly, but no speeding tickets."

Pierre headed back toward the highway. "Do you think they've found her?"

George sighed. "Well, something happened. Randall ticked them off but good."

"It sounded like he only saw one man. He told me the guy asked for her, and he said he hadn't seen her. You think they'd shoot him just for that?"

"If they knew he was lying, maybe."

"The phone call."

George shrugged. "We check the post office in Greenwood. That's all we can do."

"What if she's around here, hiding?"

"We both got out of the car, in plain view. She would have come out if she were close by."

Pierre swallowed the lump in his throat and watched for the side street that led to Greenwood. He spotted it and made the turn.

After a minute, George said, "I'm sorry. This is a blow."

"You have no idea."

"I think I do."

"The EMT said we could call the hospital later and ask about Randall."

George nodded. "I'm praying for him. He made a great sacrifice for Marie."

The lump got larger, and Pierre cleared his throat. "What if they knew about the alternate rendezvous and sent someone to Greenwood while the big guy was here?"

"I don't see how that would be possible. But…I don't see how any of this is possible."

Pierre drew in a slow, deep breath. He wanted to kick something. There must be some way to find Marie. But somehow the enemy managed to outrun them and outwit them time after time.

"Do you think they've bugged my phone?"

"Who?"

"You know who. Whoever's trying to kill Marie."

"No way."

"Come on, you've got to admit it's pretty creepy. Every time Marie communicates with us, the bad guys show up."

George sighed. "Maybe. But not your phone. I mean, when could they have done that?"

"I don't know. In Japan?"

George held out his hand, and Pierre plunked his cell phone into it. George took the cover off the battery compartment, removed the battery, and scrutinized it and the interior of the recess. "You got a screwdriver?"

"No." Pierre wished he had his knife, but he'd had to ship that too.

"They'd have to pry it apart. It doesn't look tampered with to me." George handed the phone back and took out his own, giving it the same inspection.

"Well, there's a leak somewhere."

"You're right." George held up his battery and turned it over.

Pierre blinked at him, at a loss for words. He had expected George to argue.

"So what do we do?"

George put his phone back together and placed it on the dashboard. "We keep moving."

"What if the police want to talk to us back there? Can they arrest us?"

"I'm hoping McCutcheon will cover for us."

George's cell phone trilled, and he answered it.

"Oh, hey. Just talking about you. Are you at the scene?"

Pierre glanced at him. George grimaced and went on talking.

"I know, I know. But Marie Belanger might be in the killer's hands. We had to leave. Otherwise we'd have been tied up in paperwork."

George held the small phone away from his ear. McCutcheon's incensed lecture was almost loud enough for Pierre to understand.

George cautiously put the phone to his ear again. "We're checking on the emergency rendezvous we set up with her. That's right. Our ETA is ten minutes. We'll brief you once we get there."

He slapped the phone back into the dip on the dashboard, and Pierre smiled for the first time all day.

"I'm glad I've got you at my side, George. Or should I say at my back?"

"You're just glad someone else is taking the heat for you. Old McCutcheon is not happy with us right now."

"Well, who cares about the FBI, anyhow?"

"True. But if they start complaining to the Pentagon…"

"Afraid you'll get in trouble again?"

George chuckled. "I've behaved myself for the last couple of years. Otherwise, they wouldn't have let me come."

"Oh, come on, you know you drive them crazy. Always a maverick but within regulations. The thing is, they know that when there's trouble, Hudson delivers."

"Ha! That's a good one."

"Sure. You tell everyone you're pushing paper in some cushy office in Pearl Harbor. I know you've been out on a bundle of classified ops."

"If you know so much, you know I can't tell you what I do when I'm on duty."

Pierre drove on in silence. He sent up a prayer of thanks for George Hudson. With anyone else, he'd have exploded into a million fragments by now. Somehow George held things together, just like in the old days.

They rolled into a small village, and Pierre looked around. New modular homes and older farmhouses. He found the post office without difficulty, threw the transmission into park, and jumped from the car.

George joined him, and they looked about at the placid neighborhood.

"What do you think?" Pierre asked.

"I hate to draw more attention to her, but I guess we'd better ask if anyone's seen her. You go inside."

Pierre hurried into the post office and got in line behind the two people standing before the counter. He grew impatient as the clerk searched for a particular commemorative stamp for one of the customers. He took out his wallet and glanced toward the door. He couldn't see the parking lot. Was George searching the area for Marie? More people entered and queued up behind him. At last he reached the head of the line.

"I'm looking for my wife. She was supposed to meet me here, and I wondered if you've seen her." He flipped his wallet open and showed the middle-aged postal clerk his photo of Marie.

The man peered at it through his glasses.

"Nope. Not today, anyhow. Lots of people come in, though."

Pierre sighed. "Okay. Thanks." He found George sitting on a bench outside.

"Anything?"

Pierre shook his head. "The postman hasn't seen her."

"Well, I've strolled back and forth out here, and she's not showing herself."

Pierre slumped down on the bench beside him. They didn't speak for a long time.

"What now?" Pierre asked at last.

George eyed him cautiously. "I think we need to eat."

"I can't."

"Eat anyway. You'll need your strength before the day is over."

"George, what if they got her? They'll kill her for that information. They've already killed Jenna Tarrington, and maybe Randall."

"Settle down. So far as we know, they left Randall's place empty-handed."

"Then where is she?" Pierre's lungs didn't want to take in air. "The odds are terrible."

George shook his head. "It seems that way, but remember, we can't see the whole picture."

Pierre's fingers shook. He flexed his hands and stretched them. "I'm really scared, George. I've never felt so helpless in my life."

George's hand came down firmly on his shoulder. "God is still in control of this. And He knows where Marie is right now."

Not so long ago Pierre would have rejected that, or perhaps accepted it as a general theological premise, not something that worked when the person you loved most was in mortal danger. But he'd embraced the truth of the Bible and the sovereignty of God at the bilingual church in Yokosuka. Along with Marie, he'd put his trust in Christ. And God's Word said God was in control. Always. Whether Marie was safe or in peril, whether she lived or died, God would keep her in His hand. Pierre took a deep breath. Did he still believe that?

Yes, Lord, I do. I'm sorry my faith is so weak.

"Could be she's still on her way here."

George nodded. "Could be. If she couldn't find a ride right away, we might have passed her."

"Let's pray."

They bowed their heads and prayed quietly on the bench. People went into the post office and came out carrying packages and mail. They sat in silence, watching the quiet street, and Pierre's heart ached. *Marie, ma chérie, where are you?*

Pierre's phone rang and he fumbled to get it out.

"Hello!"

"Lieutenant Belanger?"

"Yes." His heart sank at the male voice. George raised his eyebrows, and Pierre mouthed, "Heinz."

George nodded with a resigned twist to his mouth.

"What is your location now?" the NCIS special agent asked.

"We're in the town of Greenwood."

"What? I thought you were going to the Akron-Canton airport."

"We had a change of plans."

"I told them," George muttered.

"My team is on the way to the airport," Heinz said. "We expected to meet you there."

"I thought you were with McCutcheon."

"No, he stayed back at the motel, waiting for another agent to join him. They were going to drive to Akron together."

"Scratch the airport run," Pierre said. "She didn't go there."

"Are you sure?"

"Well…no. I mean, she was near there, but she had another scare. We're not sure where she is now. We had set up a second point to meet her in case something went wrong, but she's not here, either."

George's phone rang. "Hello, Agent McCutcheon."

Pierre barely registered that George was speaking to the FBI agent.

"So you designated a meeting place, but she wasn't there when you arrived?" Heinz asked.

"That's affirmative," Pierre told him.

"Do you have any leads now?"

"Not at this time."

"I'm sorry, Lieutenant." Heinz's voice was empathetic. "Maybe my NCIS team should continue to the airport and check to make sure she didn't revise her plans and book a flight after all."

That sounded as good as anything to Pierre. "We'll get back to you when we decide what to do," he said.

"Do that. And I have some news on this end that may interest you."

"Oh?"

"Yes. The NCIS agent now in charge in San Francisco tells me that Commander Tarrington cracked."

Pierre sucked in a breath. "You mean…"

"He's admitted giving his wife a computer thumb drive containing classified information. She was to pass it to a contact in the States."

"I had a feeling. Thanks. Anything else?"

"No, that's all I have so far."

Pierre hung up. George was still on the phone with McCutcheon. A uniformed woman came out of the post office and approached the bench.

"Excuse me, are you the gentleman who showed a photo and said he was looking for his wife?"

Pierre stood up.

"Yes, ma'am."

"Well, Ralph just told me. I was out on my break, but I got back a minute ago. I came in the back door."

"Can you tell me anything?" Pierre asked.

"Well, yes. A man came in an hour or so ago and asked for a woman named Marie. He had a picture."

Pierre's pulse hammered. He took out his wallet. George ended his phone conversation.

"Was it a picture of this woman?" Pierre held up the photo in his wallet.

The postal worker took the wallet and looked hard at the picture. "It might have been. It was a different picture, though. Still, it must have been her. I mean, this doesn't happen every day."

Pierre looked at George.

"What did you tell him?" George asked.

"That I hadn't seen her. Because I hadn't. But I thought you'd want to know someone had asked."

"Yes, thank you. Can you describe him?"

The woman hesitated and looked away for an instant before looking back at George.

"Well…"

George took out his wallet and flipped it open to his identification.

"Ma'am, I'm Lieutenant Commander George Hudson with the U.S. Navy. It's very important that we find this woman. Anything you can tell us…"

"He was oriental." She smiled in apology. "We don't get many Asian-Americans in this town. It's different in Akron. Chinese restaurants everywhere. But he had black hair and glasses, and—"

"A scar on his face?" Pierre asked.

"Yes, actually."

Pierre clamped his teeth together and turned toward the car. Considering the helpless rage that simmered through his veins, it was better to let George wind up the interview.

FIFTY-TWO

Marie pedaled along on her bicycle. She'd given the boy her last fifty dollars, and he got a good bargain. The tire treads were worn, and it pedaled stiffly.

She'd realized long ago that she was not headed for the town Pierre specified. Greenwood was east, and she tried to work her way in that direction, but she knew she'd gone north when she first left the auto body shop. Then she'd become completely turned around. She doubted she was anywhere near Greenwood now, and she'd been on the road almost two hours.

Ahead, she saw a cluster of houses. A church steeple rose above them, and a wave of homesickness struck her. The scene looked so New England. She decided to ride toward it and ask the first person she saw how to get to Greenwood.

What if that is Greenwood? Wouldn't that be something?

Her hopes were dashed when she stopped at a small grocery store with gas pumps.

"I don't suppose this is Greenwood?" she asked a woman putting groceries on the backseat of an SUV.

"No, that's about fifteen miles from here."

Marie managed a grim smile. "Which way?"

"Let's see... If you went down Maple Street you'd hit the state road, and then I think..."

Marie realized she was too tired to pedal for another hour. She thanked the woman and pushed the bike on up the sidewalk. The street rose gently, and every step took more energy. She stopped in the shade of a large maple tree. A robin chirped in the branches. She let her gaze rove and realized that she was almost within the shadow of the small white church.

What day is it? Not Sunday. She checked her watch. If it were Sunday, there would be cars in the parking lot now. *Lord, show me what to do.*

Her gaze settled on the small, weathered house next to the church. She pushed the bicycle across the street into the driveway and studied the house for a long minute. Before she could put the kickstand in place, the door opened.

"May I help you?"

She looked up into a kind, wrinkled face. The elderly man smiled and advanced onto the stoop.

"I'm Pastor Whipple."

Marie smiled back. "Of course."

"Of course?"

"I asked God to help me, and after all, we are next door to a church."

"Indeed we are."

She positioned the kickstand with her foot and let go of the bike. It fell away from her and crashed to the ground before she could grab it.

She scowled at it, too tired to bend over and lift it.

"Let me get that."

Pastor Whipple moved quickly without seeming to hurry. He raised the bike and rested it against the wall of the house.

"There. Would you like to come inside? My wife and I were about to have tea. We'd be pleased if you joined us."

"Tea. That sounds wonderful."

Mrs. Whipple scurried about her homey kitchen, fetching a second bone china teacup and saucer and setting it on the table beside a large white mug.

"Hello, dear. Regular or peppermint?"

"Oh, peppermint, by all means." Marie took the chair the pastor offered her.

Mrs. Whipple brought a teabag and placed it in one of the cups, and then she poured boiling water from a steaming copper kettle.

"There, now. Pastor likes honey in his tea. Will you have some? Or do you like sugar?"

"No, thank you."

Mrs. Whipple clucked her tongue and slid the delicate cup and saucer closer to Marie. She turned to the sideboard and came back with a plate of glazed cinnamon rolls. The smell made Marie's mouth water.

"Those look delicious!"

"Help yourself, child. You look hungry."

Marie reached for a roll.

"After we ask the blessing," said the pastor.

She drew back her hand.

He smiled at her and they all bowed their heads.

"Lord, we thank You for Your bounty, and for the guest You have brought our way."

"Amen," said his wife. She smiled and pushed the plate an inch toward Marie. "Now, child."

Marie felt her cheeks redden, but she took a roll and sank her teeth into it. She closed her eyes. The zing of the cinnamon tickled her nose, and the sweet icing blended with the soft, chewy bread. For an instant, the world was perfect. She sighed and chewed that first bite, lingering over it.

When she swallowed, she looked up and found the Whipples watching her with indulgent smiles.

"It's wonderful."

"Thank you." Mrs. Whipple sipped her tea, and her husband stirred a spoonful of honey into his. He helped himself to a cinnamon roll.

"Now tell us your name."

Marie opened her mouth but said nothing. Her gaze caught the pastor's. He arched his feathery white eyebrows in expectation.

"I'm not sure I should tell you."

Mrs. Whipple's eyes widened. Her husband said gently, "And why is that?"

"Because…" Marie looked down. She still held the warm, sticky roll. This house was too peaceful. Too normal. "Because I might bring trouble on you."

"Does trouble follow you?"

"Yes. Wherever I go, trouble comes. Some people have been…" She stared at him, suddenly aware of her actions. If those men came here, what would they do to this sweet old man and his wife?

She laid the roll on the edge of her saucer and pushed back her chair.

"I need to leave."

Mr. Whipple laid his hand on her wrist. "Young lady, you told me you asked God for help, and He brought you to me. Do you still believe that?"

Marie wavered. "I… Yes, I guess so."

"Then relax. Finish your tea. I won't pressure you for your story, but God placed me here to minister to people. Let us help you."

Marie licked her lips. She wanted very much to do as he proposed.

"I never had to make decisions for myself before," she whispered.

"Someone else has made them for you?" Mrs. Whipple asked.

"Yes. My husband. Before him, my father. But these last few days, I've been…" She looked into the pastor's eyes and found encouragement there. "I've been forced to take care of myself and…protect myself."

The pastor nodded. "Did something happen to your husband?"

"No. But…" She sighed. "I don't think I should tell you."

"Is it as bad as all that?" he asked.

"Yes."

"Is someone trying to hurt you?" Mrs. Whipple asked.

"Yes."

The couple was silent. Mr. Whipple sipped tea from his big white mug, and Mrs. Whipple squeezed her teabag against the edge of her china cup with her spoon.

Marie tried to gather courage, but it slipped away. A sick dread filled her, and her hands began to tremble. "If I tell you…"

"What?" The pastor set his mug down. "What are you afraid of, my dear?"

"What is the very worst thing that could happen if you talk to us?" asked his wife.

Marie sucked in a breath. "You could both die."

FIFTY-THREE

1200 Monday, near Youngstown, Ohio

"She can't have come this way." Pierre took a bite of his double cheeseburger. He was hungry after all. Very hungry. As usual, George was right, and he was glad they'd stopped at the fast-food restaurant.

"Yeah, we'd have seen her if she were walking." George popped a French fry into his mouth. "Sorry, buddy. It made sense to me to drive east. I figured she'd go east if she couldn't make the rendezvous. That's what she's done so far. She's zeroed in on Maine like a homing pigeon."

Pierre stuck a straw through the lid of his paper cup and sucked in a cool mouthful of cola. George's reasoning was as good as any, but if the enemy had captured Marie, no amount of strategy would help her.

"Okay, what have we got?" George asked when he'd finished his burger. He swept the wrappings onto a plastic tray and laid his atlas on the table. "She's been hitchhiking, and from the last place we know she stopped—Randall's Auto Body—it would be easy for her to hit this road and go east to the Pennsylvania border."

"That doesn't mean she did it."

"Right."

"But if we expect her to do it, so will they."

George nodded, stroking his chin as he perused the map. "Well,

McCutcheon is adamant we bring the Pennsylvania state police in on this. They'll search along the highway and take fliers to all the truck stops. If she crosses into Pennsylvania, they have a pretty good chance of locating her."

"Or helping those goons find her."

George winced. "What else can we do?"

Pierre shrugged. "I'm glad Heinz has a man camped out at the airport. She might try to go there after all. I mean, if she's scared and frustrated enough."

"Yeah, he says there was a plane out of there late this morning. If Marie got on it, she could connect in Philly and be in Maine in a couple of hours."

"But he doesn't think she was on it."

"Right." George sat back and raised his hands in futility. "She's surprised us before. You saw the security tape from Detroit. They're pretty sure Marie got off her flight from San Francisco wearing a beaded wig."

"I still don't think that was her." Pierre scowled and sipped his drink. The fact that he couldn't positively identify his own wife on a grainy videotape unsettled him. "I guess it could be her, but…"

"But she'd still have to use her ID to get on a plane in Akron." George closed the atlas. "Your brother's going to the airport in Bangor tonight just in case?"

"Yeah. He and Marie's sister are anxious to do something, so I told André to go."

"You never know. Then there's the classified information Tarrington was supposedly smuggling to the communists by way of his wife."

"Yeah. Now that we know for sure Jenna left Tokyo with a flash drive full of secrets for her husband's contact in California…" Pierre pursed his lips and shook his head. "Why didn't Marie tell me?"

"Maybe she doesn't know anything about it."

"Oh, come on, George. She has to. She told Rachel she thought she had something they want. And why else are they chasing her?

They got Jenna Tarrington's luggage, and they got Jenna. But they're still after Marie. She's got that data."

"If she calls again, ask her straight out."

"Yeah. I should have done that when she called from the hotel. I suppose she might have it and not know what it is. She can use a computer, but she's not techno-savvy like Rachel."

George inhaled sharply. "She wouldn't just toss it, would she? If she didn't know its significance, I mean."

"I hope not. Because if she had it and threw it away, and they're still chasing her, it's all for nothing."

"Marie's a smart girl."

"Yeah." Pierre hated the doubt in his tone. Marie *was* smart, but she used to do some pretty foolish things. Like throwing his dry clean-only dress blues in the washer when they were first married. Lately she seemed to be thinking for herself more. Their time in Japan had helped. She could have cocooned in the apartment on the base, but instead she'd sought out new adventures and absorbed the culture. "I think…at least, I hope she'd know something like that might be important." He drank the last of the cola through the straw with a loud slurp.

"You done?" George asked. "I'm going to call Rachel."

"Sure. You might as well. It's not going to do us any good to keep burning gas when we have no idea where she went."

"I think we should stay put. If we drive too far and Marie calls from the Akron area, we'll have a long ride back. She's probably ahead of us, but…"

Pierre stood up and lifted the tray with the trash. "Yeah. You never know."

FIFTY-FOUR

"Are you a believer, my dear?"

Marie nodded.

Pastor Whipple reached behind him and took a Bible from a shelf. He flipped through the pages. "Ardis and I were reading from the book of Proverbs this morning. Proverbs 28:5: 'Evil men do not understand justice, but those who seek the Lord understand it fully.'"

"Evil men." Marie searched his face. "That's what I've got. Evil men trying to kill me."

"But God knows that. He will bring justice."

Tears gushed into Marie's eyes and spilled over. She clenched her fists tight. "You don't think I'm crazy, then?"

The pastor blinked and straightened. "I never considered it. Should I?"

A tiny gasp of a chuckle escaped Marie's lips. "I believe what you're saying. About justice, I mean. They'll be punished someday. But what if that doesn't happen in this life? I'm afraid they'll do bad things to a lot of people before God hands out the justice."

Mr. Whipple reached over and patted her hand. "Easy, now. This world is full of evil, it's true…"

"You have no idea!" Marie looked at his wife and then back to the pastor. "They could come here any minute."

"Someone is chasing you?" Mrs. Whipple raised her eyebrows at her husband.

"Yes. I've been running for days. These men are killers. Just a couple of hours ago, my husband and his friend were going to pick me up at a mechanic's shop in Akron. We had it arranged so they could come get me and I'd be safe. But before they could get there, the men who've been following me came and I ran." She glanced toward the door. "I shouldn't stay here."

"James," Mrs. Whipple said, "There was a shooting in Akron this morning. I heard it on the radio while I was kneading the bread dough."

"Surely that has nothing to do with…" The pastor glanced at his watch. "It's just about noon. Let's see what the news has to say."

The Whipples rose, and Marie got up and followed. Her legs felt like Play-Doh as they entered the living room.

The pastor crossed the braided rug to open a cabinet, revealing a small television set. He snapped it on and stood back. Immediately the music of an advertisement filled the room. They stood in tense silence until a local broadcaster came on the screen.

"The governor returned today from his weekend in…"

Mrs. Whipple turned to Marie. "Sit down, child."

Marie swallowed. "I really should leave."

The older woman eased down on the sofa and patted the cushion beside her. "Nonsense. We'll talk this through and give you lunch, at least."

Marie glanced at the pastor, but his attention was riveted on the television. She followed his gaze.

"In Akron today," the reporter continued, "police say a mechanic was shot by an unknown assailant while at work in his shop." Video footage of a police car parked in front of Randall's Auto Body flashed on the screen, and Marie gasped.

"That's the place," she choked. "My husband was supposed to come get me, but I saw this other car drive in, and a man got out. Poor Mr. Randall! It's my fault."

"No, no, it's not your fault." The pastor turned up the volume.

"...was taken to a hospital for treatment and is reported to be in critical condition."

Marie couldn't stand up any longer. She plopped down on the sofa, and Mrs. Whipple slid one arm around her.

"There, now. What a fright you've had!"

Marie wanted to smash the television. She stared beyond the pastor at the screen. An inset of her passport photo appeared next to the reporter's head.

"...and police are still searching for the woman who sat next to a shooting victim on a plane from Tokyo to San Francisco Friday. Marie Belanger"—the reporter pronounced her name with a hard g, and Marie winced—"was last seen in southeastern Michigan. Authorities want to question Belanger about what happened when she and the late Jenna Tarrington left their flight at the San Francisco airport. Tarrington was found dead a short time later in an airport restroom. Belanger apparently flew to Detroit later that day. Anyone seeing this woman is asked to call the number at the bottom of the screen. She may be hitchhiking. Marie Belanger is twenty-two years old, five feet, five inches tall, one hundred twenty pounds. She has dark hair and brown eyes, and was last seen wearing jeans and a maroon sweater."

Mrs. Whipple drew a sharp breath. "That's..."

The pastor switched off the television set and sat down in a leather armchair. He studied Marie for a moment. "Let's pray. If danger is imminent, we need God's counsel."

The couple bowed their heads. Marie stared at them for a moment. Everything in her said, *This is no time to close your eyes. Keep them wide open so you can see what's coming.*

But the pastor began praying in earnest, quiet tones, and after a few seconds, she lowered her eyelids and let her chin sink forward.

"And Father, we ask that You would put an end to this wickedness. Bring the men who have committed these crimes to justice. Lord, we ask that You would protect our friend Marie and take her safely back to her family. Amen."

"Amen," said Mrs. Whipple.

Marie's lips trembled as she whispered, "Amen." She opened her eyes. Her lashes were saturated, and a teardrop fell onto her blouse. "Thank you."

"We should call the police," the pastor said.

"No. Please don't."

"Why ever not, child?" Mrs. Whipple frowned at Marie. "They want to talk to you. They can protect you from those gangsters."

"You don't understand."

The Whipples were silent, staring at her. Marie swallowed hard.

"The men who are chasing me…they want something. They killed Jenna Tarrington, that woman on the plane. They killed her for it, and now they've shot Mr. Randall. If they find me, they'll kill me like that." She snapped her fingers.

The pastor frowned. "But surely the police can—"

"No. If you call the police, those men will get here first. Every time I've tried to get help, they've found me and I've had to run. I'm scared to even call my husband again. Don't you see? I called him from Randall's, and those men came and shot the owner before my husband could get there. If I call him from here…I can't risk that. More people being hurt or…you. You being killed." She gulped and shook her head, unable to meet their eyes.

After a moment's silence, Pastor Whipple cleared his throat. "Tell me about your husband."

"He's the sweetest, dearest man on earth. He's in the Navy, and we were in Japan for two years." She hesitated. Should she tell them this? How much damage was she doing by sitting here? How much more by revealing her situation? "I shouldn't tell you anything."

"God brought you here." Mr. Whipple's gentle voice calmed her. "I believe that, and I believe He wants us to help you. Now, tell me about the airplane."

Marie took three deep breaths. "All right. But lock the door."

Mrs. Whipple rose and went to the kitchen. Marie looked into the pastor's soft blue eyes.

"Pierre is being transferred, and he gets a month's leave. I was flying home to Maine, and he was going to come later. In a couple of weeks. But in the airport in San Francisco, this woman was killed."

"How does that affect you?"

Marie hesitated. "She sat beside me on the plane, and she left her suitcase with me while she went to the restroom."

"And?"

"I think the people who killed her wanted something Jenna was carrying."

"Smuggling?"

"Maybe, but I don't think it's that exactly."

"What, then?"

Marie held his gaze and inhaled slowly. "I think it's…a military secret."

Pastor Whipple sat up straight. "I see."

"No, you don't." Marie put her hands to her forehead and pulled in a shaky breath. "I didn't know this woman, Jenna, very well, but I know her husband is high up in the Navy, and he was working with sensitive material. What if…what if he is some kind of spy? I've tried to think of another explanation, but that's the only one that fits."

"Why do you say that?"

"At first I tried to make sense of it as a domestic thing. I knew the Tarringtons fought a lot, or at least they weren't happy. When I heard she was dead, my first thought was that maybe he had someone kill her when she wasn't near him, so they wouldn't trace it back to him."

"A hit."

She nodded. She could hear Mrs. Whipple moving about in the kitchen, opening the refrigerator and moving dishes.

"Pastor, I can't tell you what made me change my mind about that. It would only bring more danger to you. But I am pretty sure now that Jenna Tarrington had something that enemies of the United States want. Or at least, something that will make us some enemies if it's discovered."

He rested his hand on his chin and stared at the window. "My inclination is still to call the state police and ask them to take you into protective custody. We don't have our own police force in our little town, but—"

"No! Please!"

"You said that whenever you've called your husband, these men show up."

"Yes."

"My dear, I don't want to insult you or anger you, but is there any chance—any chance at all—that your husband is connected to these attacks?"

"No, he couldn't be. You've got to believe me. He would never hurt me. He's rock solid. He's got the FBI and the Navy Criminal Investigative Service helping him try to find me, and I want to let them help me, but…" She shook her head. "My cell phone was stolen, and I've had to use pay phones to call him. I don't see how they could trace my calls to pay phones, do you? Of course, that one time I stopped at a motel, and I called him from there. I don't understand it. They've got me so scared, I don't dare call anyone. Not the police, not the FBI, not even my husband."

"Let us take that risk for you. God can protect us."

"No, Mr. Whipple." She couldn't hold back her sobs, and she sank back against the couch cushions. Her hot face ached from holding in her grief so long. Something soft brushed her fingers, and she blinked to focus. The pastor held a tissue. She took it and wiped her eyes.

He sat back, staring into space again, and then sighed.

"What is your plan, then?"

"To get home. Just to get home to Maine." She knew that was illogical. If she went home, wouldn't the men follow her there? But it was as far as she could think. "Right now I'm out of money, and the bike I came here on is not much good. I don't know what to do."

After another long pause, he sat forward. "Have you ever ridden a motorcycle?"

Marie swallowed and dabbed at her nose. "Yes. My cousin has one."

"Come with me."

He led her through the kitchen, where Mrs. Whipple was making ham salad sandwiches. He opened a door to a breezeway and guided Marie into the garage. They walked around the car and past a neat workbench. At the back of the garage, behind a grill and a lawnmower, sat a dusty old Honda motorbike.

Marie stared at it and then at the pastor. "Does that thing run?"

"It did the last time Ardis let me take it out. That was two summers ago. She thinks it's dangerous."

Together they moved the grill and wheeled the bike out into the driveway. The pastor threw his leg over the seat and turned the key. The motor roared, and Mr. Whipple smiled. He let it run for a few seconds before shutting it off.

"I'd be pleased to let you take it."

Marie bit her lip. "I don't have a motorcycle license."

"That could be a problem. If an officer stopped you, I mean. Of course, if they did that, you'd have other things for them to worry about."

She nodded. "How much is it worth? I'll send you a check later."

"Don't worry about it. But let me do this. Give me your husband's phone number. When you've been gone an hour, I'll call him."

Marie shook her head. "That's not long enough. Six hours at least."

He gritted his teeth. "Four. Marie, you need him."

"I know. But I've got to be far away from here when you talk to him. And you can't know where I'll be then."

"But he won't be able to find you."

"I know. But you can tell him I was here and I was safe, but I'm heading for another place."

He nodded. "All right. I just hope the old Honda doesn't quit on you." He took out his wallet and handed her several bills. "Take this. You'll need gas."

Mrs. Whipple opened the kitchen door and called, "Lunch is ready."

Marie wasn't hungry. The sugary cinnamon roll kept her feeling well fed. But she wouldn't turn down a free meal at this point, and she went inside with the pastor. She could only eat half a sandwich.

"I'll wrap up another one for you to take along," Mrs. Whipple said. "I'm so glad you're taking that old bike. I worry about James every time he goes off on it."

"The bicycle I came on…" Marie said.

"We'll give it away."

The pastor left the room for a moment and came back carrying a helmet and a worn leather jacket. "This will keep you warm while you're riding."

Marie smiled. "It's terrific, but I couldn't…"

"Yes, you could. It's a package deal."

Marie hesitated, and then she hugged him and Mrs. Whipple. "Pray for me."

"We will. Call us when you're safe."

FIFTY-FIVE

André sat in the passenger seat trying to find a place for his hands. He rarely rode with a woman driver, but Lisa had insisted they take her truck this time. He wasn't even sure why they were going to Bangor again, other than the fact that Pierre had requested it as a contingency, just in case Marie got a flight out of Akron.

Lisa shifted and whizzed out onto I-95. "I figure we should stay at the airport until the last plane lands tonight. Anything that could connect from Detroit or Akron or Cleveland or—"

"Or any other place east of the Mississippi."

"Yeah, basically."

He shifted in the seat and found the armrest. He lowered it and put his elbow on it, but that felt funny, so he put it back up and clasped his hands in his lap.

"There's a ninety-nine percent chance she won't come in on a plane from anywhere. You know that, don't you?"

Lisa's eyes widened and she threw him an incredulous look. "Yeah. There's also a one percent chance she will."

"It seems like a waste of time. She'll call if she needs a ride." He tried locking his fingers behind his head, but that didn't work.

"Well, I didn't have anything better to do tonight. Did you?"

"Not really."

Lisa punched the buttons for her cruise control, increasing their speed past André's comfort zone. "She's my sister. I think a one in a hundred chance is worth it for someone you love."

André bit back a retort and lowered the armrest again. "You're right."

"Wow."

"What, you're surprised that you're right?"

"No. I'm surprised you admitted it."

He clenched his teeth for a moment and then made himself relax. "Hey, I thought we were past that."

She nodded. "We are. At least, we were last night."

Was she blushing? He looked closer. She was definitely blushing. He felt his own color heighten. The memory of their kiss had nipped at his mind all day, making it hard to concentrate at work.

"I'm sorry, Lisa."

Her lips twitched. "I guess we're both a little edgy."

"So how'd your day go?"

"Not too bad. This morning I gave the mayor an estimate for rewiring that old house he bought on Burleigh Street."

"Woohoo. The mayor."

"Yeah. And this afternoon I found out why Mrs. Zanarian's dryer was overheating, and I fixed it."

"You probably saved her life."

"Not really."

"Yes, really. If you hadn't fixed that electrical problem, she might have had a fire."

Lisa drove on in silence, but she was smiling.

André nodded. "And all I did today was sort letters and sell stamps."

"Well, we can't save someone's life every day," she said.

At the airport they checked the arrival boards and went up the escalator to watch the passengers come in from a plane out of New York. When they'd eyeballed all the people disembarking, they moved downstairs for a commuter jet coming in from Boston.

Between that and the next plane, André suggested they check out the newsstand. When the next arrival was announced, they went to watch the people streaming through the gate.

"Another negative," Lisa sighed. "It's almost half an hour until the next flight is due in. Let's get something to eat in the coffee shop."

André insisted on paying for their sandwiches and sodas. While they ate, he watched Lisa. He wished he hadn't let his irritation show on the drive to Bangor.

She was quiet tonight. Was she thinking about their interaction too, and wondering why things felt so different now than they had last night?

"Lisa…"

She looked up at him with an expression so wistful he was determined not to disappoint her again.

"I'm sorry I was rude before."

She shrugged. "I understand. You've been on your feet all day. You're tired."

"So? That's no excuse. I'm glad we can do this for Marie and Pierre. And I'm glad I'm here with you."

She smiled. It made such a difference, the way it softened her face and brought a sparkle to her eyes. On impulse he reached for her hand.

"I mean it. I hate to think that I would never have gotten to know you like this if…if things had been different this week."

"Me too." She looked down at their clasped hands and took a short, gaspy breath. "You want to look in the gift shop?"

"Sure."

They tossed their food containers in the trash and walked across the big lounge. André took her hand again and squeezed it. An Asian man sitting alone in a row of chairs eyed them and turned back to his newspaper.

As they entered the gift shop, the clerk frowned. "We close in five minutes."

Lisa drew back, but André said, "Okay," and tugged her inside.

They walked around the small shop, looking at the souvenirs. Maple sugar. Postcards. Jewelry. Stuffed lobsters, loons, and moose.

At the T-shirt rack, André flipped through the hangers. He pulled out one with a screen printed black bear.

Lisa nodded. "That's cool."

He put it back. The next one was pink. "Oh, you have to have this."

"What is it?"

He pulled it off the rack and held it up.

Sisters are forever friends.

Lisa's lower lip quivered. She sniffed.

"Hey, I'm sorry." André caressed her shoulder, not sure exactly what he'd done wrong.

She smiled through tears. "It's okay. That's…sweet. I like it."

"Hey, we're closing," the clerk called.

"I guess it wasn't very thoughtful of me," André said softly.

"No, I love it."

"Yeah?"

"Yeah. Were you serious?"

He wasn't sure that he had been, but now he was. He nodded and carried the shirt to the counter. The clerk dimmed the lights before she took his credit card. Lisa stood next to him. Her warm fingers sneaked around his wrist, and he folded her hand in his once more.

The loudspeaker blared an indecipherable message.

"The next plane must be landing," Lisa whispered.

André put away his wallet and took the bag, and they went out of the shop. The clerk locked the door behind them. They went over to the glass wall near the secure area and stood close to the Asian man, watching all the passengers come in.

When the last travelers passed through the gate, they turned away, disheartened once more. Lisa nudged him.

André glanced at her and then followed her gaze. The Asian man was heading for the down escalator alone.

"Guess the person he was waiting for didn't show, either."

"Yeah." André guided her over to stand beneath an arrival board. "Only two more flights coming in tonight."

"You okay to stay that late?" Her eyes still swam with tears.

"Yeah, I'm fine." He slid his arm around her waist. "We'll see them all in."

"Thanks." She leaned against him.

An hour later, they went out to the parking lot together.

"You want to drive?" Lisa asked.

André was surprised that she would let someone else drive her truck. "Sure."

She pushed a button on the remote to unlock the doors and handed him the keys. He opened the passenger door for her. Before she got in, he bent and kissed her. The quick, sweet kiss warmed him to his toes. Rounding the truck to the other door, he smiled to himself. He never would have thought he'd end up with Lisa, the electrician, but it didn't seem outlandish now. Had he found the woman to spend the rest of his life with?

FIFTY-SIX

"So where you headed, lovey?" The petite redheaded woman asked, handling the big rig's transmission with ease.

Marie inhaled slowly, thinking about what she should say. "Maine."

"Aha. One of my favorite states. I can't get you there, but I can get you into southern New England. How's that?"

"Great." For three hours, Marie rode in the passenger seat, alternately nodding off and chatting with Mimsie as she drove the huge tractor. In her more lucid moments, Marie thought about what would happen if she ever got home again. Did she dare take this nightmare into the circle of her family? She wished she had confided in Pierre about the computer drive. As long as she carried Jenna's secret, she knew her family wouldn't be any safer than she was.

Mimsie's frizzy red hair wafted about her head in a cloud, and her multiple earrings comprised enough hardware to stock a small Aubuchon store. In the dim light of the cab, Marie at first pegged her for thirty-five. Then Mimsie started telling about all of her adventures on the road and three failed marriages, and Marie figured she had to be at least forty to fit all of that in. As they pulled in to the parking lot of a well-lit service stop, she decided Mimsie hadn't seen the back of forty in several years.

"Coffee first, then fuel." Mimsie parked the rig and shut the engine off. She reached behind her and pulled a thermos bottle from the dark recess behind her seat. "Come on. This place has minimal amenities and maximal good coffee."

They climbed down from the cab and met at the back of the trailer. Marie shivered in the chilly night air and sent up a renewed prayer of thanks for the leather jacket.

"The service station's probably not open." She looked up at the back door of the truck. The Honda that Mr. Whipple had entrusted to her was inside between cartons of unfinished furniture, where she and Mimsie had stowed it with help from a hydraulic lift.

"Fuel only this time of night," Mimsie agreed. "Just stick with me across Pennsylvania. When we get over into New York or Connecticut in the morning, you can find a place to work on that old bike, although I'm not sure it's fixable."

Mimsie led the way into the building. The tourist information counter was closed. Marie longingly eyed the pay phone mounted on the wall between the 24-hour coffee shop and the restroom entrance.

"Somebody you want to call?" Mimsie asked.

"Well...yeah, but...I can't."

"Why not? No money?"

"No, I..." Marie held back the sigh of misery that filled her lungs. More than anything, she wanted to hear Pierre's voice again, but calling him would put her adversaries back on her track. She didn't know how, but she was certain it would. She couldn't risk another call. Not even to Lisa. The next thing she knew, those assassins would threaten her family in Maine.

"Well, come on. Let's get coffee."

Pastor Whipple and his sweet wife came to mind, and Marie fingered the slip of paper in her pocket. "There is someone."

"Okay, go ahead."

Marie took out the small yellow square and carefully punched in the number Mrs. Whipple had written for her while Mimsie went to the counter.

"Hello?"

"Mr. Whipple!"

"Yes. Marie?"

"It's me. I'm sorry to call you in the middle of the night, but it's the first chance I've had, and I've been worried about you and Ardis."

"We're fine, my dear. No trouble here today."

Marie leaned against the wall. "I'm glad. Thank you so much...for everything. I imagined terrible things happening."

"Well, put those fears to rest and praise God. Those men don't seem to have been able to follow you here. How's the old bike holding up?"

"I'm afraid it broke down just over the Pennsylvania border. But a trucker picked me up, and we've got it in the back of the trailer."

"You be careful, Marie. Some of those truckers..."

"It's a woman, and she's kind of kooky, but nice."

"Good."

"Were you able to make the call we talked about?" Marie asked.

"I did. I waited until this evening, as you requested, and your husband was most grateful to get the news. He wanted to come here, but apparently he'd already driven on eastward. I told him it wouldn't do him any good to visit us. He was disappointed that I couldn't tell him where you'd be, but he was thankful to know you'd come through this far unscathed. Seems he and his friend went to that mechanic shop where the fellow was attacked."

"Randall's?"

"Yes. It gave them quite a scare, and they were afraid the black-guards had snatched you."

"Thank you so much for letting him know I'm all right. I can't tell you how much that means to me."

"You will contact him eventually? I mean, you must be far out of reach of those thugs by now, and—"

"I've got to get to a safe place, somewhere they can't get me or hurt anyone I'm with."

"But your husband can protect you. We talked at some length, Marie. I truly believe he's a good man, and he seems to have almost unlimited resources behind him. Let him help you. The longer you're alone, the more likely you'll come to grief."

Marie drew in a deep breath. She couldn't tell anyone where she and Mimsie were. If she could find a place where Mimsie could drop her off…but she'd still have the computer drive. "Soon. I promise, Mr. Whipple. Keep praying for me."

Mimsie came from the coffee shop carrying a small bag and two thermal cups. She handed one to Marie.

"Almost done," Marie mouthed.

"Well, snap it up. I have a schedule." Mimsie turned her wrist to look at her oversized man's watch and then jerked to keep from spilling her pretzels out of their bag.

"I'll be right there." Marie watched her go out the door. *What if she leaves without me?*

"Marie, are you still there?" Mr. Whipple asked.

"Yes, but I need to hurry."

"All right. Would you mind if I called Lieutenant Belanger again in the morning? I could let him know you've found better transportation and that you were fine as of…twelve forty-seven a.m."

She winced. "I'm so sorry I woke you."

"None of that. Take care and know that God is watching over you."

Marie saw a tractor-trailer rolling past in the parking lot beyond the glass doors, but she couldn't tell if it was Mimsie's rig.

"I've got to run! If you call him again, just be aware that someone else may be listening. Goodbye, Mr. Whipple!"

"Wait! Marie—"

She hung up and ran for the door.

FIFTY-SEVEN

André rolled over and batted at his alarm clock, but the ringing didn't stop. Cell phone. He fumbled with the items on the nightstand and knocked the phone on the floor. It rang again.

Nearly awake now, he hung over the side of the bed and picked it up.

"Hello!"

"Hey, there. Is this Mr. Andrew Blanger?"

"André Belanger. Who is this?" He frowned, trying to place the deep male voice.

"Well, howdy. This is Honeybear."

"I…beg your pardon?"

The man laughed. "That's my handle. For the CB, you know?"

"Oh, right. I guess."

"I've got a message for you, buster."

"What kind of message?" About two more seconds of this nonsense, and André would hang up.

At that moment his alarm went off. He slapped it.

"Sorry. What did you say?"

"I said, a friend of a friend asked me to contact you and give you a message when I crossed the Tennessee state line."

André's mind whirled. Why would some hearty trucker in Tennessee call him? This had to be connected to Marie. "Yeah? I'm listening."

"Good. 'Cause here's the message, and I quote: 'A package will be delivered this afternoon for Pierre at the spot where Lisa's family vacationed three years ago.'"

André's heart pounded. A coded message from Marie. It had to be.

"Could you repeat that, please?" He wished he could record it somehow. He opened the drawer in the nightstand and took out a pen as Honeybear repeated the message. André scribbled the words on the back of the payment booklet for his pickup.

"Got it, buster?"

"Yeah, I think so. Thanks. Can you tell me anything else? Like what time the delivery will be made, or who's doing the delivering?"

"Sorry. That's all I got. Over and out."

"Hey—"

The dial tone sounded in André's ear. He stared at the phone and sighed. Sitting up on the edge of his bed, he looked at the clock again. Would Lisa be up yet? Probably. He punched in her cell phone number wishing he'd put it on speed dial.

"Gillette Electric."

"Hey! This is André. Where did your family go for vacation three years ago?"

"Three…is this a trick question?"

"No. It's important. Wherever you spent your vacation is where Marie is going to be this afternoon."

"You're joking."

"I'm dead serious. Some trucker just called me with a message."

"Oh, man." He heard the excitement in her voice. "What time?"

"I don't know. He just said this afternoon."

"Can you take off from work?"

"Maybe. Let me think."

"Good. Because we're driving to Old Orchard Beach."

FIFTY-EIGHT

"You don't have to—" Marie broke off as Mimsie swerved into the exit lane.

"Hey, I don't do things by halves. I was never good at fractions. Gotta do the whole job and make sure you get there safe."

"Thanks. But you didn't have to get off the highway for me."

"No problem." The exit curled around and faced southwest for a few seconds. Mimsie reached up to her visor for a pair of aviator sunglasses.

Marie smiled across the space in the cab. "It's been nice riding with you."

"You didn't really think I was going to leave you back there at the rest stop in the middle of the night, did you?" Mimsie laughed and slid the glasses on. "I wouldn't do that." Her face sobered. "That moron you rode with a few days ago traumatized you, didn't he? That's what it was, lovey. Traumatism. You've got post-traumatism stress disorder." She nodded emphatically. "I had that once."

"You did?"

"Sure did." Mimsie flicked on the turn signal and roared off the exit into the street. Marie caught a glimpse of a sign that read "Historic Sites" pointing straight ahead as motorists scuttled out of the big truck's path. "It was after my first rollover."

"You rolled your truck over?" Marie stared at her.

"My truck? Oh, no. My first husband's Caddy."

"Oh. Did you get hurt?"

"Broke my collar bone and totaled the car. Denby never got over it. That's when he filed for divorce."

"Because you wrecked his Cadillac? Didn't he care that you were hurt?"

"Not much. Let's just say the wreck was the final straw. He'd already made up his mind to leave."

Marie was at a loss for words. She'd seen unhappy marriages at the military base, but Mimsie's words chilled her. She sent up a silent prayer for a way to speak God's truth to the hardened trucker with an aching heart.

"So let's find the post office," Mimsie said.

"I don't want you to have to go to a lot of trouble turning this rig around in a tight spot. Just let me out anywhere here."

"Well, there's a shopping center yonder. Let's take it in there. No, wait!" Mimsie pointed, and Marie saw the sign.

"Mystic Seaport. We're practically there. But the post office…"

"I'll find it. Listen, I don't know much about what you've been through, but…" Marie glanced over at Mimsie, who was adjusting the gears as she braked for a red light. "Do you believe in Jesus?"

Mimsie barked a laugh. "Jesus? You mean the one born in the cow barn?"

"Y-yes. Jesus Christ. God's Son."

Mimsie grinned. "What about Him?"

"I just wanted to tell you that…that He can help you when things are tough. He came to earth to help people like me and you."

"Oh, really?" The light changed. Mimsie eased the big truck forward into the intersection. "Is He helping you now?"

"I'd say so."

"Yeah? The way you tell it, you got separated from your man, and some creep tried to assault you so you ran. You got some old motorbike on its last legs, and it broke down on you. Now you're trying to get back to poor hubby, but you keep running and he can't find you. Does that sound providentialized to you?"

Marie winced. "It's not like that. I mean, there's more I can't tell you. But, yes, I think God is with me. He's helped me stay safe this far."

Mimsie shook her head with a smile.

Marie shifted in her seat, wishing once more she'd held on to her compact Bible. "He sent you along just at the moment when I desperately needed a ride."

"Oh, God sent me."

"Yes." Marie nodded, feeling more confident. "I'm sure of it."

"Really? Because He never told me He was sending me. In fact, I could swear it was my dispatcher who sent me. She gave me my orders and told me what route to take. Wasn't God involved nohow."

Marie set her jaw, determined not to give up. *Please, Lord, show me how to get through to her.* "God uses people, you know."

"Like me?" Mimsie flashed her a glance, but Marie couldn't see her eyes behind the dark glasses.

"Sometimes. When that Honda quit on me, I was ready to give up. And then you came along and offered not only to give me a ride, but to bring the bike along too."

"So? Lots of truckers would do that."

Marie leaned toward her. "But God didn't send just any trucker. He sent you, a woman with a tender heart."

Mimsie grunted.

"In the Bible God sent people to give messages or help other people. Sometimes He used people who didn't even believe in Him."

"Sounds overspiritualated to me. Maybe God sent that bad guy to teach you something, like *don't run away from your man.*"

Marie frowned. She'd given a brief account of her run-in with Jud to explain her appearance on the highway with no luggage, but she had omitted her original motive for fleeing and had said nothing about the men she feared were agents of the Chinese government or the attack on Mr. Randall.

"I guess it comes down to whether you believe God's real or not. Because if you believe in Him, and if you also believe He speaks to men through the Bible—"

"What about women? Does God only speak to men?"

Marie laughed. "I guess you're assuming He's real, or that wouldn't upset you. No, I didn't mean that God ignores women. He speaks to us too. And He uses His Word, the Bible, to tell us what He wants us to know."

Mimsie nodded. "Okay. I can swallow that. I've always believed in God."

"Then why are you giving me such a hard time?"

"Just checking to see if your faithliness is as real as you make it out to be."

"My faithliness?"

"You know. Some people are all talk and no action."

Marie nodded. "Thanks. I'll take that as a compliment."

Mimsie turned in at a parking lot where the sign read "Mystic Seaport Main Entrance." She drove the truck to the far end of the lot where there were few vehicles and made a wide circle, almost clipping a minivan.

Marie picked up her purse and tote bag. "Listen, I appreciate all you've done for me. And I want you to know everything's fine with me and my husband. I wasn't running away from him. I was flying home to see my family." Marie halted, wondering if she should reveal even the most innocent information. "My husband's in the military, and he was going to join me in Maine in a couple of weeks. At least that was the plan. But when I told him I was having some trouble on the way home, he flew over from Japan to try to help me. But God sent you along to help me first. And I thank you. The Bible says God is my help and my salvation. This time He used you to help me."

The air brakes sighed as Mimsie brought the big truck to a stop facing the street. She pulled off her sunglasses.

"Sorry I can't take you right to your people in Maine."

"It's okay. This is great. It's only five hours or so from home. They'll come for me."

Mimsie nodded. "Well, you take care. I've got a ninety-nine

percentiled assurance that the message got through. Honeybear's dependable."

"We'll take it on faith that he's made the call you asked him to, then."

"I like what you said, about God using me. Maybe He'll use me to help someone else along the road."

"Maybe." Marie smiled. "Just be careful who you pick up."

"Oh, I don't take no creepy lookers. Now, you tell your man where I'm taking the bike, and if he wants it—"

"Don't worry about that. I don't need it anymore, and it would be too much trouble to get it home."

"Well, hey, I might keep it to tinker with sometime." Mimsie nodded. "Mother would absolutely hate it if I took it home and put it in her garage. I think I'll do it. Of course, her chauffeur will try to scrap it as soon as my back's turned."

"Your mother has a chauffeur?"

Mimsie shrugged, and Marie chuckled. As they shook hands, she ventured, "Could I contact you after I get home?"

"Sure. I'd like to know you made it." Mimsie opened the compartment where she kept her log book and handed Marie a business card.

Marie held it up and read the dainty script. "Miriam K. Hasseldorn? How elegant!"

"Oops. That's my formal card for when I'm home. Don't know how that got in there."

Marie read on, noting the address. "Newport, Rhode Island?"

Mimsie nodded. "With my mother."

"Newport? That's…"

"Yeah, I know. High-end, wealthified real estate."

"You weren't kidding, were you? About the chauffeur."

Mimsie rummaged in the compartment. "My father made his money getting rid of other people's garbage. We weren't exactly in the top tier of Newport society, and I wasn't what you'd call debutational material. But money talks, to a certain extent. Still, after Denby and

I split, I was *persona non invita* in Newport. So I found a new life on the road. My mom likes it when I come home. She keeps a suite for me so I can crash between husbands."

"And then you hit the road again."

"You got it, lovey. I'm mostly driving all the time now. I'm good at it, and I don't get yelled at in this cab. But she's seventy-six, and she'll probably retire from this life and leave me her estate one of these days. I'll have to quit driving to take care of it or else sell it. Here's my on-the-road card."

She held up another, and Marie took it.

"Miles Away Mimsie, long-haul trucker." She laughed. "Great. I'll call you."

Mimsie bobbed her head, her many earrings sparkling. "Do that. Send me an e-mail and tell me who else God sent to help you. Now, go on. I need to hit the road."

Marie held her purse tight and opened the door, swinging down onto the running board. "Thanks. A lot."

She hiked across the parking lot to the street light. As she waited for a chance to cross to the historic village, Mimsie pulled up beside her and pulled her air horn. Marie grinned and waved at her.

Thank You, Lord. Please work in Mimsie's heart. I didn't get to say much, but You can make that little seed grow.

As the rig drove away, Marie hurried over the pavement and into a different world.

FIFTY-NINE

•

André formulated his excuse for Janet while he pulled on his clothes. He rarely called in sick. Still, he didn't think he could do that. Sunday's sermon had stuck with him, and the idea that God was with him all the time—or that he was in God's presence all the time—unnerved him. He'd feel all kinds of guilty if he lied, even to Janet. If God was looking over his shoulder, he couldn't lie. Period.

His nerves kicked up as he lifted the phone, and he laughed at himself.

"This is pitiful! Afraid of the dragon lady!" He shook his head. Even so, he shuddered as he looked up Janet's home phone number. She was going to go majorly ballistic. He could feel it.

"Yeah?" said a raspy voice on the other end of the connection.

André cleared his throat. "Janet? This is André. Listen, I have a…a family emergency. I'm not going to be able to come in today."

"You're joking, right, Belanger?"

"No. I'm serious."

"We don't do family leave."

"Janet, please. I said it's an emergency. It really is."

"Who's in the hospital?"

"Nobody."

"Then get yourself over to work."

"I can't."

"Mister, you'd better have a note signed by a doctor for me tomorrow."

"It's not a medical emergency."

"What other kind of emergency is there?"

He felt a muscle in his cheek twitch. "I have to go pick up a family member."

"You're going to the airport? Make them take a cab. We have a business to run."

"But—"

"Do I have to remind you that we are a branch of the U.S. government?"

"Uh…no. No, you don't. But this is a real emergency."

"You've got a gazillion brothers and sisters. Let one of them go pick up Grandma."

André sighed and rubbed his scratchy cheek. "Janet, I'm not coming in."

"Do you want the option of having a job to come in to tomorrow?"

"Look, I have a contract. I'm sure there's something in it about family emergencies. I could have lied and told you I was sick, but I didn't. I'm being up front about this. You're acting like it's Christmas week, for crying out loud."

"I want a note."

"From who, Janet?"

"Whom."

"All right, from whom?"

"From every member of your prolific family, stating that you were the only one who could possibly handle this so-called emergency."

"You got it."

"Fine!"

André winced at the loud clack in his ear. His hand shook so violently he almost dropped the phone.

"Okay," he told himself. "That wasn't so bad." There must be a course for management in interpersonal relationships. He'd put it in the suggestion box at the post office, except he knew Janet would be the one reading the suggestions.

Fifteen minutes later he was parked in the Gillettes' driveway. Lisa let him in and led him to the kitchen.

"Be quiet, okay? Claudia's still asleep."

"How long is she staying?"

"Until Saturday. Assuming…you know. Assuming this turns out all right with Marie."

"Did you tell your folks?"

"No, they left already. Dad wanted Mom to help him dress the windows at the store."

André sat down at the kitchen table. He wasn't sure what was involved in dressing windows at a hardware store, but obviously it meant the store owner and his wife had to leave home before seven a.m. to do it right.

"So…Old Orchard?"

"Yeah. We stayed at a dive near the beach for three nights and swam every day. Then we'd haunt the shops and concessions. Marie loved it. Pierre was on that little island."

"Frasier."

"Yeah. She wouldn't hear from him for months, and Mom and Dad wanted to do something with the whole family that would cheer Marie up and take her mind off Lover Boy."

André grimaced.

"Sorry." Lisa brought two mugs from the cupboard. "I used to call him that to make Marie mad. Coffee?"

"Sure. But we'd better go soon, don't you think?"

"The guy said after lunch," she reminded him.

"Yeah."

"Well, it will only take us a couple of hours to get there."

"True." André looked at his watch.

"Maybe we should both work for a few hours, and then…"

"Oh, no. I'm not going in now. Not after what I said to Janet."

"What did you say?"

"That it's an emergency. I don't think she'd understand a delayed emergency."

Lisa shrugged and reached for the coffee carafe. "Okay, then, we'll have breakfast and make strategy. You called Pierre, right?"

"Uh…no. Not yet."

She scowled at him. "How smart is that?"

"Well, I figured we were close to the delivery point, and he's far away."

"So we tell him, and he gets closer." She turned her eyes toward the ceiling, and the hot coffee sloshed in the pot as she shook her head.

"Sorry. I guess I was thinking he could use the sleep."

"Men."

"Oh, no. Not that again."

"Yes, that again. You want to gallop in and play the hero, and then call Pierre and announce that you've saved the day, not to mention Marie's neck."

"It's not like that."

"No? What is it like?"

He picked up the coffee mug she'd filled for him and turned it, reading the words on the side. This Old Spouse, with little hammers and wrenches all around it. Had to be Lisa's father's mug. He set it down quickly without tasting the coffee. It would be stupid to ask for a different mug, he supposed, but the mental image of him knocking it off the table and smashing it on the perfectly tiled kitchen floor waylaid him. He focused in on Lisa's warm butternut eyes.

"It's like…I want to be able to tell him he can stop worrying. That she's okay. It doesn't have to be me who makes it that way."

She sat down opposite him. "Yeah. Hey, you may think this is weird, but…maybe we could pray about it."

"Yeah. Okay." She obviously expected some action, and he was determined not to disappoint her. He bowed his head and closed his eyes. "Our Father…" He swallowed hard. "Our Father…we ask You to keep Marie safe. And help us to find her." He opened his eyes just a slit. Lisa's face was serious. Her nose twitched. He couldn't think of anything else to say. "Amen."

"Amen." She opened her eyes and smiled at him. "Let's call Pierre."

That he could handle. André took out his phone and hit speed dial.

"Hey, Pierre. It's your favorite brother. Where are you?"

"Western New York. Where are you?"

"In the Gillettes' kitchen."

Pierre laughed. "This early? I won't ask."

André tried to keep a straight face. "She makes good coffee. Hey, I've got something for you."

"What's up?"

"Big news. A truck driver called me a while ago and said a package will be delivered for you at Old Orchard Beach this afternoon."

"What? That doesn't make sense."

André sighed. Maybe Lisa had a point about men. Or maybe it was just the Belanger men. "It's Marie. The package is Marie."

"Oh." Long silence. "Are you sure?"

"Well, he said a package for Pierre—that's you—would be delivered there."

"But…Old Orchard? That's not exactly a trucking hub."

"No, but it's a public place. Maybe she wanted a busy tourist attraction where she could meet you in public and those guys couldn't sneak up on her."

"I don't know." Pierre still sounded doubtful. "How could she be in Maine already? And it's not Memorial Day until next week. Is the place even open yet?"

"Well, yeah. I guess."

"If she could get as far north as that, why not all the way home?"

"The trucker wasn't coming all the way up here, I suppose. Maybe he's delivering a load of supplies there."

"Hmm. I don't see how she could have made it that far so fast."

"Well, if she hitched a ride with a long-haul trucker and came straight through…"

"Man, I don't know," Pierre said. "This pastor called me last night from Ohio and said Marie was at his house yesterday at noon. She ate lunch with him and his wife not far outside Akron. I don't see how she could make it all the way to Maine so fast."

"Could she have flown partway? Maybe she took a plane to Portland. Or Manchester."

"Nah. That doesn't fit with what the minister told me. She wasn't going to fly. She was afraid to use her credit card. Besides, the NCIS put a man at the Akron airport yesterday. There is absolutely no way Marie flew out of there."

"Okay, someplace else, then."

"Maybe. Or maybe it's a hoax."

André looked over at Lisa. She'd risen and put on an apron and begun cracking eggs into a stainless steel bowl.

"Well, Lisa and I are going to drive down there in a little while. We'll stroll up and down the street and the beach and look for her."

"Okay. There's no way George and I could get there before four or five o'clock. We're on I-84 in New York. We drove most of the night. Pennsylvania is a big state, did you know that? But I'm serious. It'll take us hours to get to Old Orchard yet."

"We'll be there by noon. Right, Lisa?"

André looked up at her, and she nodded with a wink. He smiled at her.

"Hey, listen," Pierre said.

"What?"

"I'm not sure I want you two in the middle of this."

"What do you mean?" André felt the old, competitive younger brother resentment rising in his chest. "We can be there for her."

"I know, but… It could be the people trying to get her are hoping to send us off on a wild goose chase. Be careful, okay?"

"Well, sure." André frowned. "I know you said Marie was in trouble, but she got away from those guys, right?"

"For now. But they still want what she has, or what they think she has. Maybe you should go down there and enlist the local police force to sweep the beach with you and look for her. That might be enough to keep the people following her away."

"Well…if you think it's necessary."

"You don't have a gun."

André sat very still. "No, I don't." He glanced at Lisa. "You think it's that dangerous?"

"Could be. If you see a couple of Chinese guys—one with a scar on his left cheek—then you make tracks! Especially if they're hanging out with a big, ugly white guy. Don't stick around to find out if they're guilty. Just get as far away from them as you can."

"O…kay."

"Man, I don't know, André. I hate to think you could be walking into something nasty." Weariness pervaded Pierre's voice. "These guys shot a man in Ohio, as near as we can tell, just for telling them Marie hadn't been there when she really had."

"That's rough." It was enough to give André second thoughts about taking Lisa into the thick of it. But they couldn't leave Marie there, waiting, with no one to bring her home. "We'll talk it over, and we'll be careful. Are you holding up all right?"

"Yeah. George has been great. He's driving now. I'll tell him what you said, and we'll zip over into Connecticut and up to the Massachusetts Turnpike as quick as we can. Maybe the FBI has some agents in Portland and can get them over there."

"Good thinking. That would make me feel a little better."

"We'll see if they can help," Pierre promised. "Call me when you get to Old Orchard."

"All right, bro." André hung up just as Lisa placed a plate of eggs and toast before him. "Hey, that looks great."

"Didn't sound like Pierre thought Marie could get to the drop point so fast."

"Yeah."

Lisa brought her own plate and sat down. "What if the package isn't Marie? What if it's a real, literal package?"

André frowned. Could the cryptic message possibly be a ruse?

"And when it comes down to it," Lisa went on, "how do we know we can trust this Honeybear guy?"

André picked up his fork. "He's all we've got."

SIXTY

André and Lisa strolled along the beach. Lisa had a hard time enjoying the idyllic setting while expecting villains to pop out from behind concession stands and pier pilings. She flipped up the hood of her sweatshirt. The crisp breeze off the bay must be freezing André in his chambray shirt, but he hadn't complained yet.

"Want to go back to the shops?" he asked.

"Okay." Lisa took her peppermint stick out of her mouth. "Does it seem like there are a disproportionate number of Asians here today?"

André whirled around for a moment. "Now that you mention it, yes." They started walking again.

"But I don't remember seeing any families." Lisa frowned and licked the pointy end of the candy stick. "Just men."

André stopped dead and looked behind him. "Pierre said to be careful, and to watch out for a Chinese man with a scar."

Lisa frowned up at him. "How could you not tell me that?"

"I didn't want to worry you."

"Well, this is a fine time to spring it on me." She focused on one tourist and eyed him with critical, narrowed gaze. "See that man over there with the video camera?"

"Yeah."

"He's taping everyone who comes out of the seafood restaurant. That seems a little suspicious to me. Does it to you?"

"Yeah."

She frowned, watching the man.

André kicked at a clump of seaweed. "Too bad we can't go to Palace Playland and ride the Ferris wheel. We might be able to spot Marie from up there."

Lisa looked down the shore toward the beachfront amusement park. The taller rides were visible in the distance. "That's where Marie would be for sure, if it were open."

He smiled. "I'll bet you love the rides too."

"Yeah, I always liked the carousel. Maybe the Ferris wheel. But none of those things that throw you around, and absolutely no roller coasters." She popped the last of the candy stick into her mouth and crunched it.

André reached for her hand. "Maybe we can come back when everything's open."

"Yeah, when this is over. We can bring Pierre and Marie down for a day."

"Hey, your hands are cold." He covered her hand with both of his and rubbed it gently.

She looked up at him, wishing she knew how to tell him how great it was just to be with him. His warm hands caressing hers; his chocolate brown eyes, worried because her sister was in trouble. She wanted to say something, but the words stuck in her throat.

"Look, this is a pretty big place, even though a lot of the attractions are closed," André said. "You'd think she would have been more specific about where to meet her. Maybe if we—"

"Excuse me."

They turned to find a young woman standing behind them. The wind blew her brunette hair about her face. Her casual outfit was straight out of an L.L.Bean catalog, but she wore it with an alluring flair. Lisa stiffened. Pretty, solvent, and eager to charm André. Not fair.

"Are you Mr. Belanger?" the stranger asked.

Lisa's internal smoke alarm started that obnoxious scream. So much for the tender moment.

"Yes," André said with a smile. "But how did you know?"

The woman's smile remained fixed on her face as she pulled out a wallet. "FBI. We have access to your driver's license photo. I'm agent Kendra Swallow. You see the man picking up shells?" She pointed with her chin.

Lisa followed her gaze, and André turned to stare down the beach.

"I see him," André said.

"He's Agent Fiora. The guy over there buying a hot dog is Agent Jones. We're here to help locate and protect Marie Belanger."

"Wow." André's glowing smile made Lisa uneasy. She'd cooked him a complete breakfast and hadn't gotten that big a smile out of him.

"Could I see your identification again?" she asked.

"Sure." Swallow was about to replace the wallet in her pocket, but she flicked it open again. "We're from the Boston office. And we want you two to stay healthy, so I'm asking you to leave."

Lisa squinted at the badge and Swallow's driver's license. It surely looked real. She glanced up. André was frowning at her.

"What do you think, Lisa? We drove all this way."

"We came to pick my sister up." Lisa straightened and faced the woman. "Marie called us. She did not call the FBI."

"Well, her husband called us. Our boss says trouble follows your sister, so it's time for us to step in and you to bow out. Nothing personal. We just want to make sure no one gets hurt."

"Nothing personal to you, either, but I—"

Agent Swallow's cell phone rang, and she answered it without so much as an *Excuse me.*

Lisa glowered at André, and he held his palms up.

"Hey, what can we do?" he asked softly.

Lisa fumed as Swallow turned her back and carried on a conversation largely consisting of "Yes, sir" and "I copy."

"They can't make us leave." A fierce, black resentment grew in Lisa's heart. "Marie didn't want a big production. She wanted her family to come get her and take her home. If these buffoons get hold of her, they'll want to ask her all kinds of questions, and—"

"Sorry about that." Swallow's cheerful tone did little to mollify Lisa. "My boss says we need to get you out of here pronto."

"Well, we don't want to go," Lisa said.

"Let's not make it harder for Agent Swallow and her colleagues to do their jobs."

She turned on André, ready to freeze his affable smile.

"Come on," he coaxed. "We can go back up on the pier and look around in the shops. There was an antique shop near where we parked."

"It's best if you leave the area completely," Swallow said.

Lisa glared at her. "You don't even know whether the people following Marie are here. You don't even know Marie is here."

"Leave it to us, ma'am. We'll notify Lieutenant Belanger if we locate his wife."

André tugged gently on her arm, and Lisa turned away still simmering.

"This isn't right," she insisted.

"Hey, let's not get in their way," André said. She was about to retort when he slid his arm around her waist, and the sarcasm died on her lips.

"Can we at least call Pierre?" she whispered.

"Sure. Let's go back to the truck where we'll be out of the wind and have a little privacy." He stooped and kissed her forehead without breaking stride, and Lisa's stomach flipped. She knew she would comply with any suggestion he made.

Back at his pickup, André turned the heater on for Lisa. Unorthodox in May, but after all, this was Maine, and the sea breeze still had a bite. He handed her a bottle of water and called his brother.

"Hey, Pierre. *C'est moi.* We're in Old Orchard."

"And Marie?"

"No sign of her. Where are you?"

"Just skirting Hartford. We're heading north."

"An FBI agent just came up to us and told us to leave."

"I'm sorry. They know things you don't."

"What kind of things?"

"I probably shouldn't say, but the CIA is joining them there. They think they've spotted some enemies of the state hanging around the beach, and they're hoping to round them up."

"What kind of enemies?"

"Well…you might call them Chinese Mafia."

"You're not serious."

"I'm dead serious. They call themselves something else, but you get the picture. It looks definite that they got wind of Marie's location and started congregating in Old Orchard. You and Lisa are probably better off out of there."

"What about Marie?"

There was a long silence. Pierre's voice cracked a little as he said, "I don't know, buddy. I just…don't know."

"We've been here a couple of hours. If Marie planned to be here…"

"She did," Lisa cried, grabbing his arm. André wrapped his hand around her fingers and squeezed.

"I haven't heard from her," Pierre said. "Maybe I should call the folks and see if she's contacted them."

"More likely she'd call her own parents," André said.

"I'll call them." Lisa took out her own phone, and André smiled at the eagerness in her expression. He continued to talk to Pierre as she pushed the buttons for her parents' home phone.

"Hey, Claudia. It's me. André and I are down at Old Orchard Beach, looking for Marie." She winced. "I said we're looking for Marie. She sent a message that said she'd be here this afternoon." Lisa looked up at André with an apologetic smile. "I guess I should have left a note. What's that, Claudia? Why Old Orchard? Well, the message André got said she'd be at the place where we all vacationed three years ago."

A sudden look of horror came over Lisa's face.

"Pierre, hold on a sec," André said. He lowered his phone and touched Lisa's sleeve. "What is it?"

Lisa gulped. "Are you sure, Claud?" She eyed André in abject misery. Tears flooded her eyes. "I goofed," she choked.

"What's the matter, Lisa?"

She swallowed hard and took the phone away from her ear. "I was wrong. This isn't the place where the package will be delivered."

André stared at her. He could hear Claudia's faraway voice emanating from Lisa's phone, which now rested against the thigh of her jeans. "Hey! Lisa! You still there?"

He reached over and gently pried her fingers off the phone and took it.

"Claudia, this is André. Do I understand correctly that we're in the wrong place?"

Lisa's stricken eyes met his. "I thought…"

"Afraid so," Claudia said. "The family went to Old Orchard four years ago. Man, what a doofus Lisa is."

"Uh…may I ask where you went three years ago?" André asked.

"Let's see…the next year I was away, and they all went to Mystic Seaport, in Connecticut. I was so jealous because…"

André handed the phone back to Lisa and put his own to his cheek. He hadn't shaved this morning. That was the only real thing about this crazy situation.

"Pierre?"

"Yeah, I'm here. What's going on?"

"Change of course, I'm afraid. How far are you from Mystic Seaport?"

The pause was so long, he was afraid their call had been dropped.

"An hour at least, maybe two. It's almost on the Rhode Island border. Should we head that way now?"

André hesitated. "It's the best data I've got, for what it's worth. And I'm sorry."

"Better now than after we hit the Mass Pike."

"Yeah. All right."

"Talk to you later." Pierre hung up.

André's smile felt a little wobbly as he faced Lisa. "So. Do you want—"

Several loud pops sounded from the beach, and he heard screaming. People ran past the pickup. He stared at Lisa.

"Get down!" She dove beneath the level of the dashboard, pulling his arm as she moved. "Someone's shooting!"

André's mouth went dry as he ducked low beside here. "Are you okay?"

"Yes. But you were right."

"Oh?"

"I should have listened to that FBI woman." She squeezed her eyes shut tight.

André grasped her hand. "At least Marie isn't in the middle of this."

She opened her eyes and tears trickled down her cheeks. "Any way you look at it, this is a crummy day."

Even in the middle of his fear for their safety, André wanted to comfort her. He reached out and wiped away the tears from her cheeks and began to pray softly. At least they could ask God to see them through this crummy situation they had stumbled onto.

SIXTY-ONE

Marie sauntered through the gravel streets of Mystic Seaport, trying to appear the casual tourist. A group of junior high school students had entered the village just behind her. She tried to stay out of their way as the forty jabbering teens rushed from one point of interest to another with their chaperones dragging wearily behind.

It was nearly three o'clock. Had Pierre received her message? She'd assured herself a dozen times he could make it here by now. Maybe Honeybear hadn't called André as she'd asked. Or maybe he'd garbled the message.

She peered into the blacksmith's shop. A reenactor stood at the glowing forge, talking to a handful of spectators as he used tongs to remove a piece of metal from the fire. The cheerful scene drew her, but it would be harder for Pierre to find her if she stayed inside a building.

Trudging on down the street, she eyed each person she met from beneath her lashes. Visitors wandered, wide-eyed, from one restored building to another. Staff members walked faster, with a purpose.

Farther down the street, she found the ropewalk. She didn't remember it from that other time her family had visited the seaport, but there were so many exhibits they probably hadn't had time to view them all. Curious, she opened the door. The long building was deserted. She stepped inside, awed by the web of forty hemp strands feeding through a metal screen to be twisted into a thick cord. The rope that came out beyond the framework stretched a hundred yards down the length of the echoing structure.

The door opened behind her, and she jumped. A couple with two children entered, and Marie stepped to one side to let them in, and then she slipped out the door. Her heart thudded as she turned back up the street, scolding herself.

No deserted buildings. I've got to stay where there are plenty of people.

She meandered along, farther from the center of the village, to the pier where the ship *Joseph Conrad* was docked. A rope barrier stretched across the ramp, with a "Closed" sign dangling from it. Against the side of the vessel, a workman hung in an apparatus that looked to Marie like a child's swing. As she stepped closer, she saw that his seat was suspended by ropes, and he looked quite comfortable as he worked on the old weathered boards of the hull.

A couple moved in beside her, staring at the ship.

"It'd be great to sail on her," the man said.

"What's he doing?" the woman asked, pointing at the workman.

"Looks like he's scraping the hull. They're probably going to repaint just that section. If they were redoing the whole thing, they'd have it over at the shipyard."

Marie left them and headed back toward the central part of the village. As she rounded the corner of the long shed that held a small boat exhibit, she realized that even here, in the open, she was in an isolated spot. Clusters of people walked past, but between them were gaps when she was virtually alone. She hastened back to the busier village street and on toward the centerpiece of the exhibits—the whaling ship *Charles W. Morgan.*

The masts of the *Morgan* rose against the blue sky. Clusters of tourists mounted the walkway to the deck, and she saw that a tour group was forming. She scurried up the gangway and joined them on deck, keeping to the back edge of the group.

The guide led them around the upper deck, pointing out the rigging and the brick stoves and try-pots, where whale blubber had been heated to extract the oil. The others headed below to view the crew's quarters and the lower deck, where the slabs of blubber were cut up, but Marie hung back. She didn't want to get into a confined space.

At the gunwale, she scanned the village street, looking for a familiar figure. Would Pierre be in uniform when he came? Or was he too far away to make the rendezvous this afternoon? Would he send someone else to meet her?

Maybe Honeybear made a mistake when he took down André's phone number. She couldn't spot any policemen, or anyone who might be a security guard. But would she know a plainclothes officer if she saw one? The afternoon was half gone, and her misgivings grew into apprehension.

If he doesn't come by four o'clock, I'll find a telephone and call him.

She leaned against the old timbers and closed her eyes in prayer.

"Well, well."

She whirled around and stared into the familiar, scarred face of the Chinese man.

SIXTY-TWO

1600 Tuesday

George followed the car ahead of him, determined to stick to McCutcheon like a tick on a dog's back. When he'd called McCutcheon, the FBI agent was twenty miles ahead of them, heading for Maine, but on receiving the new report of Marie's whereabouts, he'd U-turned and clapped a portable emergency light on the roof of his car. He and his team had soon caught up with George and taken the lead.

When they entered the town of Mystic, the bubble light came off, and the two cars rolled placidly down the street to the parking lot of the reconstructed seaport village. George parked as close to the street as he could, and Pierre jumped out and ran toward the park entrance.

"Wait!" McCutcheon called.

George sauntered over to the agent's car. "You can't hold him back, McCutcheon."

"He could get himself killed."

George walked with the three FBI agents into the visitors' center. Pierre was purchasing a ticket. McCutcheon strode up behind him.

"Belanger, let us handle this."

"In a pig's eye." Pierre pocketed his wallet and scooped up the ticket.

George decided to let Pierre deal with McCutcheon and chose a brochure from a rack on the counter as he slipped the employee behind it a twenty-dollar bill.

McCutcheon clamped his hand on Pierre's shoulder.

"Listen to me. Our agent in charge up in Maine—that would be Agent Swallow, of the Boston office—just contacted me again. They've had a bloodbath at Old Orchard Beach."

Pierre turned slowly and gaped at him.

"What happened?"

McCutcheon and the other agents stepped to one side, away from the ticket counter, drawing Pierre with them. George quickly pocketed his change and ticket and joined them.

"When our people arrived, they found no trace of your wife," McCutcheon said. "We now know she never went there, but apparently a lot of other people thought she did. Our team members spotted several Chinese nationals and Asian-Americans whom they considered to be acting suspiciously. They were able to identify a man high up in a tong operating out of New York."

George edged in closer to Pierre. This didn't sound good at all. McCutcheon included him in his gaze but went on talking to Pierre.

"This leader seems to be involved in a vague scheme to overthrow Red China."

Pierre blinked hard, and George felt his own adrenaline surge. How much did McCutcheon know about the China plot, and could the Asian men he described have connections to those involved in the secret negotiations?

"That seemed strange to us, since we'd been thinking the people chasing your wife were on the other side—taking care of business for the Chinese communist government." McCutcheon stroked his mustache. "Then they realized there were representatives from both sides on the beach. That's when Swallow decided they'd better get the civilians out of there."

"My brother and Marie's sister were there," Pierre said.

McCutcheon nodded. "She identified them early. Watched them

hanging out and looking for Mrs. Belanger. At the point where she realized serious trouble was brewing, she approached them and told them to leave the beach. Her team started quietly alerting other tourists to vacate the area. A few minutes later, the fireworks started."

"You mean…"

"She said it was like the O.K. Corral."

"Casualties?" George asked.

McCutcheon's eyes narrowed. "Thanks to Swallow's decisive action, no civilians were injured, but the two contingents went at it tooth and nail. Agent Swallow and her team basically stayed out of it and let the Tongs and the Commies shoot each other up. Three dead, and a couple more were wounded. When it was over, our people rounded up five survivors. Unfortunately several others got away. Swallow's got her hands full."

"But my brother and Lisa are okay?" Pierre asked.

"I'm assured that they are."

"That's very interesting," George said, perusing the map in the brochure, "but we still need to find Marie Belanger. She wasn't waiting for us out front. This village has more than fifty structures. I suggest we fan out and show her picture to staff and visitors, and ask if anyone's seen her."

"Please let us handle it," McCutcheon began, but Pierre interrupted.

"We need to find her fast."

"Lieutenant, I understand your feelings. That little rumble up in Maine wasn't a coincidence, and we all know it. Your wife and the information she's carrying caused it. Both sides want the same thing; therefore, both sides want her."

Pierre clenched his fists. His dark eyes almost shot sparks, and George stepped in. "So how far away is the NCIS team, Mc-Cutcheon?"

The FBI agent glanced at his watch. "They should be here any minute. That's four more people."

"Great. So maybe one of your men should wait out front for them, and the rest of us should get at it."

McCutcheon eyed him testily for a long moment and then shrugged. "We need to close the gate, Hudson. We can't let any more innocent people in. There's a risk we'll see some action here too."

"But they all think she's in Maine," Pierre insisted.

"Fine. Do you suggest we page her?"

Pierre's gaze wavered. "Of course not."

McCutcheon nodded. "The odds are slim, but we have to consider that the killers could be here. I'm just trying to prevent a repeat of Old Orchard. There are more tourists here. The park up there hadn't opened for the season. This place is open year-round."

"Let's move," George said.

McCutcheon stepped to the ticket counter, ignoring the line of patrons, and flashed his badge.

"I'm with the FBI," he told the employee selling tickets. "I'm sorry to interrupt your day, but we need to close you down early today. We'll make a search of the grounds, and—"

The ticket seller dropped his jaw. "But, sir…"

George looked around for Pierre. His friend was slipping out through the door that led to the historic village. Before it closed, he turned and caught George's gaze. George winked and turned back toward McCutcheon.

"Do you think that's really necessary?"

McCutcheon glared at him. "I don't have time for this, Hudson. We need to find her before… Hey, where'd Belanger go?"

George cocked his head to one side. "He'd bought his ticket. I expect he's seeing the sights."

The employee raised his chin as he addressed McCutcheon. "I'll have to call my supervisor, sir. This is highly irregular."

"See you later." George hurried through the door, glad to put McCutcheon's sputtering behind him. He consulted the multicolored map. In the distance, Pierre was hurrying along the path toward the waterfront. On the way they'd discussed the most likely places to find

Marie. Pierre had opted for the restored whaling ship, and George had picked the gift shop. It was only a few steps away.

The young woman behind the counter smiled broadly, showing off a full set of braces. George produced his identification and the photo of Marie that he'd carried for the last four days. Marie's striking face was one people noticed. Sometimes that was good, sometimes bad. He hoped today her beauty would work in their favor.

"I'm Lieutenant Commander George Hudson, and I wondered if you've seen this woman today."

The woman studied the picture.

"Yeah, I remember her. She was the first person I waited on when I came back from lunch."

George contained his elation and kept a neutral tone. "What time was that?"

She patted her hair with one hand, frowning. "Quarter to one, maybe?"

"Did she buy anything?"

"A couple of postcards. Said she wanted to send one to a friend in Newport."

"Anything else you remember about her?"

"I asked if she wanted a bag, and she said no. She put the post-cards in her purse."

"That's it?"

"Well, I think she asked me directions to the post office." She smiled and shook her head. "I'm not sure. We get a lot of people in here."

"I understand."

George headed outside and strolled toward the tall ships. Pierre had specifically mentioned the *Morgan*, the pride of the exhibits. George spotted him on deck, talking to a staff member dressed in denim.

Near a huge anchor set up as a sculpture, George stopped a couple and showed them Marie's picture. They shook their heads and went on. George took the gangway to the ship in a few strides, and Pierre met him at the side of the deck.

"She was here." Pierre's dark eyes gleamed. "The sailor saw her."

"How long ago?"

"Maybe an hour. He was doing a group tour and lost track of her. But he's pretty sure it was her."

George nodded. "Okay. She was in the gift shop too, but earlier. I guess that clinches it. Have you been below?"

"Not yet."

"Maybe we'd better take a quick run-through."

"You do it. I'll wait here. It's a pretty good view." Pierre rested his elbows on the rail and surveyed the shifting crowd that passed below them in the dirt street.

George did a quick sweep of the deck and then went down the companionway. He peered into each tiny cabin. And he'd thought his shipboard quarters were small! It made him thankful to live in the modern world.

He followed a group of children and their parents into the hold and back up another set of stairs. No place for her to take refuge. He thought she'd stay out in the open, anyway, where she could see them arriving.

Pierre was in the same spot where he'd left him.

"Nothing," George reported. "What now?"

Pierre inhaled deeply. "I heard someone say there's a museum building where they have films and artifacts."

"You want to check it out? I can head down the other way and ask around the houses and shops."

"Yeah. But, George…"

"Hmm?" They climbed the steps to the gangway together.

"Did you notice what McCutcheon said?" Pierre asked.

"Yeah."

"We didn't tell him any of that."

George watched his face as they reached the ground. "He made it sound like they've been watching these Chinese. Someone at their headquarters may have made the connection."

"But the plot," Pierre said. "How could they know that? It sounds more like CIA than FBI. I mean, this thing has been really hush-hush."

"Yes, but a lot of people have worked on it."

Pierre stopped in the street. George pointed across to a large building. "There's your museum."

"Tarrington turned," Pierre said.

"Yes."

"Someone else might have too."

George nodded. He'd seen it before, and he knew it was true. Someone you thought was true to the core flipped and went over to the enemy.

"You know, Marie and I were just going to start a normal life," Pierre said softly. "We were going to get back into the States and settle down at some base and start a family."

"That can still happen."

Pierre looked doubtful. "Do you think McCutcheon closed the park?"

"I don't know. I haven't heard any announcements yet."

"You think they'd clear out all the visitors?"

"Maybe."

Pierre sighed, and his shoulders sagged.

"Hey, let's move," George said. "We'll find her."

SIXTY-THREE

Marie was hauled out of the car and shoved. Unable to see through the blindfold, she tripped over a step or a curb, and a rough hand grabbed her arm. She caught her balance. After the long ride, it was a relief to be out of the confines of the car.

"You walk."

She walked.

The blindfold stuck to her skin where her tears had dried. The noises of traffic and many voices surged around her. She inhaled cautiously. Diesel fumes. Cooking oil. Fish. Cigarette smoke.

She was guided inside a building, and almost at once the noise quieted and the scents became spicy. The food smells were stronger. Incense? A hand led her, and she shuffled along, sensing a person ahead and another close behind her. After twenty steps, they stopped.

"Down stairs."

She reached out cautiously and felt a wall, then groped until her hand found the top of a railing. With the toe of her sneaker, she sought the edge of the first step.

"Go down."

She went down slowly, feeling each step. There were twelve. Her knees trembled, and it was hard to keep her balance.

At last she was told to stop, and fingers worked at the knot in her blindfold. When the cloth came away from her eyes, she blinked. They stood in a small, windowless room furnished as an office.

"Sit."

Two people occupied the room with her. She turned and saw a swivel chair behind her. The nearest man nodded, so she sat down.

Her two companions stood in silence. Questions filled her mind, but she said nothing. The man with the scar was nowhere to be seen. One of her guardians was stout, the other thin, and both had black hair and dark eyes, with unmistakably Chinese features. She took a deep breath and exhaled carefully. Her pulse had slowed during the ride, and she had decided one couldn't sustain terror for long. Still, a faint nausea clung to her, and she couldn't shake a certainty of impending doom.

The door opened and the scar-faced man strode in, holding up her purse. At least, Marie thought it was her purse, but the leather bag he held was limp and slender.

He shook the empty purse before her face.

"Where is it?"

Marie's pulse raced. She opened her mouth, but no sound came out. Maybe you could stay terrified, after all. She swallowed hard.

"Where is it?"

"What?" She managed.

"You know what. The computer drive that Jenna Tarrington passed to you. What did you do with it?"

She closed her mouth and stared past him at the stout man.

The leader slapped her.

She gasped and raised her hands to her face.

"You tell me!" he shouted.

"I...don't know anything about your business."

"You lie."

He stormed from the room.

She gulped in air but kept her gaze lowered, fearful of catching the notice of the two remaining men. She sat shivering, although the air was not cold. She hugged her arms around her chest and tried to sit still.

After several minutes, two women entered the room. Marie began to tremble, although neither was the one who had shot Jenna. The older woman spoke to the guards, and the men went out.

"Stand up," she said to Marie.

Marie stood, and the younger woman reached out and began to unbutton her blouse. Stepping aside, Marie slapped at her hand.

"Stop. What do you think you're doing?"

The older woman planted herself squarely in front of Marie and glared into her eyes.

"You be quiet. We search you and take your clothes away. You put this on." She held up what appeared to be a black bathrobe.

"What if I won't?"

"Then we call them in." The woman jerked her head toward the door.

Marie pressed her lips together and tried not to quake. Plainly she was going to lose her clothing whether she wanted to or not. She'd already lost the tote bag she'd bought at the thrift shop in Ohio. She supposed they had gone through it thoroughly, as they had her purse, in hopes of finding Jenna's flash drive.

She looked deep into the Chinese woman's eyes. "Please, do we really have to do this?"

The woman just stared back. Her companion waited.

Marie sighed. "All right. Just let me undress myself."

When they had left with every stitch of clothing she'd worn, she sat down in the chair again, shivering and holding the black garment close about her.

After a long time, the young woman returned and handed her a bundle of her wadded up clothing. She left, and Marie dressed quickly, her hands trembling. She tried to keep an eye on the door every moment, fearing that the two men who acted as guards would come back.

She was tying her sneakers when the scar-faced man returned. The other two men followed him in and stood near the door.

"Are you ready to talk?"

She avoided meeting his gaze.

"You led us on a long chase. You can see that we do not give up. Now tell me what I want to know."

Marie couldn't help touching her cheekbone gently. The bruise hurt, and she was sure he could see a red mark where he had struck her.

"Tell me." His voice was soft, coaxing.

"I don't know what you want."

"I want the item Jenna Tarrington agreed to carry through customs for us. In San Francisco, she refused to give it up. She gave us her computer, but the information I need was not on it."

Marie clamped her teeth together. He made it sound as if Jenna had handed over her computer willingly.

"Our contact threatened her, and she said she no longer had what we needed. For that, she lost her life. I got her traveling bag, but it was not in there, either. In Detroit, I got the two suitcases she had checked, but again, it was not there."

Marie lifted her chin. "Perhaps she did not have it in the first place."

He shook his head. "Her husband says she did. And now the Americans have him under guard. We cannot talk to him. But he swore on his life she would bring it to us. She walked away from him at Narita with it in her bag. But she got off the plane in San Francisco without it."

"You have no proof she took it out of Japan."

He slapped her again, and Marie sobbed. She could feel him staring down at her.

"Why do you care?" he asked.

She didn't answer.

"I will tell you why." The scarred man paced the small room, and the other two men glided out of his way.

He whirled and pointed at her.

"You care because you know what she had. If you did not know what she carried, you would not care, and you would tell me anything I asked to save your life."

A foul taste rose in her throat, choking her.

"Yes, I said your life. That is what you will pay with. Just as she did."

He pivoted and marched from the room before she could speak.

The other two men approached her and seized her wrists. Marie writhed and gulped for breath as they bound her hands before her. The stout man brought the black blindfold.

"Please don't."

The man grunted and wrapped the cloth around her head, tying it tightly in the back.

With great effort, Marie held back a sob. "Please. I don't have what he wants. Why is he doing this?"

One of the men said, close to her ear, "You think Xian is evil? You go to the boss. Then you will know evil."

"He...he is not the boss?"

The man chuckled. "Xian is the man who would like to be boss."

The other man laughed with him.

Marie pondered that. So they were not going to kill her immediately.

Thank You, Lord. Please give me wisdom. Show me what to do.

They took her up the stairs again. The cooking smells sickened her now. The men led her outside. The air was much cooler, and she thought it must be evening.

"Quick, now," one of the man said, pushing her forward.

A squeal of brakes startled her, and there was a sudden slamming of car doors and the pounding of running feet. She heard muffled shouts and grunts, and the impact of something hard on flesh.

No one restrained her for a moment. She put her hands up and ripped off the blindfold. Dark-clad figures brawled on the sidewalk and in the street. Someone grabbed her from behind and dragged her away from the building. She struggled, but he shoved her, and she fell headlong. Harsh hands lifted her and propelled her toward a dark van.

SIXTY-FOUR

They drove for more than an hour, maybe two. Her new captors did not blindfold Marie, and she was allowed to stare out the window. The man sitting next to her held a gun trained on her midsection. She prayed silently and tried to memorize the signboards.

Canal Street. The signs on most of the businesses were in Chinese characters. Tokyo had prepared her for some of the sights of a huge city, but still she gaped at the skyscrapers and lights. The Chinese signs gave way to English only. The signs soon told her they were leaving Manhattan by the Queens Midtown Tunnel. She had no clear notion of where they were, no image of Long Island in her memory, but she knew they were going away from the city and toward the Atlantic.

The three men in the car didn't talk to her during the ride, and she kept quiet, watching. Her head ached, and the bruises on her cheek throbbed. The tunnel brought on an unexpected claustrophobia. She closed her eyes and then snapped them open again. She had to pay attention.

When they emerged from the artificial twilight of the tunnel, she exhaled. Long Island. Soon they left the tall buildings behind and zipped past thousands of single-family dwellings. So many houses! The miles sped by, and the neighborhoods changed. The houses were farther apart, and bigger. They turned onto a quiet, tree-lined street and stopped before an iron gate. It opened, and they rolled into an exclusive community. The contrast to the crowded tenements of Chinatown stunned her.

At last the driver pulled up before a huge stone mansion and stopped the van. Her guard opened his door, climbed out, and then motioned with his pistol for her to follow.

She eased across the seat, keeping an eye on his weapon, and lowered herself to the pavement. Her tired legs trembled.

"Inside," the man said, and she turned toward the house. Slowly she climbed the steps. Brass lights gleamed on either side of the wide front door. One of the three men who accompanied her pushed the doorbell, and it opened at once. A black-clad Asian man bowed to them and stood aside. Marie entered the hall.

I wish Pierre could see this place!

She couldn't help staring. It almost seemed as if her parents' whole house could fit in the entrance hall, and the peak of the roof wouldn't touch the glittering chandelier far overhead.

The man with the gun prodded her, and she followed the one who walked ahead of her into a side room. At their bidding, she sat gingerly on the edge of a sofa upholstered in thick red velvet. The chamber was more Marie's idea of a formal drawing room than a comfortable place to live. Gold swirls decorated the dark wallpaper, and several large paintings hung about the room. Most were floral still lifes, but over a marble fireplace hung an oversized portrait of an Asian woman in a yellow gown. She was in her fifties perhaps, although her skin was unwrinkled and her hair a lustrous black. Her haughty eyes gazed down on Marie.

The men stirred, and she looked toward the doorway. A very fat man came in slowly, rolling along with short steps. He stared at her for a long time, and she shivered. Finally he waddled to a large padded chair and sat down. Marie sank into the couch cushions.

"You know who I am?" he asked.

She shook her head. "No, sir."

He inhaled through his nose while studying her once more. "Perhaps that is best. But I know who you are, Mrs. Belanger."

Her mouth went dry at his tone.

"Please, sir…" It came out a whisper, and she cleared her throat.

"Speak up! You wish to say something?"

Marie hesitated. "Forgive me. I am…ignorant. I do not know why your people have brought me here."

"I find that hard to believe."

She said nothing but looked down at the lush wool rug.

"Tell me what Wing Fu got from you."

Marie looked up at him in confusion. "Wing Fu?"

"The leader of the communist cell. His men took you to Chinatown. What did you tell him?"

"I didn't tell them anything. And I didn't meet anyone named Wing Fu. At least, if I did, I didn't know it. There was a man called Xian. One of the others said he wanted to be the boss."

The fat man smiled. "Yes. I know this man. You are fortunate my people found you when they did."

Marie's throat constricted, and she swallowed hard. Who was this man? Could she trust him? "Thank you. I appreciate your assistance. But I would like to get back to my family."

"Not so fast, Mrs. Belanger." He crossed his pudgy legs. "Your husband is a naval officer."

"Yes, sir."

"I understand he has been on the fringe of an important operation concerning American relations with China."

"I don't really know. My husband never tells me what his work entails. I mean, I know that he performs certain duties, but he would never tell me anything specific."

The man nodded. "I see. But you understand about classified information."

"What do you mean?"

"Your husband and the men he worked with had access to certain secrets."

Marie sat up straight. "I'm not sure what you're implying. And if he did have secret data, he wouldn't tell me about it."

He smiled and raised one hand. A servant in black-and-gold silk moved silently toward them, his padded gold slippers soundless on the carpet. He stopped by the master's chair and held out a tray with a glass on it. The man took the glass and waved the servant away. Marie was offered nothing. She watched in silence as her interrogator sipped the liquid in the glass.

"So." He shifted his position and set the glass on a small bamboo table. "You claim you know nothing about the information our nations are trying so hard to recover."

She took a deep breath and blew it out slowly through her mouth.

"I don't know that there is any such information. I have wondered. All I know for sure is that a woman was killed and someone has been chasing me, but I don't know why. Are you telling me all this has something to do with my husband's work?"

"Only indirectly. You have heard of the man Commander Christopher Tarrington?"

"Yes."

"Your government has arrested him. You know this?"

She shook her head. "I haven't heard much news this week. But I do know that his wife was killed."

"That is correct."

"But I don't know why."

"Why do you think she was killed?"

Marie could not hold his gaze. "I...don't know."

"She did not pass you information before her death?"

"She barely spoke to me at first. Then we sat together on the plane. She ignored me for most of the flight, but we talked a little about our families. When we got to San Francisco and went through customs, all of a sudden she wanted to walk with me to the next gate. We were to be on the same flight to Detroit."

"All of this I know. I have eyes and ears everywhere. You were seen with Mrs. Tarrington in the San Francisco airport."

Marie remembered the men who had watched her. How did she

know this man wasn't part of the communist regime? He might even be the "boss" Xian's men had spoken of. Perhaps the street fight was staged to trick her.

She cleared her throat. "The airport has many cameras. Everyone knows by now that Jenna Tarrington and I were together for a short time. The police have put out bulletins saying they want to find me."

"Ah, but you have been very good at eluding them." He lifted his glass and took another drink. "So. You use a computer?"

His change of subject startled her. Where was this conversation leading? Her headache was worse, and her stomach rumbled.

"I'm not very good at it. My husband has a computer, and I use it for e-mail. Sometimes I write a letter on it."

"You are familiar with the small, portable data storage called a flash drive?"

"Xian asked me about that. I have never used one."

"They are called by other names, but you understand what I am talking about?"

"I think so. It holds extra memory for a computer?"

"Precisely."

She nodded. "I don't know much about that type of technology, but I can see its usefulness."

"Oh, yes. It is very useful."

"That's what all of this is about, isn't it? Someone put data on one of those, and Jenna was supposed to give it to someone else, and she didn't. And now you think I have it."

He pursed his lips. "You see? You are not so ignorant as you claimed."

"But…"

"What?"

She wished she hadn't spoken. "Nothing. I just wondered why, if someone had information that important, he wouldn't just e-mail it to the person he wanted to have it."

He lifted his glass once more, took a sip, and then set it carefully down on its coaster. "This particular information could not be passed easily, not even by e-mail. You see, some documents are very closely guarded, and the people who have access to them are watched. If anyone had tried to send this data out of the military base in Yokosuka, the sender would have been discovered quickly and arrested."

She nodded, applying what he said to Commander Tarrington's situation. "But that person could ask a civilian to carry it into the United States for him."

They sat without speaking, and the man watched her. Marie wondered again which side he was on. What sort of information was Tarrington trying to export? If this man were on Tarrington's side, then he wanted that information badly and had probably paid for it. But that would also mean he was an enemy of the United States. If he were on the opposite side, however, he was on the side Pierre's crew worked for. The patriotic, pro-American side, whatever it was they were trying to accomplish in the Far East. Why would he want to get the flash drive? Instantly a logical explanation popped into her mind—he wanted it to keep it from the other side. But in that case, he was an ally and wouldn't harm her.

Marie sent up a swift prayer. Would boldness help here?

She stood. At once the servants standing about the perimeter of the room moved closer, and the fat man sat forward.

"Sir, may I go home now?" she asked.

"I should think not."

"But why? I don't have that flash drive you care so much about."

"I know that."

"You do?"

"Xian had you. If the flash drive was on your person, he would have found it."

She flushed at the memory of the humiliating search and the way Xian's hand had shot out to strike her.

"That...did not happen."

The fat man nodded. "Good. I believe you, and I am extremely happy to hear it. If Wing Fu got hold of this information, thousands of Chinese people would die."

Marie sucked in a breath.

"That surprises you?"

"Yes. I told you, I have no clue what sort of information we are talking about."

He nodded. "That may be so, or it may not. But as to your question, Mrs. Belanger, no. You may not go home yet."

"But…you don't work for the government, do you?"

He smiled. "I work for myself."

"Then why do you want me? I have nothing of value to you."

"But you did have it, didn't you?"

An odd, tingling feeling spread through her arms and legs. It was important not to tell him. For some reason, she knew that. If this man were on the up and up, he would let her go. But he wanted that data for his own purposes.

She stared at him. "If I did have it, I would not give it to you."

SIXTY-FIVE

1730 Tuesday, Mystic Seaport, Connecticut

Pierre trudged past the tall ship *Joseph Conrad*. It was closed to tourists. He couldn't see any crew members on board, but a man hung over the side in a bosun's chair, wielding a paintbrush. He doubted that fellow had noticed a pretty girl passing by. He quickly looked in the boathouses and sheds and headed back around toward the main gate and the visitors' center.

George was nowhere in sight, so he ambled along the lane he'd already traveled, past the restaurant and general store. The park closed and the vacationers gradually left, but the search went on until the sun set. Pierre was hungry and frustrated. George came out of the apothecary shop and met him in the middle of the street. Neither asked if the other had news.

"Maybe we should have had them page her."

George shook his head. They'd discussed the pros and cons of that strategy, and it was too late now. "Come on. It's time to meet the others back at the gate."

They turned and headed for the visitors' center. Pierre dragged his feet. George turned around and walked backward, watching him.

"Tired, *mon ami?*"

"Yes."

"We've done everything we can."

"I know. But she was here. She was, George."

"Yes. But she's gone."

Ahead Pierre saw Heinz and his NCIS team members lounging on the steps to the ticketing area. He grabbed George's sleeve and stopped him.

"Wait a sec."

"What is it?"

"Remember what we talked about earlier? When I mentioned it was funny McCutcheon seemed to know all about the China operation?"

"Maybe he doesn't really. Maybe the CIA operatives told the FBI in very general terms that there's some buzz about China, and he's trying to sound important and make us think he knows all about it."

Pierre shook his head. "Think, George. Put that brain of yours on this for me. Every time Marie called one of us, the killers got ahead of us."

"Well…"

"And we had Heinz look at our phones. They aren't bugged."

"Right. So that means no one was hearing our phone conversations with Marie."

"Exactly. And she called from a different phone every time—mostly pay phones."

George nodded. "So no one learned her location through wire taps."

Pierre glanced toward the building. McCutcheon and his team came out through the door. The FBI agent began talking with Heinz.

Pierre turned his back to them. "I'm telling you, George, the only way those assassins could find Marie before we did is if Marie told them or we told them."

· George's eyes glittered as he looked toward the men on the back porch of the visitors' center.

"Hey, Hudson," McCutcheon called.

"Be right with you." George leaned closer to Pierre. "I hear you, but I'm not convinced. Yet."

"Well, keep thinking about it."

"What about Ohio? We got to Randall's Auto Body a half hour ahead of McCutcheon."

"Yeah. We'd left them behind at the motel."

"And Heinz didn't even know about it," George said. "He called us when we were in Greenwood, and he still thought we were headed for the Akron-Canton airport."

Pierre nodded. "Yeah. But when we left the motel, you called McCutcheon and told him where we were headed."

George inhaled, his eyebrows drawing down in a scowl. "That was after your brother called us."

"Right. We left the motel thinking Marie was going to the airport. McCutcheon said he'd send the NCIS there, but he waited in Cafford for his own men to arrive. He was planning to catch up with us, but we left Randall's garage before the FBI got there."

"Yeah, okay. I follow you. I told him about the emergency rendezvous. And the Chinese man with the scar beat us to it."

"My point exactly. Who told him about the emergency rendezvous?"

"But the killers were ahead of us, at Randall's and at Greenwood."

"Yeah. If McCutcheon tipped them off as soon as we told him, and they were already ahead of us when we left the motel…"

George clenched his teeth. "I don't even want to think this."

"*Mon copain,* there is no other explanation. Think about the preacher. He told me Marie was okay, but not where he lives. And she had already left there. The killers did not go there. Why? Because we did not have that knowledge to pass to McCutcheon."

The FBI and NCIS men left the porch and came toward them.

"What's up?" Heinz asked. "You didn't find anything, did you?"

"No," George said. "Just trying to figure out where we go from here."

"I don't know as there's much more we can do tonight," Heinz said.

McCutcheon nodded. "Unless we get another lead, we might as well find a place to sleep."

Pierre bit back a retort. No way could he sleep, wondering if the killers had Marie now. But then, if his suspicions were correct, McCutcheon probably knew whether or not they had her. He might know exactly where she was. He might even have kept them here for hours searching the village while those thugs took Marie to a secure location to…what? He felt sick. They would try to make her tell them where the flash drive was. If she didn't give it to them, they would kill her as they had Jenna. And if she did? He didn't believe for one second that they would turn a witness loose.

SIXTY-SIX

"Take her to the boat," the fat man said. His chair groaned as he pushed himself upward. "Keep her there until I send word. Two guards at all times." He stood for a moment, panting from the exertion.

"Excuse me," Marie said.

He gave her a disinterested look.

"I'm hungry."

His eyes narrowed, and Marie's heartbeat accelerated. Was she pushing him too far? Some instinct told her that he would respect courage. She managed to meet his stare without flinching and ignored the fluttering in her chest.

"Take her to the kitchen first and tell Jacques to feed her." He turned and ambled from the room with his peculiar, rolling gait.

Two servants came toward her. She recognized one as the man who had held the gun on her in the car.

"This way." He went ahead, and Marie followed him into the foyer with the other man behind her. They went down a paneled passageway and stepped into a huge open room with gleaming appliances as large as those in restaurants. A man dressed in white stood at a worktable, covering dishes of food.

"Mr. Lu says to feed her."

Marie looked down at the floor, afraid that if any of them caught her eye she would give away her thoughts. The fat man had deliberately not given her his name.

"Qu'est-ce que c'est?"

She jerked her chin up, astonished. The man in white had spoken in French, asking, "What's that?" Their eyes met, and she quickly lowered her lashes.

"Feed the lady," the Chinese man said with exaggerated enunciation.

"Ah, oui. C'est bon. Elle a faim."

"Whatever," said the guard. "How about some tea?" He and his companion pulled stools up to the worktable.

"Sure, sure. I get him for you." Under his breath, the chef said in French, "When the boss isn't looking, you goons do whatever you want."

Marie almost laughed. She bit her lower lip to stop its twitching. She saw another stool in a corner and edged toward it.

"May I sit here?"

The talkative guard eyed her and then shrugged. "Just don't try anything."

She sighed as she sat down. They were between her and the kitchen door, but she was behind them, and she hoped they wouldn't turn around to stare at her. She also hoped they were far enough away that she could perhaps hold a tête-à-tête with the chef.

He served the men tea first and set a plate of sweets before them. Then he began filling a porcelain plate with food from the dishes on the worktable.

"Mademoiselle likes the leftovers?" he called to her, smiling at her over his shoulder.

She wanted to respond in French, but instead said, "Anything you can give me will be appreciated, sir."

He nodded and added a few more items to the plate, and then he took it across the room to a microwave oven. While the plate warmed, he poured a glass of water and carried it to her, along with silverware and a linen napkin.

"Here, mademoiselle. Sit right up at this little table. I will bring you the dinner, yes?"

"*Oui.*" She smiled up at him.

He paused with the fork in his hand and stared at her.

"Shh," she whispered.

A smile slowly curved his lips upward.

"*Mademoiselle parle français?*"

"*Un peu.*"

"*C'est magnifique.*" He glanced at the two guards, but they were chatting and eating cookies. He raised his voice. "I am sure you will enjoy the food. I am, after all, a master chef."

"It's an honor to eat in your kitchen, sir," Marie said.

The microwave's buzzer sounded, and Jacques left her to fetch the plate. When he returned, he set it before her with a flourish. "Be careful. It is very hot." In French, he whispered, "The guards, they barely speak English. They will not understand if we talk in French. And why is mademoiselle a guest in this house?"

"I am not a guest." Marie shot a glance at the guards. One of them was looking her way. "It smells delicious," she said louder. When the guard turned back to his conversation, she said in rapid French, "Mr. Lu had me kidnapped. Can you help me?"

He rolled his eyes toward the ceiling. "Aie! Mademoiselle asks much." In louder English, he said, "The scallops are delicious." He kissed his fingertips to the air.

One of the guards looked toward them.

"Hey, Jacques! You got leftover scallops? Give us some of those."

The chef left her and served the two guards more food, grumbling all the time. "You mustn't eat it all. The master, he is likely to wake up in the night and want a reprise of his dinner. He must feed the belly, no?"

Marie drank her water and then went to work on her plate. The dishes, although warmed over, had been expertly prepared, and broiled scallops in a butter sauce fairly melted on her tongue.

Thank You, Lord, she prayed silently. *I haven't been thanking You enough for things like food and water and air and...breath.*

She held up her empty glass and called, "Could I have more water, please?"

Jacques came at once to take it from her hand.

"Please," Marie whispered in French. "I think they are going to kill me."

"Pourquoi?"

"Why?"

He nodded.

"Thank you, sir," she said in English. She whispered, "He thinks I have something valuable, but I don't have it. He doesn't believe me. And he won't let me go."

"One moment, mademoiselle." He took her glass away and filled it. When he returned, he said, *"Voilà.* The water. *Je ne pense pas que je peux t'aider."* I do not think I can help you.

Marie felt tears forming in her eyes. She knew her fatigue and her desperation were working against her.

"Please!"

Jacques frowned. He looked over at the guards, but one appeared to be telling an involved story in Chinese.

"I hate working here," Jacques whispered. "I think it is some sort of Asian mafia den."

"Then why do you stay?"

He shook his head. "I lost my last post at a restaurant after one of the patrons got food poisoning. But that was not my fault. Still, the restaurant closed, and I had trouble finding a new job. This position was open, and it pays well, so I took it. But I did not know then what sort of man the master is."

Marie looked up into his sad, gray eyes. "What sort of man is he?"

"Ruthless."

She winced.

"He does not do the dirty work, as they say, but he has many men to do it for him." Jacques picked up her plate and said cheerfully, "So. Mademoiselle has finished? You would like some tea now? Or perhaps coffee?"

She didn't really want either, but decided it would enable her to continue talking to Jacques. The more things she asked for, the more time he could spend at her table.

"Tea please. And honey. And do you have any lemon?"

"Of course, mademoiselle."

When he brought the honey pot, she said, "Mr. Lu told them to take me to a boat."

Jacques nodded and said in French, "That is his yacht. He anchors it at Bayshore. Sometimes they take people there and we never see them again."

He went to the big brushed steel refrigerator and took out a lemon, which he sliced on a butcher block. He scooped the wedges into a small dish and brought them to her table.

"You've got to help me," she said.

"How is this possible?"

"My husband is looking for me. I'll give you his cell phone number."

Jacques looked toward the guards once more, his brow creased with worry. "I will get the tea."

He prepared it in a white china pot decorated with blue flowers.

"It is a lovely teapot," she said when he set it down, along with a small cup without handles.

He dropped the stub of a pencil behind the teapot and whispered, "There is a phone book in the drawer of the table. Write the number at the bottom of the first page. I promise you nothing."

"Merci!"

He left her again and busied himself putting the food away. Marie examined the side of the table and found the small drawer.

Jacques held a plate with two buns on it up to the guards. "It is a shame to put away these two little buns. Who can eat them?"

The guards accepted them eagerly, and while their attention was diverted, Marie cautiously slid the drawer open a few inches and raised the corner of the phone book cover. She printed the number hastily, with her pulse pounding in her throat.

When she finished, she pushed the drawer in and picked up her cup.

Three more men entered the kitchen, and one of them asked the guards, "Why have you not left? Mr. Lu wants to know if you have got her at the boat yet."

"He said to feed her," one of them said with an injured tone.

The other turned and demanded, "Hey! Are you ready?"

Marie stood.

"Come," said the first guard, removing a pistol from his pocket. "Don't try anything, or we tie you up."

Her legs felt heavy as she walked toward the door.

"Oh, *monsieur*," Jacques said, stepping between her and the guard for a moment, "I have prepared the coffee for you, in case there is none on the boat." He handed the man a vacuum bottle.

When he turned, Marie looked directly into his eyes. *"N'oublie pas,"* she whispered. *Don't forget.*

SIXTY-SEVEN

The creaking of the cabin door awakened her. Marie sat up quickly, nearly banging her head on the bulkhead above.

A large man filled the doorway of the sleeping cabin, and she caught her breath. She didn't recognize him, but his cruel mouth and muscular form were enough to send terror through her veins.

"You. Come out here."

He turned and left the doorway. Marie fumbled for her sneakers. She pushed the light button on her watch. Five a.m. Although her headache had receded, her cheek was still sore. She wondered where Pierre was. Had he ever received her message? He must be frantic.

Cautiously, she stepped into the larger cabin that served as a lounge. The boat shifted and she staggered, realizing the motor was running and they were under way.

"Where are we going?"

"I will ask the questions." The big man stood between her and the stairs that led up to the deck. After staring at her for ten seconds, he formed a fist and began gently punching it into the palm of his other hand. "Mr. Lu wants to know if you are ready now."

She gulped. "For what?"

"To tell him where the computer part is. The one with information on it that interests him. He said you know what he means."

Marie considered her options. She could see only three: Lie, tell the truth, or try to stonewall it.

"I don't have what he wants."

His hand zipped out and struck her temple, harder than Xian had hit her. She crashed onto the padded bench. Her skull banged against the wall. As she tried to break her fall, she succeeded only in smashing her right forearm against the edge of the bench.

She pulled herself onto her knees and lay with her head and arms on the cushion, panting. The pain in her arm was annoying, but shocks pounded in her head. She counted them and decided her pulse determined their regularity.

"Get up!"

She lifted her head and fought nausea. Trying to slow her breathing, she waited for the sickness to go away.

He seized her arm and pulled upward. Marie twisted and tried to stand but fell back to the floor. After looking down at her for a long moment, he went up the stairs.

She lay there until she could breathe steadily. Slowly she put her hands to her head. The inside pounding still rocked her. She considered trying to get back to the bunk they'd given her and gave up. Her efforts to form a prayer in her mind took too much strength.

Sometime later, she heard footsteps and opened her eyes just a slit. One of the guards who had brought her to the boat stooped and touched her shoulder.

"You okay?"

"No," she whispered.

"When Jing come back, you talk. Tell him what he want to know."

"Who...is Jing?"

"The man who give you this." He pointed to her face, and Marie assumed he indicated her latest bruise.

"Please help me." She struggled to sit up. The pain assaulted her anew, and she leaned her back against the bench and closed her eyes.

"If you don't tell, you don't go home."

Her mouth went dry. She pulled air in through her nostrils, then with sheer determination opened her eyes and looked at him.

"Where are we going?"

"We go out. Off the shore. One mile, maybe more. No one find you."

She stared into his cold, black eyes.

He stood up. "You tell him."

"I don't have what they want."

He shook his head. "Too bad. Tell him something."

A moment later the huge man was back. Jing. Marie couldn't look at him, but she heard his fist softly striking his palm.

"Where is the computer part?" he asked softly.

"I don't have it."

"Mr. Lu knows you don't have it. Where is it?"

She brushed her hair back and pressed her hand to her throbbing temple. "I got rid of it."

He stood still and waited.

She sighed and looked up at him. "I didn't know what it was at first. My cell phone was stolen, and I was looking for it in my suitcase. That's when I found the flash drive." She closed her eyes again, but they flew open when Jing kicked her ankle. She drew her knees up, bringing her feet away from him.

"What did you do with it?"

"I kept it for a long time. I saw a girl using one in the airport, and I guessed it had something to do with a computer. But I didn't know where it came from or who it belonged to. Then I thought maybe Jenna—the woman who was killed in the airport—maybe she had put it there."

"What then?"

"I ran."

"Sit up there." He nodded at the bench behind her.

Marie took a deep breath and pushed herself upward. She was able to sit on the edge of the bench and turn to face him.

"Now tell me the rest."

"Will you let me go home?"

"That is up to Mr. Lu. But if you do not tell me, this is the end for you."

Tears spilled down her face. Her left cheek smarted, and she realized the skin was broken.

"Some men kept chasing me. I don't know who they were. There was a Chinese man with a scar, and a big white man. Another Chinese man too. At least three of them. I…I thought maybe they were in it with the woman who…" she swallowed and wiped her face on her sleeve, "…who killed Jenna."

"Communists." Jing's mouth curled as he said it. "They use a woman to do that."

"They…were not friends of yours?"

He snorted. "If you gave it to them…" He raised his fist.

"No! I didn't." She shifted and rested her sore right arm on her thigh. "I didn't know what they wanted, but I was afraid they would kill me too. After a while I realized that little computer drive was what they were after. I thought of giving it to them so they would leave me alone. But I was afraid to do that. I thought they must be evil men."

He said nothing, but his mouth was a thin, cruel line.

"Then I thought about just throwing it away."

His eyes widened. "You didn't?"

"No."

"Then where is it? You have kept many men busy for several days. It is time to end this."

She sighed and looked down at the floor. "I…" She sobbed. What awful things would happen if she revealed the truth?

Jing stepped toward her, his fist raised. She held her curled hands in front of her face.

"Please don't. I'll tell you." She swallowed hard and prayed silently, *Forgive me, Lord. I can't go on with this. Please don't let Pierre hate me.* She looked up at Jing. He towered over her, his face a menacing mask.

"I mailed it."

He blinked. "You mean, in a package?"

"Yes."

"Where to?"

Marie's lips began to tremble. *I can stop running, stop worrying.* "I sent it to my husband."

"Your husband? In Japan?"

"No. I addressed it to him at his parents' home in Maine."

"And your husband knows this?"

"No. I haven't talked to him since yesterday. I mean Monday. What day is it?"

He ignored her question. "When did you mail the package?"

"When I got to Mystic. Yesterday, I guess. Around noon."

He wheeled and mounted the companionway.

They would try to get the package, she was sure. What would they do to Pierre's family? She couldn't think about that.

The man who had spoken to her earlier came down the stairs. He opened a cabinet and rummaged inside.

"Here. You go back to your berth."

He handed her a small cellophane package of peanuts and a granola bar.

"Can I have some water?"

He opened a small refrigerator she hadn't noticed before and brought her a can of Dr. Pepper. He tossed it on the cushion beside her and went up the stairs.

Marie slumped back against the wall, letting her tears bathe her cheeks. The engine started, and she felt the boat turn in a wide arc.

SIXTY-EIGHT

0955 Wednesday, Mystic, Connecticut

"We need to get out of this town and do something." Pierre shoved his hands in his pockets and stared out the motel room window.

"As soon as we know what to do," George agreed. "At least we know Mr. Randall's going to make it."

"Yeah. I'm glad." Pierre's cell phone rang, and he leaped to the nightstand for it.

"*Allo, allo!* Lieutenant Belanger?"

"Yeah?" Pierre plugged his right ear with one finger while listening with his left ear. "Who is this?" He couldn't place the heavy Parisian accent.

"My name, it is not important. But I must tell you, and very quickly, that your wife, she needs you."

Pierre's heart seemed to stop for an instant and then thundered on. In French he demanded, "Who are you? What do you know?"

George was sitting in an armchair across the room, with maps spread out on the small table. He looked over at Pierre with raised eyebrows.

Pierre tried to catch every word of the excited Frenchman's rapid-fire delivery.

"The pretty lady, she gave me your number. I would have called you last night, but it was too dangerous. But now I think she needs your assistance very fast, *monsieur*. I heard them talk during the breakfast this morning, and I learned your name. They have your wife on a yacht."

"*Pardon!* Did you say a yacht?"

"*Oui.* It is the master's boat. He keeps it at the Long Island Yacht Club, but I heard this morning when the men say they have gone out to sea. They take your wife out there until she gives them what they want."

"I don't understand."

"Welcome to the club of the bewildered, *monsieur.* I cannot talk long. I am taking the risk as it is, but I told them I needed a fresh onion and ran down to the market. I cannot call from the big house. I don't think they suspect anything, but I must hurry. *Comprenez-vous?*"

"*Oui, je comprends.* But this boat—what's it called? Who does it belong to?"

The Frenchman whispered, "It is worth my life to tell you, but…oh, she is a pretty girl. But he will kill her anyway. He cannot let her tell the authorities what they have done."

Pierre's heart lurched. "Who is he? Is he a communist?"

"No, no! He is an American citizen, and he hates the communists. He is a businessman. Owns more real estate in Manhattan than Donald Trump. The men, they say he grabbed your wife yesterday from out of the communists' hands in Chinatown."

"His name," Pierre said through his teeth.

There was a hiccup of a pause, and the Frenchman hissed, "Mr. Lu. The boat, she is the *Eugenie.*"

There was a click, followed by a dial tone.

Pierre turned to George. His friend was already on his feet.

"A boat, Pierre?"

"A yacht. Long Island Yacht Club."

"Where?"

"Long Island, I guess."

"Long Island is huge."

"Well, we can't ask McCutcheon to look it up on his laptop."

"Agreed." George's brow furrowed. "Time to make a decision. Either we trust Heinz and the NCIS, or we lose a lot of time."

Pierre nodded. "They've got her, and they're threatening to kill her. Let's do it."

George grabbed the hotel phone and punched in Heinz's room number.

"Special Agent Heinz? We need you in room 236 immediately. Please come alone, and don't tell anyone where you're going."

SIXTY-NINE

1015 Wednesday, Mystic, Connecticut

"I don't know. That guy's been with the bureau a long time. He's supposed to be one of their best." Special Agent Heinz shook his head. "Can I at least get some coffee?" He looked longingly toward the hotel room door.

"We don't have time," Pierre said. "Every minute could mean the difference between life and death for my wife. If you're not with us, we're on our own. Just don't, please, tell McCutcheon or anyone else what we've told you."

Heinz gritted his teeth. "I like you guys, but I'm just not sure..."

"It's a serious accusation, we know," George said. "But this can happen. It *has* happened in the past, and you know it as well as I do. Someone you think you can trust, who has a glowing record, goes rogue. Maybe he's desperate for money, maybe he's disillusioned. Whatever the motive, he flips. And then nobody's safe."

Heinz nodded slowly. "Okay, I'll agree to help you test him, but I'm not committing myself beyond that. If it turns out he's okay, then we keep working together."

Pierre grimaced. "How long is this going to take? Because we've already wasted ten or fifteen minutes. We should be on the way to the Long Island Yacht Club."

George squeezed his shoulder. "I think we can expedite that, buddy. Special Agent Heinz has the authority to call in a helicopter for us, don't you, Heinz?"

"Absolutely. If we're sure."

"We'll never be sure until Marie is under our protection," George said. "This is the best tip we've had since Mystic. Heinz, we've got to run with this."

Heinz inhaled, not looking at them. "Oh, man, I hope you're not wrong about this, Hudson."

"I'm not."

Heinz nodded. "Okay. There's a Coast Guard station not far from the yacht club. They'll help us. What do you want me to do first?"

"The chopper," Pierre said.

"Right." Heinz walked to the window and pulled the drapes back. "They could land in the parking lot here. But we should use my room for the setup, not yours. I don't want anyone finding unauthorized equipment in your room. You guys don't need the headaches that would cause you."

"Do it," George said. "As soon as you call the Coast Guard, we'll set McCutcheon up, and we'll prove to you that he's not on the level."

SEVENTY

André worked quickly, sorting the Express Mail packages. He made out yellow slips for two going to post office box patrons and piled the rest into bins for the carriers. While he worked, he tried not to think about yesterday—how close he'd come to leading Lisa into the middle of a gun battle under the misguided notion that they could find Marie and bring her home. He shuddered every time he remembered Lisa's terrified face.

The address on one small padded envelope stopped him. Lt. Pierre Belanger. His parents' address. Marie's handwriting.

He glanced around the workroom. No one was looking. It was against regulations, but he had a funny feeling about this one. He dashed to the locker room, stowed the package in his locker, and went back to work.

His cell phone rang late in the morning shift while he was taking money from a customer. He glanced over at Janet. She was busy, but he knew she'd be angry if he took a personal call while working.

He handed the woman her change and pulled out the phone, giving the next customer an apologetic glance. He turned away from the lobby, with his back to Janet, and looked at the screen. His parent's number showed. He grimaced and punched the receive button.

"Ma, I'm working."

"I know," his mother said. "I'm sorry, but your father's gone to Augusta this morning, and there are a couple of motorcyclists hanging around."

André frowned. His mother wasn't usually jumpy. "What do you mean, Maman?"

"These two guys on motorcycles. I was hanging out clothes, and they drove by twice. The second time the motor noise cut off, so when I went in the house, I looked out the mudroom window, and they're stopped down by the corner. Just sitting there."

André didn't like it. He looked at the clock. "Ma, it's only eleven o'clock. I can't leave yet for lunch. Maybe at noon…"

"Okay. I just wanted to tell someone. They're making me nervous."

"Call the police."

"Oh, I couldn't do that. I mean, they haven't *done* anything."

He sighed. "I'll see if I can come now."

He hung up, served the next customer, and then put up the "THIS WINDOW CLOSED" sign.

"Janet—"

"Don't tell me. A family emergency."

"Yeah. I promise to be back in an hour."

When he turned onto the road where his parents' farmhouse lay, he saw the bikers lounging under a tree within sight of the Belangers' driveway. He was tempted to stop and ask them what they were doing, but as he came even with them, one hung his helmet from his bike's handlebars. He looked up as André's pickup passed, and André felt a stab of apprehension. The man was Asian.

He almost ran from the truck to the house. His mother met him at the door.

"Hi. That was fast."

"Hi." André locked the door behind him. "I saw them. Call the police, Ma."

"Wha—"

"Just call 911."

She turned and went for the phone. A few minutes later, peering from behind the café curtain in the mudroom, they saw a local patrol car pull up. Two officers got out and questioned the cyclists.

André held his breath. He was glad the PD had sent two men. Elation filled him when he saw the officers pat the men down and take a pistol from one of them.

"Yes!"

"Oh, André," his mother said. "Those are bad men! They might have robbed us."

"Yeah, they might have."

"I'm so glad I called you. I didn't want to call the police and have them think I was paranoid."

"You're not paranoid, Maman. A little neurotic, maybe."

They watched for a few more minutes. Another patrol car came, and the officers put the two bikers in the second car. The first car rolled up the road and into the driveway.

"You called us about the suspicious loiterers?" the officer asked when André opened the door.

"Yes, sir. My mother did. She was kind of nervous with them sitting there so long, and she called me at work. I decided I'd better come out and see what was going on. I didn't like the look of them."

"Well, I don't know what they were up to, but we'll keep them a few hours. And we'll take their motorcycles into impound just for security. Don't want to leave those fancy bikes sitting there. But the only things we could find to charge them with were a concealed weapon—the guy claims he has a permit in New York, but he's supposed to have it on him. Probably hasn't really got one. Oh, and one of them had an expired registration."

André nodded. "Well, hey, I know my mother will feel a lot safer now. Thanks a lot."

The patrolman nodded. "Glad to do it. We get people in from out of state like that, and when they don't move on, it usually means they're up to no good. Drugs, most likely, though we didn't find anything like that on them. This will show them we're on the ball in Waterville, though."

He touched the brim of his hat and went out to the cruiser. The rural mail carrier was just stopping at the Belangers' mailbox. André remembered the package he had put in his locker. He opened his mouth and then closed it. His mother had had enough worry for one day. If things went well, Pierre would soon be home, and André could give him the package in person. And if things went bad…worse, that is, than they were now, with Marie still lost out there and gangsters shooting up the state's tourist attractions…well, then, that package would probably be the least of their worries.

SEVENTY-ONE

Marie awoke with a massive headache. She left the bunk and staggered through the larger cabin to the head. When she emerged a few minutes later, the Chinese guard was setting a plate and mug on a table that folded down from the wall like a shelf. The boat swayed gently, but the engine was silent.

"You eat," the guard said.

Marie sat down on a stool and reached for the mug. "Where are we?"

"We a ways out. Mr. Lu say we stay out until he get the package you sent."

"Will he let me go then?"

The man shrugged. "How long it take to send a package to that place?"

"I...don't know."

The man frowned. "We bet on it. How do you say...a pool?"

She stared at him. "What do you mean?"

"We bet on when they get the package. Some say today. I don't think today. Is too soon. I think a week. Some say two, three days."

She inhaled sharply. No, she would not bring up the subject of Express Mail.

The man shrugged. "Whoever guess closest gets the bets." He nodded at her plate, which held a bagel and a dish of canned peaches. "When you done, you can go on deck. But don't think you swim. We too far out. And there be sharks."

Marie shivered. "All right. Thank you."

The bagel crunched when she tried to bite it. Stale. The peaches went down smoothly, and she sipped the hot, strong coffee.

A few minutes later she mounted the stairs and poked her head above the hatch. She saw three men, one in the bow and the other two up in a wheelhouse. She'd heard the motor chug during the night, but still she'd expected for some reason to see masts and sails. The power yacht was bigger than she'd realized when they brought her aboard in the dark, longer than her parents' house. She wasn't good at estimating distance, but she guessed it was at least sixty feet. She wondered how many crew members were on board.

As she stepped cautiously onto the deck, the man in the bow noticed her. Marie froze for an instant before she recognized him as the one who had told her that she would be permitted above decks.

The sun shone overhead, and its rays felt good on her face. The breeze was chilly enough to cause goose bumps to rise on her arms, though. She walked a few steps to the rail and looked out over the water. Nothing but sea. She crossed the deck, looking to see if the men above her noticed. One man watched her but made no move. She stared out on the other side of the boat. Far in the distance she made out a smudge of shoreline, and off to one side she glimpsed a ship.

"Don't try any tricks."

She whirled at the voice and found the huge man Jing behind her.

"What could I do?"

He nodded and walked aft, where he sat down and watched her. She tried to blame her shivering on the cool wind, but she couldn't deny that the man was scary.

The man who had brought her breakfast wasn't exactly friendly, but he was less terrifying than Jing. Slowly she walked toward the bow.

She noticed a small boat hanging from its lowering gear just off the side of the yacht. Even that dinghy would be more than she could handle alone. She eyed the tall, arched brackets fastened to the side of the yacht. From them a pulley and rope system was suspended, holding the dinghy aloft. The crew could lower it from its position level with the yacht's deck to the surface of the water below, but she couldn't do it. The people working the mechanism would have to be on deck, not in the dinghy, she was sure. Too complicated.

The guard had stepped to one side and was looking out to sea. She flipped back a corner of the tarpaulin covering the dinghy. There was room for her to hide in there, under the tarp. But the men would find her. That would be one of the first places they would look.

Several items lay in the bottom of the dinghy; a life preserver, oars, a toolbox, and some yellow nylon rope tied to eyebolts in a short black board. Marie looked over her shoulder again. No one was watching her. Pulling the edge of the tarp higher, she saw a locker on the far side of the boat with a red cross on it. First aid kit. Next to that a plastic case marked "Orion" was mounted below the gunwale. There seemed to be more lockers beneath the seats.

Lisa could probably figure out a way to use those things and find a way to escape. Pierre could do it for sure. Marie replaced the tarp and lingered, studying the brackets supporting the dinghy and sighed. No way. She'd rowed a boat a few times on Messalonskee Lake in Maine, where her family's friends had a cottage, but she wasn't very good at it. The guards would catch her before she got the oars into the oarlocks.

She walked toward the bow. Along the cabin wall, through locked grill doors, she could see air tanks and wetsuits hanging in a locker next to a spear gun and several fishing rods. Hanging on the wall outside the door were a pair of surfboards.

The sight of the recreational equipment brought home to her the desperateness of her situation. These people could commit murder and then go sailing.

The Chinese man was coiling a rope. As she approached him, he finished and hung it against the bulkhead.

"Mr. Lu says we have to stay out here all day?" she asked.

His eyes narrowed. "They don't get package, we don't go in."

She nodded. "So...tomorrow, maybe? You don't seem to have a lot of food on board. Will someone bring more food out to us?"

He shook his head. "You don't worry about that."

"Do you..." She hesitated, and the man stooped to pick up a beer can from the deck. "Please tell me the truth. Will Mr. Lu let me go when they retrieve the package?"

The man turned away without answering.

SEVENTY-TWO

1045 Wednesday, Mystic, Connecticut

Special Agent Heinz nodded at George and Pierre. "All set. This room and the bathroom are bugged worse than the Kremlin." He handed George a headset. "You guys am-scray and I'll get Mc-Cutcheon over here."

"What if he won't make the call from in here?" Pierre asked.

"Then we've got nothing."

Pierre sighed. "There's got to be a foolproof way."

"There is, but it would take more time than you want to give me."

George eyed Pierre. His friend, whose disposition was usually placid, was close to losing control.

"Pierre, why don't you get on down to the lobby and get a cup of coffee? If you see McCutcheon, tell him you're waiting for me, and we're planning to check out. He'll buy it."

"Okay, okay."

Pierre gave Heinz one last bleak stare and went out.

"Good, Hudson," Heinz said. "He's on the brink. You know that, don't you?"

"Why do you think I sent him away? Pierre's an excellent officer, but he's been through too much this week. I think it's best if I sit in our hotel room alone to listen to the show."

Heinz nodded. "We three are the only ones who know about this. I didn't even tell Cucci, and he's my right arm in field operations."

"I appreciate it," George said.

"Right. So if this goes bad…"

"It's not going to."

George went out the door and closed it softly, looking up and down the hallway. No one in sight. He took the stairway down to the next floor and entered his and Pierre's room, and then he put on the headset.

A few seconds later he heard Heinz dialing and then a greeting from one of the FBI men. Heinz asked for Agent McCutcheon.

"Hey, Heinz, whatcha got?" McCutcheon asked.

"We just received a tip I think is worth following."

"What is it?"

"Can you come to my room? I'd rather not discuss it over the phone."

"Right."

George sat down in an armchair and waited. Half a minute later, he heard a muffled knock.

"Thanks for coming so fast. Come on in. Hello, Packard."

George grimaced. McCutcheon had taken one of his operatives with him to Heinz's room. He could plainly hear the door closing and Packard's greeting.

"Where are Belanger and Hudson?" McCutcheon asked.

"They went downstairs for coffee. I told them I'd brief you, and we'll meet them down there. They're anxious to get going."

"Of course. Did Mrs. Belanger call her husband or what?"

"No, someone else called. Someone she'd been with."

"And?"

George held his breath. He didn't want it to be true, he realized. The only good solution to this was for Pierre to be wrong. But then, what could explain the way their enemies had defeated them time after time?

"There's a chance she could be in Hartford," Heinz said.

"Hartford?"

"Yeah. We think they took her to Hartford yesterday. A guy called a few minutes ago and said Marie is being held at a mansion just south of the city. Gave me the address."

"But…" A pause followed.

"I don't know how reliable this source is," Heinz said, "but he told Belanger these guys aren't the ones who nabbed her at Mystic. They got her in Chinatown, he said."

"And the reason he's telling us this is…?"

"The informant works for the guy in charge, and he doesn't like the way they're treating her. She begged for help, and he agreed to make the call for her. He says the leader will kill her if she doesn't give up what he wants by noon."

"Noon? We've got to hurry." McCutcheon's voice had a worried, urgent tone. George began to feel guilty. What if Pierre was wrong? How much time were they wasting?

"Here's the address," Heinz said. "Why don't you get your team together? Call them from here if you want. I'm all packed, and I'm going down to meet Hudson and Belanger. Just shut the door when you're done, and meet us in the parking lot."

"All right."

George heard the door close. He exhaled in relief. Whether McCutcheon used his cell phone or the house phone, they'd hear him now. He got up and went to open his own door.

"Packard, go to our room and get packing." McCutcheon's voice was still clear. "I'll call the others and be right with you."

As Packard made his exit on the floor above, George waved a silent greeting to Heinz. The NCIS agent entered the room, set down his suitcase, and put on his own headset.

"He sent Packard out," George whispered.

Several seconds of silence were followed by quiet footsteps and then a clack.

"He's closing the drapes," Heinz said.

George nodded.

"Hey," McCutcheon's voice came, low and insistent. "Who have we got in Hartford? Yeah. The word is, she's there. Can you people get over there? I'll give you the address. No, I think it's legit. Whoever called Belanger said they grabbed her in Chinatown. Who else would know that? All right, you get over there fast, and I'll delay things here as long as I can. But you won't have more than a fifteen-minute start, I'm guessing." McCutcheon gave the address George had conjured out of thin air.

Heinz pulled off his headset and took out his cell phone. "Cucci! I need you at our room now! If McCutcheon's coming out, keep him there."

George stood in the doorway, watching Heinz run for the stairs. On the headset, he heard McCutcheon finish giving his instructions.

"All right. Don't call me. Just get her and disappear. I'll call you in two hours. We need to get that data from her and put an end to this game."

After a pause, George heard him say, "Nelson, we just got a tip. You guys get your things and meet us in the lobby. We're heading out."

Next came the rattle of a lockset as a door opened.

"Oh, hey there. Did you forget something?"

Special Agent Heinz's voice was crisp and authoritative. "Put your hands on the wall, McCutcheon. We've got it all on tape."

George exhaled. Time to go down and give Pierre the news. He heard a faint whirring that quickly grew louder. Through the window he saw a helicopter approaching from the west. He grabbed his duffel bag and Pierre's and headed for the door.

SEVENTY-THREE

Marie stood on deck facing the shore and thinking. She knew the men were communicating with people on land. Several had cell phones, but the boat must have radio equipment as well. That was probably up in the wheelhouse, where there always seemed to be at least two men.

The wind had picked up since she came on deck and she shivered, glad she had the pastor's leather jacket over her thin cotton blouse. Clusters of clouds sped overhead, throwing shadows on the gray waves. She eyed the jet trails dissipating in the sky. Kennedy International Airport, she supposed, though she couldn't see the distant coastline well enough to orient herself. Maybe it was part of Long Island, but who could tell from here?

She considered going below deck again to make a search. There could be a radio down there. It seemed logical to her that the galley area would house communications gear.

Checking the positions of the crew, she noted Jing heading for the stairway. No, she did not want to come face-to-face with him below deck. She had counted at least four other men. They left her alone for the most part, but it seemed someone always had an eye on her.

The sun was past the zenith now. If that package didn't reach Maine today, she'd be here for at least another twenty-four hours. But the postal clerk had assured her that Express Mail was guaranteed. That's what the exorbitant price got you—overnight delivery. Pierre's mother had probably already brought in the mail for the day. Had Lu's men gotten there first? An image of Annette, Pierre's youngest sister, checking the mailbox and encountering the thugs who had waylaid her in New York sickened Marie. She would not, could not, consider that. After all, it was a weekday, wasn't it? Annette and Eloise would be at school.

She tried to figure out exactly what day it was and gave it up. But she was certain of one thing: This nightmare had gone on long enough. With the jacket, she wasn't cold, and she figured she had a better chance of learning something if she stayed topside.

They'll let me go as soon as they have it, she told herself. But that wasn't true. If they didn't get it, they would kill her. They'd made that plain. The only reason they kept her alive now was the off chance she'd lied and they needed to beat more information out of her. Once they had the package, they wouldn't need her anymore. She began to tremble and grasped the rail.

One of the men called out, and she turned to see what was happening. Had they heard from Mr. Lu? A guard stood by the stairway holding something in his hand and yelling to someone below. What was he holding? He turned and called to the men in the wheelhouse and waved the object. A deck of cards. One of the men swung down the companionway to join him, and they disappeared into the hold.

Marie caught her breath. Only one man remained on deck, fishing off the bow, and one in the wheelhouse. If the three below were going to have a card game, they might not resurface for quite some time.

The stiff breeze whipped her hair, and she turned her back to the wind. No way would she go below and walk through the room where the three thugs were playing cards.

The yacht bobbed up and down with the swells. She looked longingly over the side at the dinghy again. If only she knew how to launch it and had the confidence to try. Better get away from it. The crew might think she was planning to escape and send her back to her sleeping quarters.

The wind tugged at her clothing as she went forward to the middle of the deck. The cabin wall blocked the wind. She sat down with her back against it and closed her eyes.

A sound drew her attention to the bow of the yacht. The fisherman was standing, bracing himself against the gunwale. He had a bite! The impulse hit Marie before she had time to analyze it. All she knew was that she had to try to get away, and she might not have a better chance.

Fear washed over her as she considered the plan that had come to her mind, and she almost dismissed it, but remembering Jing's fists and the other guard's chilling words was enough.

"Heavenly Father," she whispered, "I have to try. If You want me to succeed, You'll have to keep them distracted."

She flattened herself against the cabin wall and then eased along it, hoping the man above in the wheelhouse couldn't see her. She tiptoed along the side of the dinghy. Opposite it on the bulkhead was a locker labeled "Life Raft." Inflating that would draw attention too soon. But the surfboards…

She held her breath as she took hold of the lower one. It hung on a rack but was not locked in. Carefully she lowered it to the deck, not letting it bump against the wooden floor. The bright yellow color was perfect for what she had in mind. A quick look forward told her the fisherman was still occupied. She tiptoed aft, lugging the awkward board. Near the stern, she hurried around to the other side of the yacht, climbed up on a built-in bench, and wrestled the surfboard up to the rail. Looking down, she almost lost her courage. What if this didn't work? Would the wind and waves cooperate to aid her?

She glanced over her shoulder. The man in the wheelhouse was standing, craning his neck to watch the fisherman land his catch. With a silent prayer, she stood.

With all the force she could summon, she shoved the surfboard over. It plummeted beneath the waves, then popped up again, shooting out several yards from the side of the boat. Marie gulped and hopped down off the bench, ducking low, and made her way back to the apparatus that held the dinghy alongside the yacht. The man in the wheelhouse was still watching the fisherman. She crouched low, waiting.

"Please, Lord."

She almost made her move but held back. If they looked at the wrong moment...

A shout reached her. The fisherman turned and yelled up to the pilot in frantic Chinese, gesturing wildly at the waves ahead and to the starboard side. More shouting, and then feet pounded up the companionway. The card players stormed onto the deck and ran directly to the bow. The four men leaned over the railing talking and waving their arms.

Marie jumped up and scrambled over the port rail into the dinghy. She pulled the tarpaulin into place and lay still for a moment, trying to calm her breathing. Then she began cautiously feeling the items in the bottom of the boat. The crew would not be so easily convinced that she'd leaped overboard. They would search the yacht from top to bottom. She couldn't stay here.

SEVENTY-FOUR

1430 Wednesday, Atlantic Ocean, off Long Island

George and Pierre stood at the bow of the Coast Guard cutter, looking ahead with binoculars as they ran south of Long Island, searching for the *Eugenie*. The wind tore at their clothes, and George's ears were cold. He counted on their intelligence reports being correct. If so, the ship would soon overtake the yacht.

"There." Pierre pointed.

George changed his focus slightly. On the horizon he located a gleaming white Hatteras power yacht. It had to be the *Eugenie*. He wished they were still on the helicopter that had flown them to the Coast Guard station. They could zoom out there and confirm that this was the vessel they sought, but he knew they were in a better position to help Marie by approaching her prison on the hundred-foot law enforcement cutter.

"So that's how the other half lives," Pierre said.

"Yeah. Must be nice."

Pierre gave him a thin smile, resting his binoculars against the rail. "When you retire, maybe you can get a job sailing one of those babies for some rich guy."

"As if."

"Oh, that's right. You and Rachel are going to start a horse ranch."

"That's the plan," George said, studying the yacht. "She's going to fly over and meet me in California to look at land."

"When did this happen?"

"This morning. When I called her, she told me she'd got a week's leave."

"Wow. You're looking at property now? You've got a couple more years until you retire."

"Yeah, but Rachel's getting out next April. We figure it's time to start thinking about where we want our kids to grow up."

Pierre raised his binoculars again. "I know what you mean."

"You two starting a family soon?" George asked.

"We want to. After this...hey, I'll do anything Marie wants. If she wants me to resign my commission, I will."

"No, don't do that. I mean, not unless she really *needs* you to." They were close enough to the yacht now that George no longer needed the binoculars, and he let them hang from their strap. "The Navy will take care of you. Just...at your next assignment, get a little house off the base somewhere and have a baby. Don't wait until you can retire. Life's too short."

They both stood in silence for a minute. They drew close to their quarry and could make out several figures moving on the deck. The drifting yacht straightened suddenly and began to move.

"They started their engine." George felt the deck vibrate beneath his feet as the cutter's pilot increased speed.

Pierre shot him a sidelong glance. "Are you praying?"

"Yes."

Pierre nodded. "Thanks. You know, if things don't go the way we hope..."

"Don't think that way," George said.

"I try not to, but everything's been so crazy this week. If today is true to form, she's not really on that boat."

"She's there."

Pierre grimaced. "Well, however it turns out, you need to leave. Go to Rachel."

"Buddy, I'm here for you until this is over. Rachel understands that."

Pierre's facial muscles worked, and he started to raise his binoculars but let them drop.

"We're on target!" Heinz strode toward them across the deck. "She's the *Eugenie,* all right."

"Can they outrun us?" Pierre asked.

"No way. They won't get up to speed before we're on top of them."

"Quite a vessel," George said, staring at the luxurious yacht.

"Yeah, they say Lu is worth half a billion, give or take a few mil. This is his weekend getaway."

The cutter surged through the waves, coming up on the starboard side of the yacht.

They heard the voice of the Coast Guard officer on the bridge, aided by a speaker. "This is the U.S. Coast Guard. Heave to and prepare to be boarded."

No response came from the *Eugenie* except a steady increase of speed. She changed course to port, but the cutter was already abreast and soon overtook her.

"Heave to," the skipper commanded.

A few seconds later, when the *Eugenie* continued at full speed, a gun thundered, sending a shell across the bow of the yacht. Almost at once, the pilot cut the engine of the *Eugenie* and brought the boat around in the water so that its starboard side paralleled the big cutter. Four men stood on the deck staring across the fifty yards of water between them, their hands raised.

Pierre fidgeted as they watched the cutter's crew hurry to launch a small boat for the boarding party. Of course he wanted to be in that group, but they'd fought that battle already and lost. The skipper had refused to take Pierre or George onto the yacht until his men secured it. The two friends leaned on the rail beside Heinz and watched the skipper and three petty officers lower themselves over the side into the launch and run across to the *Eugenie.*

Pierre tensed, watching every move as the four Coast Guard men climbed the boarding ladder. George knew these few minutes were torture for Pierre.

"Take it easy," he said. "They'll let us aboard soon."

Pierre nodded.

Ten minutes later the skipper returned with one of his petty officers and five prisoners in the launch. All five appeared to be of Asian or part-Asian descent. One of them was a huge, burly man whose face was a study in surliness. George had a bad feeling about that man, but he said nothing. No sense upsetting Pierre.

The cutter's crew took the *Eugenie's* men in hand, and the skipper handed over several weapons they had confiscated from the yacht. Then he approached the spot where Pierre, George, and Heinz waited.

"Lieutenant Belanger, I'm sorry to report that we found no trace of your wife in our initial search of the boat."

Pierre's face blanched.

"We made a cursory search of all cabins and decks. We believe all of the crew surrendered, but we didn't find anyone else aboard. I'm going to let you board with four more of my men. Special Agent Heinz and his team can accompany you. Make a thorough inspection of the vessel, but…I'm not hopeful at this point. I'm sorry."

George clasped Pierre's shoulder. "You all right?"

Pierre nodded. "Did you question the crew?"

"They denied having a woman on board. Some of them either don't speak English or pretend they can't. I will continue to question them while you go over to the yacht."

They climbed down into the launch and made the short ride in silence. George was glad they didn't have to go far on the choppy sea. As they gained the deck of the *Eugenie,* one of the petty officers met them at the top of the ladder.

"Sir," he said to Pierre, "We found these near the rail on the starboard side of the boat."

George stared at the worn sneakers in the officer's hand.

Pierre's hand shook as he reached for them. He turned them over, staring at them, then looked inside one.

"She had a pair like this."

"Are you certain they belong to your wife?"

"No. But the size and the brand are right."

The petty officer nodded. "I'll take them across to the cutter. We can ask the crew about them. Unless they have very small feet…well, I doubt they'd fit any of those men."

Heinz and his team, along with the remaining Coast Guard men, fanned out over the deck. Several men went down the stairs.

"They would have kept her below," Pierre said.

"Go with Heinz," George told him. "I'll look around up here, just to be sure."

Pierre hurried toward the hatch, and George walked the edge of the deck, between the bulkhead and the rail. He stared down at the spot where the petty officer had found Marie's sneakers. Why would she take off her shoes? If they'd thrown her overboard, it didn't make sense. But if she'd leaped over the side on her own…

He looked over the side, but saw nothing in the water between the *Eugenie* and the white hull of the cutter. Slowly he walked aft, searching the deck at the stern of the boat for something, anything. He came around to the port side and started forward. A small dinghy hung from davits over the side, its rail even with the yacht's. The canvas tarpaulin had been thrown back. No doubt the officers had already searched the dinghy. It was a logical place for a person to hide. It was empty except for oars and a few miscellaneous pieces of equipment.

"Hudson!"

George looked up. Heinz and Pierre came rapidly toward him from the hatch.

"What is it?"

Heinz pulled up before him. "One of the Chinese told the captain they had Marie on board, but she jumped overboard half an hour before they spotted us."

George swallowed hard.

"Are they sure?"

"They saw a surfboard that had been hanging on the wall there—" he pointed to the bulkhead where a red surfboard hung next to an equipment locker. Below the red one was an empty rack for another board. "They saw the board floating in the water and searched for her. When our man took her shoes over to the cutter, that's when he cracked. He admitted they'd seen her shoes on the deck. But if she jumped in after the surfboard, she didn't make it. They watched the board float away but couldn't spot her. They went over the boat from stem to stern and found nothing."

"I'm...very sorry to hear that." George eyed Pierre. His friend was staring at the open Atlantic. *So close,* George thought. *We were so very close.*

"Did they tell their boss?"

"They were going to," Heinz went on. "They were afraid to tell him, but after they were sure she wasn't on the boat, they didn't know what else to do. So they called his home, and someone there told them the house had been raided and Mr. Lu was taken away in handcuffs."

"That would be your man, Cucci."

"Yes. Special Agent Cucci's a dependable man. They gave him three more agents, and they carried it off the way we planned."

George nodded, unable to watch Pierre's face any longer. He looked down at the dinghy. "I hoped..." He checked and stared, and then he reached for the rumpled tarp and pulled it back farther. "What's that?"

Pierre's glazed eyes focused. "What?"

"That line." George climbed into the dinghy. A yellow nylon line was tied to a cleat inside the gunwale. It ran over the port side rail of the dinghy, hanging taut.

"We approached them on the starboard side," George said. "We never got a look at their port side."

As he leaned out over the off side of the small boat, he heard

Pierre suck in a breath. George's heart skipped as he looked down. A bosun's chair hung from the yellow line, and clinging to the ropes that made the sides of the swing, her lips trembling and her face pale, was Marie Belanger.

SEVENTY-FIVE

1455 Wednesday, Atlantic Ocean

"Ma chérie!"

Pierre leaned so far over the side that the dinghy tipped precariously. Marie moaned and flinched. Slowly she turned her face up toward him. She didn't smile or speak. Tears streamed from her eyes.

Pierre's mind leaped, but George was ahead of him.

"Help me, Pierre. Heinz, get the launch underneath her. We can't bring her up from here."

"Chérie, hold on!" Pierre called. "We're here, and we're going to lower you down. Just don't let go."

George untied the line that held the bosun's chair in place. Pierre grabbed the rope further down and held it firmly, in case George lost his grip.

"Hold it, now," George warned him. "Let them get into position."

A hail came from below, and they began to pay out the line. Pierre wanted to look over the side and watch, but he couldn't. One of Heinz's men leaned over the *Eugenie's* rail and reported on their progress.

"Just a couple more yards. Easy! She's swaying. Okay. A little more." At last the call came. "They've got her!"

Pierre dropped the line, scrambled out of the dinghy, and ran to the ladder. He climbed halfway down and waited impatiently until the petty officers brought the launch back over to let him aboard.

He sprang down into the boat and made his way over the thwarts to the seat where Marie huddled in a silver emergency blanket the Coast Guard men had wrapped around her. She looked small and miserable. His gut twisted as he saw how the left side of her face was swollen and bruised, with a cut over the cheekbone.

"Mon amour!"

She sobbed and lifted her arms to him. Pierre sank to his knees and pulled her into his embrace.

"*Chérie, chérie*, it's over."

She clung to him fiercely. "They were going to kill me."

"Oh, my love, I'm so sorry. You were very brave."

"No. I was scared the whole time."

"But you did a very smart and courageous thing."

"I was desperate. And I saw the swing. At first I didn't think about what it was, but I'd seen a man using one at Mystic."

Pierre gasped. "I saw that guy! On the *Conrad*."

She nodded. "But I couldn't hear anything once I was down there. Someone was shouting, but I couldn't tell what was happening. And I wondered if I'd be able to get back up again."

"I'm sorry it took so long to find you."

She burrowed her face into his jacket front. "Take me home," she whispered.

"I will." The launch began to move. He looked up and saw George gazing down at them from the yacht's deck. Pierre raised one hand in a brief salute before enfolding Marie more securely in his arms.

SEVENTY-SIX

André pushed the disconnect button on his phone and smiled at the people gathered in his parents' living room.

"Well?" his father asked.

"She's safe."

The combined Gillette and Belanger families cheered and clapped. Lisa threw her arms around him and kissed his cheek. André couldn't stop grinning.

"When will they be here?" Mrs. Gillette asked.

"Probably late tomorrow. Pierre is taking her to a hospital to have her checked over. If she's okay, they'll get a hotel room there in New York for tonight and drive up tomorrow."

"Can't they fly up?" Claudia asked.

"Marie doesn't want to fly."

"Well, that's understandable," Lisa muttered. "I can't wait to hear her whole story."

"Oh, there's another thing. I need to call Janet and have her unlock the post office for me in about an hour."

"What for?" his mother asked. "You're not working overtime, are you? I thought that was only in December."

André chuckled. "No, it's for the U.S. Navy. Pierre says they're sending an officer to collect a very special parcel."

They all stared at him in bewilderment.

"You know how Marie said some men were chasing her?" André asked.

The family members looked at each other with troubled eyes. That mystery had bothered them all.

"What's it about?" his father asked.

"Well, someone on Marie's plane put something in her luggage, and these men have been after her all week, trying to get it back. That's why she was running. And, Mom, it's also why those motorcycle thugs were hanging around here this morning."

His mother's jaw dropped. "You mean, they were the same people who… How can that be?"

André shrugged. "Not the same men chasing Marie, but friends of theirs. Or more likely, employees of theirs. Marie had put the item they wanted so badly in an Express Mail package and sent it here, to Pierre. I saw the package this morning when I sorted the mail, and I set it aside. I didn't know then what was in it, but I guess that's what the two bikers were watching for."

"Hey, Mom," Claudia crowed, "you called the police on some international terrorists! Right on!"

"But Marie is all right, isn't she?" Lisa asked.

He smiled down at her. "Yeah. Pierre says she's shook up and she has some bruises, but he thinks she'll be okay, and we'll see them tomorrow."

"Terrific." Lisa's hand wriggled into André's, and he squeezed it.

"Want to ride over to the post office with me?"

"While you give the package to the Navy? I'd love to!"

"Wear a sweater," her mother said.

"Yes, Mom."

"And, André, don't keep her out too late," Mr. Gillette added.

"Dad, I'm twenty-five." Lisa's cheeks flushed, and André smiled. She was downright cute when she was embarrassed.

"Don't worry, Mr. Gillette. I'll take care of her."

Eloise Belanger brought Lisa her jacket. They didn't really need to leave yet, but André didn't mind. More time alone with Lisa.

In his truck, he buckled his seat belt and then took out his phone to call Janet.

"What do you mean, you need to get into the post office tonight? Absolutely not!"

"Janet, it's an—"

"I know. One of your emergencies."

"Well, it is."

"I'm not buying it."

Lisa, in the passenger seat of the truck, watched him with sympathetic eyes. André grimaced at her and said sweetly into the phone, "Okay, Janet. Don't worry about it. I'll just tell the admiral that the postmaster refused to open up for the special unit the Navy sent to get their property. They can put the whole detail up in a hotel, I'm sure, and get their package in the morning. If it's not too late to stop the international crisis they're trying to prevent."

Silence.

"Janet? You there?" André asked.

"Belanger, you are such a liar."

"If you think that, then you'd better not come to the post office. The admiral's men will be there at eight o'clock sharp, and you won't want to hear their language when I tell them we can't get in. You know how sailors swear."

Lisa clapped a hand over her mouth to stifle the laugh that burbled out.

"Eight o'clock?"

"That's right. You're not feeling sick, are you Janet? You sound kind of off your feed."

"I'm sick, all right. I'll see you at 7:59. Not a minute before."

André smiled. "Let's see, if the admiral calls, I'll tell him 1959. That's the way they say it, isn't it? Or would it be eight bells? No, a minute before eight bells."

Janet hung up. André shrugged and pushed the disconnect button.

"Women."

Lisa erupted in laughter. "She is going to make you miserable for the rest of your career."

"Nah. I found out this morning she's transferring to the Auburn post office at the end of June. She only has to put up with me for another month."

Lisa's smile held a tinge of regret. "No thanks to me. I almost got you killed yesterday."

"Hey, don't do that. We agreed God was watching over us."

She nodded.

"You okay, Lisa?"

"Yeah."

"It was pretty awful, but it wasn't your fault. And the FBI is glad they caught several gangsters because of our mistake."

She winced. "Just call us the bumbling heroes."

André looked at his watch. "We've got time to get ice cream before we meet them."

Her eyes took on a subdued gleam. "Gifford's?"

"Sure. You like the good stuff, huh?"

"I hope they have peppermint."

"No, black raspberry."

"Peppermint."

André started the truck engine and then leaned over to kiss her.

EPILOGUE

Six weeks later, Norfolk, Virginia

Pierre sat in his new commanding officer's tiny workspace on the base, balancing his hat on his knee and sweating. His nerves always made a major assault when he had to talk to someone higher up, but combined with Virginia's July heat and a sporadic air-conditioning system, he was miserable.

"Because of your close involvement in Operation Lion Gate, you're entitled to know that op has been scrubbed."

Pierre averted his gaze, though he wanted to stare at the captain. He stared at the file cabinet instead. All those clandestine trips into China. The danger, the anxiety, the Chinese nationals who risked their necks for freedom.

"Any questions?"

Pierre cleared his throat. "Completely scrapped?"

"For the time being, at least." The captain leaned back in his chair. "I'm told that the way things came down, the opposition became aware of our intent, if not any details. Besides that, we've got several hot spots flaring up in the Middle East again. Right now it seems unwise to add an unstable China to the mix. Our diplomats have their hands full trying to pacify the Chinese government and convince them to continue business as usual with the U.S.A."

Pierre nodded slowly. That was it. All over.

"So...my new assignment stands?"

"Yes, you'll be here with us for at least the next year." The captain straightened and handed him a large manila envelope. "I expect you'll be a great asset to our training staff, Lieutenant."

"Thank you, sir."

The captain nodded. "All right. I'll be in close contact with you. You'll have a yeoman to do paperwork for you and an office, if you can call it that, in the Parker Building. Get settled. If you have any questions, give me a call."

He stood, and Pierre jumped to his feet.

"Thank you, sir."

He hurried out to his car and headed for the main gate. Home. He was still learning the streets and seeking out alternate travel routes between the base and the new house. Shortcuts. Detours for high-traffic days. Twenty minutes later, he turned onto the street where their house nestled between two others just like it, amid a newish development. It wasn't a bad house; it just lacked the character of the old farmhouse his parents had lived in for thirty years.

Marie didn't meet him at the door, and he called her name.

"In here!"

He tossed his hat on the table and went through the family room to the bedroom. She was standing on a chair, adjusting a curtain rod.

"Here, let me help you."

He reached up and hooked the end of the rod on its bracket.

"Thanks." She looked down at him and smiled, that gentle, amazing smile that still sent shivers through him. "At last, I'm taller than you." She placed her hands on his shoulders and bent to kiss him.

Pierre wrapped his arms around her waist and lifted her from the chair, setting her on the floor without letting go.

"You like the curtains?" she murmured.

"Mmm."

"No, really." She pushed away from him. "Step back, take a good, hard look, and be honest. Because you'll spend a third of your life in this room for as long as we're in Norfolk."

"At least a year."

"It's official?"

"*Oui*. I am now an instructor of things I can't tell you about."

She smiled. "Terrific. No long cruises or secret missions."

"Well…not so far. You never know."

"Come on, look at the curtains."

They were curtains. Green with a gold thread woven in. He stepped back near the doorway and looked at them from there. He could see that they went with the green-and-white quilt Marie's mother had made.

"I like them."

"Yeah?"

"It's a good color."

She came into his arms again. "George and Rachel called."

"Oh?"

"Yeah. I told them."

He smiled and nuzzled his nose into her hair. It smelled faintly of citrus and ginger. "What did old George say?"

"He was happy for us. Maybe a little wistful."

"They'll be parents soon. Rachel's still getting out in the spring, right?"

"Yeah. She's looking forward to being a civilian again, although she sounded like she'd miss the animals she's been working with."

"She'll have babies to keep her busy."

"Yeah. She said to tell you congratulations, and she hopes we can all get together before too long. And we're under orders to send pictures."

He pushed her away and placed his hand on her tummy. "You don't look pregnant yet."

She giggled. "It takes a while. He's only, like, a quarter of an inch long."

Pierre nodded. Just thinking about the baby made him smile. He touched Marie's cheek, where the bruises had been in May. They had morphed into yellow, purple, and brown, and then they faded over a matter of weeks. When they arrived in Norfolk, she'd plastered on the makeup so people wouldn't ask questions. But now she didn't need it anymore, and he loved the way her soft, supple skin felt.

She smiled and pushed his hair back off his forehead. "You hungry?"

"Ravenous."

They went to the kitchen together, and she opened the refrigerator.

"I heard from Special Agent Heinz," Pierre said. "You know, the NCIS officer?"

"Yeah? What did he say?"

"They raided that Chen Trading Company in San Francisco."

Marie turned toward him with a package of pork chops in her hand, her dark eyes huge. "That's the place Jenna called from my cell phone?"

"Right. He said they'll send the phone back to you."

"Did they find the woman? The one who shot Jenna?"

Pierre shook his head. "Not yet. Sorry."

She exhaled heavily. "I wish we knew they'd found her."

He took the package from her hand. "They arrested several people they think were involved in the espionage, though. They may send someone here with photos for you to look at. If you can identify any of the men who chased you, it will help them a lot."

She nodded. "Can you be with me when they come?"

"Absolutely."

She turned back to the refrigerator. "Oh, Mom called too. She wants to fly down for a week in September."

"That'd be good. Can we have the guest room ready by then?"

"You mean the baby's room?"

"Well, you've got eight months to turn it into a nursery. Your mom can sleep in there without a crib and a rocking chair, I assume."

Marie laughed. "I'm sure she won't mind if we don't have baby furniture yet. She can help pick it out."

"Oh, she'll love that."

"Yeah. She's hinting that Lisa and André might make an announcement soon."

Pierre blinked and sat down at the table. "You mean, like an engagement?"

"Uh-huh."

He shook his head. "I'd about given up on André."

"Well, they seemed pretty serious when we were home."

"Yeah." He smiled. "I'm glad they've both started going to church and thinking about their spiritual lives."

Marie plunked several containers on the counter and opened a cupboard door. "Me too. As far as Mom is concerned, it's a done deal with those two. I'm surprised she hasn't bought her mother-of-the-bride dress yet."

"If it's that serious, I'll bet my mother's doing the happy dance too."

"For sure. And my mom's already saying, *It's too bad we can't find a nice young man for Claudia.*"

"Nah, she's a career girl." Pierre stood and went to the counter. He opened one cupboard and closed it, and then did the same with another. "Where do we keep plates?"

Marie chuckled. "Next one over."

He found them and took two down.

"Of course, your brother Mathieu is still single." Marie turned on a burner and opened the meat container, sliding two chops into the frying pan.

"Mathieu? He's still getting over that breakup with Michelle, isn't he?"

"That was months ago."

"Yeah, well…do you really think lightning could strike three times in the same place?"

She looked up at him, her brown eyes sparkling. "Three sisters marrying three brothers? It's probably been done before, but you're right. That would be unusual."

"This family doesn't do anything the normal way." He went to stand behind her and twined his arms around her waist. "*Chérie,* I'm so proud of you."

"Of me? What for?"

"Because of who you are."

She wriggled around in his arms to face him, setting her spatula down carefully on the stovetop.

"I'm just…me."

"I know. But it's been…what? Almost five years since I proposed to you. And way back then, I could see that you would become this wonderful, stunning, competent, remarkable woman."

"That's a lot of adjectives."

"Not to mention gorgeous."

She hugged him and laid her head against his chest for a moment. "I love you."

"*Je t'aime, chérie.*" He thought back to how close he'd come to losing her, and of all the people who had helped Marie come home to him. He stroked her hair, feeling tears sting his eyes. No, this time was too good to dwell on the possible past. He sent up a quick prayer of silent thanks.

She turned back to the stove, dreamy-eyed. "Sit. This will be ready in a minute."

Pierre opened the refrigerator. "I'm getting you a glass of milk. For the baby."

"What do you think of the name Miriam?"

He stopped with the jug in his hand. "I thought it was a boy."

"We don't know yet."

"I guess not."

"So what were you thinking?"

"George, maybe?"

She smiled. "Not Michael, for your father?"

"Well…"

"I guess we should think about it for a while."

They sat down together. Pierre asked the blessing, and as they dished up the food, he knew what he would do first thing in the morning. He'd stop at a bookstore along his alternate route and buy a baby name book. And when he got to his new desk in the cubicle in the basement of the Parker Building, he would open the yellow pages and look up a florist. Roses for the mother of his son. Or daughter.

Marie raised her eyebrows as she reached for the salad dressing. "What are you thinking about?"

"Nothing."

"Yes, you were. You were smiling."

"I'm just happy, *chérie*."

This is it, he wanted to say. *This is everything I begged God for when you were missing, and everything I agreed to give up if He would just bring you back to me. He's given it all to us.*

But he wouldn't say those things to her. Not yet. The memory of that time was too fresh. Someday they would talk about it, maybe during their prayer time together, while Marie held their baby. He would tell her how much it meant to him just to be here with her.

She smiled, and his heart flipped. She knew all that was in his heart. Of course, she knew.

ABOUT THE AUTHOR

Susan Page Davis is the author of several novels, spanning categories such as historical, mystery, young adult, and romantic suspense. A former news correspondent, she and her husband, Jim, are the parents of six and the grandparents of four. Susan and Jim make their home in Maine.

Visit Susan at her website: www.susanpagedavis.com

Harvest House Publishers
For the Best in Inspirational Fiction

Mindy Starns Clark

SMART CHICK MYSTERY SERIES
The Trouble with Tulip
Blind Dates Can Be Murder
Elementary, My Dear Watkins

Roxanne Henke

COMING HOME TO
BREWSTER SERIES
After Anne
Finding Ruth
Becoming Olivia
Always Jan
With Love, Libby

Sally John

THE OTHER WAY HOME SERIES
A Journey by Chance
After All These Years
Just to See You Smile
The Winding Road Home

IN A HEARTBEAT SERIES
In a Heartbeat
Flash Point
Moment of Truth

THE BEACH HOUSE SERIES
The Beach House
Castles in the Sand

Susan Meissner

A Window to the World
Remedy for Regret
In All Deep Places
A Seahorse in the Thames

Craig Parshall

Trial by Ordeal
CHAMBERS OF JUSTICE SERIES
The Resurrection File
Custody of the State
The Accused
Missing Witness
The Last Judgement

Debra White Smith

THE AUSTEN SERIES
First Impressions
Reason and Romance
Central Park
Northpointe Chalet
Amanda
Possibilities

Lori Wick

THE TUCKER MILLS TRILOGY
Moonlight on the Millpond
Just Above a Whisper
Leave a Candle Burning

THE ENGLISH GARDEN SERIES
The Proposal
The Rescue
The Visitor
The Pursuit

THE YELLOW ROSE TRILOGY
Every Little Thing About You
A Texas Sky
City Girl

CONTEMPORARY FICTION
Bamboo & Lace
Every Storm
Pretense
The Princess
Sophie's Heart
White Chocolate Moments

FRASIER ISLAND

Will Rachel's first top secret assignment prove to be her last?

After specialized underwater training, Ensign Rachel Whitney of the U.S. Navy is posted to a remote island in the North Pacific, a tiny scrap of rock guarding a highly classified secret. She could love her new assignment if her commanding officer, Lt. George Hudson, weren't so difficult to please.

Despite George's first reaction to her presence on the island, Rachel sets out to prove she is perfect for the job. She doesn't dream of being a heroine—or falling in love— but when word leaks out about the prize they are guarding, Rachel and George find that they have few resources besides each other and their faith in God to thwart an enemy attack that could endanger all of America.

Let this romantic and exciting adventure take you to a place where fear meets faith and weakness is exchanged for unexpected strength.